SHATTERED

JADE

BOOKS BY
LARRY ALEXANDER

STANDALONE NOVELS

Shattered Jade

76 Hours

NONFICTION

Bloody Ridge and Beyond (with Marlin Groft)

A Higher Call (with Adam Makos)

In the Footsteps of the Band of Brothers

Shadows in the Jungle

Biggest Brother

SHATTERED JADE

A NOVEL OF SAIPAN

LARRY ALEXANDER

BLACK
STONE
PUBLISHING

Printed in the United States of America
Originally published in hardcover by Blackstone Publishing in 2024

First paperback edition: 2024
ISBN 979-8-212-89377-0
Fiction / Historical / World War II

Version 1

Blackstone Publishing
31 Mistletoe Rd.
Ashland, OR 97520

www.BlackstonePublishing.com

This book is dedicated to the memory of the many thousands of soldiers, sailors, and civilians who perished in the twenty-four-day Battle for Saipan. They are all Shattered Jade.

PROLOGUE

The olive-drab staff car, a US Army Plymouth captured in Manila in 1942, rolled along the unpaved coastal road, then slowed to a halt amid a swirl of dust. An enlisted man popped out and quickly opened a rear door. Major Tadashi Tanimura stepped from the vehicle, followed by his friend and aide Captain Kisaburo Hanaya. A gaggle of officers standing a few feet away sprang to attention. One man broke away from the group and approached Tadashi. Tadashi knew him to be Colonel Hikoki Kogiwara, who commanded all the engineer units on the island.

"You come from General Saito," Kogiwara said, returning a perfunctory salute.

Tadashi, island commander Yoshitsugu Saito's aide-de-camp, nodded, then said, "The general wishes a status report on our defenses."

Tadashi slid a rolled document from a brown leather case carried by Hanaya and spread it out on the hood of the Plymouth. The document was a map of Saipan. Tadashi always

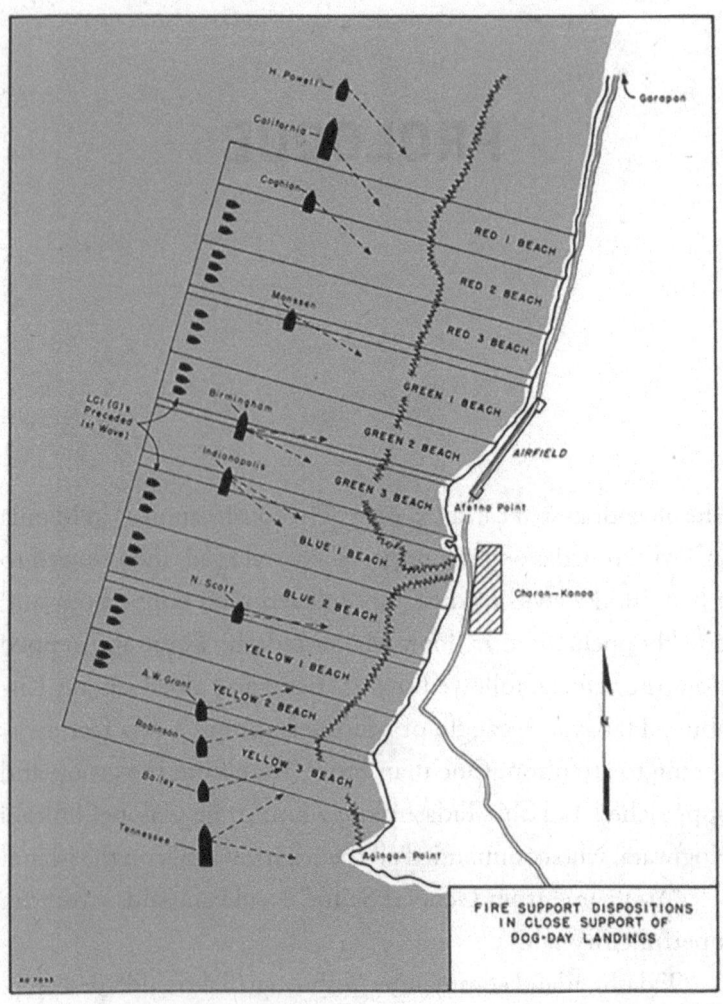

FIRE SUPPORT DISPOSITIONS
IN CLOSE SUPPORT OF
DOG-DAY LANDINGS

thought the island looked very much like an eastern-facing bear sitting on its haunches, with Kagman Peninsula as the front paws and Nafutan Point as the rear. On the map were four defensive zones traced in red ink.

Within these four zones, dug in and waiting for the Americans to arrive, General Saito and his naval counterpart, Admiral Chuichi Nagumo, could count some thirty-five thousand men determined to defend Saipan to the death.

Tadashi tapped his finger on the map at the location where he now stood, which was on the coastal highway about three hundred yards inland from where the Pacific Ocean washed the western beaches. He turned and glanced back over his shoulder. A few yards beyond the road lay the steel rails of the narrow-gauge railroad that in peacetime had carried tons of sugarcane from the fields to the refinery at Charan Kanoa. Some two thousand yards beyond that rose up a jagged limestone ridge that bristled with caves. Hard work and long hours by a legion of sweating laborers had transformed many of these natural fortifications into formidable bunkers for artillery pieces. Most of these guns, deadly 75mm weapons, were placed in such a way that they could be fired, then pulled back into a cave to reload. This also protected the guns from enemy shells and bombs.

But it was here on the beach, amid the undulating wilderness of tall grass, gnarled trees, and sugarcane fields, where the first fighting would occur. Here the men of Nippon had to hold back the American juggernaut that had been rolling westward across the Pacific since Guadalcanal fell nearly seventeen months ago.

"You have been working on our beach defenses, our first line against the Americans," Tadashi said. "How are your preparations coming along?"

Kogiwara began to describe the greeting he had planned for the American landing forces, starting with the lagoon itself.

"Before a single American boot tramps on our shore, the killing of our enemies will be well underway," he said with obvious pride. "I've had swimmers out in the water all day planting small red flags. These will mark the channels through the barrier reef that the American landing boats must take. These flags are aiming points. Our machine guns and coastal guns are zeroed in on them."

Tadashi nodded.

Kogiwara continued.

"We are fortunate that Saipan's rugged coastline leaves the American devils with few choices on where to land," Kogiwara said. "Saipan has fifty-four miles of coastline, but very few of those miles contain suitable landing beaches. Mostly these are along the western and southern coasts. It's almost certain that they will storm the western beaches between where we now stand and south to Charan Kanoa. It is here that their troops will be harshly punished."

He began to describe how almost every yard of beach would be subjected to intense mortar and artillery bombardment. Equally deadly would be scores of machine guns, both heavy and light, whose interlocking fire could sweep the entire shoreline. Then there was the long but narrow tree line about twenty yards from the water's edge.

"The few Americans who survive the beach will push into that wide band of scrub trees and vines, where our snipers will take a heavy toll," Kogiwara said. "Those woods also contain more machine guns as well as men in cleverly secreted spider traps ready to take the Americans under fire from the rear as they pass by. Beyond the tangle of the woods, of course, we have a wide swath of open ground, where the Americans will find more rifle pits, trenches, machine guns, and pillboxes. Our intention is to turn the invasion area into an American graveyard."

Wrapping up, Kogiwara's outlook now reflected deep concern.

"When they come, we will certainly kill many," Kogiwara said. "I know the general wants the Americans destroyed on the beach and pushed back into the sea. But I realistically don't see how we can prevent the enemy from gaining a toehold before darkness falls."

"We can't," Tadashi confirmed. "But a toehold is just what General Saito wants. All our beach defenders need to do, Colonel, is keep the American invasion contained. The more men they jam onto a narrow and confined beachhead, the easier it will be to destroy them when we launch our counterattacks. Between our six batteries of guns on the ridge plus our howitzers, we'll have almost seventy field pieces laying down fire on their heads. Nowhere on that beach will they find safety. To make things worse for them, Colonel Goto has ninety tanks ready to crash through their lines."

Kogiwara understood that but said, "That is all well and good, Major. But how long will our defenses hold? Our fortifications may seem daunting, but many of our bunkers are not as strong as they should be to withstand the punishment the Americans can throw against them. As General Saito is aware, we have done our best with what we have, but our resupply efforts have been strangled by American submarines. We cannot strengthen the fortifications appreciably unless we can get more materials. If I don't get that support, I cannot promise how long our defenses will stand."

"The men will have to work harder," Tadashi suggested, taken aback by Kogiwara's fall from exuberance to borderline defeatism. "Use as many men as you need."

"We already have every spare soldier working," Kogiwara said. "Work crews are working two twelve-hour shifts. I have Korean workers and also islanders, both Japanese civilians and native Chamorro. But the Chamorro are undependable unless we apply the lash to their backs. We even have girls from the Girls' School of Saipan helping. But no matter how many workers I have, the lack of materials leaves them nothing to do but sit around with their arms folded. I respectfully ask that General Saito address this shortage of construction materials immediately."

Tadashi was well aware of the problem. Earlier, on his inspection tour, he'd spoken to Captain Sake Oba, who had over one hundred men digging gun positions in the hills overlooking the town of Garapan. Oba expressed shock at the lack of materials, including concrete and explosives, plus a complete absence of tractors.

"Your points are well taken, Colonel, and I will pass them along to General Saito," Tadashi replied. "Unfortunately, the Navy reports that the Americans have left Eniwetok. That's only two thousand kilometers east of us. Saipan is their most likely target. General Saito is aware of the handicap you are forced to work under, but know that when the Americans get here, we will fight, and any shortages of materials will be offset by the code of Bushido, where every Japanese soldier swears to kill ten Americans before he dies. General Saito knows the value of our holding Saipan. This island and all the Marianas are key elements in Japan's outer ring of defenses. Losing it would doom any hope we have of emerging from this war victoriously."

"What about the Imperial Fleet?" Kogiwara asked. "Do you think they can arrive in time to defeat the American Navy in the Decisive Battle?"

Tadashi was silent. Unlike many of his peers, Tadashi had little confidence in the Japanese Navy's "Decisive Battle" scenario, where the Combined Fleet would do battle with the Americans and crush them. Yes, the Navy had *Yamato* and *Musashi*, the two most powerful battleships in the world, each packing nine 18-inch guns with a maximum firing range of twenty-six miles. Still, he no longer believed that the Navy had the sufficient strength, particularly in aircraft carriers.

After a brief silence, he said, "The general has told Imperial Headquarters that Saipan is absolutely invincible. And so it shall be."

With a final salute, Tadashi returned to the Plymouth. Hanaya was by his side.

"Tokyo misinformed us, my friend," Tadashi told Hanaya as the driver opened the car door. "Our leaders assumed we would not have to face a possible invasion before November. How we could've used those five extra months to more fully prepare."

"Maybe Tokyo was wrong about where the Americans are heading," Hanaya said.

Tadashi shook his head.

"A troop convoy is known to be sailing on a westward course," he said. "The only logical place they could be bound for on that particular heading is the Marianas. They're coming for us, my friend."

CHAPTER 1

Peter "Hardball" Talbot glanced at his Timex. All around him, US Marines in full battle array were clomping down the iron staircase that led into the bowels of LST 968. Below them on the tractor deck, two dozen amphibious landing craft, amtracs, waited impatiently to ferry the men to the shores of Saipan.

It was 0625.

Reveille had sounded at 0400, and the Marines had been herded into the compartment that passed for a mess hall aboard this Large Slow Target, as the sailors dubbed the LST. Men whose appetites hadn't been squelched by seasickness or outright terror wolfed down the traditional steak and eggs breakfast, with a coffee chaser served scalding hot and blacker than Satan's soul.

At 0542, the loudspeaker bellowed, "Land the landing force. Marines, lay up to your debarkation stations." Outside, the rumble of naval guns roared. The preinvasion bombardment had begun.

Wordlessly, the Marines filed down the iron stairs into the

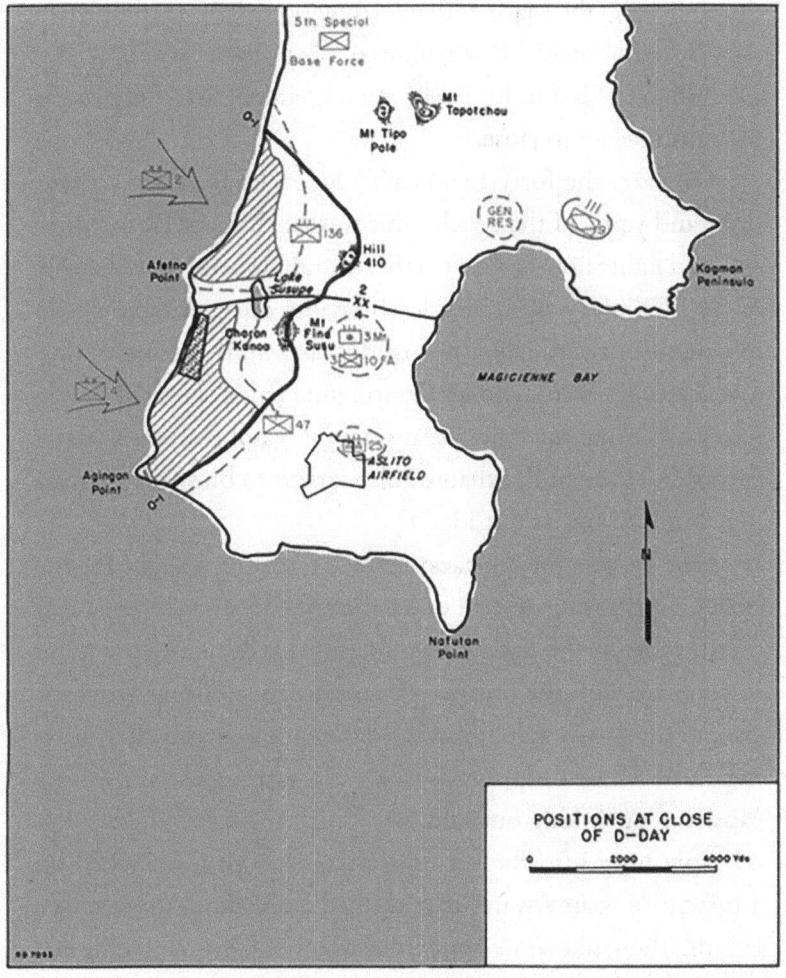

POSITIONS AT CLOSE
OF D—DAY

0   2000   4000 Yds

dimly lit, cavernous hold. The steel bulkheads echoed amid the clamor as Marines boarded the boats using the rear-mounted ramps. It was like being inside a church bell on Sunday morning. What sounded like the ringing of a telephone jangled three times, alerting the Marines that loading needed to be completed.

"Second Squad," Pete bellowed. "Let's move ass!"

When the last of his twelve men boarded, Pete followed as the ramp began to close.

Outside, the forty-two heavily laden LSTs closed to four thousand yards of the beach. This was the Line of Departure.

Red lights now flashed overhead, and buzzers blared harshly as the LST's forward doors slowly swung open. A ramp began to extend outward, then sloped down toward the wave tops. Twenty-four seven-cylinder Continental engines roared to life, heavily scenting the stale, sweaty air with gasoline fumes. Along each side of the hull, exhaust fans worked to blow the increasing clouds of fumes outside.

One by one the amtracs advanced, scaling a slight incline before the dizzying descent down the ramp. Each vehicle paused on the ramp so the coxswain could time his drop into the water to coincide with the four-to-six-foot ocean swells. Missing the crest of the wave could mean the difference between safely leaving the LST or dropping into a watery trough and possibly capsizing or sinking outright.

Splashing into the sea nose first, each amtrac kicked up a torrent of foamy water that washed back along the vehicle's length. Then, like some ponderous water bug, the craft churned away from the LST to clear the way for the next.

After finding its assigned spot in the gathering armada, Pete's amtrac began to circle monotonously, awaiting the signal to head for the shore. In the distance, Pete could hear the crash of naval guns; the sharp bark of the cruisers; and the distinct, deep-throated thump of the behemoth barrels aboard the battle-ships. Overhead, the ripping sound of large-caliber shells made inexperienced Marines flinch instinctively.

This was day three of the naval bombardment of Saipan. Now it was invasion day, and the Navy had allotted just three hours for softening up beach defenses. This fire was to be delivered by two battleships, two cruisers, and seven destroyers at a range of just over two thousand yards.

At 0630, the rhythmic drumbeat of the naval guns suddenly ceased, replaced by the drone of airplane engines. Within moments, the sky became alive with dive-bombers, both older Dauntlesses and the newer Helldivers. These were accompanied by F6F Hellcat fighters. As the Marines watched, clouds of fly-boys approached at treetop level, strafing and dropping bombs on the Japs' heads.

An angry ball of fire roiled skyward after a plane buzzed over the island.

"Think they hit an ammo dump?" Corporal Walter "Honey-bun" Hullihen asked Pete.

"Them's napalm bombs," one of the boat's forward-mounted .30-caliber machine gunners shouted above the engine's rumble. "It's new. Like an airborne flamethrower."

"Ah'll be gawdamned," Pfc. William "Reb" Marshall said with awe. "What'll they think of next?"

Carrier planes continued zooming above the Marines, when suddenly objects began falling from the sky, pummeling the men in the landing boats. Many of the Marines cowered in terror. Pete and two other NCOs—Reb Marshall and First Squad's Sgt. Bill "Biff" Hodges—yelled that the objects raining down on them were spent brass casings ejected from the wing-mounted machine guns on the fighter planes. Still, many of the men calmed down only when the deluge from above ceased.

Pete leaned his back against the amtrac's steel ramp as the vibrations from the engine coursed through the craft's steel carcass. Pete studied the twelve men he'd be leading into battle.

He'd been given command of the squad on May 7, immediately upon his return to the company. He'd been gone nearly five months for recuperation and rehabilitation after having his right leg peppered by Japanese grenade shrapnel, suffered two hours before Tarawa fell. He was no sooner off the truck that had brought him to Camp Tarawa on Hawaii's Big Island, when Master Sgt. Thomas O'Leary wrangled him into a tent that bore a hand-painted sign that read: "2nd Div., D Co. HQ."

Inside the tent, behind a desk that looked as if a grenade had exploded on it, sat Captain Thomas Jackson Stacey, a tall, athletic Virginian lovingly called "Stonewall" by his men. The nickname pleased him, though he'd never let them know it. Beside the captain, First Lt. Woodrow Long sat in a wooden straight-backed chair, his long legs stretched out casually. Hailing from Daytona Beach, the lanky Floridian commanded First Platoon and had served as Stacey's executive officer following the death of First Lt. Ed Pfeffer on Tarawa. Seated to Stacey's left was an officer Pete did not recognize. What caught Pete's attention was that the man looked Japanese.

"At ease, Talbot," the smiling officer joked, noting a look of surprise in Pete's eyes. "I'm as American as you are. I was born on Maui, and I root for the Boston Braves."

"This is Lt. Shimada, my S2 intelligence officer and Japanese interpreter," Stacey said. "Pull up a chair, Hardball. Light up if you want."

Pete gratefully fished a pack of Camels from his blouse pocket and lit one. Uneasy with Stacey's informality, Pete removed the wedge-shaped garrison cap, or piss cutter, settled into a wooden straight-backed chair, and lit a Camel. Lt. Long and Shimada also fired up scrags. Stacey didn't smoke.

"The leg's okay?" Stacey asked.

"It's not a hundred percent yet," Pete replied, "but I'm fit for duty."

"Not surprising that it's still sore," Long observed. "Jap grenades are ugly. They break apart in larger fragments than our pineapples and do more damage."

"Scuttlebutt says you married that redheaded gal while you were recuperating," Stacey said.

"Yes sir," Pete replied. "I decided my kid brother was right. He made a pain in the ass of himself trying to convince me that Aggie and I were meant to be together, and I finally decided he was right."

Pete thought briefly of his little brother entombed inside a sunken submarine in the Solomon Islands for just over a year.

"Congratulations," Stacey said. "And welcome back. With you, Rosie, and the replacements who came in with you, the company is finally back to full strength, but you're going to see a lot of new faces."

Lt. Cornwall, Pete's platoon leader, entered the tent, followed by Gunnery Sergeant Earl Nicholson. They shook Pete's hand and then pulled up chairs and sat down. Pete was glad to see them but couldn't help feeling something unpleasant was coming his way.

"Why do I feel like I've been called into the principal's office?" Pete said.

"We just know how you like to bitch whenever you're handed a new job," Nicholson injected.

Cornwall spoke next.

"I'm putting you in permanent command of Second Squad."

"Excuse me, sir," Pete injected. "Corporal Aldrich is a damned sight smarter than me, and he's been doing the job since I was hit. Why take it away from him? He's more than qualified."

"The Professor knows about this and agrees to hand command back to you," Cornwall said.

"He would, the sonofabitch," Pete snarled.

"We all talked this over and agree that you're the best man for the job, so the matter's closed," Stacey told Pete. "You led the squad for over two days on Tarawa after McDougal got hit, and you did a commendable job. During that long night, when we were under repeated banzai attacks, you kept moving along your line, talking to your men, keeping up their spirits. That's part of what a good leader does. When you led your men against that Jap pillbox and dislodged the entire right of the Jap line that was holding up our advance, you proved you have guts and that your head works under pressure. You earned that Silver Star."

Pete knew there was nothing left to say.

Stacey now told Pete how the division has been restructured and how platoons were being divided into four-man fire teams.

"Your Second Squad's been trimmed back to twelve men, besides yourself, and divided into three fire teams, each led by an NCO," Cornwall added. "Sgt. Aldrich will be your senior fire team leader and second in command."

Pete nodded his approval.

"The other two teams will be led by Harnish and Hullihen, both of whom are now corporals," Cornwall added.

"Nothing against Bucket," Pete said, using the nickname Harnish earned in boot camp. "But why not give the lead to Marshall? I think Reb's a little more solid."

"He is, but he's also proven to be a damned fine AW man, which is the backbone of the fire team," Nicholson replied.

"One more thing, Talbot," Stacey said, reaching into a desk

drawer. "If you're gonna run one of my squads, you'll need these." He handed two patches to Talbot. "Sew those on and take charge of your men . . . Sergeant."

Pete scowled at the two patches, each with three chevrons trimmed with red piping. "You and the gunny are dismissed."

Pete and Nicholson rose, saluted, and left. Outside, Pete slipped the piss cutter back on his head and glowered at the stripes as the two men walked along the dusty company street.

"I didn't ask for these," Pete grumbled.

"The Polish Marines call that toughski shitski," Nicholson replied with a grin.

Arriving at his squad tent, Pete immediately had the men fall in. What he saw did not encourage him.

Red-haired, freckle-faced Ken Goodman was a farm boy whose family ran a dairy farm near Harpers Ferry, West Virginia. He looked nervous, but beneath that boyish exterior, Pete sensed a toughness honed by hard work.

Standing next to Goodman and hailing from Bethlehem, Pennsylvania, was blonde-haired Samuel Dubbs, a Feather Merchant who stood about five foot seven. Yet he was solidly built, sort of like a football lineman. As a teenager earning money for college to become a teacher, he had labored hard in coal mines, so there was muscle under the sleeves of his blouse. Pete read the man as an eager beaver.

At age eighteen, Vivian Miller looked like a fifteen-year-old. A product of the small town of Portageville, New York, on the Genesee River, Miller's dad was the local pharmacist, and his son served as the home delivery boy. Miller did not smoke, nor did he drink, which sat well with the man beside him.

Of the six new men, Donald Dembrowski was the only experienced Marine who was wise enough to call dibs on Miller's beer rations. A gravel-voiced Chicagoan, Dembrowski had worked in an auto scrapyard cutting apart old cars and engines. This earned him the nickname "Scrap Iron."

He'd joined the Marines before Pearl Harbor and well before anyone else in the squad. His past work experience landed him in the motor pool until his request for a combat assignment. His personnel file showed discipline problems. He would need to be watched. But then again, Pete thought, his own 201-file read pretty much the same way.

Chico Morales, who was whispering something to Dembrowski, was a Feather Merchant like Dubbs, except that his olive complexion made Pete think of his best friend, Ted Giovanni, now lying under a white cross on Tarawa. A Los Angeles native, Morales drove a taxi. Effusively friendly, he urged everyone to call him by his nickname: "Hack."

The last of the replacements was Wilmer Baumgartner, who, like Miller, was older than he appeared. Baumgartner was from Louisville, Kentucky, where his dad worked at Hillerich and Bradsby manufacturing baseball bats.

Baumgartner was a draftee, a status that made him a pariah to some of the veterans.

Dismissing the new men, Pete quickly confronted his veterans when he heard them grumble.

"Listen up, all of you," Pete said, addressing the half dozen old-timers. "I'll have none of that shit in my squad."

"For Chrissake, Hardball," Reb replied. "Draftees! Our buddies left on Tarawa are rollin' in their graves. Last year it was women Marines, now it's draftees. Sweet Jesus, what's the Corps comin' to?"

"Hardball is absolutely correct," Aldrich chimed in. "We can't have this animosity in the squad. These new men are here to help us do a job, and how they got here doesn't matter."

"Ah knew ya'll'd be soft on 'em, Professor," Reb said, unconvinced. "But Hardball heah knows better."

"Don't you ever tell me what I know and don't know, you fuckin' hayseed," Pete snarled. "All of you listen to me. Every squad in every platoon of every company in this division is going through the same thing after our losses in November. I didn't want this squad leader job, but I got it, and by God I will run a tight unit. If any man—*any man*—has a problem with that, I will personally tag you with a leather medal. And if my boot in your ass doesn't help, I'll find other ways of convincing you."

Now looking over his squad as they headed for battle, Pete thanked God that his lambs were being shepherded by men of experience. Corporals "Honeybun" Hullihen, Bernie "Rosie" Roseblum, Charles "Bucket" Harnish, and Pfc. William "Reb" Marshall were Tarawa veterans who—with the exception of Rosie, who'd been wounded by a Japanese bayonet—had endured seventy-six hours of the most brutal combat in this war. Pete could depend on these men.

But most of all he could depend on Steve Aldrich. Not only had he become Pete's right-hand man during the fighting on Tarawa, but he'd also overcome Pete's tendency to self-isolate himself from those around him to become Pete's most trusted friend and confidant. Dubbed "Professor" after his two years at Towson College, Aldrich had run the squad from the time of Pete's wounding on November 23 until his return.

By Pete's watch, it was now 0700. The Navy planes had expended their payloads, so with ammo trays empty, they headed back to their carriers. The naval guns resumed. For another thirty minutes, the Navy pummeled Saipan, walking their high-explosive shells along the beach and the ground up to one thousand yards inland.

With the thumping of the naval guns as a backdrop, Pete wormed his way through the crunch of men, wanting to make one more round of his squad, particularly the newer men. Approaching Steve Aldrich, he winked at his best friend, then lightly punched "Rosie" Roseblum on the shoulder and stopped in front of Stanley Potter.

"How are you holdin' up, Potts?" Pete asked.

Potsy had been wounded at Tarawa. Struck while still in the landing boat, he never made it ashore. The young Virginian smiled.

"I just wanna get a crack at 'em this time," he said.

Pete grinned, nodded, and moved on to Wilmer, who was muttering, "Tay oh gat sab tay ko. Boo kee oh oh toe say."

Then he repeated the phrases again.

"What the hell are you doin'?" moaned Honeybun, who was standing next to the boy.

"I'm trying to learn those things we were told to say to get a Jap to surrender," he stammered.

"Hell, boy," Honeybun said. "Ain't no Jap gonna put up his hands and drop his weapon just because you ask him to. Just shoot the bastard. You'll live longer."

Pete reached out and unsnapped Baumgartner's helmet strap.

"That's a good way to lose your head, kid," Pete said. "Keep it unsnapped till we get ashore."

"My boys are a little nervous," Honeybun told Pete.

"We all are," Pete said, then looked at "Scrap Iron" Dembrowski, who seemed to be focused on the Thompson cradled in his arms.

"You ready to use that thing?" Pete asked.

"I've been waitin' two years for this chance," he said.

Pete stepped closer to the man and lowered his voice. "I want no hotdogging," he said. "You're part of a team, and I want it played that way. I've read your record. You've had discipline problems, but that's in the past. Before Tarawa, a lot of officers and NCOs felt the same way about me. But you're starting in this squad with a clean slate, so don't fuck it up."

Pete moved on to Goodman.

"Missing Harpers Ferry about now, huh?" he asked.

"Yeah, Sergeant," he answered. "Shoveling cow crap looks a lot more attractive right now. Are you missing home, too?"

"Missing Chester?" Pete replied with a smile. "Hell no."

Pete noticed that Sammy Dubbs looked pale and sickly.

"If you're gonna puke, do it now over the side," Pete said. "Once the Japs open up on us, keep your head down. Then you can puke on the deck if you must."

Standing right next to Dubbs, Vivian Miller took Pete's advice. He hoisted himself up, hung his head over the side, and threw up into the water. Pete helped him to lower himself to the deck.

"Feel better, Miller?"

"Don't know," he gasped. "Scared to death."

"Just the jitters," Pete said, trying to calm the young man. "Once we get ashore, you'll be too damned busy to be scared."

A light began blinking from one of the transports.

"That's the signal!" the LVT's coxswain called out from his seat behind the sloping armored shield. "We're goin' in."

Pete gave Morales a confident wink and a grin.

As the circling landing boats spread out to form individual waves, Pete glanced toward the island. So far, no opposing fire had come from the enemy, but Pete knew that would change.

Well out in front of the first wave of LVTs, Pete spotted a half dozen Landing Craft Infantry boats closing on the shore. These 158-foot craft, designed to carry as many as 210 men into battle, were part of a twenty-four-boat armada of LCIs pressed into service in a totally different capacity. Carrying not armed men but 81mm mortars and racks of 4.5-inch rockets, these crafts churned through the gentle swells.

The men in the landing boats tensed as every turn of the screws pushed them closer to the ominously silent shore. Still almost a thousand yards away, Pete unslung his Thompson and yanked back the cocking lever.

"Second Squad, lock and load," Pete called out.

He watched as his men set the safeties and slid clips into their weapons, followed by the metallic sound of bolts being snapped closed.

"Mean lookin' buncha killers ya got there, Hardball," said the man standing beside Pete. It was machine gunner Cpl. Moxley Pope. Hailing from Demopolis, Alabama, Pope nonchalantly loaded a short belt of .30-caliber ammo into his light machine gun.

Pete was glad Pope was attached to the platoon. Pete knew Pope—along with his ammo and tripod carrier, Pvt. Sidney Hoskins, a Yankee from Park Falls, Wisconsin—could be relied on when things got tough.

Pope was one of two MGs detached from Weapons Company to the Second Platoon, the other being Pfc. Riley "Yaz" Yastremski, a Cleveland, Ohio, native, and his assistant, Pfc. Paul "Wheels" Wealand of Allentown, Pennsylvania. Pete didn't envy Pope dragging that thirty-one-pound weapon around.

The boats continued churning toward shore when an ear-splitting sound like the ripping of thousands of bolts of fabric temporarily drowned out the naval gunfire. Ahead, Pete saw the LCIs wreathed in smoke as they began launching nearly a thousand rockets from launchers that numbered from 24 to 120 tubes. Pete watched the flaming black dots of the rockets leave the launchers and arc skyward. Smoke and debris blossomed into the air as the missiles smothered the shoreline.

"How could any Japs live through that?" Dembrowski said, awe in his otherwise gruff voice.

"Not only can Japs live through that," Pete replied, recalling the intense, yard-by-yard pounding that tiny Tarawa took, "but you can bet your ass that for all the smoke and noise there'll still be a lot of Japs waiting to greet us."

After the smoke-shrouded LCIs fired all their rockets, the mortars on board went to work, dropping high-explosive and white phosphorous rounds on the landing beaches.

So far, the enemy response to the invasion had been almost nonexistent. That changed as the amtracs closed to within five hundred yards of shore. The first inkling that the Japs on Saipan weren't about to roll over came when waterspouts blossomed among the landing boats. The erupting shells became more numerous as the boats plowed closer to the island. As the Marines closed the distance, the booming of the shore guns became clearly audible above the racket of the amtrac engines. Then a new sound was added—the metallic ping of machine gun rounds smacking into the steel plating of the landing boats.

"Here it comes," Pete heard Potts muttering. "Sweet Jesus, here it comes."

Pete understood that Potter was having flashbacks to the last time he was in this position, and shrapnel pierced the bulkhead on the landing boat and tore into his body. Pete pressed close to Potter.

"Take it easy, Potsy," he said. "This isn't a wooden Higgins boat."

Potts nodded, but the fear remained.

The pinging became more incessant. Meanwhile, the rounds that missed whined and whistled overhead. The number of hits bouncing off the boat made Pete wonder why these Jap gunners seemed more accurate than those on Tarawa. Had they been somehow pre-zeroed in?

Like a thunderclap, a large-caliber shell splashed into the water close to Pete's boat. The amtrac, nearly swamped by the resultant waterspout, was jarred, throwing men down in a tangle. Several Marines splattered their breakfasts all over the deck, themselves, and their comrades.

An ear-shattering roar off to port caused Pete to look skyward. He saw a bloody plume of water hurled skyward, carrying with it pieces of equipment and parts of men as an unfortunate amtrac took a direct hit. Horrified, Pete realized it was the amtrac carrying Lt. Woodrow Long, Dog Company's XO, and elements of First Platoon. Dubbs saw it too and threw an arm across his face as he sobbed. Honeybun put a hand on his rifleman's shoulder and shook him none too gently.

"Snap to, Marine," he barked.

Dubbs stared wide-eyed at his fire team leader and swallowed hard. The sobbing stopped.

At about the same time Dubbs was stifling his fears, the starboard .30-caliber machine gun operator on Pete's amtrac was struck in the chest several times, his body jerking rhythmically as his life was ripped from him. The man's blood splattered a half dozen Marines, including Vivian Miller, who had crimson smears on his face and shoulder. Any breakfast that Miller might've had left was puked onto the amtrac's deck.

Before the young man could panic, Reb removed a canteen from his web belt, poured water into his hand, and washed the red smudges from the youth's face. Miller nodded his thanks, but the revulsion in his eyes remained.

Pete sagged against the steel bulkhead of the amtrac, stunned by the sudden loss of Long and his men. As Japanese bullets clanged off the steel body, Pete became grateful that the Marines had made hundreds of these vehicles available for this operation.

Pete noticed Pharmacist Mate First Class Ryan Magruder, the medical corpsman who patched up more than a few Dog Company Marines on Tarawa, including Pete, double-checking supplies in his Unit 2 medical bag. He looked up and saw Pete watching him. Magruder smiled.

"How's the leg holding up, Hardball?" he called out over the battle racket.

Pete gave a thumbs-up, and Magruder nodded.

Sgt. "Biff" Hodges wended his way through the mass of men, coming from the front of the amtrac. He stopped beside Pete.

Leaning toward Pete's left ear, he said, "Coxswain told me the beach looks all fucked up. Jap fire is stopping everything, so forget about ridin' inland as planned. He's droppin' us on the beach."

"Just like Tarawa," Pete snarled. "Snafu."

Pete withdrew into a sullen silence. He jerked back to alertness when up in the front of the amtrac, the coxswain held up a hand with three fingers extended.

"Three minutes," he shouted.

"Second Squad, listen up," Pete called out. "When you debark from the ramp, fan out. Don't bunch up, but don't get separated from the squad. Keep moving. Off the beach if possible. The Japs'll have it zeroed in for mortars and artillery. Keep an eye on your NCOs. I'll see you all onshore."

Pete turned to face the ramp at the rear of the amtrac, then hunkered down and waited.

The amtracs—144 of them in the first wave, minus those that sat crippled or burning—closed relentlessly on the beach. Overhead, a Marine Corsair roared, machine guns pounding.

At 0840, all along the three-and-a-half-mile beachhead,

some three hundred LVTs began dropping the first Marines on the shore of Saipan. Eight thousand men splashed ashore within twenty minutes. The beach itself was a scene of chaos. Wrecked amtracs littered the sand as others tried to fulfill their mission of carrying troops to designated positions inland. All the while, the landing zone was being pummeled by Japanese artillery rounds fired from 75mm guns as far away as the ridgeline twenty-five hundred yards inland. Even targets not visible to the gunners on the high ground came under galling fire directed by artillery spotters high atop the smokestack of the sugarcane refinery at Charan Kanoa, which afforded them an unhindered view of the entire landing zone.

At the bow of Pete's amtrac, the coxswain leaned back.

"Thirty seconds!" he shouted above the roar of battle.

Christ, Pete thought. *I'm leading twelve men into battle. Please, God, don't let me fuck up.*

CHAPTER 2

As he prepared to set foot on the beach to a hot Jap reception, Pete recalled the day the invasion convoy slipped out to sea without fanfare, but any thoughts that their mission was unobserved soon vanished.

"You Marines of the Second and Fourth Divisions now heading toward Saipan," cooed Tokyo Rose, her sultry voice flowing from LST 968's public-address system. "What are you boys fighting us for? Wouldn't you rather be home with your wives and sweethearts? Why don't you quit now? Otherwise, I'm afraid you're all going to die."

Her prediction earned her a chorus of hoots and obscenities, but her warning was clear. Were the Marines charging into a trap?

Pete set his eyes on the ramp to the rear of the amtrac. Beneath him, he could tell that the vehicle's tracks were no longer churning water but rolling on the sandy bottom. Japanese bullets pinged off the armored sides like steel-jacketed hornets.

"This is as far as I can go!" the coxswain yelled.

The ramp dropped.

"Follow me!" Pete hollered.

Exiting the amtrac, he scurried across the wet sand. A quick backward glance told him that his men had rushed from the boat and were behind him, fanning out as directed. Invisible Japanese rounds punctuated by red tracers whizzed and hummed around his ears, some kicking up sandy geysers at his feet. Marines from earlier landings were all around, some digging in furiously, trying to burrow deep to avoid flying bullets and shrapnel. Others plunged ahead toward a four-foot-high sandy dune line that ran the length of Red Beach about fifteen yards inland from the water's edge. Not all made it. A number of Marines lay scattered on the beach, some nursing wounds and shouting for a corpsman and others dead, the uncaring sand soaking up their lifeblood.

As he hastened across the open beach, Pete heard a cry to his left as a Marine from First Squad was stitched by several rounds from a machine gun. Blood spurting from his wounds, the man collapsed. Beyond that, Pete saw an exploding artillery round catapult two Marines into the air.

The enemy fire grew in intensity as more artillery and mortar shells dropped among the invaders. Running full out, Pete heard a dull thunk, and something tugged at his waist, but he kept going. Realizing they'd never get off the beach ahead, the limited protection afforded by the ridge of sand beckoned.

"Take cover!" he cried. "Dig in!"

Reaching the long dune line, Pete dropped, hugging the sand as Japanese bullets zinged overhead and chewed at the crest. The rest of the squad followed, grateful for the meager protection. All, that is, except Wilmer Baumgartner. About three paces from the dune, shrapnel from a Japanese mortar round punched into his right side just above his belt. With a loud grunt of pain, he spun and fell. Aldrich saw the youngster go down and hurriedly crawled out to the man. Without a word, he grabbed Baumgartner by the straps of his pack and dragged him to the shelter of the sandy ridge.

"Corpsman!" he hollered. "Corpsman!"

Crouching low, Pete scurried to Aldrich's position. Baumgartner lay crying, clutching his bloody side.

"I don't wanna die," he pleaded. "Am I gonna die?"

A medical corpsman from Third Platoon was the first to respond. He knelt by Baumgartner.

"Take it easy Mac," he told the youth. "I got you."

He was rummaging through his Unit 2 bag when a Japanese bullet punched through his helmet. The man spun and lay facedown in the sand.

"Goddammit," Pete snarled. Then called, "Corpsman! Corpsman!"

Magruder arrived.

"Thank God," Pete said. "Just keep your head down."

Shoving the legs of his dead comrade out of the way, Magruder knelt by Baumgartner and began his work. As he fished for a syrette of morphine, Baumgartner sobbed, "Am I gonna die?"

"Not if I can help it," Magruder replied as he jabbed the boy in the left thigh.

"Don't worry," Pete told the young man. "Magruder here patched me up on Tarawa. You'll soon be back home making baseball bats again."

Baumgartner gave a drugged smile as he drifted into a morphine-induced haze.

Pete asked, "How is he?"

"As soon as I can, I'll get him loaded onto an LVT," Magruder answered. "We have two transports rigged up as temporary hospital ships, so they'll take him out."

Magruder saw the concern on Pete's face.

"Go easy, Hardball," Magruder said. "I don't think the wound's fatal—that is, if I can get him care."

Pete nodded.

The situation on the beach was pandemonium. Bodies of dead Marines as well as a number of Japanese corpses lay about in profusion. Scattered among these dead, friend and foe alike, was a maze of wrecked and burning LVTs, discarded weapons, and abandoned equipment.

Japanese machine gun bullets puckered the sand, while mortars and heavy artillery rounds dropped in hurling shards of steel in all directions. Pete was certain the artillery was located on the looming mass that on maps was identified as Mount Tapochau, the highest point on Saipan. But much of the Jap machine gun and small arms fire was coming from the tree line just ahead and the network of trenches that crisscrossed the fields beyond.

A tangle of trees lined the beachhead some twenty yards from the surf. Some of the trees lay shattered by the preinvasion bombardment, but many more remained, their bullet-scarred trunks standing amid a tangle of vines.

Pete glanced at his men. Most were crouched down, safe from bullets but still vulnerable to bursting shells. A few returned a feeble fire on the tree line, hoping to hit their tormentors. Pete was contemplating his situation when Lt. Cornwall and Gunny Nicholson materialized from a cloud of smoke billowing from a burning LVT.

"Thank Christ," Cornwall huffed as he dropped to the sand. "I was wondering where everybody was."

"Same here," Pete said. "First Squad is to my left, but that's all I know."

"Third Squad's with me," Cornwall said. Then he snarled. "Dammit. What a fuckup. That crazy current in the bay threw off our boats. We've got guys from the Eighth Marines landing on our beaches, and some of our guys have landed on the Sixth's beaches. Captain Stacey is trying to sort things out. But hell, half of First Platoon is missing, including Lt. Long."

"I think they're dead," Pete said somberly. "At least some of them. I saw Lt. Long's boat take a direct hit. Last I saw, it was on fire and sinking."

Nicholson turned to face Cornwall.

"Damn!" he snapped. "That's gonna be a blow to the skipper."

Cornwall looked at Pete.

"Stonewall wants a quick meeting," he said. "Get Hodges and then have your two squads follow me. Where are Pope and Yaz with those damned coffee grinders?"

"I think they're with Hodges," Pete said. "I'll make sure they come along."

Dispatching Potts to fetch First Squad and the two machine guns, Pete got his men ready for the move. Once the squads were together, Cornwall led them along the beach, keeping the dunes between them and the Jap-infested trees.

They found Stacey at his temporary HQ behind a disabled LVT. After placing their men along the dune line, Pete and Biff Hodges joined the other officers and NCOs gathered around the captain. As expected, Stonewall was shaken by the news of the loss of Lt. Long. He turned to young Second Lt. Michael Jones, who had joined the company two weeks before the division departed from Hawaii.

"Looks like you're First Platoon's new skipper, Lieutenant," Stacey said. "How many men do you have?"

The young man, whom Pete guessed was about the same age as his younger brother Charlie, gulped.

"I don't know, sir," he replied. "Maybe one squad."

"I don't want a maybe," Stonewall replied. "When we dismiss here, I want a number." He turned to the others. "We'll keep this brief before the Japs find us. We gotta get off this beach. Fast. The Japs have their artillery zeroed in, and there are more waves of Marines on the way. If they get here before we get off, we'll be like a lot of fish in a barrel. We gotta punch through that tree line."

"I thought the amtracs were supposed to take us through the trees and a few hundred yards beyond," said Third Platoon's leader, First Lt. Raymond Pickering.

"Yeah," Stacey replied. "And Santa Claus was supposed to come down my chimney last Christmas."

"Can we count on any supporting fire?" Nicholson asked.

"Doubtful," Stacey answered. "The whole regiment is attacking. We'll have our machine guns lay down a base of fire, but for now, no mortars or armor. We don't think there are a lot of Japs in those woods, and the tree line isn't very deep. But trust that the Nips will be well dug in—snipers, spider holes, maybe a small bunker or two. Hopefully, one of our bazooka teams can handle those."

"If we get through the tree line, then what?" Cornwall asked.

"Our objective for right now is the narrow-gauge rail embankment that skirts the coastal road," he said. "Once it's secured, the entire regiment will push inland." He fished out a silver whistle attached to a leather cord around his neck. "When I blow this, we go. Get your men ready."

Pete and the others rejoined their commands, crawling on hands and knees along the line of dunes. Back with Second Squad, Pete found a few of his men exchanging fire with unseen enemies in the trees. He briefed his three fire team leaders.

"When we move, we all go together," he said. "Lead 'em,

scream at 'em, kick 'em in the ass, whatever you need to do, but keep them moving."

Settling back, Pete risked a glance over the dune at the deadly open expanse between his squad and the trees. His men would not be the first Marines to try to force their way across. At least a dozen corpses in Marine battle dress lay sprawled on the sand between him and the trees. This did not make for an encouraging sight.

As he awaited the signal, Pete watched more landing boats make their way toward the beach. A few Higgins boats had come in, and Pete watched a gun crew manhandling a 37mm anti-tank gun through the shallow surf. His heart gladdened when, further along, two Sherman tanks and a half-track mounting a 75mm gun rolled ashore.

Pete's throat was parched from the heat. He felt it had to be at least eighty degrees already, and it was only ten o'clock in the morning. Pete pulled out one of his two canteens. Filled just before he left the ship, he wondered why it felt so light. Then he saw the hole and recalled the thunking sound and tug at his waist. A Japanese slug had punched clean through. He tossed the worthless canteen away.

To his right, Pete watched Sammy Dubbs. The boy was kneeling in the sand, hands clasped, eyes tightly closed. When he opened them, he saw his sergeant looking at him, and he smiled meekly.

"You prayin', Dubbs?" Pete asked.

"Yes, I am, Sergeant," he replied. "I'll say one for you, if you'd like."

"Thanks, kid," Pete answered. "I'm okay." He paused. "You're from Pennsylvania. Bethlehem, I think you said?"

He wanted the boy to focus his mind on something else.

"Yeah," he replied, eager for the diversion. "Christmas City,

USA. Every Christmas the town goes all out with decorations. Lights. The works."

"Sounds nice," Pete said.

An anxious look came over Dubbs's face.

"I'm scared, Sergeant," he stammered. "People are dying all around me. I've never seen people killed before."

"Only a fool isn't scared," Pete said. "I pissed my pants at least twice on Tarawa."

"You, Sergeant?"

"Yes, so there's no shame in being scared. Just follow your training. When we go, keep moving. Always remember a target standing still is easier to hit than one moving."

Just then, Second Battalion's .30-caliber machine guns began chattering all along the dune line. Firing short bursts to keep from burning out the barrels and having to replace them under fire, the Brownings raked the trees and swept through the overhead branches as fast as the loaders could slap in new ammo belts. Pete watched smoke and splintered wood shower forth from the tortured trees and wondered if any Japs were being hit.

Then came Stonewall's shrill whistle.

With a shout of "Let's go," Pete and Second Squad rose up along with the rest of the battalion. As the squad closed the distance, a few desultory shots rang out, but return fire was a lot lighter than anyone dared hope. With surprising ease, the battalion reached the wood line. Plunging into the trees, the men had to clamber through a stand of dense underbrush and tangled roots that snagged their clothes and twisted around their boondockers. As he pushed forward, Pete was startled when a bullet slammed into a tree just inches from his head. The shot that buzzed his ear came from above, so Pete lifted his Thompson and emptied half a thirty-round stick into several of the nearest trees. There was the sound of splintering wood, and something heavy thudded to the ground. The Japanese soldier who had come close to canceling Pete's ticket tried to painfully roll over, until Pete fired a three-round burst into the man.

A few feet to Pete's left, Honeybun Hullihen flinched as a bullet tore through the left sleeve of his shirt. He noticed a section of the ground drop, then slowly rise again. A rifle barrel appeared, but before the man could sight in for a second try, Hullihen took three quick paces forward and kicked the rifle aside. With the muzzle of his Garand, he threw back the camouflaged lid of the spider hole and fired four rounds into the startled face of the man inside.

Cleverly concealed beneath downed tree branches, a Japanese soldier sprang to his feet, and with a snarl, lunged toward Dembrowski, his bayonet-tipped rifle thrust forward. Reacting quickly, Dembrowski fired off a six-round burst from his Thompson. At close range, the heavy rounds ripped through the man's torso, sending out a spray of blood as he was slammed over backward.

A Japanese soldier also leaped out at Potter, but, alert after his being hit on Tarawa, he squeezed off two rounds from his Garand, and the enemy soldier dropped to the ground like a sack of grain. However, Potts did not see the second man. Potter fell, dead before he knew he'd been shot.

Aldrich saw his comrade die and blasted his attacker with his Garand. He knelt by Potter and felt for a pulse even though he knew he'd find none.

"Goddamn it," sighed the Professor, who never swore. Then he removed one of Potter's identity tags and moved on.

As the Marines pushed through the woods, the defending Japanese retreated rearward like partridges flushed from a thicket. Marines, eager to lash out at their tormentors, fired at the fleeing enemy, dropping a few.

Continuing their attack, the long line of Marines from Second Battalion advanced out of the trees and into a gently rolling field. They'd gone about twenty paces when they walked into a wall of small arms fire. The unexpected fusillade ripped through the ranks, and men fell, some writhing from wounds, others in the silence of death. Those unscathed dove to the ground to find what meager protection the grassy meadow could offer.

Now it became evident where the fugitives from the tree line had been heading. About five hundred yards ahead, the Japanese had constructed a long trench. Helmeted heads popped up. They opened with a volley of rifle fire and were soon joined by Type 96 machine guns emplaced in sandbag-protected revetments along the trench. Their five-hundred-round-per-minute rate of fire was especially devastating, forcing the Marines to pull back to the trees for protection, dragging their wounded along. Cries of "Corpsman!" sang out from the American line.

The firing from both sides was heavy even though most of the Marines realized that at this range, it would take an incredibly lucky shot to hit so small a target as a Japanese head. Keeping low, Pete moved along the line of his squad, encouraging the men—especially the new ones—by telling them to "keep firing" and "pour it on 'em." And they did. Pete heaved a sigh of relief when he saw Nicholson approach through the trees.

Crouching behind a small knoll, Pete said, "I was never so glad to see you. What the hell are we gonna do? We can't sit here all day just burning powder. We're sitting ducks."

Nicholson offered Pete a Lucky Strike, but Pete shook his head. Nicholson lit up.

"Captain's on the horn now," Nicholson said through an exhale of smoke. "Pogey Bait's mortars are setting up behind us, and Stonewall's trying to get some Navy destroyers to drop some 5-inch stuff on the Nips. Once that starts, have your boys keep their heads down. Naval fire is notorious for firing shorts, and there's no Purple Heart for being nicked by friendly fire."

Pete nodded.

"Then what?"

"On Stacey's whistle, we advance across the field and kick the asses of any Japs still standing," he replied. Then he added, "How'd your squad fare so far?"

"Baumgartner got hit back on the beach," Pete said. "Doc sent him to the rear. Other than that . . ."

Aldrich, who was hunched by a spindly ironwood tree, said, "Not quite."

He held out an identity tag and tossed it to Pete, who read "Stanley Potter."

"Damn," Pete said. "He was on Saipan less than three hours. After Tarawa, that just doesn't seem right."

"Some guys got no luck," Nicholson observed. Then he reached for the disk. "I'll give this to the captain. One more letter he'll have to write."

"No," Pete said. "He was one of mine. I'll write that letter."

"Okay," Nicholson said. "I'll tell the captain so he can log it into the company record."

Then he was off.

After Nicholson departed, Aldrich said to Pete, "Are you sure you can write that letter? He was on my fire team. I'll write it if you'd like."

"No," Pete said. "I'm in charge of the squad, so this is something I gotta learn to do."

The back-and-forth firing persisted for another twenty minutes when a telltale "whump" announced that a 60mm mortar had just launched its rocket. More followed. The first round fell short, dirt and debris blossoming upward a good fifty yards in front of the trench. The next volley straddled the trench, after which the mortars found their range. A whoosh overhead announced the arrival of Navy shells, whose detonations just a hundred yards in front of the Marines forced men to involuntarily duck.

The next volley fell closer to the Japanese line. The third volley hit the trenches, but by that time, there were few targets to hit as the occupants headed for the rear.

Stacey's whistle sounded.

"Let's go! Let's go!" came the call up and down the battalion line. The Marines emerged from the woods and swiftly rushed forward. The mortar and naval fire lifted as the Marines closed the gap between them and the enemy. They'd covered more than half the five hundred yards to the trench when the Marines discovered that not all the Japanese had run. Machine gun fire from a pair of Type 96s erupted from a low pillbox directly in front of Third Platoon. Three men, including the platoon's CO, First Lt. Pickering, were hit in the initial burst, and everyone else dove to the ground.

On the far left of the battalion line, the remnants of First Platoon, down to sixteen men after the loss of Woody Long and almost two entire squads, tried an end run, banking on the machine gunners not being able to traverse their weapons far enough. However, as they closed to within a hundred yards, they came under unexpected heavy fire that reduced their number by two men. With both Dog and Easy Companies now stymied by the pillbox, the entire battalion attack was bogged down.

A sudden explosion blossoming in front of the pillbox announced the arrival of armor units rolling in from the beach.

The shell came from one of two Sherman tanks just now emerging from the tree line. Even as Pete watched, the second tank's 75mm gun barked. The well-aimed shell scored a direct hit on the pillbox, which, evidently lacking concrete reinforcement, blew apart in a ball of flaming debris.

The attack order renewed, the Marines lifted themselves and surged ahead. With the destruction of the pillbox, many of the remaining defenders fled. A few held their posts as Marines jumped into the trench. Bayonets flashed and rifles discharged at close range as men of both sides grappled in a life-or-death struggle.

Young Private Goodman leaped into the trench and landed squarely on a hunched-over Japanese soldier, and both crashed to the dirt floor. The enemy soldier, who looked as young as Goodman, regained his feet first. Both men looked at each other in shock and surprise, but it was the Japanese man who had the quickest reaction. With his rifle knocked from his grasp by the fall, he slid his bayonet from its scabbard. Goodman's gaze was transfixed on the menacing weapon, with its fifteen-inch blade and nasty-looking J-shaped quillon at the hilt. Instinctively, he raised his Garand and fired two unaimed rounds into the man's chest. The Japanese soldier's face took on a look of astonishment as he collapsed backward against the trench wall. Goodman watched the man take his final breath, then he sank to the ground and wept.

Securing the trench took just five minutes, and every enemy soldier who chose to die for his emperor did so. But the Marines had no chance to take a much-needed breather. With the enemy in flight, the way was open to the coastal highway and the rail embankment just beyond.

"Come on! Come on! Let's go!" officers and NCOs shouted as they urged their men onward.

Pete found Goodman sitting on the ground crying. He grabbed the young man's arm and lifted him.

"Let's go, Goodman," he said. "We gotta push on."

"I killed him," the boy wept, pointing.

"You had to," Pete said. "We'll talk about it later. We gotta go."

Reluctantly, Goodman stumbled forward.

Within minutes, they were running across the hard-packed dirt road to reach the railroad tracks. The Marines dropped to the rail line, huffing and puffing from their exertions amid the humid air of what was rapidly becoming a very hot day.

Their respite was short-lived. Before the men were fully dug in, some of the Japanese 75mm guns on the ridge that had been firing on the beach shortened their range and began dropping shells along the Marines' newly won ground. Men flattened themselves as shards of shrapnel sang through the air around them.

The barrage was furious but brief because the Japanese artillerymen soon had worries of their own. A flock of Navy Hellcats providing air cover for the beach landings came swooping down, attracted by the smoking cannons. As they skimmed the ridge, what appeared to be black pods fell from their undercarriages. Wherever the pods struck, thick balls of orange flame and greasy black smoke boiled up from the earth. The flames seemed to cling to the ridge. Artillery fire diminished noticeably as enemy gun crews not roasted hastily towed their pieces back into the protective mouths of the island's caves.

"If I knew who invented that stuff, I'd recommend him for a medal," Aldrich said.

Not under fire for the first time since landing, the men relaxed. Pete raised his head to scope out the ground ahead. What he saw was a wide field of brush, which soon merged into a patchwork of sugarcane fields. Some of the cane was flattened, some burned, probably by the Navy to deprive the enemy of cover, while in other fields the cane stood tall. What looked like a small village stood at the far edge of the cane fields. Beyond was a large patch of woods before the ground sloped upward to form the foothills of Mount Tipo Pale. Rising just to the east of Tipo Pale was the formidable slopes of Mount Tapochau.

It was midafternoon by now, and the sun was on its downward track. The entire Second Regiment formed an arc on the coastal plain, while its right was bent around to link up with the Sixth and Eighth Regiments coming in from other beaches. Ahead lay Saipan's coastal plain, which sloped upward, gently at first, from the beach to the foothills of Mount Tipo Pale. Their move was not uncontested as Japanese fire from entrenchments straight ahead and from the ridge now on their right tore at the advancing men. After pushing forward a hundred yards or so, the advance ground to a halt. Pete saw Nicholson coming along the line. He knelt by Pete.

"Have your boys dig in—two men to a foxhole," he said. "I think this is home for tonight." He looked around. "You know this is almost the same spot the amtracs were to take us before letting us off. This is the Tractor Control Line." He pointed to the ridge still smoldering from napalm. "That was our Day One objective."

"Must be wonderful to be an armchair general in some HQ three thousand miles from the flying bullets," Pete said. Then he added, "I saw Lt. Pickering get hit. How is he?"

"Bullet grazed his shoulder," Nicholson replied. "Doc patched him up."

"You know the Japs are gonna hit us tonight," Pete said.

"Yep," Nicholson answered.

"You also know we're open on our left flank all the way to the beach," Pete noted.

"No problem," Nicholson said. "First Battalion finally arrived.

Their amtracs missed our landing area. They'll be filling in on the left and anchoring our line. Have your guys get some rest now. Once the sun goes down, I want a hundred percent alert."

Pete nodded, then asked, "With Lt. Long gone, who did Stonewall tap as his XO?"

"Lt. Cornwall," Nicholson said. "He's gonna miss Long. They were tight. Did you know that back in '40, Long drove stock car in the Daytona Beach Road Course?"

"No shit?" Pete replied.

"Yeah," Nicholson continued. "It was at a place called Ponce Inlet. Damned shame."

He departed, and Pete began checking on his guys, starting with Goodman.

He found the youngster leaning against the foxhole he shared with Honeybun. He still looked shaken.

"I know this can get under your skin," Pete said. "But you gotta put it behind you."

"I keep seeing his face," the youth replied.

Pete fished a pack of Camels from an ammo pouch and lit one up.

"When I was coming ashore on Tarawa, my best buddy got killed right in front of me," he said. "I fell to my knees and bawled like a goddamned schoolboy."

"Really, Sergeant?"

Pete described dragging Ted ashore and spotting a Jap tank on the beach.

"A Jap soldier was on top," Pete said. "His eyes met mine, and for a second or two we stared at each other. He saw what I was doing for my buddy, and the bastard saluted me. I couldn't believe it. Then we both went back to the war. But for the rest of the battle, I could not get that man's face out of my mind. It haunted me. It still does."

"You haven't heard the best part," Pete continued. "Two hours before Tarawa was secured, we'd just wiped out about fifty Nips who staged one last banzai. We think they're all dead, when suddenly, out of the smoke, there's this lone Jap standing. He's got no rifle, just a grenade. But as he's about to throw it, his eyes met mine. It was the same damned Jap who was haunting my brain. He saw it too, and he hesitated for just a second. But in that second, he got shot. His grenade fell short. It killed a buddy but only wounded me. Had he not hesitated, his grenade probably would've punched my ticket. The Jap did die, but lived long enough to salute me again." Pete briefly paused. "I still wonder who he was, where he lived, about his family. Was he married? Did he have any kids? All questions I'll never get answered. But the war has moved on, and now you need to put that man behind you just like I've had to do. Think you can do that?"

Goodman nodded.

Pete patted Goodman on the shoulder and continued to move along the squad line. Reaching Fire Team Three's part of the line on the left of the platoon, Pete dropped to the ground beside Bucket Harnish.

"Everything good here?" Pete asked.

"Yeah," Bucket replied.

Charles Harnish had earned the odd nickname in boot camp when, as punishment, he was forced to stand on the parade ground with his bucket on his head and sing kids' songs like "Baa, Baa, Black Sheep" and "Mary Had a Little Lamb," until the DI, "Bull Moose" Blakely, told him to stop. If he didn't sing loud enough, Blakely would whack the bucket with his nightstick and yell, "Louder."

"Say, Hardball," Reb Marshall asked from the foxhole he shared with Vivian Miller. "Is it true that Potsy bought it?"

Pete nodded.

"Damn! Tha' there boy had the evil eye on him."

The Second Battalion line remained relatively quiet for the remainder of the afternoon and into the evening hours, while Japanese guns on the slopes of the hills out in front continued to pound the congested beach area. Even regular attacks by napalm-toting planes didn't stop the threat.

It was well into the evening hours when the sound of anti-aircraft guns from the harbor began to rattle. From his position, Pete watched as about half a dozen Japanese planes, probably from the Nip base at Truk, soared over the fleet and began dropping bombs and launching torpedoes.

"Looks like it's the Navy's turn to duck," Harnish said.

An explosion sounded, and dense black smoke rose into the sky. Pete could not see what was hit, but it seemed to burn fiercely.

"Whoa," Pete said. "Something got nailed."

Men cheered as they watched one, then another, and finally a third enemy plane fall toward the water, trailing smoke.

The aerial display had been over about an hour when Pharmacist Mate First Class Ryan Magruder approached from the direction of the beach.

"Everyone okay up here?" he asked.

"So far," Pete said. "You corpsmen seem to know everything. What happened at the beach?"

"An LST out beyond the reef took a torpedo," he said. "About ten guys got killed, and the thing sank. They also hit a light carrier that had to head away for repairs."

"Baumgartner?" Pete asked.

"He's aboard one of the three hospital LSTs," Magruder said. "But they're all loaded to capacity. We've had almost two thousand casualties today so far. Three hospital ships are on their way here. They should arrive in a day or two."

Pete nodded somberly and looked toward the woods a thousand yards ahead.

They'll hit us tonight, he thought. *The casualty list is just beginning.*

CHAPTER 3

With his binoculars pressed tightly against his face, Major Tadashi Tanimura scanned the glasses across the panorama of war laid out before him. His perch was a camouflaged thirty-foot observation tower on Mount Tipo Pale southeast of the town of Garapan.

"They have much power," said Lt. Col. Yukimatsu Ogawa, commander of the 136th Infantry Regiment, as he watched the Americans battle their way ashore.

Colonel Ogawa had been Tadashi's commanding officer before he was plucked from the regiment to serve as the Forty-Third Division's aide-de-camp under then commander Prince Kaya Tsunenori. Tadashi remained in that job when the prince was replaced by Lt. General Yoshitsugu Saito. Then the third man in the tower spoke.

"*Maryland*," Vice Admiral Chuichi Nagumo muttered half to himself as he peered through large naval binoculars. "*Pennsylvania. Tennessee. California.*" He lowered the glasses and turned to the other two men. "At Pearl Harbor, my airmen sank or heavily damaged all four of those battleships. Now here they are. I wish I could resurrect *Akagi, Kaga, Hiryu*, and *Soryu* so easily."

There was much sadness in Nagumo's voice. The commander of the Central Pacific Area Fleet lamented the loss of four of Japan's precious aircraft carriers during the Midway operation. After that defeat, it seemed as if *Yawata*, the *kamisama* of war, turned his back on Nagumo. The admiral looked older than his fifty-seven years. In 1941 he'd been lauded as a hero when his fleet of warships, the powerful *Kido Butai*, or Mobile Unit, smashed the US Pacific Fleet at Pearl Harbor. When *Kido Butai* itself was smashed at Midway six months later, he had to be talked out of committing suicide.

That disaster had been kept secret from the civilian population. Many in the military—and even for a time the emperor himself—had not known. But it had crushed Nagumo's spirit. In March of 1944, he was put in charge of Fourteenth Air Fleet and Central Pacific Area Fleet, covering the Mariana Islands. It was a figurehead position that left him more or less marooned here on Saipan.

With all due respect to the man and his rank, Tadashi said, "Admiral Ozawa will soon be here with the fleet, and the Decisive Battle will alter the course of the war."

Tadashi had spent much of the day moving on foot along the slopes inland of the invasion beaches, talking to unit commanders and observing the opening phase of the fight in order to report conditions back to his boss, General Saito.

Tadashi wasn't particularly impressed by General Saito, seeing him as indecisive and possibly even inept. Tadashi had much preferred serving under Saito's predecessor, Prince Tsunenori. However, the prince was a cousin of Empress Nagako, so when the division was being transferred to Saipan, it was decided that having a member of the Imperial Family possibly die in battle would never do.

Tadashi, however, was happy to be sent to Saipan. As a boy, he had lived on the island for many years. Nagumo knew of Tadashi's connection. Even though the young major was in the Army, the old sailor looked on him fondly, so much so that he often tacked the polite "san" at the end when he spoke to Tadashi.

"This is very difficult for you to watch," Nagumo mused.

Tadashi nodded.

"The happiest years of my life were spent here," he replied.

Tadashi's father, Hideo, came from a wealthy family. He had a keen interest in farming, and his social position allowed him the opportunity to study agriculture in the United States at the University of Nebraska. After graduating in 1911, he moved back to Tokyo. In Japan, Hideo took a position in the Ministry of Agriculture. With his knowledge of increasing crop yield, the Ministry sent him back to America in late 1914 to learn American techniques. In early 1923, Hideo Tanimura was transferred to Saipan, where the sugarcane industry was just gaining momentum.

Tadashi pointed toward the shore and a cluster of buildings that comprised Garapan.

"We had a house on the eastern side of the town," he said, recalling the well-manicured gardens, fountains, and ornate bridges often accessed through traditional *torii* gateways, all mimicking a Japan he had never seen until he entered the Army preparatory school, *Rikugun Yonen Gakko* in Nagoya, in 1932.

"You're a well-traveled young man," Ogawa said. "Tell Admiral Nagumo about how you also lived in America. And about your mother."

That was a part of his life Tadashi did not wish to delve

into, especially with American Marines storming ashore with every intention of killing him and his comrades. But there was no escaping the fact that when his father returned from America after college, he brought along not just his knowledge but a young American wife, Peggy Driscoll, who had been studying to be a teacher but became enthralled by the bespectacled young man from halfway around the world.

"Honto, Tadashi-san?" Nagumo asked.

"Yes, it's true," Tadashi said. "My mother was an American who met my father in college. My mother is—was—Christian, although she and my father were married in a traditional Shinto ceremony. We lived in the United States for about eight years. I started school and had American playmates. I speak English fluently."

"Were you born in America?" Ogawa inquired.

"I was born in Japan, just before we sailed for America."

"Have you thought that some of those men out there might be your friends, Major?" Ogawa asked.

"It would not matter if they were," he replied. "My loyalty is to Japan and the emperor."

In his years here on the island, Tadashi had explored its numerous caves. He had many friends, including among the native Chamorro. Many of his Japanese friends scoffed at him. To them, the Chamorro, most of Spanish descent, were culturally and ethnically inferior. Inwardly, he detested how the occupying soldiers of Nippon used the Chamorro as slaves and pack animals to build island defenses. Regardless, Tadashi continued his friendships.

One Chamorro man he especially liked was named Fernando Casio. Well into his fifties, Fernando, whose entire wardrobe seemed to consist of tattered trousers, a sleeveless shirt, and a broad-brimmed straw hat covering unruly black hair, operated one of the island's narrow-gauge steam engines on its sugarcane run. Oftentimes Fernando let the boy ride along on his rounds. At each stop, Tadashi aided Casio and the other farmers to load harvested cane stalks onto the open rail cars. In early May 1944, when Tadashi returned to Saipan as a soldier, he quickly looked up his old friend. Fernando was overjoyed to see Tadashi, even allowing him to once again ride along in the steam engine.

Two weeks later, American carrier planes strafed the island's airfields and bombed the sugarcane fields in an attempt to burn the stalks and give Japanese soldiers fewer places to hide when the invasion began.

One of the American planes caught Fernando's little train chugging along near the village of Tanapag with a load of harvested cane. After the all clear, Fernando was discovered slumped over in the engine, his dead hand still clutching the throttle of the bullet-riddled engine.

"Where is your family now, Tadashi-san?" Nagumo asked.

"My father was called back to Japan in 1936. I had come back in '32 to attend the Army preparatory school," Tadashi said. "They returned to Tokyo, although my mother was sick by that time. She had a bad heart. She died in 1938. Father has retired and moved back to Yonezawa, where we had lived when I was born. It's just him and me now. I had no brothers or sisters."

"Were you glad to get back to Japan?" Ogawa asked. "I'd have been overjoyed."

"I had no memories of Japan," Tadashi said. "It was almost like a foreign country. The only good thing that happened to me, aside from the prep school and the Army academy, the *Rikugun Shikan Gakko*, is that I met a girl."

He smiled sheepishly as he fished a photo out of his rucksack and passed it around. The image was of a shy-looking maiden in a traditional kimono and holding an ornate fan. "Her name is Kokoro. It fits her perfectly. She has a good heart and clever mind, but she is also emotional."

"She looks as gracious as a willow," Nagumo said.

Tadashi fished into a breast pocket of his tunic and brought out a half pack of Hikari cigarettes, a parting gift from Prince Tsunenori. He had vowed to himself to smoke them sparingly, but this seemed like a fitting occasion. He fired one up, then put the glasses back to his face.

"I wish the Americans had given us more time," he mused. "I was ordered to look over our defenses, then I reported to General Saito that it would take us six months to properly defend the island. With American submarines sinking so many of our transport ships, we received insufficient supplies."

He puffed on the cigarette and continued, "General Saito seemed satisfied. Some planner in Tokyo told him the Americans would not be in a position to strike us until November at the earliest."

Despite Tadashi's report, Saito was confident of success.

"Take this down," he had told Tadashi. "It is a general edict I want sent out to all the troops."

Tadashi began writing as the bandy-legged former cavalryman dictated, "It is expected that the enemy will be destroyed on the beaches through our policy of tactical command based on aggressiveness, determination, and initiative.

"When the enemy elements are attempting to land, our main firepower will be directed at the landing forces prior to their arrival on the beach. Taking advantage of the confusion we will inflict on them, the enemy will rapidly be destroyed by our counterattacks, mounted from all sectors wherever the opportunity presents itself.

"Should the enemy succeed in getting a foothold on the beach, intense fire will be concentrated. When the time is right, determined counterattacks will be launched with the aid of our reserves and our tanks. Although the advantages of surprise will be lost, the enemy landing forces can be dealt with by further attacks after nightfall."

Saito's confidence in success was shared by Tadashi. He was sure of victory despite the fact it was sheer chance that he reached the island at all. In preparing for its departure for Saipan, an insufficient number of transports meant the Forty-Third Division was sent in two echelons. The first, which included Saito and his staff, arrived safely. The second echelon was less fortunate. On June 5, torpedoes from an American submarine sent the *Takaoka Maru* to the bottom. Carrying men of the 118th Infantry Regiment, the ship sank quickly. Most of the soldiers managed to escape, but a sizeable contingent perished.

But the worst was yet to come. American submarines struck repeatedly over a two-day period, during which five more transports were sunk. Tadashi was dockside when what was left of the convoy dropped anchor at Charan Kanoa. He was gladdened that eighty percent of the men from the torpedoed ships had been rescued, but they were a sorry sight to see. They had lost all their equipment and weapons. Their uniforms were torn and rumpled and oil-stained from being in the water among sinking ships.

Taking another look at the invasion beaches, Nagumo's eyes went skyward as a trio of American warplanes passed overhead.

"Have you seen what you needed to see, Loyal and Faithful Servant?" Nagumo asked Tadashi, using the translation of the young major's name.

Tadashi nodded.

"Then we'd best get out of this tower before one of those accursed flyers sees us."

A staff car, the captured Plymouth, was concealed under some trees, waiting to take Tadashi and Nagumo to Saito's command center.

The day before the invasion, Saito relocated his headquarters from Charan Kanoa inland to a cave about two miles from the village of Tsutsuran. Tadashi found his commander in conference with Colonel Matsutake Suzuki, who served as both commander of the 135th Regiment and Saito's chief of staff. The three men were leaning over a table and studying a well-worn map, on which was scribbled notations outlining four defensive zones traced in red ink. One zone extended from the west shore at Flores Point and the seaplane base about a mile and a half north of Garapan to the east coast just above Hashigoru. The zone was commanded by Suzuki.

Another zone ran along the east coast south to Mount Tapochau, then extended west to the coast below Garapan. This area was defended by Colonel Ogawa's 136th Regiment. Directly south of that zone to the north of Charan Kanoa was the Central Sector, defended by Lt. Col. Saku Nakai. The largest defensive zone indicated on the map was the Southern Zone, which defended the entire lower third of the island. This zone was defended by Yoshira Oka's Forty-Seventh Independent Mixed Brigade as well as elements of the Twenty-Fifth Antiaircraft Regiment centered around Aslito airfield.

A varied assortment of other smaller units, plus marooned survivors whose ships had been sunk, rounded out the defense, giving Saito and Nagumo some thirty-five thousand men to defend the island.

Upon entering the cave, Nagumo walked directly to the map table. Tadashi waited patiently just inside the cave's mouth for Saito to acknowledge him. As the three officers conversed in low tones, in the background Tadashi was aware of the steady drumbeat of bombs and artillery coming from the invasion beaches two miles to the west.

Finally, Saito looked up.

"Major," he greeted. "Please come."

Tadashi bowed to the senior officers, then walked to the table. Saito indicated the map.

"Please," the general said. "Tell me what you observed."

Tadashi swept a hand along the west coast of the island, pointing out that the Americans had a beachhead extending from just south of Garapan almost to Charan Kanoa.

"They are coming ashore in great numbers," he said. "I am guessing, but at the present rate, they could easily land as many as ten thousand men by nightfall."

"How far inland have they gotten?" Suzuki asked brusquely. It was no secret among the staff that Suzuki viewed Tadashi with disdain. Vehemently anti-American, he was deeply suspicious of Tadashi's family ties to the United States. Tadashi had learned to shrug off such impolite insinuations. His breeding was hard to disguise. At six foot one, he stood out in a land where the average height for a man was eight inches shorter. His deep blue eyes were another giveaway, a trait he inherited from his American mother.

"Since the Americans began landing this morning, I spent time with both Colonel Ogawa and Colonel Oka, as the landings are in their sectors," Tadashi said. "From what they tell me, the Americans have made inroads. Some have gotten as far inland as the Lake Susupe area, and their troops have taken the outskirts of Charan Kanoa. At the northern end of the invasion area, the Americans have advanced to the tracks of the sugar train. But nowhere have they moved inland farther than half a mile. Meanwhile, they continue to stack up on the beaches."

"Colonel Oka and Colonel Ogawa," Suzuki said, "did you think to ask them if they can hold their ground for now and prevent the Americans from advancing inland any further?"

"They've both taken heavy losses," Tadashi said, ignoring the jab. "But they have a firm hold on the ridges and high ground overlooking the beaches, and both, especially Colonel Ogawa, have more than enough men and more than enough guns to hold the enemy in place for twenty-four hours. Maybe longer."

Saito nodded with satisfaction. He walked slowly to a nearby cabinet and removed a half-empty bottle of Suntory whisky. Pouring a glass, he offered the bottle to Suzuki, Nagumo, and Tadashi.

"Twenty-four hours is sufficient," Saito said after taking a sip of the mahogany-colored liquid. "It will give us time to gather our troops and tanks. They know what is expected of them?"

"Yes sir," Tadashi replied. "When he is fully moved into position, Colonel Ogawa will send his 136th Regiment at the center of the American lines. Also, Colonel Goto expects to have sixty tanks ready to join the attack. Colonel Yakazo will send his troops against the American left flank."

Saito nodded, then took another thoughtful sip of the Suntory.

"If we can tear a hole in the American perimeter and get into his rear, we can do him mortal damage," Saito mused.

"Are you sure it will be enough?" Suzuki asked. "You heard Major Tanimura say they could have ten thousand men on that beach. Ogawa and Yakazo together can muster no more than four thousand, and that's if they throw in every man. Among other scattered units in that sector, six thousand men would be the most, unless we strip troops from other sectors."

Tadashi's jaw dropped. He hadn't known that Saito had

allocated so few men to what he clearly saw must be an all-out effort.

"General," he said, knowing that what he was about to say, contradicting his commanding officer, was almost akin to an insult. "Do you not think we should commit as many men as we can get our hands on?"

The other officers stood in silence over this brash statement, but Saito seemed not to notice.

"What we lack in numbers we more than make up for in courage and night-fighting ability," he said. "You all know that the Americans' decadent lifestyle makes them poor soldiers. They have no Bushido code to guide them. They lack honor."

Tadashi was troubled by Saito's confidence. Did the man not remember Guadalcanal? Bougainville? Tarawa? Did he not know that just recently, Kwajalein and Eniwetok in the Marshall Islands fell?

"This is where the Navy comes in," Nagumo chimed in. "Even as we speak, Admiral Ozawa's Mobile Fleet is lifting anchor and steaming toward a rendezvous. They should be within striking range in three or four days. It will be a great battle. They will smash the American fleet. The transports, those not sunk by our planes, will flee like scared children, and those men on the beach will have no choice. Cut off, they must either choose death, for which they have no stomach, or disgraceful surrender."

Tadashi stood silent. He had pushed his luck. He dared not disagree again.

Saito finished off his whisky and sat the empty glass firmly down on the center of the Saipan map.

"The Mariana Islands are a key part of the Empire's Absolute Defense Line," he said roughly as the sound of battle echoed in the distance. "From here, Tokyo is thirteen hundred miles, and while no bomber I know of can reach our homeland from here, the fall of Saipan will give the Americans a base from which to capture islands that will put Tokyo within bombing range. That cannot be allowed to happen. We must hold at all costs. Our bodies must become a bulwark of the Pacific. For if we fail, I fear America will win this war."

Tadashi nodded soberly. He and Saito finally agreed.

CHAPTER 4

June 16 was a day of waiting for the thousands of Marines already onshore. "When are they coming?" was the question most asked.

But outside of a doomed charge by a few hundred Japanese sailors, the First Yokosuka Special Naval Landing Force that was broken in blood on the coastal road, the Japanese did not come. Instead, by order of General Saito, they silently marshaled their forces in preparation for what all felt would be a crushing attack on their hated enemies.

Pete used the time to mingle among the squad, especially the rookies, and put them at ease.

He remembered how he had been tough on them that first day they'd met at Camp Tarawa.

Calling the new men together, he said, "My name is Sgt. Talbot. I am your squad leader. You may hear some of the veterans call me Hardball, but you men have not yet earned that privilege. You will call me 'Sergeant' or 'Sgt. Talbot.' Don't think

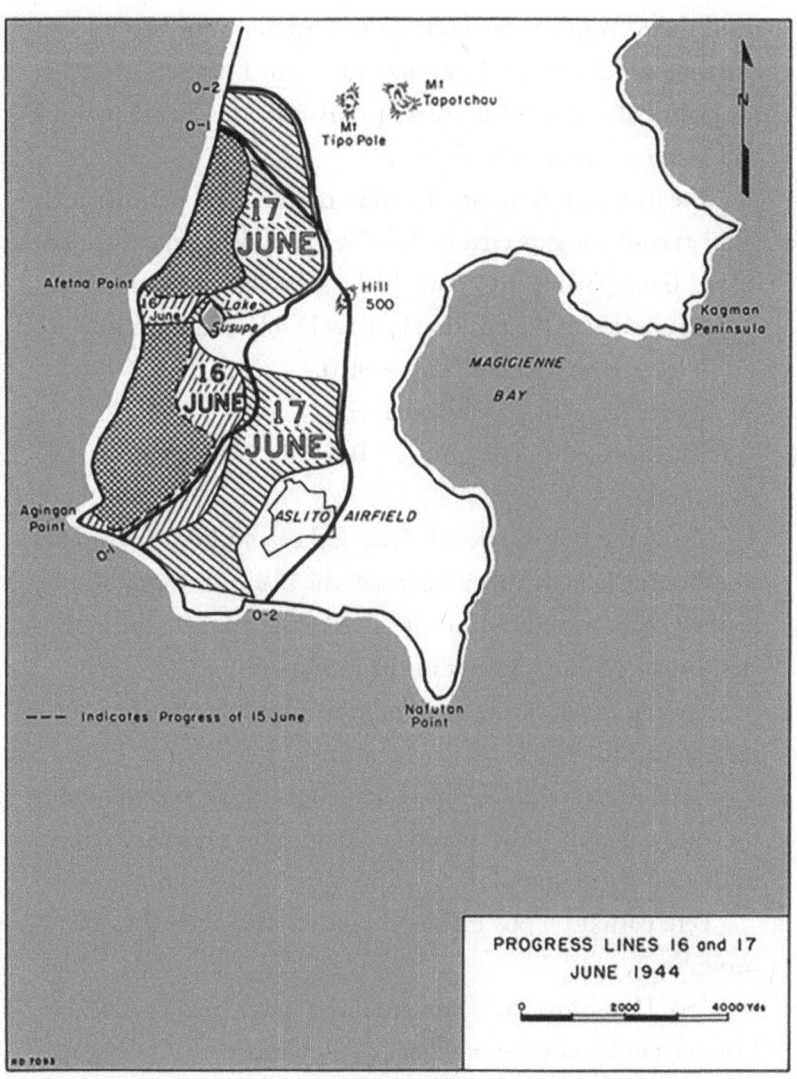

PROGRESS LINES 16 and 17
JUNE 1944

that because boot camp is over things will get cushy. You will train hard and be pushed to the limit. You will work side by side with the veterans, who've been battle-tested. Talk to them. Learn from them. Your life depends on it. Give me your best efforts, and you and I will get along just fine. But I have no stomach for eight balls who think they can just slide by. Try that and I will land on you with both feet."

The new men responded well in training and performed as good as could be expected on Red Beach under enemy fire. The loss of Baumgartner and Potts had a sobering effect on them.

He crawled to the position held by Dubbs and Dembrowski.

"How's it going here?" Pete asked.

"Fine, Sergeant," Dubbs replied.

"You worked in coal mines," Pete said. "Were your family all miners?"

"No," the boy answered. "My father and both my uncles work for the Lehigh Valley Railroad, the Black Diamond Route, hauling coal—mainly anthracite—from the mines to the foundries. I worked one summer in the mines."

"Going down into a coal mine would scare the crap outta me," Pete said.

"It wasn't too bad," Dubbs said. "I was trying to earn money for college, but then the war came along, and I enlisted. I wanted to defend my country."

Pete patted Dubbs on the shoulder, then turned to Dembrowski.

"So, Dembrowski," Pete said. "I've never been to Chicago. I understand you were practically neighbors with Al Capone."

"I grew up about five blocks west of what we called Capone's Castle," Dembrowski said. "I was eight when his gunsels mowed down seven of Bugs Moran's Northside Gang in that garage on North Clark Street on Saint Valentine's Day, 1929."

"I thought Philly was tough," Pete said and moved on.

At Fire Team Two, Pete found Miller dug in beside Reb. A good-looking kid, Miller's face bore the faint pockmarks of once having chicken pox.

"So where in New York is—what's the name—Portageville?" Pete asked. "I've never heard of it."

"I'm not surprised, Sarge. It's a very small town," Miller said. "Have you ever heard of the Genesee River? Portageville is right alongside it."

"No," Pete answered. "But I once drank a bottle of Genesee beer."

"That brewery is about forty miles from my home," Miller said. "I have an uncle who works there."

"Do you drink Genessee beer as well?" Pete asked.

"Oh no, Sergeant," Miller quickly said. "I don't drink at all."

Just beyond, Pete found Chico Morales. He was small, perhaps even shorter than Ted "Feather Merchant" Giovanni. Pete figured that for Morales to pass the minimum height requirement of five foot six, he must've stood on his tiptoes. A wiry man, his skin was deeply browned, his broad nose appeared to flatten as it spread out across his face. That face was accented by vivid brown eyes and high cheekbones.

"You're from Los Angeles, Morales," Pete said. "How long have you lived there?"

"I was born in LA, Sergeant," Morales said proudly. "I'm an American citizen."

"How'd you get into the taxi-driver business?" Pete inquired.

"My pop drives a hack," he replied. "I love to drive, so over the summers I'd often ride with him. I soon knew pretty much all of LA. Driving a hack seemed to be a natural."

Pete returned to his foxhole.

As darkness descended on day two of the invasion, Pete,

like everyone else holding the line in anticipation of a major Japanese response, endured a second night of nervous agitation.

The constant pounding of the beach by enemy artillery experienced during the landings was now relegated to just the occasional crash of rounds intended less on destruction and more on depriving the Americans of sleep. Everyone knew that would change with the rising of the sun. Meanwhile, anyone in need of leaving his position to take a piss had better know the password, which was any month of the year, to be answered by naming another month.

Nicholson appeared from the night whispering, "June."

"August," Pete replied.

"How are your boys doing, Talbot?" Nicholson asked as he slid into Pete's foxhole.

"It's the waiting," Pete said. "Why the hell don't they come?"

Nicholson smiled grimly.

"There was a halfhearted attempt on the 2/6's sector a little while ago," Nicholson said. "I hear the gyrenes killed about two dozen of the Nips. But they did the same thing to us on Tarawa. Remember that first night? We expected them to try to push us back into the lagoon, but they never came."

"I remember," Pete said. "And if they don't come to us, I guess we'll have to go to them."

Nicholson smiled grimly.

"That decision is above my pay grade," he said. "You know, this whole damned island that I've seen so far reminds me of the Philippines. I was posted there from '32 to '37, before I got sent to China."

"Good thing you got out of there when you did," Pete said. "Did you like it?"

"It was good duty," Nicholson said. "We were based on the Bataan Peninsula, which stank because all the good bars were in

Manila. That meant when we got leave we either had to take the long overland route on trucks or go to Balanga and cross Manila Bay on the *Don Miguel*. She was an old interisland steamer, half iron, half rust. I heard the Japs sank her, which was probably the best thing they could've done. Oh, some information on First Platoon: Tom Woodson is taking over as platoon sergeant."

Talbot nodded. He knew Woodson. The two of them, plus Linus Parsons, had all been promoted to corporal on Tarawa.

"What about Parsons?" Talbot asked.

"No one's seen him," Nicholson replied. "Evidently, he was on the same LVT as Lt. Long. Anyway, it's going on 2200. If the Japs don't come before sunrise, the captain is calling a meeting for the platoon leaders at 0500. After that, I'll fill you in on what's going on."

With that, Nicholson faded into the darkness.

Pete again moved along the line of foxholes to bolster the men's morale and ease jangled nerves. He found young Goodman sharing a foxhole with Hullihen. Pete squatted down by them.

"You okay, Goodman?" he asked. "I mean about that Jap and all."

"Yes, Sergeant," the boy said. "I'm sorry that got to me. I was scared, I guess. I'm still scared."

"You're not alone," Pete said. "We're all scared. You'll do fine with old Honeybun here."

"So tell me about Harpers Ferry," Pete said to get the boy's mind off his fright. "Isn't that where that slavery thing happened? John Brown or whoever?"

"Yeah. That happened in 1859," Goodman said eagerly. "Our farm is on Loudoun Heights overlooking the town. Before the Battle of Antietam in 1862, Stonewall Jackson himself posted some of his guns on our land."

"I think I just had a history lesson," Pete said. "You and

Honeybun here should get along fine. Didn't your uncle ride with Jackson, Honeybun?"

"You know damned well it was Jeb Stuart," growled Hullihen, who'd been watching the ground ahead.

"That's right," Pete said, shooting a sly wink at Goodman. "I get those two guys confused."

"Like hell you do," Pete heard Honeybun say as he moved on.

The next foxhole was occupied by Dubbs and Dembrowski. Both men were lying against the forward edge of the hole, staring intently into the darkness. They both glanced at Pete when he stopped beside their position.

"When are they coming, Sergeant?" Dembrowski growled. "I want another crack at them slant-eyed bastards."

"Stand easy, Dembrowski," Pete said. "They haven't forgotten we're here." He paused. "Scrap Iron, you said."

"That's what they call me," he answered.

"Seems fitting," Pete said. "Makes you sound tough."

"Where I grew up, you don't survive if you aren't tough," he replied.

Moving on, Pete stopped briefly with Harnish and young Miller, who both gave him the "okay" signal to his greeting.

In the next foxhole, he found Reb vigilantly watching the ground in front, while Morales was saying in a low voice, "I tell you, Corporal, after the war you come to Los Angeles, and I'll give you a free tour of Hollywood."

With his left hand atop the BAR and his right index finger near the weapon's trigger, Reb replied, "Now why in the hell would ah wanna come to Cali-fuckin'-fornia?"

"Are you kidding, amigo?" Morales replied. "Everyone should come to California. It is *muy excelente*."

"Forget it, Morales," Pete said. "To that good old boy, there's nowhere like Georgia."

"Ah," Morales said, waving a dismissive hand at Reb. "How about you, Sergeant? Come to California after the war. I know where all the stars live. You like Myrna Loy? I have her address."

"I'll have to clear it with the wife, although I admit that Loy is some dish," Pete joked, then pointed toward the darkness. "Keep a sharp watch."

Pete returned to the position occupied by Aldrich and Rosie.

"All your chicks safe and secure?" Aldrich asked.

"For now," he said. Then he removed his helmet and ran a hand through his sweat-soaked hair. From the webbing of his helmet liner, Aggie's smiling face beamed up at him. Aldrich saw it.

"Aggie's a pretty girl," the Professor said.

"I miss her," Pete said. "Maybe getting married right now wasn't a good idea."

"Do you love her?" Aldrich asked.

Pete nodded.

"Yeah," he said. "More than I ever imagined."

"Then it was a good idea," Aldrich said. "Did your folks come to the wedding?"

"My mother did," Pete replied. "We sorta patched things up. Aggie saw to that. My old man didn't want to come, which is fine. I wasn't about to invite the sonofabitch. Besides, it was a small wedding—Aggie's folks, my mom, a couple of Aggie's girlfriends, my uncle Dick and aunt Mae from Boston, and my cousin Tommy, my uncle's son who's a Doggie. He served as best man. By now, he's probably in France kicking Hitler's ass," Pete snorted. "What a wedding party we made. Me in my dress blues, Tommy in his Army Class A uniform, and the chaplain in his Navy best. All we were missing was a goddamn flyboy."

Pete lapsed into silence, recalling his wedding day in the base chapel at the Philadelphia Navy Yard. Aggie was radiant as she walked down the aisle in her mother's silky wedding gown, her red hair accented sharply against the white mesh of the veil. Until that moment, he didn't truly realize how beautiful she was. Pete could see the joy in Kathleen Barnoffski's smile and the gleam in her eyes. Even Aggie's father, Aloysius, looked proud. It was never any secret that he thought his daughter could do better, a fact Pete mentioned to Aggie one night during their honeymoon.

———

It was during their second night together. Lying in bed, his arm tightly around Aggie's bare shoulder, he drew her as close to him as possible and remarked on how pleased her father looked.

"Daddy?" Aggie said as her face nuzzled Pete's neck. "He's changed his tune. You're now 'my Marine son-in-law, a decorated war hero.'" She added that last bit, trying to mimic her father's gruff voice. They both laughed.

Pete chuckled again at the thought.

But it wasn't just his new in-laws who seemed happy with this union. Pat Talbot, who had little enough to smile about after life with a drunken, abusive husband and the loss of a son in war, seemed to glow.

Hugging him before the ceremony, she said, "I am so happy today, Peter. Aggie and you were meant to be together. She's good for you. I've known that since you were kids."

"I think everyone knew it but me," Pete said.

"You knew it too," Pat Talbot replied. "That's why you never pushed her away like you did other people."

"I had to come to grips with who I am and understand how temporary and how fragile life can be," he replied.

"I wish your father had come along," Pat said.

Benny Talbot did not attend his son's wedding. He had been

"out of sorts" of late, as he put it, and begged off. Just as well. Pete didn't want him there anyway.

"And Charlie," Pat whispered. "My dear, sweet Charlie."

Yet Charlie had been there. Pete felt his presence during the ceremony, and it gave him a feeling of ease, a sensation he mentioned to Aggie that night.

"Funny you should say that," she said in a hushed tone. "I felt him there too. So maybe he was. He's happy for us, Peter. I know he is."

Pete nodded and hugged Aggie closer.

———

Pete smiled at the memory and replaced the helmet atop his head, settling back into his foxhole. That's when the bugles sounded.

Jolted to action, Pete spun around and gazed up the length of the darkened coastal road, where even now he could hear the cries of "Banzai."

Quickly exiting his foxhole, he moved along the squad line.

"Here they come," he said. "Wait for the Navy to light the place up, and make your shots count."

He was no sooner back in his foxhole when the first star shells burst overhead. They revealed a swarm of running men, most carrying bayonet-tipped rifles; officers were swinging swords. The command cry of "Open fire" rang out. Scores of charging men dropped in their tracks, but the horde kept coming. The momentum of the attack brought them to within fifty yards of the battalion's line, but there the wave was smashed. Bodies piled up as the Japanese returned what fire they could before they began to pull back. As the tide receded, three Japanese tanks rolled onto the scene, but rather than fire on the Americans, they seemed disoriented by the falling back of their comrades.

From behind his position, Pete heard the "whoosh" as a bazookaman fired his lethal tube. The rocket streaked through the air and slammed into one of the tanks, a light *Ha-Go*, which seemed to leap off the ground before being engulfed by flames. The two remaining tanks renewed their efforts against the Marines. Braving small arms fire, the pair rolled through the Marine line on the battalion's right flank. Grenades finally stopped one, but the third nearly reached battalion HQ before a bazooka ended its life. Now it sat there smoldering.

An eerie stillness descended over the field. As the last star shell flickered out, Pete viewed a landscape heavily dotted by corpses. No matter how many such attacks he endured, he could never get used to the sight of so many dead men lying sprawled, sometimes in blood-soaked heaps. Hurriedly, he checked on the squad.

"Stay in your holes," he ordered. "They'll be back."

Close to an hour after the first assault, the Japanese struck the far left of the Marine line. Star shells again lit up the landscape, and the roar of small arms and the screams of angry and wounded men pierced the night.

All along the squad's line, the men nervously awaited the outcome of the battle.

"Stupid, stupid," Dembrowski muttered to himself.

"You say something, Scrap Iron?" young Dubbs asked.

"Naw," he replied. "I'm just kicking myself in the ass because I volunteered for this. The motor pool was too damned boring. This'll teach me."

Two foxholes farther along, young Vivian Miller was bemoaning fate.

"I wonder where Baumgartner is," the youth said. He and the Louisville boy had become tight.

"Probably on a hospital ship with a pretty nurse," Bucket replied.

Miller laughed briefly.

"You know, Corporal," he said. "I'd have liked to have been made a corpsman. I mean, my dad owns a drugstore and knows about medicines and even first aid. I really feel I have a knack for that."

"Corpsmen are all Navy guys," Harnish said.

"I know," Miller replied. "After I was drafted, the powers that be assigned me to the Marines."

"I'd never be a corpsman," Harnish said. "I've seen too many get shot. I think about that guy who was killed treating Baumgartner, and about Doc Magruder. He must have nine lives. When those guys get a call, they gotta go, regardless of how much enemy fire we're under."

Off to the left, the battle finally died away, and the waiting resumed.

At 0545, about an hour before dawn, bugles again sounded all along the battalion front. The Japanese came again, this time in greater numbers and with more determination. Star shells streaked skyward, illuminating a human wave. Worse, at least a dozen tanks, some carrying infantrymen, rolled along in support.

The Marines' line bristled with fire that ripped into the mass of attackers. Again, Japanese fell in windrows, there to lay and be trampled under the feet of the men behind them. Most gruesome of all were the dead, and even some wounded, who lay in the path of the tanks, their bodies mashed by the tanks' ponderous weight. Suddenly, the brightly lit battlefield went dark as the demand for illumination rounds outstripped the Navy's supply. Now cast into darkness, the battle turned even more deadly. At the left end of the squad line, Yastremski's machine gun chattered loudly as he traversed the weapon back and forth, leaving dead Japanese in heaps. Reb's BAR took down half a dozen attackers, while Dembrowski's Tommy gun cut down three men running toward his foxhole. One enemy soldier reached the foxhole as Scrap Iron was reloading his Thompson. Sammy Dubbs met the attacking man with his outstretched rifle, its bayonet plunging into the enemy's chest. Both Dubbs and the Jap fell to the ground, where Dubbs quickly untangled himself from the corpse. Horrified by what he'd just done, the boy vomited.

The infantry attack began to falter, but the armor pressed on.

Three tanks—two medium Type 97 *Chi-Ha* vehicles and one light Type 95 *Ha-Go*—rolled toward the squad. The *Ha-Go* moving well ahead of its two heavier companions made for the hole occupied by the Professor and Rosie. In the darkness, Aldrich popped up.

"Rosie, on me," he said.

Together the two men left their foxhole. Pointing to a heavy branch that lay near a shattered ironwood tree, the two men scooped it up and charged the tank. Closing on the vehicle, they jammed the branch into the vehicle's bogey wheels, bringing the tank to a jolting stop. The driver tried in vain to rock the vehicle back and forth to clear the obstruction. Failing that, the Dutch door–style top hatch popped open, and the tank commander lifted himself out. By now, Pete had dashed out to assist his friends and, firing his Tommy gun, killed the man. Aldrich climbed aboard the *Ha-Go* and dropped a grenade down the open hatch. He leaped off the turret as the grenade exploded inside the tank's confined space. The tank sat still, smoke billowing from the open hatch and gun slits.

Aldrich and Rosie scurried back to their foxhole, chased by

a hail of Japanese bullets. Pete jumped back into his as well as the two medium tanks continued forward, their 7.7mm machine guns blazing away.

As they drew closer, Pete saw that one of the *Chi-Ha* tanks bore eight infantrymen on its steel engine deck. The vehicle now rolled along the squad line, raking the Marines with machine gun fire. Pete heard Rosie's BAR go to work, and all eight Japanese were swept from the vehicle. The tank itself spun in the direction of the Marines. To his horror, Pete saw the tank making straight for him. With nowhere to go but down, Pete burrowed himself against the bottom of his foxhole. Curled into a defensive ball, Pete prayed that he'd dug deep enough and that the ground was solid. In his imagination, he saw the tank stop above him and then gyrate left and right, grinding down the earth and crushing Pete with its fifteen-ton weight as it tried to bury him alive in his own foxhole. Pete's eyes were squeezed tightly shut as he sensed the tank above him, its steel underbelly just inches from his torso. The roar of the twelve-cylinder Mitsubishi engine was deafening and the diesel fumes nearly suffocating. He felt hot splashes of engine oil from the tank's crankcase splattering his uniform and skin, and he could swear he felt his helmet being lightly brushed by the passing vehicle.

Then it was gone. It had not stopped to crush him but rolled forward into the American rear. It didn't get far. Less than twenty yards beyond Pete's badly marred foxhole, the whoosh of a bazooka rocket was heard, and the tank exploded, flames shooting from its hatches. The third tank of the attacking trio turned and headed rearward.

Pete slumped down in his foxhole, his body shaking uncontrollably as he watched the tank burn. He no longer cared about the battle still raging above and about him. Maybe that was just as well, for he did not hear the screams of pain or the shouts of "Corpsman" when "Bucket" Harnish got hit.

Harnish and Miller had been fighting desperately against an attacking knot of Japanese. Eight men charged Bucket and Miller with screaming fury. Bucket had cut down three of them when his Garand jammed.

"Damn!" he yelled, trying to clear the weapon. "Get 'em, Miller. Get 'em."

The boy from Portageville, New York, did just that. He shot down three of the five survivors. As a fifth man closed in on the foxhole, Miller swung the rifle and smashed its butt into the enemy's startled face. Working on sheer adrenaline, he swatted a sixth man, who fell, then scrabbled away like a sand crab. Miller turned and finished off the man with the broken jaw with a single shot.

Bucket was a victim of the third enemy tank. In retreating, it swung left along the squad's line. While doing so, the vehicle's commander traversed his turret toward the Americans. Harnish, panicked by the steel monster, saw only its menacing 57mm gun.

"Get out, Miller," he yelled.

He leaped from the hole and began to run for the rear. The tank loosed its shell, which zipped over the foxhole where Miller crouched and struck the ground just yards from Harnish. Miller was quickly by his side.

"Oh my God," he cried as he saw Harnish's torn and bloody body, his left leg attached to the torso by a few strands of flesh. "Oh my God."

Instinctively, he applied pressure to Bucket's torn leg above the grievous wound and hollered, "Corpsman! Corpsman!"

Pete was still in his foxhole, dazed by his experience. The next thing he was aware of was Aldrich shaking him.

"Come on, Hardball," he was saying as he shook his friend. "Come on."

Rosie was there as well.

"Jesus Christ," he said in an awed voice as he saw the tank-tread gouges on both sides of Pete's partially collapsed foxhole. "Jesus Christ."

Slowly, Pete became aware of his surroundings. He could hear no shooting. The fight was over. The Japanese had pulled back, leaving hundreds upon hundreds of their comrades dead on the ground. The tank that tried to crush him still stood twenty yards away, flames crackling from its bulk, machine gun bullets inside the turret popping.

Aldrich continued shaking him.

"Snap out of it," he said.

Pete swatted the Professor's arms away.

"Quit shaking me," he moaned. "I'll be okay."

"Come on. Bucket got hit."

That snapped Pete awake, and he and Aldrich hurried along the squad line. Bucket lay on his back, surrounded by several men from the squad. Doc Magruder was hunched over him, working feverishly. He'd already called for a stretcher. Pete saw young Miller sitting by Bucket's side, blood smearing his clothes and hands.

"Miller okay?" Pete asked Magruder.

"Yeah," he replied. "That's Bucket's blood all over him. The kid did the right thing. He applied pressure until I got here. He might've saved Bucket's life."

"We were just talking about that a little while ago," Miller said in a subdued voice. "I was tellin' Corporal Harnish that I'd have liked being a corpsman."

"Ya done good, kid," Dembrowski said.

"Is he alert?" Pete asked, indicating Harnish.

"I gave him morphine, but he should be partly conscious," Magruder said.

Pete pointed to the shattered leg, his eyes asking the question he dared not say in case Bucket overheard. Magruder shook his head no.

Pete knelt beside his friend.

"Bucket," he said. "You still with me?"

The eyes fluttered open.

"Yeah," he said in a weak voice. "I panicked. I shoulda stayed in my foxhole."

"Don't worry," Pete said. "It happens."

"My left leg," Bucket said groggily. "It hurts like hell."

"You're going home, Bucket," Pete said. "Back to St. Albans. Back to them maple trees."

"Sorry to leave the squad, Hardball," he said, his voice slurred. "And the guys."

"Don't worry about it," Pete said. "We'll catch up after the war. I want some of that maple syrup you're so damned proud of."

"You got it," Bucket said, a weak smile creasing his lips.

The stretcher arrived, carried by a pair of mortarmen pressed into emergency service. Pete helped to gently lift Bucket onto the stretcher much the same way Harnish had helped lift him after being hit on Tarawa. Then he watched as his friend was carried out of the war.

Pete turned to Miller.

"Well done, Miller," Pete said.

The boy smiled for the first time since Bucket had been hit.

"Back to your positions, everyone," Pete said. "I don't think they'll be back anymore before dawn, but you never know."

Pete turned to Reb, who was watching Bucket get carried away.

"You take over Fire Team Three," Pete said.

Back in the solitude of his foxhole, Pete stared upward. In the growing light, Pete could plainly see the tread marks straddling his position. Examining his helmet, Pete saw a small smear of engine oil at the very top of his camouflage helmet cover. The realization of nearly being crushed hit Pete hard. That, combined with the image of Bucket Harnish with his leg nearly blown off, caused Pete to shake uncontrollably.

Then, for the first time since he held Ted Giovanni's dead body in the lagoon on Tarawa, Peter Talbot wept.

CHAPTER 5

At Tsutsuran, about a mile and a half southeast of where Pete and Dog Company had fought for their lives, Tadashi Tanimura lay on a blanket in a small tent tucked away under some trees a few paces from General Saito's headquarters cave. Outside, dawn was streaking the sky, and though Tadashi was tired from the exertions of the past twenty-four hours, sleep eluded him.

Initial reports indicated that the night attacks had not gone well. Casualties had been substantial, and nowhere had the American line been seriously pierced. Commanders laid the blame on the enemy's heavy use of illumination rounds.

General Saito considered the setback less serious than Tadashi did. He sent out orders that the attacks be renewed after dark, but again did not stress an all-out effort.

Tadashi was greatly troubled over General Saito's decision not to attack the Americans with full strength right away. Instead, by giving the Americans another day to solidify their foothold, Tadashi was convinced that the much-anticipated counterstrike would fail. Tadashi felt Saito was inviting catastrophe by his vacillation.

Even the civilians back in Japan understood the island's importance. In his pocket, Tadashi carried the last letter he'd received from his father. Hideo Tanimura was a member of his neighborhood's civil defense organization, or *Tonarigumi*.

"Our *Tonarigumi* is making preparations in the unlikely event that the enemy seizes our Mariana Islands bastion," he wrote. "We watch constantly for enemy bombers, and we have learned how to identify each type of aircraft. We pray the gods will show us favor but are ready for the worst."

"Our spirits are quite high," his father assured him. "Even the children are unafraid. They have a song they enjoy. 'Why should we be afraid of air raids? The big sky is protected with iron defenses. For young and old, it is time to stand up. We bear the honor of defending the homeland. Come on, enemy planes. Come on many times.'"

He said the brave words did his aging heart well, and he sought comfort in the knowledge that Tadashi's American mother was not there to see this war between America and Japan.

"She loved America like she loved Japan," he wrote. "So did you, but now you have a higher duty to our emperor. *Gisei, giri, meiyo, hokori, sekinin.*"

Yes, Father, you're correct, he thought. *Sacrifice, duty, honor, pride, responsibility.*

Tadashi knew the letter by heart, and it saddened him. He doubted he'd ever see his father again. Or Japan, for that matter.

He looked at his tentmate, who was sound asleep just a few feet away. Captain Kisaburo Hanaya was as close to being a brother as Tadashi would ever know. They had been cadets together at the Army academy. After Tadashi was chosen to serve on Prince Tsunenori's staff, he recommended Kisaburo as well for his keen organizational skills.

Tadashi realized both of them were destined to die. Yes, it was a soldier's duty to die for the emperor, but not if living meant fighting on to victory. Dying needlessly did not benefit the nation or the emperor. Yet, Tadashi thought, dying needlessly is the fate to which Saito assigned every man under his command. He thought about a passage in a book of instruction soldiers received upon induction. *"Ikite ryoushu no hazukashime wo ukezu."* A soldier must never suffer the disgrace of being captured alive.

Pete felt someone shaking him.

"Hardball," Steve Aldrich whispered urgently.

Pete jolted upright, then realized he'd cried himself to sleep.

"Jesus Christ," Pete muttered, rubbing a sleeve across his eyes. "I'm sorry. I . . ."

"Don't worry," Aldrich said. "You had a terrible night. You got run over by a tank. I wanted to give you a heads-up. Gunny's making the rounds."

Pete nodded, then saw Nicholson approach. In tow he had Sgt. Marty Manson, leader of Third Squad. Before the war, the burly Californian had worked as an assistant gaffer for Warner Brothers. The last movie he boasted about helping to install the electric wiring for was the spy film *Across the Pacific*, which starred Humphrey Bogart.

"Bogey was a nice guy," Manson liked to say whenever he had the chance. "He wasn't so uppity that he couldn't take time to josh with the crew."

As he approached, Nicholson took in the sight of Pete sitting in his hole, flanked on both sides by the deep ruts from tank treads that led to the smoldering wreck to the rear.

"You're one lucky sonofabitch," the gunny said.

Nicholson gestured for Pete to follow. They moved to the left and the portion of the line held by First Squad and Biff Hodges. As the three squad leaders knelt around Nicholson, they were joined by Sergeant Ed "Pogey Bait" Baker, now in command of Dog Company's mortar teams. Baker had earned his nickname because he always carried a pack of Charms candy on his person.

Last to join the group was Cpl. Moxley Pope, a Bronze Star winner on Tarawa who now led Dog Company's machine gun section.

"Here's the score," Nicholson began. "At 0800, Second and Third Battalions are moving forward. First Battalion will be in reserve and watch our right flank. We'll have some tanks. Not as many as Stonewall would like, but we have to take what we can get. Our main goal is that low ridge ahead." He pointed across the corpse-laden battlefield of last night at an ominous-looking ridgeline nearly two thousand yards away.

"It's gonna stink to high heaven with all those dead Japs out there," Yaz commented.

"Bad-smelling dead Japs will be the least of our worries," Nicholson said. "We have to cross that ground as rapidly as we can. Most of the battalion will be cleaning out the cane fields. D Company's objective is a farm village by the base of the ridge. You can bet the Nip bastards have several machine guns and plenty of infantry waiting for us there." He turned to Baker. "That's where you come in, Pogey Bait. Blast that village as we close on it. Also, be ready if we hit any unexpected resistance crossing the field." He glanced around. "We've gotta break out of this beachhead. Everything is jam-packed, and the Twenty-Seventh Division is set to start landing today. Any questions?" Hearing none, he added, "There's some hot joe at the company CP. Not a lot, but enough for half a canteen cup apiece, so if you want, send a couple of guys back."

After Nicholson departed, Pete assigned one man from each fire team to get coffee for his buddies, then briefed his fire team leaders. After the briefing, Pete pulled Aldrich aside.

"I'm sorry I fell asleep," Pete whispered. "I don't know what happened."

"It's okay," Aldrich said. "I got you covered."

"It's not okay," Pete replied. "I fucked up. Christ, I'd ream the ass of any squad member who doped off." Then he realized Aldrich must've heard him bawling.

The Professor saw Pete's obvious discomfort.

"It's a new day," Aldrich said. "Let's just get back to work."

At 0800, whistles blew. Major Richard Clarkson led Second Battalion across the open ground, with men spread out about ten paces apart. Gingerly, the advancing Marines stepped over and around the bodies of the Japanese slain the night before. Not so nimble were the five tanks—three Shermans and two light Stuarts, which led the way for the battalion. Their treads ground uncaringly over the men who lay dead in their paths. Pete watched the bodies being so callously crushed and thought how that nearly happened to him.

The first inkling of what was to come occurred when sporadic mortar rounds began bursting among the advancing men. Then artillery shells of various calibers from 37mm to 105mm rained down on the Marines, who quickly hit the dirt. While the infantry advance stalled, the armor continued to clank forward. As they neared the first cane field, a swarm of Japanese emerged from concealment.

"Don't let 'em get the tanks!" Lt. Cornwall called to the men.

One Sherman was thirty yards ahead of Pete's squad, and he hollered, "Shoot 'em! Shoot 'em!"

Even as he yelled, he leveled his Thompson and cut down two Japanese closing in on the Sherman, both carrying bottles whose stems were aflame. As they fell, one man's Molotov cocktail shattered. The resultant burst of fire caused the second explosive device to rupture, setting fire to the earth around the two bodies. The tank halted as the driver, realizing his peril, shifted into reverse. Another pair of Japanese charged, both toting fiery bottles, and again both were dropped before their lethal projectiles could be thrown. The wicks quickly burned down, and both exploded, setting the grass afire and incinerating the men who'd carried them. A single Japanese soldier charged and managed to lob his cocktail before he was shot down. The bottle of flammable fluid burst on the tank, and flames quickly spread across the vehicle's armored hull. Hidden behind a cloud of black smoke, a second Japanese soldier tossed his cocktail, then disappeared into the cane field. His bottle broke on the tank, and the flames roared furiously across the engine deck. The hatch atop the burning Sherman popped open, but the tank commander immediately realized there was no escape that way. Moments later one, then two, then all five crewmen emerged from under their stricken vehicle, fleeing through the escape hatch. Outraged, five Japanese charged, firing their rifles. One tanker was struck in the back, spun, and fell. A second crewman was also hit and fell. Both men were mercilessly bayoneted by three of the screaming Japanese soldiers before Dog Company's fire bowled over all the attackers.

The other tanks, realizing their vulnerability, stopped. With all machine guns blazing, they began rolling rearward. Shooting down a number of the enemy, the Shermans made it back to the cover provided by the infantry. One of the Stuarts wasn't as fortunate. Steve Aldrich saw a Japanese soldier charge the tank, carrying a round metallic object. Recognizing it as a magnetic mine, he aimed his Garand with the intent of firing several rounds at the man. Instead, after one shot that missed the running target, the n-clip sprang from the breech of his M1, and the bolt remained open.

Knowing he didn't have time to fish a new clip from his bandolier, ram it into the breech, and slap shut the operating rod, he pointed and yelled, "Magnetic mine! Get him, Rosie."

Rosie did, but not before the metal mine clanged against the steel hull. The blast blew the dying soldier in two as the fifteen-ton tank shuddered to a halt, then sat still, sending up a cloud of smoke. None of the five men inside emerged.

Marine gunfire had taken down at least thirty of the enemy, and the survivors filtered back into the sugarcane. As for the Marines, the shellfire they were enduring grew worse as machine guns from unseen enemy positions began chewing up the ground around them. Some of that fire, Pete noted, was from the cluster of shacks that was to be D Company's objective.

The Japanese aim was spot on, and more than two dozen men from the battalion were struck. Cries for corpsmen kept medical personnel busy. Pogey Bait's mortars were working by now, spitting out 60mm and 81mm rounds that blossomed among the cane and around the wooden shacks. But the deadly Japanese fire persisted.

Advancing would have been costly but not impossible, except that just about then, further up the battalion line, Major Clarkson took a round square between the eyes. His death unnerved his staff, and Clarkson's XO called the attack to a halt.

Grudgingly, the Marines began falling back. Grabbing any meager cover, such as small clumps of brush, random trees, a few small ripples in the earth, even piles of enemy corpses, the men resisted stubbornly. But their momentum had been lost, and they ended up almost back where they had started.

The entire fiasco had lasted over an hour. A brief period of time in a war, but long enough that Second Battalion suffered thirty-eight casualties, including eleven dead. Third Battalion had similar losses, and all that had been gained was about a hundred yards of sun-parched grass and a few spindly trees that a bird wouldn't build a nest in.

Once the Marines were dug in, Japanese fire slackened, then faded altogether.

The sun had slipped past the noon hour, and the Marines, having little if any shade, baked under its rays. Nicholson had checked in with Pete once and, satisfied that the squad was okay, moved on to First Squad. Hodges hadn't been as lucky. One of his men—a recent replacement named Rippley or Ripton, Pete wasn't sure—had been shot in the gut. He'd been a bloody mess when he was lugged off to the rear by mortarmen drafted to serve as stretcher-bearers.

"That boy is in bad shape," observed the Professor, who had dropped by Pete's foxhole. "I don't think he's going to make it."

Pete shrugged, then he reached into his rucksack and removed a blue-and-tan K-ration box labeled "Dinner" in black lettering. Unsheathing his Ka-Bar, Pete slit open the rectangular card stock box. The first thing he came across was a pack of four Chesterfield cigarettes. He thought about Robert Sherrod, the *Time* magazine newsman he'd gotten to know on Tarawa. He'd heard that Sherrod was somewhere on Saipan and briefly considered saving the Chesterfields in case he ran into him. Then he reconsidered, finding the idea that he'd run into Sherrod highly unlikely and decided to smoke them as a way of conserving his Camels.

With the small key attached, he opened the can of processed cheese, then used his Ka-Bar to spread it on his biscuits. Munching the nearly tasteless meal, he said, "What I wouldn't give for a home-cooked meal. Maybe a pot roast and fresh potatoes, with some carrots thrown in."

"What I wouldn't give for any kind of hot meal," Aldrich replied.

Pete said, "I remember Nicholson telling me that on the 'Canal the Army got K-rations while the Marines were expected to clean up the C-rations left over from the last war. But Marines being Marines, they raided Army supply depots during air raids, when all the dogfaces were in bomb shelters."

On the ridge twelve hundred yards from Pete's company, Major Tadashi Tanimura and Captain Kisaburo Hanaya watched the Americans attack and repulse with satisfaction.

"Maybe that will knock some of the arrogance out of them," Hanaya told Tadashi as he lowered his glasses.

"Yes," Tadashi said with a nod. "I just pray that we gave them a sound enough thrashing that they will be content to hold what they have and won't venture out before nightfall. The beach must remain jammed."

As the sun rose higher and higher into the sky, temperatures rose as well. As everyone in the battalion had feared, the sweltering heat swelled up the many corpses scattered across the landscape, emitting a terrible stink and becoming a gory feast for millions of flies. By now, it was estimated that as many as seven hundred Japanese lay dead on the field.

If any man present thought it couldn't get any worse, that notion was disabused when Japanese artillery and mortars began to periodically drop their lethal rounds on the Marine position. Men spent time deepening their foxholes.

Around midafternoon, Lt. Cornwall called a meeting of his NCOs in his new HQ, an abandoned Japanese machine gun pillbox. Constructed of thick logs and coral and firmly packed with sandbags, it could withstand almost anything but a direct hit by a 5-inch or larger gun. When Master Sgt. O'Leary and Capt. Stacey entered, everyone snapped to attention.

"As you were," Stacey said. "Smoking light's lit."

A few of the men fired up scrags as Stacey faced his men.

"I'm going through the company platoon by platoon to brief everyone so you all know what's going on," he said. "Right now, the Twenty-Seventh Division is coming ashore near Charan Kanoa, where they will link up with elements of the Fourth Marines to take a small airfield just outside the town. The rest of the Fourth, along with the 2/8 on our far right, will start to push east. Their goal is to cut the island in two. Then they will secure the southern portion of the island. Some units will head south while others pivot north. From that point, we will all push north, with the Fourth Marines on the right, the Twenty-Seventh in the center, and us on the left."

"Does that mean the Army will be between us and the Fourth?" Nicholson inquired.

"Yes," Stacey said. "Look, I know what you're thinking. The Army, by the nature of its commanders and its training, is more cautious than our own and may slow us down, but General Smith has vowed to make their CO, who is also named General Smith, keep up."

"What are we to do, sir?" Cornwall asked.

"For one thing, there's the high ground in front of us," Stacey said. "While the 2/8 will mostly be responsible for Mount Tapochau, we will have to concern ourselves with Mount Tipo Pale and its foothills. We'll encounter rugged ground with ravines, rocky peaks, and about a million caves. Japs will have dug into most of them, but also civilians, which is going to complicate our job. We're not here to kill civilians, especially old men, women, and children. Instead, we're going to have to convince them to surrender. But from reports we're getting from civvies who have already come into our lines, the Japs have told them we will murder their families and rape their women, so the people are terrified of us."

His face grew somber.

"Another thing we must prepare for," Stacey continued. "We've already had cases where attacking Japs have driven civilians in front of them to use as human shields. If that happens, you'll have to steel yourselves and do what needs to be done. Is that clear?"

Everyone nodded.

Pete raised a hand.

"What about that city?" he asked. "Garapan or whatever."

"That's still on our to-do list," he said.

"Anyway," he said in conclusion. "We're not going anywhere today, so tuck in tight. Air recon has reported seeing fairly sizeable numbers of Japs in the hills above us, and they seem to be heading our way. Tanks too, so they may attack again tonight. Difference is, tonight we'll have tank support plus a battery of 37mm anti-tank guns. Also, the Navy has laid in a new supply of star shells, so we won't be in the dark. Questions?"

Seeing none, he and O'Leary ducked out of the bunker.

CHAPTER 6

A steady rain began falling around midnight as a heavy squall blew in from the sea. On a wooded slope on the southwest face of Mount Tipo Pale, four men stood close together under a canvas fly strung between four trees. Before them, along a narrow dirt path turned to muck by the rain, a seemingly endless stream of men filed silently past. Some of the men wore rain ponchos, most did not, but all wore a look of excitement. These warriors of the 136th Regiment were en route to meet the enemy, and their sense of confidence overcame the miserable conditions of soggy clothes and mud-caked *jika tabi* shoes.

Major Tadashi Tanimura watched the passing men intently as the rain drummed down on the canvas overhead. He knew these men. He had been one of their officers until called to serve as a staff officer. They were a proud component of the Forty-Third Division, the *Homare Heidan,* or Honor Division. These veterans had chased the British the length of the Malay

Peninsula to Singapore in 1942. Others had taken on the Australians in New Guinea. They had never tasted defeat.

"They look strong and full of fight," said Hanaya, who was standing beside Tadashi. "I feel sorry for any Americans who get in their way."

"I hope so," Tadashi said as men continued sloshing by. "General Saito has great expectations for this attack."

"The attack time is 0330," Tadashi continued. "Your men should be in position no more than thirty minutes prior. Can you do that?"

"They'll be ready," Ogawa stated confidently.

"And Commander Karashima's naval landing force on your right?" Tadashi asked.

"He says he'll be ready," Ogawa replied. "His men have farther to go, so they are being loaded onto trucks. Some of my men coming in from the General Reserve near the village of Chacha are also loading onto trucks."

Tadashi nodded, then turned to the fourth man under the fly.

"And your tanks, Colonel Goto," Tadashi said. "How are they faring? They made a poor showing last night."

"The rain has created some movement problems," the grizzled tank veteran said, irritated by the slight thrown in his face by the young upstart major. "But I'm sure most of my armor will be up when the charge commences."

"Most satisfactory," Tadashi said to all present. "Remember: After your men push through the American front lines, they are to fan out left and right. We don't want to just push the Americans back into the sea. We want to destroy their ammunition and supply dumps in the rear."

"My officers have been so instructed," Ogawa said.

Tadashi nodded his approval as he watched two crews of

artillerymen manhandle a pair of 37mm anti-tank guns along the boggy track. Silently, he prayed to *Yawata*, the *kamisama* of war, to grant these men success. Then he said a quick prayer to the Christian God his mother had told him about. Even though he could never reconcile in his mind the two ideologies, it didn't hurt for one to cover all eventualities.

"You are troubled?" Hanaya asked his friend, leaning close and keeping his words low.

"No," Tadashi answered. "I just wish we'd have struck them harder last night."

"You're not questioning General Saito's wisdom, are you?" Hanaya asked. He was aware that a number of officers shared Col. Suzuki's suspicions about his friend's loyalties.

"No," Tadashi replied. "It just would've been my preference. We are fortunate though. The rain will cover the sounds of so many men moving into position."

Tadashi had lied to his friend about his questioning Saito's judgment. He felt a deep dread for the coming attack.

About three-quarters of a mile from where Tadashi watched the men of the 136th Regiment move into position, Pete huddled inside his soggy foxhole. He sullenly listened to the distant karumpf of artillery and rattle of small arms coming from some distance to the south.

Relocating from his semicrushed position, Pete spent time deepening his new foxhole. Now he wasn't so sure going deeper was a good idea. The rain saturated the sides of the hole, causing mud to slide down on him. Knees drawn up and feeling miserable, Pete listened to the rain drum on his helmet and camouflage poncho as he tried to stay as dry and comfortable as conditions allowed.

About an hour earlier, Pete had been summoned to another

platoon meeting with Lt. Cornwall in his CP. The interior of the pillbox was cramped and uninviting, but at least it was dry.

Cornwall began without preamble.

"I want your boys on full alert," he said. "No one sleeps. Stonewall calls this Jap weather, and he's convinced they'll come tonight. If they do, the Navy is prepared to light up the field with star shells, so the Nips will have to attack through a god-damned light show."

"Air recon was up earlier and spotted Japs moving along the faces of Tipo Pale and Tapochau, but that's not un-usual," Cornwall continued. "What does bother me is there was some evidence of tank movement. G2 is certain the Japs have a couple of armored battalions on this island, and as they proved last night, this ground we're sitting on is ideal tank country."

"What about our armor?" Sgt. Hodges asked. "Stonewall said earlier we'd have armor support."

"If we need 'em, Biff, they'll be here," Cornwall said.

"I'd rather those tanks were here now," Pete said.

"There are two platoons of Shermans just behind our pe-rimeter," Cornwall said. "They can get to any hot spot in the line quickly. There will also be some anti-tank guns positioned behind us. It'll be easier if this damned rain lets up."

The group was dismissed and headed back to their squads. As Pete sat in his soggy foxhole, he thought about some advice Nicholson had given him the day he returned to the company. As Nicholson guided Pete through the maze of tents that was Camp Tarawa, the gunny halted.

"Before we go back to the platoon, a word of advice," he said. "You're a squad leader now, so it's no more just lookin' out for number one. You've got twelve men to think about, so get to know them. Learn how to read them. Find out their strengths and weaknesses—what a man is capable of doing and what he's not, especially in combat."

Pete was confused.

"Half my guys are veterans," he said.

"True, but things are different now," Nicholson said. "You're in command. You've got to look at them from that viewpoint. Take Rosie, for example. He was seriously wounded. How will he react when he gets back in action? The Professor, Hullihen, and Harnish are team leaders. How will that responsibility affect their judgment? You've got to consider all of this."

At around 0200, the rain let up almost as abruptly as it began. Feeling cramped after spending much of the last hour in his saturated foxhole, Pete climbed out, unfolded himself, then moved carefully to his right, where he found Aldrich sitting on the muddy lip of his foxhole, staring ahead in the darkness.

"What's up?" Pete inquired.

Aldrich shook his head slightly.

"Thought I heard something," he said, pointing. "Out there. Pretty far away."

Pete heard nothing and said so.

Aldrich would not be put off.

"There it is again," Aldrich said in a harsh whisper. "Soft and far away."

Pete strained, then he heard it too—an engine or multiple engines growling ever so lowly in the distance. Even as he listened, the sound slowly grew louder and louder, until every man could hear it. After a short while, the engines sounded steady, not advancing or retreating. Minutes later they seemed to recede.

"Trucks or tanks?" Aldrich asked.

"Trucks," said Dembrowski, who had just come up through

the dark to Aldrich's foxhole.

"What are you doin' here?" Pete snapped, perturbed that Dembrowski left his position.

"Came to see if you heard that," he answered. "Those are truck engines. I've been in motor pool long enough to know the difference. They brought something up, unloaded, and now they're leaving. I'd say they brought up troops."

"Thanks, Scrap Iron," Pete said, using Dembrowski's nickname for the first time. "Now get back to your foxhole and get ready."

Now a new engine noise was faintly heard.

"Tanks," Nicholson whispered as he approached through the night. "Captain says the Japs may be moving into attack positions."

Even in the dark, Pete could see Nicholson's eyes harden.

"Get your boys ready, but have them stay in their holes," he said. "Pass the word along to Hodges. Have Yaz and Pope get their rattle-and-tats ready. I'll send a bazooka team this way."

He left, and Pete turned to Aldrich. The two men stared at each other, both thinking the same thing: *Holy shit.*

Things began popping off shortly after 0300. Off in the distance, beyond the Marine line that was dug in across the coastal road, came the blaring of trumpets. Even at this distance, yells of "Banzai" and "We drink Marine blood" could be distinctly heard. These cries, however, were soon drowned out by the rattle of gunfire as the Marines met the charge with a bloody fusillade.

The distant struggle roared for some thirty minutes before subsiding. For Pete and the others, it was like having five-cent seats for a Joe Louis fight.

As the fighting diminished, the men in Dog Company's

portion of the line seemed to share a sense that the next blow was coming at them. Pete left his foxhole and moved softly along the rear of the squad's line.

"Fix bayonets," he ordered. "Stay in your holes. When they come, the Navy will light up the field. Pick your target."

At the end of his section of the line, Pete found Yaz Yastremski watching his loader, Pfc. "Wheels" Wealand, feed a belt of .30-caliber rounds into the gun's receiver.

"You all set to go to work, Yaz?" Pete asked.

Yastremski indicated four metal ammo boxes at the rear of his dug-in position, each containing 250 rounds.

"I got over a thousand little love notes for Tojo," he said with a wicked grin as he yanked the bolt handle, cocking the weapon.

By the time Pete got back to his foxhole, the bazooka team dispatched by Capt. Stacey had arrived and took up position between Second and Third Squads.

Now came the waiting.

It wasn't long. At 0330, bugles blared again, only these were not on the far left. They came from directly in front of Second Battalion. Next came the shouting and the shuffling of feet on the muddy ground. Cries of "Marines go to hell," "Death to Roosevelt," and the inevitable *"Tenno Heika Banzai"* knifed through the air as the advancing soldiers wished their emperor a long life.

More ominous than the shouted threats were the accompanying sounds of engines and the clank of treads as tanks advanced with the infantry. Beyond that veil of inky predawn blackness, death was approaching in waves. The curtain of darkness was suddenly lifted as two streaks of light arched through the night sky. Both burst high overhead, emitting a flare that bathed the earth below in an intense greenish glow. The two blazing parachuted flares slowly drifted down, revealing a wall of men several hundred yards away moving briskly toward the Americans. There seemed to be a thousand of them. Spaced out along this human wave Pete saw several tanks, some out in front of the infantry, others farther back.

Pete's guts tightened. This attacking force was far larger than anything he had experienced on Tarawa. Could they be stopped? If this attack looked overwhelming to him, how would it be for the new men in the squad who'd never been subjected to the fury of a banzai assault by men reconciled to the idea of dying?

As the overhead flares petered out, more star shells erupted as the offshore destroyers *Halsey Powell*, *Coghlan*, and *Monssen* did their best to keep the enemy well-lit. Naval support now included the battleship *California*, which sent its half-ton 14-inch shells screaming inland to burst among the advancing enemy. Under the glow of the star shells, Pete could see men tossed into the air by the explosions.

With the Japanese within three hundred yards of the Marines, the American line roared to life. Running figures fell like rows of wheat, but the rest kept coming, their shrill cries of "Banzai" getting louder with every step. As he fired his Thompson, Pete saw one Japanese tank erupt in a ball of fire after a direct hit from a naval gun, the vehicle's turret somersaulting into the air. The burning hulk seemed to shed blazing debris, but as Pete looked closer, he saw the debris was actually soldiers who had been riding on the tank.

Another Japanese tank exploded and then another, this time victims of Sherman tanks that roared up from behind the Marines.

Some of the Japanese tanks drew to a halt, turning sharply to face this new challenge. Their passengers leaped off. Once on the ground, these men tried to rush forward but came under a deadly hail of Marine fire that stopped them cold. Men fell in heaps, some lying still, others writhing in agony. In his foxhole, young Private Goodman, who had fretted so badly over the Jap soldier he killed yesterday, would later be amazed at his actions today. Emboldened by the presence of Corporal Hullihen by his side and with the adrenaline pumping through his body, he feverishly fired three rounds from his Garand into a man coming straight at him with a bayonet. All three bullets struck home, and the man fell facedown in the mud, almost to the edge of the foxhole. Ignoring the corpse, Goodman sought new targets.

By Goodman's side, Honeybun saw an NCO heading for his foxhole, a sword in one hand, a grenade clutched in the other. As the NCO activated the grenade by slamming the arming rod against his helmet, Honeybun's slugs hit the man. He fell, the grenade falling from his hand and into the mud. There it exploded, finishing off the NCO and an unfortunate soldier who just happened to be running beside him.

Vivian Miller was terrified by the number of attacking Japanese and also because, with the wounding of Harnish, he was left to face the charge alone in his foxhole. He worked the Garand as quickly as he could, firing until the empty clip popped out, then snatching a new one from his bandolier, reloading, and firing some more. He had shot down at least four men, so far as he could tell, hoping his pharmacist dad would understand.

In their foxhole, Scrap Iron and Sammy Dubbs made a good team. Between Dembrowski's Tommy gun and Dubbs's M1, there was a pile of dead Japanese in front of them so high that Dembrowski had to get out and drag corpses aside to clear their field of vision. Dubbs watched Dembrowski's act of courage in awe and marveled.

Reb Marshall's BAR was so hot from firing that his hands

had first-degree burns after accidently touching the barrel. Still, the automatic rifle barked, dropping enemy soldiers in appalling numbers. Beside him, Hack Morales dropped one Jap, then a second, and then a third in rapid succession. He was reloading his Garand when two Japanese bullets struck him, one in the right shoulder, the other in the throat. Blood spurting from the latter wound, he fell backward against the foxhole and began gasping. Reb heard Hack get hit and turned. He was sickened by the amount of blood. He ceased firing to put pressure on the wound.

"Corpsman!" he hollered, hoping to be heard over the battle racket. "Corpsman! Doc!"

Realizing the danger both men were in, since neither were defending the foxhole, he reluctantly picked up the BAR and resumed firing, still calling, "Corpsman!" between bursts. He thanked God when Magruder arrived.

"It's Hack, Doc," he yelled. "Take care of him!"

The assault continued for well over half an hour, then unexpectedly seemed to lose steam. Rather than charge into certain death, more and more enemy troops preferred to hold their ground, dropping to a knee or lying prone to exchange fire with the Americans. All the while, the constant barrage of star shells kept them well outlined and made them easy targets.

The tanks, however, pressed on. Yet even their attack seemed to grow confused, and they meandered aimlessly, firing their guns in the general direction of the Americans but seemingly without any specific targets. Pete watched one tank, a light Type 95, try to approach. As its commander hand-cranked his turret around in an effort to bring its 37mm gun to gear, there came a loud boom from behind the American line. The Japanese tank shuddered under a direct hit, smoke and flames pouring out of its hatches. The commander, screaming, tried to climb from the top hatch amid the flames. Then an internal explosion popped the man out like a champagne cork. The death blow had been delivered by a Sherman coming up from the Marines' rear. Half a dozen Shermans rolled through the American position and into the fray against the stalled Japanese charge, their 75mm rounds slicing through the more lightly armored enemy vehicles.

The Japanese tanks, even the medium *Chi-Ha* types similar to the one that tried to crush Pete the night before, were no match for the heavier Shermans. One *Chi-Ha* was hit head-on by a round from a Sherman. The explosion ripped the tank open and lifted the turret into the air, causing it to land cockeyed on the chassis.

A light *Ha-Go* was hit by an American 37mm anti-tank gun. It rolled to a stop, burning furiously twenty yards from Aldrich and Rosie's foxhole.

The tank battle swirled for more than twenty minutes as armored vehicles were suddenly converted into burning hulks. But not all the losses were Japanese. One Sherman was struck from the rear by a *Chi-Ha*, whose 57mm round sliced into the Sherman's engine compartment, bringing the thirty-ton beast to a halt, its crew abandoning the vehicle.

Another Sherman advanced about fifty yards out in front of Second Squad when a round from a light Japanese tank struck the rear bogey wheels. The blast crippled the tank as one tread snapped. Almost instantly the tank was surrounded by a dozen Japanese soldiers, who began climbing on board to pry open the hatches. Remembering the butchery of the stranded tankers he had seen the day before, Pete jumped from his foxhole and charged forward about half the distance, spraying the Japanese with his Thompson. Along with him went Rosie, whose BAR seemed to sweep the enemy soldiers off the tank as if they'd been washed off by a hose. All twelve were dead within moments.

Now five men crawled out from under the tank from the emergency hatch, one man clutching a bloodied shoulder from metal shards caused by the exploding shell.

"Covering fire!" Pete heard Aldrich yell, and the squad responded as Pete, Rosie, and the grateful tankers scurried back to the line.

"Oh, Jesus," the tank commander sighed with relief. Then he looked at Pete. "Thanks, Mac. That took guts."

By now, nearly an hour had passed since the attack commenced, and the enemy wave finally receded. The tortured landscape took on the appearance of a field of harvested corn whose stalks lay about in profusion. More than a dozen ruined Japanese tanks and three Shermans remained, many smoldering.

Star shells now ceased to glow, and darkness returned to hide the horrid scene. The tank commander shook Pete's hand, then led his men rearward. However, as he walked back to his foxhole, Reb ran up, blood on his hands and clothes.

"It's Morales, Hardball," he gasped. "He's hit bad. Doc's with him."

Pete hurried to Reb's position, where he found Magruder bent over his patient.

"He's gone, Hardball," he said heavily. "He was all but dead when I got here. He bled out. I couldn't stop it."

Pete's guts churned as he stared at the now silent Hack Morales. Pete recalled the happy-go-lucky kid who was eager to give him a taxicab tour of the stars' homes in Hollywood.

Magruder handed Pete Chico's identity tag, then used Morales's poncho to cover the body.

Aldrich joined Pete. Pete looked at his friend, then at the

disc in his hand that would join the one in his pocket that had belonged to Stanley Potter. Pete saw young Vivian Miller sitting on the edge of his foxhole. He was weeping quietly as he stared at the poncho-covered body of his squad mate.

Pete turned to Aldrich.

"I can't do this," he said bitterly. "I had twelve guys with me when we landed; now I've lost four."

"Do you think any of us enjoys killing men and watching friends get maimed or killed?" Aldrich responded. "It's just the way of the world right now, and we have to do what we're forced to do. Don't feel sorry for yourself. This squad needs you."

Pete nodded somberly. Then he looked out into the darkness over the field of dead men and burning tanks.

"They'll be back," Pete stated firmly. He looked to Aldrich. "Get the guys ready. Hundred percent alert."

It was as if Pete was reading Tadashi Tanimura's thoughts. The young major was furious.

At a makeshift command post located behind the Army's main jump-off position, he glared at the assembled officers.

"This was not what General Saito expected," he raged. "The attack was well launched. It had advanced admirably. All the elements—infantry and armor—seemed to be in lockstep. Then, as they closed on the enemy, everything fell apart. Everything! It was like watching headless chickens. There was no coordination. No leadership. Where were the officers? Where was the *Yamato Damashi*?"

Tadashi knew he was on thin ice, speaking to superior officers as he did. However, he was speaking for Saito, and it was his job to let the others know the general's thoughts.

"I caution you on your tone, Major," Ogawa said, restraining his voice. Inside, he bristled at Tadashi's words. His pride did not appreciate being spoken to so harshly by a man of junior rank—a man with known American ties.

"I am not here as an officer junior to you, Colonel Ogawa," Tadashi tersely replied. "I am the representative of General Saito, and my tone is exactly the tone he'd be using if he were here. A perfect opportunity was squandered, hundreds of men dead, and over a dozen tanks destroyed, all for nothing."

"I think it was the illumination shells," injected Hanaya. "Just like last night."

"Nonsense, Captain," Tadashi shot back. "We knew they'd use illumination shells."

"But not so many," Hanaya insisted. "The field was never in darkness."

Tadashi pondered this. Then he turned to another officer.

"Colonel Goto," he barked. "Where were your tanks? It was expected that you'd have sixty or more, but you only committed about half that number."

"It was the weather, Major," he said. "The rain caused vehicles to get bogged down. But they'll all be up within the hour."

Tadashi recalled just before he left HQ earlier in the evening, he'd dispatched a radio message to Tokyo in Saito's name that read: "After dark this division will launch a night attack in force, and we expect to annihilate the enemy in one swoop."

That had not happened.

"General Saito has great confidence in you, Colonel Ogawa," Tadashi continued. He had put Ogawa down as Saito would have wanted him to, and now it was time to bring the man back up and restore the colonel's face. "He is fully aware of your courage and skill in leading your men."

Ogawa briefly bowed at the compliment he had just been given by a man who was known throughout the division as Saito's most trusted aide.

"You will all have the chance to redeem yourselves in the eyes of General Saito," Tadashi said. "We're attacking again. At 0530, an hour before dawn. This time you will drive through the Americans and reach their landing beaches and supply dumps. You will destroy everything in sight or die trying."

"I will lead my tanks forward personally," Colonel Goto vowed. "We will grind the Americans under our treads."

Tadashi nodded with satisfaction. His bloodlust was up.

CHAPTER 7

Later, Pete and his men would argue over which they heard first—the harsh blare of the bugles or the roar of Mitsubishi diesel engines—but none could deny that a mammoth attack was rolling across the field toward them at precisely 0530.

As they had done two hours earlier, parachute flares lit up the sky to reveal a tidal wave of enemy soldiers interspersed with at least forty tanks, many overflowing with men piggybacking on their steel hulls.

"Doesn't this ever stop?" Pete asked himself.

Naval gunners began to ply their trade, and the air above the Marines was split as a volley of 5-inch rounds from offshore destroyers soared overhead. Thundering explosions wracked the air and pillars of fire and smoke blossomed among the attackers. Under the glare of the star shells, Pete could see body parts tossed carelessly into the air. As Pete had seen all too often, this carnage did nothing to slow the attack.

A 14-inch shell from the *California* exploded in front of

the Japanese, all but vaporizing one man while knocking down several others and snapping the track of a nearby *Ha-Go* light tank. The vehicle was left to spin helplessly on its single remaining track.

As he lifted his Thompson in preparation of the command to fire, Pete was shaken when another shell from the *California* slammed into the ground almost midway between his foxhole and that shared by Rosie and Aldrich. The sudden impact jolted everyone. The unexploded "short" stuck nose first into the rain-softened ground, its hot steel skin sizzling and sending up a steamy mist.

"Jesus Christ," Pete heard Rosie gasp as he gazed at the projectile that, had it not been a dud, would have killed them all.

After the initial shock, Pete got angry. First he was run over by a Jap tank, and now an American battleship shell almost canceled his ticket.

Turning his attention back to the assault, Pete saw this one was different from the first. Unlike that charge, this time very few men stopped to fire their weapons. Instead, they carried them waist high, bayonets pointed toward the Americans.

As the Japanese drew closer, 75mm and 105mm guns of the Tenth Marines positioned behind the battalion line went to work, their shells arcing over their embattled comrades. Razor-sharp shrapnel sliced through the enemy ranks. Interspersed with the artillery discharges was heard the "thunk" of mortar rounds being dropped.

All the while, the sky was lit by flares, giving the Marines a front-row seat to the butchery going on to their front. Then it was their turn.

"Open fire!" officers and NCOs called out.

For the second time during that long, gruesome night, the Marine line exploded, mowing down enemy soldiers like blades of grass. Yet even as he heard the firing and saw Japanese soldiers fall in droves, Pete knew the gyrenes would not be able to stop this charge. These determined attackers would break through. So would their tanks. It was just a matter of how many and how big a breach they would make.

Colonel Takashi Goto saw that as well. Standing up in the turret of his *Shinhoto Chi-Ha* medium tank as it rolled forward, the island's overall armor commander knew they'd break the American line. This was the opportunity he had longed for over the past forty-eight hours.

Grinning, he ordered his tanks to charge ahead, with him leading the way.

The rattle of gunfire was deafening. Suddenly, Japanese troops burst through the American lines. Rosie fired a last burst from his BAR before being bowled over by an enemy soldier. The two scrabbled under the harsh glare of an illumination shell until Rosie found himself underneath the attacker. Desperately grasping to free his Ka-Bar, Aldrich spared him the effort by freeing his own blade. Swiftly, he lifted the intruder's head and slit his throat, the man's blood spurting onto Rosie as he struggled free.

Pete fired a burst from his Thompson that quickly dropped three men. His weapon empty, he dropped the spent magazine and grabbed a thirty-round clip, inserted it, and yanked the arming lever just in time to shoot two more Japanese. One man, however, got through this hail of bullets and plowed into Pete. The Thompson jarred from his grip, Pete fought the Jap with one hand while with the other he tried to free the .45 from its shoulder holster. The enemy soldier shoved a hand into Pete's face, attempting to get a stranglehold, but Pete managed to free the .45, shove the Colt up under the man's chin, and sent a bullet crashing into his brain. Pete was in sheer survival mode. He automatically rose to his knees, holstered the automatic, located his Thompson, and resumed firing.

"Farmer" Goodman had never liked bayonet practice in boot camp and, much to the ire of his DI, had difficulty learning the fundamentals of parrying the enemy's jabs and thrusting his own weapon.

The gangly redhead from Harpers Ferry learned it now. He had just shot down two attackers when a third ran up, bayonet gleaming in the harsh artificial moonlight of the flares. As the Jap soldier thrust at him, Goodman slammed the Arisaka aside with a parry to the left, then swept his Garand upward to smash the butt plate up under the man's chin. Stunned, the enemy soldier fell to the ground, where Goodman plunged the bayonet into his chest. The blade stuck, so Goodman, recalling another lesson, fired off a round to blow the bayonet free. After suffering trauma the day before over a soldier he'd slain, Goodman was suddenly aware that, when necessary, killing could be easy. It was an unsettling thought.

Private Vivian Miller was glad when he'd been invited to share a foxhole with Reb after Morales's death. He fired his weapon, reloaded, then fired and reloaded again. He did not know how many men he had shot, or if they were dead or alive. That didn't matter right now.

Then he saw the tank headed straight for their foxhole. Reb saw it too. As the vehicle, a light *Ha-Go*, churned toward their position, Reb yelled, "Miller! Bail out!"

Reb rolled out of the foxhole on his side, and Miller did the same on the other end as the tank chewed the earth over their position, its track missing the boy's left foot by four scant inches.

Worried that there might be Japs riding the tank, Reb was

relieved to see the hull was barren of men. Then he recalled that Jap tanks, especially light ones, have a weakness to small arms fire if that fire is directed at a bracket by the bogey wheels. Concentrated fire on that point could jar the track loose, so he opened up on the tank's tread area with his BAR. It worked. With a loud snap, the track broke free, and the *Ha-Go* rolled to a stop.

"Fire at the eyeholes," Reb shouted to Miller.

As Miller aimed for the eye slits, Reb climbed onto the rear of the tank, looking for the vulnerable oil portal with the intent of dropping a grenade inside. He did not find the portal, but the tank commander saved him the effort. The man lifted the hatch to inspect the damage, only to have Reb bash him with his BAR's heavy butt. As the man fell back into the turret, Reb dropped in a grenade. It went off with a loud hollow bang as Reb jumped clear.

Close by, Scrap Iron saw Reb take out the tank and muttered, "Crazy bastard." Still, he couldn't help but grin. Casting aside any second thoughts that he might've made a terrible mistake transferring out of the motor pool, Dembrowski now knew he'd made the right choice. This is what he had volunteered for.

Sammy Dubbs was reloading his Garand when two Japanese hurried forth. Working quickly, Dubbs dropped one of them, but the second got off one round. Luckily, after firing his rifle, Dubbs flinched just enough that the Jap's bullet cut through the sleeve of his shirt and passed clean through the fleshy part of his upper right arm close to the shoulder. Dubbs fell back against the foxhole, and the Japanese soldier, perhaps thinking he'd killed the American, ran past and into the Marines' rear. There he died from .30-caliber machine gun fire as he attacked a Sherman coming up onto the line.

Scrap Iron saw Dubbs get hit and sprang to his side.

"You hurt bad, kid?" he asked anxiously.

His teeth clenched in pain. Dubbs could only shake his head no.

Dembrowski yelled for a corpsman. He patted Dubbs on his good shoulder and then rejoined the battle.

Further along the platoon's right flank, the situation had grown dire. Japanese overran the machine gun position defended by Moxley Pope and his loader Sidney Hoskins. Bayonets flashed, and a sword wielded by a Japanese officer came down on Hoskins's neck. Their job done, the enemy continued rearward toward Cornwall's HQ, nearly overrunning it until five men from First Platoon countercharged. They shot down the attacking Japanese, including the officer. However, one man, as he died, lobbed a grenade toward the pillbox. Cornwall felt as though his legs were on fire as he was thrown to the mud.

Eyes wide with pain and terror, the young officer from Binghamton, New York, reached out to shake O'Leary, who lay next to him.

"O'Leary! O'Leary!" he called, trying to rouse the man. But Master Sergeant Thomas O'Leary was beyond hearing, a shard of shrapnel lodged in his brain.

Colonel Goto's tank had just silenced an American 37mm gun position, blasting the weapon and its crew with two well-aimed rounds. Now he watched as American tanks rolled forward, passing through the Marines' line to engage the Japanese armor. This sight thrilled Goto. He longed to do battle with these beasts and turned his *Chi-Ha* toward the tank battle now forming. His *Shinhoto Chi-Ha* was superior to other Japanese medium tanks, with a five-man crew instead of four and a high-velocity 47mm gun with more penetrating power than the standard 57mm piece in most *Chi-Ha* versions.

As his vehicle closed the distance, Goto ducked back inside

the steel safety of his three-man turret and ordered the driver to turn right. His first target was an American Stuart light tank that was cutting across his field of vision. As his loader shoved a round into the main battery, Goto sighted in.

"*Hai!*" he yelled.

The cannon roared, and the tank shuddered slightly as the shell streaked from the barrel. It struck the lighter Stuart tank with such force that the resulting explosion caused the fifteen-ton tank to roll onto its side, fire belching from its interior.

A grin creased Goto's face as he spun the turret again. Now he sighted a heavier tank, a Sherman, approaching from his left. The Sherman got off the first shot, but it was hastily aimed, and the round fell short. Rolling past the burning hulk of the Stuart, Goto fired his main gun. Like the Sherman, his aim was off as the shell caromed off the Sherman's steeply sloping front, creasing the armor plate but not exploding until it struck the earth thirty yards to the rear. The Sherman seemed to shake off the blow as the commander traversed the turret slightly, lifted the barrel, and fired again.

In his final moments, Goto knew this one would not miss.

"*Dai Nippon, Banzai,*" he yelled, wishing his nation a long life a brief second before the American shell penetrated his tank's armored skin and exploded.

The *Shinhoto Chi-Ha* drifted to a stop, its flaming steel corpse converted into a crematorium for the colonel and his crew.

The sun was well above the horizon and beginning its morning climb when the fight finally ended. After more than three hours of desperate fighting, hundreds of Japanese survivors, many of them wounded, staggered rearward. Among them was a growing disillusion. They had expected an overwhelming victory, not a stunning repulse.

Exhausted Marines gazed out across the field, where the aftermath of two vicious night assaults lay strewn in twisted heaps. Among this human wreckage, no less than thirty-five enemy tanks stood silent, except for the crackle of flames, casting black clouds of smoke that rolled across the field of corpses like a shroud.

Pete dragged the body of the dead Japanese soldier he'd killed out of his foxhole and left it a few yards behind his position. Then he made the rounds of the squad.

He saw Magruder at Dembrowski's foxhole and headed there first. Doc was bandaging Dubbs's arm and shoulder as Scrap Iron looked on.

"Is he hurt bad?" Pete asked.

"Naw," Magruder said. "His arm's gonna hurt, but that's the extent."

"I'm not leaving the squad, Sarge," Dubbs said. "I can still fight."

Pete nodded.

"You ain't getting out of it that easy," he said.

Dubbs chuckled.

"Besides," Pete said. "The Twenty-Seventh Division has begun landing so maybe they can give us a bit of a breather by shouldering the load for a few days."

Dembrowski snorted.

"Yeah, the Army," he sneered. "They're as worthless as tits on a bull."

Pete turned to Magruder.

"How'd the platoon fare?" he asked.

Magruder grew somber.

"Japs overran Pope and Hoskins's machine gun," he said as he rewrapped unused bandages and stuffed them back into his Unit 2 bag. "Pope got bayoneted four or five times, but I think that tough son-of-a-whatever is gonna make it. But a Jap sword nearly sliced off Hoskins's head. I'll never get used to seeing that." He paused. "And Lt. Cornwall got hit. Grenade shrapnel in both legs. I had him taken off to the field hospital on the beach. And Master Sergeant O'Leary is dead. Same grenade."

That hit Pete hard. He had the highest regard for Captain Stacey and Lt. Cornwall. Now Cornwall was out of it. But he was struck even harder by the death of O'Leary, a grizzled veteran with twenty years in the Corps.

"Overall, we lost about one hundred forty guys, killed and wounded," Magruder said. "But they say along the battalion front there are some three thousand dead Japs."

"Good God," Pete said. "That's almost as many as the Japs had in total on Tarawa. How long can the Nips hold out with those kinds of losses?"

"They're tough bastards," Magruder said. "In the First Battalion sector, a lot of the dead were Navy men, Special Landing Force. We know what they're like from Tarawa."

Pete nodded in agreement, then checked in with the rest of the squad. He stopped by the battered foxhole belonging to Reb and Miller and noted the damage from its being rolled over by a Jap tank.

"You two okay?" he asked.

"Thas a fact," Reb drawled. "Unlike our fearless leader, we was smart enough to get out of the way before we ended up under that blamed tank."

Pete smiled and moved on.

Goodman and Honeybun were munching on the dried fruit bars they'd removed from their K-ration breakfast boxes when Pete arrived. Honeybun inspected the dark-colored fruit bar he held in his hand.

"Did you ever wonder what kind of fruit they use in these

things that it can be unrefrigerated for years?" he speculated. "I'll bet my uncle Walter ate these same fruit bars when he was riding with old Jeb Stuart."

Pete moved on.

After the squad check, Pete returned to his foxhole, where he was soon joined by Aldrich. Pete told him about Cornwall and O'Leary.

"We have other concerns too," the Professor said. "I checked with the squad; we burned a lot of ammo last night."

Pete nodded.

"I'll check with Gunny," he said. "Now get these bodies cleared away before they start to stink."

Back in the observation tower overlooking Garapan, Major Tadashi Tanimura was crushed by the repulse of this latest attack, and appalled at the losses. Yet he was not surprised.

After the withdrawal of the attacking force was complete, Tadashi located Colonel Ogawa, who was equally devastated by the setback. With tears in his eyes, he gazed at the men now going into bivouac to get some rest from the night's exertions. The inability to demolish the American line had left them disheartened and frustrated.

"What happened?" he asked Ogawa. "Our men reached the American lines. Why did we fail?"

"Their proficiency with artillery is maddening," Ogawa said dully. "It's like their shells have eyes. But even worse are their illumination shells. My men are second to no one in night fighting, but how can we use that to our advantage when the Americans seem to have an endless supply of those damned star shells?"

"Do you have any idea of your losses?"

"No," Ogawa said. "But they are substantial."

"Have you heard from the Navy sector?" Tadashi asked.

"Only rumor," Ogawa said. "But it seems the First Yoko-suka did no better than us. I did hear that Colonel Yakazo died at the head of his troops."

"And our tanks," Tadashi said. "What have you heard from Colonel Goto?"

"Nothing," Ogawa answered. "The colonel is missing. He was last seen leading his tanks into the enemy lines."

Tadashi nodded sadly.

Unable to report in person in a timely manner to Saito, Tadashi used Ogawa's radio to dispatch the sad news of the overnight disaster to HQ. Saito had been stunned by the set-back. His consolation was that his men died with honor, but the mere fact of their deaths brought the Americans that much closer to success.

Upset but far from dispirited, Saito seemed to find a new aggressiveness.

"In your absence, I am dispatching a message to Imperial Headquarters informing them that our attack failed because of enemy tanks and firepower," Saito told him. "I am adding that we are reorganizing and will attack again."

Tadashi wasn't sure that Saito's plan to launch another as-sault was correct. Perhaps, Tadashi thought, it was unwise to keep smashing their heads against that wall of American steel. The problem was that Tadashi, no matter how fond Saito was of him, dared not question his commander's tactics. He just hoped Saito would realize the futility of head-on attacks before it was too late. Gazing down from the tower to the rooftops of Garapan a mile to the west, he felt exhaustion from the night's action and the stress of his responsibilities.

Climbing from the tower, an urge overtook Tadashi. He turned to address his friend Hanaya.

"I am tired, Kiso-san," he said, using his pet name for his

friend for the first time since the invasion. "Let me invite you to my home," he said and led his friend toward Garapan.

On this hot, sunny Saturday, Garapan was a far cry from the bustling town of busy islanders Tadashi had known as a boy. The sturdy concrete post office on Middle Road near the main town square stood relatively unscathed, with just a few cracks and chips and a lot of broken windows. Oddly, in the rear courtyard lay the stiffened carcass of a water buffalo. Other buildings of concrete and wood bore the scars of heavy naval shelling during the preinvasion softening-up. Some suffered various degrees of damage; others had collapsed walls; and a few were roofless, hollowed-out shells.

Main avenues that Tadashi remembered as busy roadways, with names like Kalachucha, Flooris, Bukiki, and Puti Tainabia, were clogged by mountains of debris. Side streets like Floris Rosa and Kadena Di Amor, once lined with neat shops and houses, were heaped with charred and twisted sheet metal roofing, chunks of concrete, splintered utility poles, and various articles of household furnishings. Once used for peaceful purposes by humble people, the rubble-strewn remains of these structures now concealed Japanese sailors of the First Special Naval Landing Force and Fifth Special Base Force, their machine guns and anti-tank weapons awaiting the inevitable arrival of the American Marines.

On the southeast corner of Middle Road and Kopa Di Oru Street, the two men came upon Sugar King Park. Here Tadashi recalled playing American baseball with his friends on the park's lush lawns. Now those lawns were torn apart and cratered and crisscrossed with trenches.

Careful not to be too visible to the American fighter planes zooming overhead, hungry for targets, Tadashi led his friend along Middle Road, then turned right along Sugar King Road. This eastern side of the town was home to many of the island's affluent families, and that included Tadashi's parents. In his position with the Ministry of Agriculture, Hideo Tanimura represented the emperor and was provided with a fine house for himself, his wife, and young son.

Walking along, Tadashi sometimes pointed out the home of a family he knew as a boy. Many suffered battle damage, and a few were demolished. He recalled his playmates, especially his best friends Yasuyuki Umeza and Matsutake Nakamoto, killed respectively on Tarawa and the Philippines.

The house just off Sugar King Road stood almost unscathed. Another family had moved into the house after Tadashi's parents returned to Japan in 1936, but the house was now vacant and ill-kept. Passing through the *torii* gate, he and Hanaya walked along a crushed coral pathway, skirting around what had been an ornamental garden and koi pond. What water remained was brackish, and any fish it was home to were long dead. The lawn, and especially the gardens his mother so loved, reflected long-term neglect.

"My mother loved her garden," Tadashi said as much to himself as to his friend. "It would make her sad to see it shriveled and dying."

Tadashi felt a warmness of coming home as the two men entered the house. That warmth vanished when he found himself in a large family room peppered liberally with broken wicker furniture, smashed wall hangings now lying on the floor. Everything was liberally coated in the dust of neglect. This was not the elegantly furnished room so meticulously tended by his mother, and it saddened Tadashi immensely. Even the family's Shinto shrine, the *Kamidana*, was gone.

Tadashi wasn't sure what condition he'd expected the house

to be in since he'd lived here, but this wasn't it. He had hoped to go into the bedroom that had been his own, but now this unkempt house repelled him. His honored mother, who always felt out of place in her husband's society, had loved this house. Now it was dead and decayed.

"This is not my home," he said more to himself than to Hanaya.

He turned and walked out, leaving Hanaya to catch up.

"My mother believed in the Christian God, in a spiritual life after death," he said. "Before she died, she told me her spirit would watch over me. I didn't understand, but her words still comforted me. I hope she is not here with me right now."

He left and did not look back.

The sun beat down on the field of the dead. As expected, the hot rays caused the Japanese bodies to swell, and the stench of decay permeated the air. Navy Seabees manning bulldozers attempted to mitigate the smell by scooping trenches in the earth and then shoving in as many corpses as would fit.

Pete sank back in his foxhole. Rooting through his haversack, he took out a waterproof pouch, opened it, and removed a black-and-white photograph his mother had recently sent him.

The photo was of his brother Charlie. Wearing his white Navy uniform and smiling to the camera, Charlie was leaning against the .50-caliber deck gun mounted to the rear conning tower of the submarine USS *Grampus*. On the reverse side, in Charlie's neat handwriting, was the inscription: "Brisbane, February 1943." Pete gazed at the confident smile on his brother's face, the smile of a young man who was blissfully unaware that he had less than a month to live. Pete cherished this photo and the accompanying letter from his mother. She had written that the photo had arrived at their home with a package of personal effects sent to her by the War Department a few months after the submarine had officially been declared lost.

Pete was about to replace the photo in his haversack when he saw Nicholson approaching in a low crouch so as not to entice any Japanese snipers.

"You look like a man with problems," Pete observed as Nicholson joined him in his foxhole.

"You've been readin' my mail," Nicholson replied. "We had some tough fighting overnight. Colonel Riseley, the battalion CO, directed some of it while sitting on a log beside his CP puffing on a cigar." Nicholson chuckled. "He called it a five-cigar counterattack."

"I heard about Lt. Cornwall and about O'Leary," Pete told the gunny. "So what's the score? Who's leading the platoon?"

"For right now," Nicholson said, "Skipper is sending us an officer from his staff. Lt. Stehman."

"Rodney Stehman?" Pete moaned. "He's the goddamned S4. A fuckin' supply clerk. Is he supposed to make sure we're well supplied with condoms?"

"I agree, he's not commanded troops in combat," Nicholson said. "But he's seen action, and he's a Marine officer first and a supply officer second."

"Who'll be platoon sergeant?" Pete asked.

"Hodges is senior," Nicholson said. "I'm just on my way now to give him the good news."

"Fine with me," Pete replied. "I was afraid you were going to volunteer me."

"No," Nicholson said. "But you better hope Hodges stays healthy."

"Damned shame about O'Leary," Pete said.

"Yeah," Gunny said. "It's going to hit Maudie pretty hard. But she's a tough lady, and she has three kids to help her."

Nicholson saw the photo still in Pete's hand.

"A photo from that new wife of yours?" he asked.

"Huh? No," Pete said and handed it over. Nicholson looked at the photo with interest. "My mom sent it to me. It came in the last mail call."

"I admire those submariners," Nicholson said as he studied the picture. "You couldn't get me to go down in one of those things."

"Me neither," Pete admitted. "My little brother had more courage than I ever gave him credit for."

Pete went quiet. Nicholson handed the photo back and gave Pete a sympathetic slap on the shoulder.

"By the way," Nicholson said. "A couple of LVTs brought up some supplies—ammo, fresh water, and some rations. They dumped the stuff by the company CP, so rotate your men to go back and get what they need."

He went to look for Sgt. Hodges.

CHAPTER 8

Pete didn't like it, but orders were orders.

Those orders had come down about an hour earlier, when Nicholson and First Lt. Rodney Stehman called a meeting of all Second Platoon squad leaders at his assembly point, which was the CP he had inherited after Lt. Cornwall's wounding.

"At 1500," Stehman began without preamble, "the battalion is moving forward. Our objective is that ridge ahead." He pointed at the looming high ground ahead in the shadow of Mount Tipo Pale. "We'll be moving forward in route column. Our platoon has been ordered to take the advance position." He turned to Nicholson. "Who do you suggest for point, Sergeant?"

"Hardball," Nicholson said. "You take point. You'll be accompanied by a Sherman, so you won't be out there bare-assed."

Stehman nodded.

"First squad will provide the connecting files between your squad, Sergeant Talbot, and the rest of the platoon. Dog

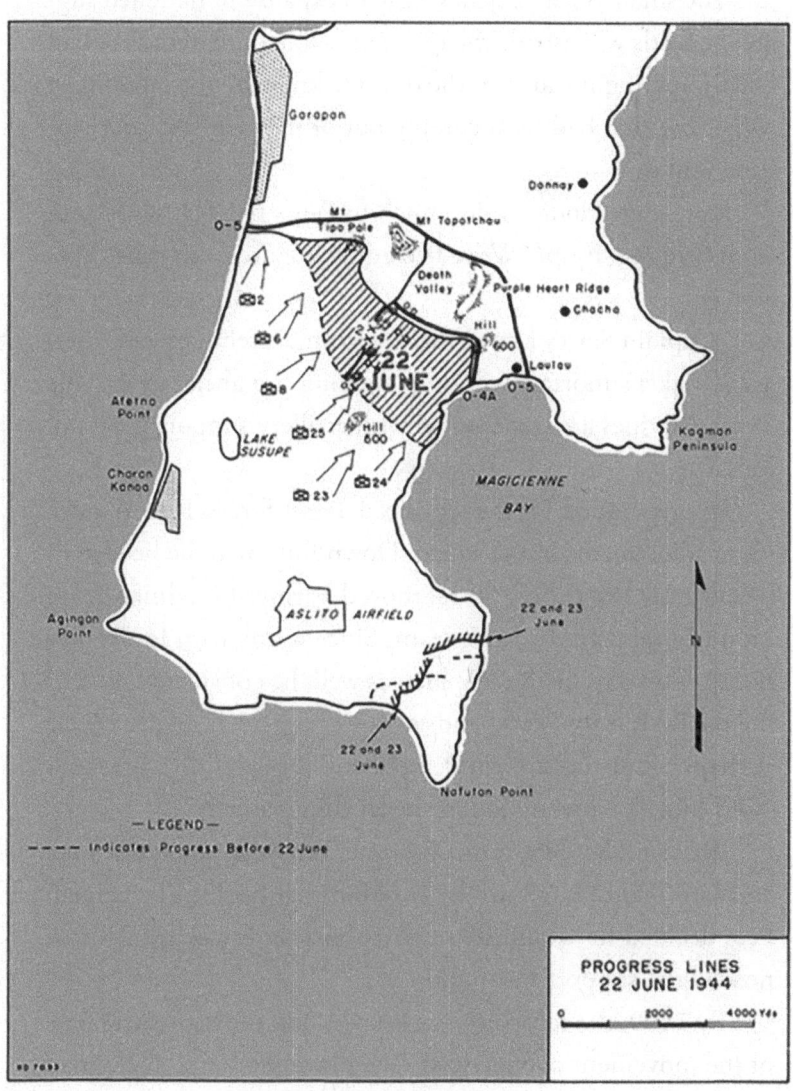

PROGRESS LINES
22 JUNE 1944

Company's first task is to seize and neutralize that cluster of shacks dead ahead."

The small village beyond a broad expanse of flattened sugarcane fields was astride the company's line of march; Pete had been watching it much of the day. He knew by the amount of sniper fire that had been coming out of that area that the Japs were well dug in.

"Sir," Sgt. Hodges said, much to Pete's relief. It saved him from bringing it up. "We've been drawing fire from those huts all day."

"Captain Stacey knows that, Sergeant," Stehman said. "Sergeant Baker's mortars will drop walking fire ahead of us. The Tenth Marines are standing by with artillery support if we call for it."

In preparation for the job ahead, losses forced Pete to make some adjustments in the squad. Down four men, he needed to balance his fire teams. So he moved Farmer Goodman from Honeybun's team to Reb's team. Since a fire team leader was not supposed to be the AW man as well, he considered switching the BAR from Reb's hands to one of the other men—Miller perhaps—but did not think Reb would peacefully surrender "Old Jube" to anyone else, so he let things stand.

That shift left Fire Teams Two and Three each short one man and Fire Team One down by two, but that couldn't be helped. Pete decided he would fill in that shortage himself if Aldrich needed the support in a fight.

By 1400, the company was formed, and the approach phase of the movement commenced. The promised tank, a Sherman with "Daisy Mae" painted on its turret, led the way, with Fire Team One, Aldrich, and Rosie directly behind. Fire Team Two, Honeybun, Scrap Iron, and Dubbs formed a wedge on the left, and Fire Team Three, Reb, Miller, and Goodman did the same on the right. Pete positioned himself between Fire Teams Two and Three and behind Aldrich.

As the column started, the rest of Second Platoon walked about a hundred yards behind the point, with three men forming the connecting link between point and the advance team. Another hundred yards further back was the main body, comprised of Headquarters Section, First Platoon, Machine Gun Platoon, and the Mortar Section. Two squads spread out to each side served as right- and left-flank guards. Further back behind the main body came the Rear Party, and thirty yards behind that the Rear Point, with three men spread out as the connecting file, followed by one lone fire team.

As the formation crossed the fields where burial details still worked, the most prevailing sound other than the tank engine was the crunching of Marine boondockers as they stepped on the felled sugarcane stalks.

"I don't see anything," Aldrich said to Pete, speaking loudly to be heard above the Sherman's engine. "But I know they're watching us. I can feel it."

As the tank and Pete's point guard closed on their goal, "Pogey Bait" Baker's mortar crews went to work, and the ground ahead blossomed with bursts of fire and smoke. Through the clouds of dust and spent powder, Pete could see the village. A dirt road previously unseen approached the village from the west and passed between two rows of huts. There were at least nine houses Pete could see—four on the south side of the dusty roadway facing five houses on the north side. A couple of the structures looked sturdy, constructed of stone or concrete, while the rest were of wood, with thatched roofs made from woven palm trees. Unlike the stone and concrete homes, which boasted doors and were built on ground level, these cruder structures were mounted on thick wooden stilts, putting them about three or four feet off the ground, doubtless to guard against unwanted visitors, such as snakes and rats.

As Pete's men closed to within forty yards of the village, the friendly mortar fire lifted. Pete spotted movement in one of the houses. He opened the phone box mounted on the right rear of the tank and got the commander on the line.

"First house on the right," Pete told the tank commander. "There's someone home."

As Pete raised a hand, signaling the entire column behind him to halt, the turret of the tank slowly traversed to the right just as a Type 96 Nambu machine gun began to chatter, its 6.5mm slugs bouncing off Daisy Mae's steel body. With a terrifying "whoosh," a tongue of liquid flame shot from Daisy Mae's snout. The Japanese inside the wooden house realized too late that she was what the Marines dubbed a "Zippo." They tried to flee, but Daisy Mae's hot breath quickly enveloped the small house, and the aged wood burned swiftly. Screaming figures, their clothes alight, scrambled from the house. They weaved drunkenly for a few moments, only to drop dead on the road or in the gardens.

Daisy Mae slowly resumed rolling forward as more gunfire erupted from more buildings. The men of Second Squad rallied behind the Sherman, popping out to return fire, then ducking back.

A hundred yards to the rear, the rest of Second Platoon fanned out. Converting depth into width, they hurried forward to aid their comrades. Stacey held the bulk of Dog Company in its position unless Second Platoon needed assistance. The gunfire became a steady crackle as Daisy Mae entered the village, passing through the line of huts, with the men of Second Platoon hot on her heels. Daisy Mae rolled onto the roadway, crashing through a wooden fence, her fiery tongue first incinerating a house on the left side, then swiveling her turret to immolate a house on the right. Japanese soldiers, some on fire, began leaping out of bungalows while others crawled from beneath the elevated houses. Fleeing, they fired their weapons wildly at the Americans. A number of these men were shot down, while the rest fled before the flaming wrath of Daisy Mae. Marines continued to sweep through the village, tossing grenades through windows and doors to flush out any stragglers.

Pete saw Reb Marshall drop to a knee and spray the area under an elevated shack while young Miller lobbed a grenade into a window. Honeybun and Dubbs raced across the dirt street and burst through the doorway of a hut, firing their weapons as they went. Each shot a Japanese soldier as three more jumped out of a rear window. Dembrowski was waiting there with his Tommy gun leveled and cut the trio down.

Pete ran up to one of the stone houses. Hearing movement inside, he pressed himself against the outside wall by the door. Taking a grenade from his web belt, he yanked the pin and lobbed the pineapple inside. The explosion was like a thunderclap, followed immediately by a bizarre wailing sound inside the hut. Pete burst in through the front door, Thompson raised and ready. Three Japanese soldiers lay dead just inside, their bodies torn open by his grenade. Carefully, Pete stepped inside. The wailing he had heard continued, but now he recognized it as children's voices. Cowering in a far corner, Pete discovered a withered old man, a middle-aged woman, and three small children all under age ten. The adults looked terrified, while the children screamed as they clutched the grown-ups.

"Gaijin!" a little girl cried. *"Gaijin!"*

Pete stood, not knowing what to do. Then he realized that their terror might be in part because he was still pointing his

Tommy gun at them. He lowered the weapon, hoping to allay their fears, but to no avail.

"It's okay," he said as calmly as he could. "It's okay. Professor! Get in here."

"What's up?" Aldrich asked as he entered the house, then he saw the civilians. "Oh."

"Yeah," Pete said. "Do you remember any of that Jap lingo they tried to teach us on the ship? They think I'm gonna kill 'em."

Aldrich nodded, then slung his rifle over his shoulder.

"Shimpai shinaide," Aldrich said. *"Korosanai."*

"What are you telling them?" Pete asked.

"I hope I'm telling them not to be afraid—that we won't kill them," Aldrich replied. Then to the civilians he again said, *"Shimpai shinaide. Korosanai."*

He fished into his light marching order pack and took out a K-ration box.

"These people look like they're starving," Aldrich said.

Aldrich opened the box, a dinner, and removed the can of stew he found inside. Opening the tin with the attached key, he carefully moved forward and offered it to the woman. Initially, she cowered even further into the corner. Then hunger won out, and her hand, shaking like a leaf, came out cautiously and accepted the food.

"Domo," she said, weakly. *"Domo."*

She doled out some of the food to the children.

Until that moment, Pete did not see that the woman and two of the still crying children were bleeding. Their skin and clothes were so dirty that it hadn't been evident. Since the blood seemed fresh, he guessed that their wounds were from his grenade.

"Dammit," he said and went to the door. "Corpsman! Corpsman!"

As always, Doc Magruder arrived quickly.

"What's up, Hardball?"

Pete pointed.

"Some of them are wounded," he said. "My grenade."

"They wouldn't be the first civvies on this island to get in the way," Magruder said as he opened his Unit 2 bag and knelt by the children. At first the kids were afraid of the strange man. Then he showed them his Red Cross armband. The woman spoke softly to the children as Magruder went to work on their injuries.

As Doc ministered to the civilians, Aldrich examined the rest of the house.

From the other side of the room, Aldrich said, "Hardball, you didn't walk over here, did you?"

"No," Pete replied. "Why?"

Stepping over debris, Pete crossed the room and looked down. Half buried under the rubble was the body of an old woman, the blood on her as fresh as it was on the others. She looked about the same age as the man. Pete stood horrified.

"Oh, Jesus Christ," he moaned. "I did that."

Aldrich put a hand on Pete's shoulder.

"You had no way of knowing."

"I killed the kids' goddamned grandmother," Pete said angrily. "This is all such bullshit."

He stomped out of the house, across the front garden, and sat down on a low stone wall that separated the house from the road. He lit a Camel and seemed engrossed at the treads of a Sherman that clanked along the road.

The entire village was now overflowing with Marines. Daisy Mae was at the far end of the village, having left in her wake one smoldering concrete house and three fiercely burning wooden structures.

The shooting over, about thirty enemy dead lay on the

roadway and in the gardens around the houses. Ten civilians who had been found hiding were marched outside. Hands held high as they stumbled along, they looked as terrified as the family Pete had discovered.

Pete was on his second cigarette when he saw a man running along the street in the direction of the Marines, both hands in the air, one of which held a crucifix.

"Chamorro, Chamorro," he called out. "Francisco."

His fear was relieved when Miller approached him. The young private fished his own crucifix out from beneath his shirt and showed it to the man, who smiled with relief.

"Gracious, gracious," the man repeated over and over. *"Ve con dios."*

Nicholson approached Pete, noting the pained look on his face.

"What's up with you?" he asked.

Pete's only response was to thrust an arm in the vague direction of the doorway. Nicholson went inside. Moments later he was back. He'd obviously spoken with Magruder.

"Put it behind you," Nicholson said, standing over Pete. "We're finding civilians all around the village, and about eight or nine were accidently killed by our guys. They could've evacuated, but they chose to stay."

"I know that," Pete said. "But it was their grandmother."

Nicholson's expression hardened.

"You have to shape up," he snapped. "Isn't that what you'd say to one of your own men? Cry all you want on your own time, but right now you have a job to do, Sergeant."

"You can be a bastard. Do you know that?" Pete said.

"Goddamned right," Nicholson replied. "Now see to your squad. It seems we're going to be here for a while. We've hit stiff resistance in these hills, so we're going to sit tight and secure what we have. Since we headed the battalion today, Easy and Fox Companies are moving forward. We're battalion reserve."

Nicholson left.

Aldrich walked up to Pete and sat down on the wall beside him.

"Since O'Leary got hit, Nicholson's the top NCO in the company," the Professor said. "That must weigh heavy on a man like him, who takes the life of each Marine seriously."

Pete wasn't sure if he needed to respond or not. But he never got the chance as Rosie called out, "Look what I got!"

What he had was a very young, very skinny Japanese Army private who, in an ill-fitting uniform that sagged from his thin frame, looked as terrified as the civilians. Rosie half marched, half dragged the man toward Pete. Dembrowski suddenly snatched the youth from Rosie's hands and slammed him to the ground. He then raised his Thompson.

"Dembrowski!" Pete snapped. "As you were!"

"We're here to kill these bastards," Dembrowski snarled. "I'm just doin' what the Corps is paying me to do."

"You disobey my orders, and so help me God, I'll drop you where you stand," he said in as mean a voice as he could muster.

Dembrowski lowered the submachine gun and stared at Pete, anger burning in his eyes. "They nearly crushed your ass under a tank yesterday," Dembrowski growled. "Your buddy Harnish got his leg blown off. So when did you become a Jap lover?"

Just then Captain Stacey arrived.

"You talk to a superior like that again, and I'll have you court-martialed," he said.

A woman broke away from the group of civilians who had been rounded up and ran to the Japanese soldier. She threw her arms protectively around him and glared at Dembrowski.

Stacey's S2, Lt. Shimada, approached the young men.

"Onamae wa nan desu ka?" Shimada asked.

The youth, clearly dumbfounded to see a Japanese man in a Marine uniform, spoke back.

"Kashigura Yoshi desu," he said.

"He says his name is Yoshi Kashigura," Shimada said, then listened as the man chattered some more. "He is sixteen and lives in this village. He said he and other islanders have been conscripted into the Japanese Army. This is his mother." The man chattered on. "He says he was placed in the 136th Regiment under a Colonel Ogawa and that his comrades are forming a new defensive line."

"Where?" Stacey asked.

"Doko?" Shimada inquired.

"Wakaranai," the man replied.

"He doesn't know," Shimada reported.

The mother now began speaking, and Shimada translated.

"She said her son is not truly a soldier and wants to take him home with her," Shimada said.

"No," Stacey said. "He's still a POW. Tell him—and his mother—that we have to hold him but will not harm him. G2 may want to talk to him."

Shimada did as ordered, and the man meekly allowed himself to be taken back. His mother cried and was led away by a sympathetic neighbor.

"Sir," Pete said to Lt. Shimada. "There's a family inside this house—an old man, a woman, and three kids."

Pete described what happened.

"Would you talk to them, sir?" he asked.

Shimada smiled to Pete.

"Sure, Hardball," he said.

"Tell them I'm . . ." he paused. "Tell them I'm so damned sorry."

Shimada clapped Pete on the shoulder and walked inside the house.

Pete returned to the wall, where Aldrich was waiting. He sat beside his friend.

"That old woman really got to you," Aldrich said.

Pete thought for a moment. There was a time when he'd have been outraged at Aldrich for poking his nose into Pete's past. But no more.

"The thought of those kids seeing their grandma die reminded me of my own grandmother, who died of cancer," Pete said.

He turned to Aldrich.

"Get the squad settled in," he said. "Fifty percent alert just in case. I want to be alone for a while."

Aldrich nodded and left.

It was growing dark by the time Tadashi Tanimura and Kisaburo Hanaya made the exhausting trek from Garapan to Saito's headquarters at Tsutsuran. The increasingly loud rumble of artillery was evidence that the Americans had broken out of their beachhead and were pushing east to cut the island in two. Tadashi knew that Saito had to move his headquarters very soon or face the indignity of being cut off and possibly captured.

In anticipation of this, Tadashi had previously scouted out a number of potential locations, the nearest being a cave two miles north of Chacha. Now, Tadashi knew, that move was necessary.

As the shift was being readied, Tadashi found Admiral Nagumo fretting over the movements of the Mobile Fleet and Admiral Jisaburo Ozawa, the man who had succeeded Nagumo in command of that proud arm of the Imperial Navy.

Code-named Operation *A-Go*, the fleet, built around nine carriers and five battleships and supported by twenty-four submarines, had sailed from Tawi-Tawi on Mindanao on June 13.

Granted, the force only had 473 aircraft scattered among those carriers, but two of the battleships, the behemoths *Yamato* and *Musashi*, each sporting a dozen 18-inch guns, could sink any vessel the Americans possessed.

If they were on schedule, right now the fleet would be slowing in order to refuel from the seven accompanying oilers. If they were on schedule, that is.

"Where is Admiral Ozawa?" Nagumo fretted while he stared down at a situation map of the South Pacific spread out on a table. "Where is he? Is he keeping to the schedule? Timing is everything."

"Admiral Ozawa will be on schedule if he has to invoke the winds and waves himself," Tadashi assured the admiral.

"Yes," Nagumo said. "But my biggest worry is that the fleet will be spotted by American submarines as they make the passage through San Bernardino Strait. Surprise is our biggest ally."

General Saito fished a pack of Kinshi cigarettes from his pocket and lit one up.

"Admiral Ozawa will be here, and the great battle will begin," Saito said. "Be patient, Admiral."

"I know he will," Nagumo replied. "When I spoke with him last, he told me he burned with a desire to destroy the enemy and place our Imperial Country on safe ground."

He poured two fingers of Suntory into a glass, then held up the bottle to see how much of the fine whisky remained.

"I must go easier on this." He smiled sadly. "It's my last."

"My biggest concern is the power of the enemy fleet," Saito said. "Colonel Oka of the Mixed Brigade told me his men had captured an American pilot near Charan Kanoa. Under torture, the man told Oka that the Americans have fifteen carriers and nearly a thousand planes. The American prisoner was then executed, of course."

Nagumo nodded, then took a sip of whisky.

"Yes, they also have seven battleships and outnumber us in cruisers and destroyers," Nagumo said. "But we have a number of advantages over them. Because our planes are lighter, we can perform aerial reconnaissance over a five-hundred-mile area, while they can do so only over three hundred miles. Also, Ozawa will approach from the east, so the prevailing winds will allow him to more easily launch and recover his planes. The Americans sailing east to west have to reverse course to launch and recover."

"Admiral Ozawa and I are both also expecting assistance from at least five hundred planes from our bases on Tinian and Iwo Jima," Nagumo continued. "In fact, those planes will be ordered to strike the Americans today and cripple the fleet before Ozawa arrives to finish them off."

Saito poured himself a glass of sake from a bottle on a side table. He preferred the smooth, fine rice wine over Nagumo's harsh-tasting whisky.

"Then there is this," Nagumo said as he began to pace. "The American commander, Admiral Spruance, is overly cautious, and he lacks experience in carrier warfare. Like most Americans, he suffers from a lack of aggressive spirit. His main concern is supporting the landings, so it's doubtful his planes will range more than a hundred miles out." He turned to Tadashi.

"Do you not agree, Tadashi-san?" the admiral asked.

"Yes sir," Tadashi said.

Tadashi revered Nagumo, more so than he regarded Saito, but in his soul, he felt Nagumo was wrong. How could the admiral forget that it was Spruance who commanded two of the three American carriers that smashed Japan's forces at Midway?

Saito spoke next.

"Major Tanimura," he said. "How long do you think before we need to relocate our headquarters?"

"The Americans have one division pushing north and two divisions thrusting across the island and moving to the south," Tadashi replied. "I think we need to make the shift to Chacha as soon as possible."

Saito nodded.

"We will depart now," he said. "Make preparations."

Nagumo mulled over Tadashi's report.

"Three divisions," he mused. "Once Ozawa crushes the American fleet, that will leave a lot of stranded enemy soldiers for us to mop up."

Tadashi stared at Nagumo, and a deep sadness welled up inside him. Contrary to what Nagumo believed, Tadashi knew the Americans had plenty of aggressive spirit. He also strongly suspected that it was Ozawa's fleet that would be crushed.

He hoped he was wrong, but he was certain that all of them—Saito, Nagumo, and himself—were destined to die on this island.

He hoped his mother's spirit would be with him.

CHAPTER 9

None of the Dog Company Marines in the newly captured village recalled what time the shooting started, but it was after midnight when all hell broke loose out on the water. A few hours earlier, there had been a spate of gunfire from the area where Fox Company was dug in, and also some random firing further up in the hills, probably patrol action. However, the booming and flashes offshore from the direction of Garapan meant business.

They were naval guns. Not cruiser or battleship caliber, but most likely 4-inch weapons mingled with 20mm and .50-caliber fire. Shells left flaming wakes as they slashed across the night sky, and a few flares popped to illuminate the watery battlefield.

"Somebody's catchin' hell out theah," Reb mused as he, Pete, Aldrich, and a few other men from the squad watched the light show and listened to the rumble.

The performance raged for nearly thirty minutes. Occasionally, an especially bright light flared up at sea as a shell found a juicy target. The shooting finally sputtered out.

Pete fished his watch from a pocket. Aggie had bought him the timepiece as a wedding gift.

"The hands glow so you can tell time in the dark," she told him excitedly. "I thought it could be something useful, you know, when you have to go back."

"I love it," he replied and kissed her. He didn't have the heart to tell her that a watch with luminous hands and numbers could mean death for the wearer if worn at night. So Pete only wore the watch during the daytime or, like now, when he was not eyeball-to-eyeball with the enemy. Otherwise, he carried it in an ammo pouch.

Aggie's gift told him it was 0150.

"Don't get too comfy," Pete told the men, pocketing the luminous watch. "We got OP duty in ten minutes. There are two Ops, so I need four volunteers. Honeybun, your team will take the first watch at 0100. The rest of you will take over at 0300. Third platoon will relieve you."

"Volunteers," Reb chided. "Tha's what ah like about the Marines."

After dispersing Honeybun's squad at the observation posts, Pete spent the next hour struggling to compose letters to the families of Stanley Potter and Chico Morales, careful to avoid any words or phrases that might fall prey to the censors. Potter was easier. He had known "Potts" since joining the regiment. Still, the words didn't come easy. You can use phrases like "he was a good Marine" and "he had a lot of buddies in the squad, and we all liked him" and "he managed to kill several of the Japs and fell facing the enemy," but would those words of praise for their son soothe the grief over his loss? Pete doubted it.

Morales was a harder letter to write. He had only known "Hack" for about a month, and while he enjoyed Morales's stories about driving his taxi in Hollywood, he knew little about the man. Pete worked through it the best he could, writing what he felt the family—any family—needed to know about the loss of their loved one. Finishing, he stuffed the letters into his LMO pack and resolved to run them by the regimental Holy Joe at the next field church service, whenever that might be.

Four miles directly east of the Second Battalion line in the hills just above the village of Chacha, a small convoy consisting of Saito's captured Plymouth and seven well-worn trucks drew to a halt. Camouflaging the vehicles in a small grove of trees, Saito and his party prepared to strike out on foot.

Their destination was a large cave at the base of Kagman Peninsula. It was a sturdy-looking cave protected by several large slabs of rocks overlooking Magicienne Bay. General Saito and Admiral Nagumo glanced around briefly, then entered the cave. Saito nodded approvingly. Wordlessly, his staff began to set up the command center.

Lying on his cot and feeling lonely, Tadashi dipped into his knapsack and drew out the last letter he had gotten from Kokoro. A nurse working in a Navy hospital in Yokohama, she told him of the suffering of the men she was treating and how much their misery made her fear for his safety. Instead of her words comforting him, they only served to increase his loneliness. It was highly unlikely that he would ever see her again.

"If you keep reading and rereading that letter from Kokoro, you're going to wear the paper thin," Hanaya said jokingly.

"No matter," Tadashi said without looking up. "I know most of it by heart."

"So what does she say?" his friend asked.

"She worries about her sister Yoshi," Tadashi said. "Since 1942, she has been working at the Mitsubishi airplane factory in Nagoya. She says the workers are made to work ten to twelve hours a day. Instead of going home, many just sleep on straw mats at their work area. They get three days off a month."

Hanaya's voice grew serious.

"Criticism like that could be construed as defeatist," he said. "Kokoro should be careful."

"Relax, Kisaburo-san," Tadashi soothed. "Kokoro is only worried about Yoshi's physical health. Yoshi was never the strongest of Kokoro's sisters. She also greatly fears that if Saipan falls, not only will it be the death of me, but America could get close enough to Japan so that bombers will strike the plant in Nagoya."

"That will never happen," Hanaya said scornfully. "The Yankee devils will never desecrate the Land of the Gods."

"It happened once," Tadashi reminded his friend. "Remember April 18, 1942?"

"Yes. That was the day of the cowardly American raid by the criminal Doolittle," Hanaya said. "We were too complacent. That will never be repeated."

"Did I tell you that was the day I met Kokoro?" Tadashi said. "I was on leave and going home to visit my father, and she was also going home to visit her parents, so we were both at Shimbashi Station at the same time, both headed for Yonezawa. When the alert was sounded, everyone went to the shelter. I was shoved from behind by an overeager man and crashed into this young woman and nearly knocked her off her feet. I apologized profusely but was mesmerized by her beauty."

Consumed by fond memories, Tadashi folded the letter and put it away. He thought about the sea battle that was most likely happening right now hundreds of miles away.

Admiral Ozawa is carrying our fate in his hands, Tadashi thought.

It was shortly after sunup that Nicholson made the rounds of the company, checking with platoon and squad leaders. Nicholson entered the squad's hut and looked around.

"Cozy," he observed. "But don't get used to it. As soon as we get the word, we're moving up to replace Fox Company on the line. They seem to have found a hill they can't climb."

"What was the Navy shooting at last night?" Pete asked.

Nicholson took out his pack of Lucky Strikes, lit one, and drew the smoke in deeply.

"Japs tried an end run," he said through a cloud of exhaled smoke. "About thirty barges filled to the gunnels with troops came out of Tanapag Harbor after midnight. They were those big bastards, about fifty feet in length. It's believed they intended to land troops behind our lines. Some Navy gunboats caught them off Flores Point and poured fire on them. Reports say they sank about a dozen barges, and the rest turned back."

Nicholson got back on his feet.

"By the way," Nicholson said. "They're sending us some replacements. I'm not sure when they'll arrive, and I don't know how many. You're down four men, Third Squad is down three, and First Squad is down four as well. What's coming to us has to be divvied up, so I can't promise to bring you back to full strength."

"Beggars can't be choosers," Pete said.

Nicholson left. Pete addressed the squad.

"Get your shit together," he ordered. "When we get the word, we're moving up on the line."

"This fight ain't got no fuckin' line," Reb grumped.

While his men began stuffing their gear back into the

LMO packs, Pete removed a toothbrush from his shirt pocket to clean the sand and grit from his Thompson. As he cleaned around the trigger mechanism and bolt area, Honeybun, seated a few feet away stowing away his personal gear, said, "It'd make old Bull Moose Blakely's heart flutter with pride if he saw you now."

"Yeah," Pete chuckled. "If he was a stickler on anything, it was proper care of your weapon. I can still hear him yellin', 'Worship your weapon, ya goddamn bunch of Boots. Keep it clean, keep it close, nurture it, and memorize every part of it down to the smallest screw. You take care of it, and it will take care of you. That's more than any dame can promise.'"

After finishing his task, Pete rinsed off the toothbrush with canteen water and placed it back in his pocket.

As the Professor finished cleaning his Garand, he said, "It's funny what we remember. For me, it was the table manners in the mess hall. My mom taught us kids to be polite, to eat with our mouths closed, and to ask for food to be passed. So here comes boot camp, and it's like flophouse rules, with guys reaching across in front of me for food, chewing with their mouths open, and flecks of food flying out as they talked while eating. I think the worst was guys grabbing food off the platters before the mess stewards even set them on the table. The Marines could use my mother."

As he packed his LMO, Pete drew out an object that caught Aldrich's attention. It was a string of rosary beads with a silver crucifix attached.

"You're a lot of things, Hardball, but Catholic isn't one of them," he observed. "I've seen them before." Then it hit him. "Giovanni was fingering them while we waited offshore at Tarawa."

Pete glanced down at the onyx beads he held, then looked at Aldrich.

"Yeah," he said. "I took them off the Feather Merchant after he died. I carried them through Tarawa and during multiple hospital stays. I handed them to his mom when I visited her just like I promised him."

A brief but thick silence followed. Then Aldrich said, "That must've been incredibly painful. I have an extensive vocabulary, but I'm not sure I could've found the proper words to use in that situation."

"I never did anything so difficult in my life," Pete said. "Even when Charlie died, the grief was mine, and I kept it to myself. But in that house, I had to share that grief with a family even more torn than me. Before I left, his mom handed me the rosary and told me to keep it and think of her son."

Pete put the rosary away.

"Maybe instead of carrying it with me I should've given the rosary to Aggie," he mused. "She's Catholic, although she'd say a lapsed Catholic."

"Keep it for good luck," Aldrich said.

"It didn't bring the Feather Merchant much luck," Pete observed.

"Consider this," Aldrich said. "So far you've been run over by a tank and nearly killed by an American battleship shell."

"You have a point," Pete said.

Then he became aware of a lot of chatter outside. He stuck his head out of the hut and spotted Ed Baker, the leader of the platoon's mortar section.

"What's up, Pogey Bait?" Pete asked.

"The Navy is gone," Baker said.

"What do you mean gone?" Pete replied.

"I mean gone," Baker answered. "Just gone. Carriers, battleships, cruisers, the whole shebang. The only thing left offshore is a few transports and some gunboats. This is just what happened at the 'Canal. The fuckin' Navy turned tail and ran. There are a few thousand pissed-off Marines between here and the landing beaches. They left us practically bare-assed. Again."

Pete emerged from the hut, followed by Aldrich.

"There has to be a reason for that," Aldrich said. "As I understand it, at the 'Canal, the Jap Navy beat up on our fleet and sank four or five cruisers because the swabbies were just goofin' off and not paying attention. I've heard 'Canal vets like Nicholson call Savo Island the Battle of the Five Sitting Ducks. But there was no naval battle here. We probably would've heard it, just like the gyrenes on the 'Canal heard the Savo fight."

Pogey Bait wasn't convinced. He turned to Pete.

"Then how do you explain the goddamned Navy buggin' out?" he complained.

"I can't, but I'll check into it," Pete replied.

Placing his helmet on his head, he headed off for the company CP.

There he found Captain Stacey; Sgt. Nicholson; several lieutenants, including Shimada and Stehman; and three platoon sergeants. Stacey was on the radio. Nicholson indicated Pete should wait but remain quiet.

"Yes sir," Stacey said into the handset. "But it would've been nice if we'd been told. My men, especially my veterans, are having cows over this." Pause. "Yes sir, I understand about security." Pause. "Yes sir, I know Japs may be eavesdropping on our communications, but we have runners, don't we?" Pause. "No sir, I wasn't being critical. I just wished we'd have been forewarned." He hung up the handset. "Fuckin' staff colonels. Who the hell needs them?"

He turned to the gathering that had collected around the CP.

"The Navy did not bug out," he said. "They did not leave us high and dry. Only the newer battleships and fleet carriers are gone and will return. Eventually. The rest are standing by just over the horizon line. It seems our picket subs around the Philippines are tracking a large fleet of Jap warships that has left San Bernardino Strait and is heading across the Philippine Sea straight at Saipan. The Jap fleet includes carriers and two of the biggest battleships in the world, and part of our fleet has gone to intercept. That's all I can tell you because that's all I know."

"So they'll be back when they've trounced the Nips," Biff Hodges said.

"But what if the Navy gets trounced?" Sgt. Tom Woodson said. "Like at Savo."

"Then kiss your ass goodbye," Hodges answered.

"They won't get trounced," Nicholson said, assurance ringing in his voice. "The Navy is on its toes this time. There'll be no more Savo Islands."

"Oh," Stacey said. "More good news. 'Howlin' Mad' Smith came ashore today at Charan Kanoa and set up his HQ in a schoolhouse the Jap CO, General Saito, had occupied. Inside, they found abandoned documents outlining defensive plans, the number of tanks the Japs have, and troop numbers. You'll be glad to know that G2 got the troop numbers wrong. Instead of fifteen thousand to twenty thousand Japs, like they told us, there are over thirty-five thousand on the island."

"I wish G2 would come here and fight them," Nicholson mumbled.

"They also estimate that the Japs have as many as ninety tanks," Stonewall continued. "If I get any more encouraging news, I'll let you know."

The group broke up. Pete walked back to his squad. Corpsman Ryan Magruder caught up to him. He asked Pete if everyone in the squad was okay.

"We're fine for now anyway," Pete said.

"Glad to hear it," Magruder replied. They began walking together. "I can use a break. Do you realize our division has had thirty-five percent casualties so far, including almost four thousand wounded? We've had wounded guys waiting twenty-four to thirty-six hours for treatment. We have two hospital ships out there, *Solace* and *Bountiful,* who've been receiving patients still wearing field dressings. Shit, as soon as *Solace* dropped anchor, they took on about five hundred eighty patients just like that." He snapped his fingers. "They filled every bed and began putting some guys in the crew quarters. *Bountiful* took on five hundred patients, and three hundred fifty of them required beds. Hell, some Higgins boats carrying wounded out to the ships have been turned away and sent back to shore to our field hospitals."

"Sounds like a truly fucked-up operation," Pete said.

"That's putting it mildly," Magruder said. "Then there's those poor bastards assigned to retrieving bodies from the water. They're using grappling hooks to snag floating corpses and drag them to the boat. If the body is American, they bring it on board. If it's a Jap, they just push it away and go on looking. It's not much easier for burial details onshore. Blackening of the skin and bloating on some of the corpses means the only way to tell a dead Jap from a Marine is by the leggings, the belts, or the helmets."

Magruder's description of the treatment of the wounded made Pete angry. He thought about Baumgartner, and especially Bucket Harnish, and hoped they were being well taken care of.

"Two more hospital ships, *Relief* and *Samaritan,* are on the way," Magruder said. "But until then, some wounded are being taken aboard makeshift hospitals on transport ships. Those guys who die from their wounds while on the ships aren't being turned over to Graves Registration for burial. They're being taken out a couple of miles and buried at sea."

"Aren't you just a regular Shirley Temple," Pete growled.

"It makes a man think," Magruder mused as they walked. "I watched them working on the Second Division Cemetery behind the invasion beaches near Charan Kanoa. The bulldozers were scooping out a trench fifty feet long, ten wide, and six deep. Then the bodies were wrapped in ponchos and laid in the trench, which is then covered up. I was thinking tomorrow that could be me. Or you, Hardball. Or any of us. And suddenly, I'm thinking I just wanna go the hell home."

"The war isn't a total waste," Magruder continued. "I did get this."

He held up his left arm to show Pete a steel wristwatch. Slipping it off, Magruder showed Pete the gleaming steel back of the case, which bore a small anchor on the top right side and on the top left an indistinguishable etching. At the bottom were the letters "SKS." The watch was attached to a brown leather band.

"It's a *Seikosha* watch," he said. "I showed it to Lt. Shimada. He seemed impressed. I think he called it a *Tensoku Dokei*, or Celestial watch, and said it's a pilot's watch and that this figure on the back is the guy's initials. A wounded Marine I was treating gave it to me as a thank-you for saving his ass. He didn't need it, he said, since the arm he wears watches on was blown off by a Jap mortar round. He said he got it off a dead Jap near the Charan Kanoa airstrip."

By now, they were back with the Second Squad. Four men stood around a fire, where Rosie was brewing coffee in a steel helmet he had placed directly on the coals.

"Hot joe, Hardball," he said. "You and Doc want some?"

Magruder begged off and walked on. Pete retrieved his cup

from his canteen and held it out to Rosie. With his hands protected by thick swatches of fabric he'd picked up somewhere, Rosie took the helmet and tipped some strong black coffee into Pete's cup.

"After the war, you'll make someone a great wife, Rosie," Pete said after his first sip.

"So what the fuck is goin' on with the Navy buggin' out?" Baker snapped.

"Don't get your skivvies in a knot, Pogey Bait," Pete said. Then he told the men what he and Capt. Stacey had discussed.

In the command cave overlooking Chacha, there was a strong feeling of confidence and a renewed sense of impending victory after a runner brought the news that the American battle fleet had departed.

"They've taken the bait," Nagumo crowed. "Admiral Ozawa will be like *Ryujin* as the dragon emerges from the sea to smash the enemy fleet."

The analogy of the god dragon of the sea crushing the enemy brought grins to many faces, including General Saito, who seldom smiled. But it did not bring a smile to Tadashi. He would much sooner place his faith in *Yawata*, the *kamisama* of war and the divine protector of the Japanese people. Although he wasn't sure that even *Yawata* could protect them now. Yes, the Mobile Fleet was powerful and included nine aircraft carriers. However, those nine vessels only carried a few aircraft mostly flown by young pilots with insufficient hours of experience. As for Ozawa, expecting additional help from planes on Tinian and Iwo Jima, Tadashi had his doubts. He feared that Ozawa, as well as Nagumo, were being overly optimistic as well as overly confident. Tinian was only three miles south of Saipan, and Tadashi was sure the planes there had either been flown somewhere safer, or else had already been pulverized by American naval fire. If not, then why hadn't they attacked the American fleet anchored so close to their home base? As for Iwo Jima–based planes, Tadashi doubted they had the range, and even if they did arrive in time to attack the US fleet, would they have enough fuel to return to their base?

Pitted against that, it was known that the US fleet had fifteen carriers, including seven fleet carriers, which alone carried close to one thousand planes. They outnumbered the Japanese in every other class of ship as well, *Musashi* and *Yamato* notwithstanding. It would take more than a mythical sea dragon to defeat that enemy force.

Keeping silent, Tadashi watched as Saito spread out a well-used map of the Mariana Islands and the surrounding waters. He pointed to a patch of open ocean west of Saipan.

"By now, they should be somewhere around here," he indicated a spot on the map. "That would put Admiral Ozawa within seven hundred miles of Saipan. By now, he has deployed his submarines. Their deadly Long Lance torpedoes will strike first. Whatever ships remain after those attacks will run up against our air strikes long before the Americans are in range to launch strikes of their own." Nagumo paused, a thin smile creasing his lips. "I think sometime tomorrow will be fought the Decisive Battle we have all been anticipating."

Saito, caught up in Nagumo's eagerness, chimed in.

"It is a fact that, so far, the battle has been going against us," he said. "It is also true that they have taken the small airfield at Charan Kanoa and are making it operational for their land-based planes. Even more serious, the Americans are on the verge of reaching Magicienne Bay, which will cut off the lower third of the island, making it more difficult for us to coordinate with our comrades to the south. But that will change.

After the American fleet has been dealt with, I anticipate that our ships will come here to shell the American forces and destroy their supply dumps with their food and ammunition. Our forces here on the island will then go on the counterattack on multiple fronts simultaneously. Once we defeat the enemy here, we will have broken the back of the American advance in the entire Central Pacific."

Everyone was grinning in anticipation.

Tadashi did not smile. He felt his commanders had duped themselves into believing the impossible. Yet he dared not challenge the misplaced optimism of his superiors. No, karma was karma, and his was to remain silent, serve his masters as best he could, and, when the time came, to die with honor.

Tadashi walked outside. Looking up into the blue sky, his thoughts turned to *Amaterasu*, the sun goddess, the primary Shinto spirit.

"Great spirit who shines in the heavens," he whispered. "I place my fate in your hands."

Then the image of his Christian mother passed through his mind, and for her, he added, "Amen."

CHAPTER 10

The move to relieve Fox Company was not issued, and as evening set in, Dog Company settled in for another night in the village.

Pete was seated on the rickety veranda of the squad's hut when an enemy barrage came crashing down. Pete sprang to his feet, yelling, "Take cover! Take cover!" The boom and crash of the shells sent shards of metal, comingled with rocks and gravel, hurtling through the air. Pete hunkered down by a low stone wall beside the hut. He was joined by several other men from the squad.

Somewhere in the direction of Third Platoon, a cry for a corpsman rang out.

The barrage of mortar fire was intense but short, lasting just five minutes. All around the village, men stood up, brushed themselves off, and surveyed the damage. Most of the rounds simply carved craters into the ground. Some already damaged huts were stricken again, and an adobe structure that had been reduced to a hollow shell earlier had now totally collapsed.

The steps leading to the veranda Pete had been sitting on had been damaged. Aldrich commandeered an empty wooden box that once held Japanese rations to serve as a makeshift step to replace the ones the mortars had blown into kindling.

"Let's go inside. I have something for you," Aldrich said.

Inside the hut, Aldrich smiled and reached into his haversack.

"You have a birthday coming up soon, don't you?" the Professor said.

"If you call July 7 soon," Pete answered.

The Professor drew his hand out of the bag. In it, he held a brown glass bottle.

"It's Sapporo," Aldrich said. "It's a beer made by Japan's oldest brewery. Happy early birthday."

Pete's eyes lit up.

"Where the hell did you find that?" he asked, awestruck.

"I took it from a dead Jap NCO," Aldrich said. "He didn't want it anymore." He paused. "It was the only bottle he had. I looked."

"Ooohhh," Pete said softly. "I'll treat it nice and gentle. Just like I treat Aggie."

Having no opener, Pete took out his Ka-Bar and whacked off the cap and top of the bottle. Holding it up he said, "Would you like some?"

"It's all yours," Aldrich said.

"I knew you'd refuse," Pete said. "That's why I asked."

Between slugs, Pete said, "You know you could've sold this to some gyrene for a ton of money."

"What good is money here?" Aldrich said. "Besides, I want to keep our fearless leader happy."

Within a few minutes, the Sapporo was just a pleasant memory, and it was just as well, for at almost the same time Pete chugged the last drop, Gunny Nicholson arrived outside the hut.

"Talbot!" he barked. "Get the hell out here. I got a gift for you."

Pete came out onto the veranda, along with the Professor. There the two men saw that Nicholson had with him three young Marines. Their fresh faces and clean uniforms told of their status as replacements fresh off the boat.

Nicholson pointed to each man from left to right.

"This is McCready, Simpson, and Perkins," he said.

"No," the man on the right said. He pointed to the center man. "He's Perkins. I'm Simpson."

"Just so the two of you know the difference," Nicholson said. Turning back to Pete, he said, "I know you're down four men, but this is the best I could do for now." He gestured to the trio. "Do what you can with them. We're moving up tomorrow morning around 1000. Stonewall is calling a meeting of all NCOs tomorrow at 0700. Be there."

He stalked off. Pete turned to eye the new men.

"Welcome to Second Squad," he said. "I'm Sgt. Talbot. I'm your squad leader, and this is Sergeant Aldrich, my assistant."

He pointed to the man who called himself McCready. "I have this nasty habit of wanting to know who I'm fighting beside, so tell me a little about yourself, McCready."

"My first name is Robert," he stammered under Pete's gaze. "I'm from Jamestown, New York. There's a movie star who was born there. Lucille Ball. Maybe you've heard of her." Pete gave no sign of recognition. "She recently married some orchestra leader named Desi Arnaz."

"Never heard of either," Pete said.

"I worked as a copyboy with the *Jamestown Tribune* since graduation last summer," he said. "My dad's an editor."

Pete looked the boy over and noticed that he carried a 1903 Springfield and a pouch containing an M1D scope.

"Sniper?" he asked.

"I shot expert in boot camp," he said. "Top score in my graduating class. My dad used to take me deer hunting. I got good at it."

Pete turned to Reb and Honeybun, who had joined the discussion.

"Reb," Pete said to Marshall. "I'm going to move Goodman back to Honeybun's team and give you McCready. He's a sniper, so treat him well."

Pete stepped in front of Simpson next.

"You are?" he inquired.

"Eddie Simpson—I mean, Edgar," the boy said. "I'm from Cape May, New Jersey."

"Any hidden talents?" Pete asked. "Did you go deer hunting too?"

"No, Sergeant," he replied. "The only wild game we hunted in Cape May was tourists."

Pete turned to Reb.

"I'm going to assign Milton Berle here to you as well," he said and moved on to the third lad.

"Hope you're not another jokester," Pete said.

"No, Sergeant," the boy snapped. "My name is Paul Perkins. I'm from Eagle Lake, Florida."

"And what did you do in Eagle Lake, Florida?" Talbot inquired.

"I worked in a citrus-packing house," he said. "I was trying to earn tuition for college. I want to go to Palm Beach State College and become a teacher."

Pete turned to Aldrich.

"I'm giving Perkins to you," he said. "He's right up your alley. Joe College. Between the two of you, maybe you can solve the world's problems."

Turning back to the new men, Pete asked if anyone had questions.

"I do, Sergeant," Simpson chimed. "How does a fella go about gettin' a samurai sword? I promised my brother a Jap sword."

Pete stared at the new men.

"Listen up, all of you," Pete said sternly. "There'll be no souvenir hunting. The Japs just love souvenir hunters, so they rig grenades to swords, weapons, flags, even their own dead, just hoping to blow the head off some greedy Marine. They also will not hesitate to wrap themselves in the guts of dead comrades and play dead until you walk by. Call me a bastard if you want—I've been called worse—but I won't lose a man because he was after loot. Is that understood?"

The new men were silent, so Pete turned up the volume.

"I'm not talking just to hear my voice," he said. "Is that understood?"

"Yes, Sergeant," they said in chorus.

Pete turned to his fire team leaders.

"Get 'em ready," he said. "We're moving up tomorrow morning."

As the sun began to dip below the horizon, there was an intense feeling of anxiety in the headquarters cave of General Saito. Every man knew that hundreds of miles away, across the darkening ocean, their fate was being decided.

To the south, the battle was slowly turning against Saito's forces. As predicted, the Americans were sweeping eastward from Charan Kanoa and had reached Magicienne Bay. Some had also wheeled south to push toward Nafutan Point at the bottommost tip of Saipan, while the rest of the Americans turned northward. Best intelligence reports were that Saipan's defenders from Garapan north to Marpi Point were now facing elements of three American divisions.

The bitterest pill was the fall of Aslito airfield and the drubbing the emperor's men had taken in the valiant but ultimately
doomed assaults of June 16–17. These men had never lost a
battle before, not in China or Southeast Asia. Now they seemed
unable to win. Their attacks were pressed forward with vigor,
only to be beaten off as the numbers of their dead grew steadily.

That was the reason so much of the defenders' hopes rode
on the approaching Mobile Fleet.

"It is my sincere hope that Admiral Ozawa could be within
striking range of the Americans shortly after midnight," Nagumo
said. "Our men are the best night fighters in the world. Our torpedoes are the most deadly, and our ships the largest. So much
is in our favor that victory must be the outcome."

Tadashi was not convinced. He was one of the few Japanese
other than the late Admiral Isoroku Yamamoto, who dreaded
war with the United States, having once been the Japanese Naval
attaché in Washington, DC.

In 1940, Tadashi had the honor of hearing Yamamoto speak
out against Japan's signing the Tripartite Pact with Nazi Germany
and fascist Italy. It was as if the great man was speaking Tadashi's
own thoughts. War with America would lead to tragedy, Yamamoto had said. It was certainly the cause of his death, and it was
almost certain it would lead to Tadashi's demise as well.

Tadashi heard Yamamoto speak again, this time shortly after
he had joined the staff of Prince Tsunenori. Prior to that, then
Lt. Tanimura had been assigned as a platoon leader and had
seen two years of fighting in Nanking, China. Japanese soldiers
had gone on a killing spree that left tens of thousands, if not
hundreds of thousands, of Chinese civilians dead. As a soldier,
Tadashi was fully prepared to kill the enemy. But the Christian
side of him, his mother's side, left him repelled and shamed by
the carnage.

Now Tadashi watched the orange sun teeter on the thin horizon line. With sadness mingled with love for this island, he recalled watching the sun set many nights. He was almost certain that the news coming from Ozawa and the fleet would be bad, and wondered how many more sunsets he would enjoy.

Pete was watching the same sunset. To the north, the breeze blowing down on him carried with it the rattle of small arms fire and the karump of exploding mortar rounds. Tomorrow he'd be facing that fire himself.

Steve Aldrich strolled up and took a seat beside Pete on the stone wall.

"'And dusk crept over the sky from the eastern horizon,'" Aldrich said. "'And darkness crept over the land from the east.'"

Pete looked at him.

"Very poetic, Professor," Pete said.

"Yes, but not original," Aldrich said. "That's Steinbeck. *The Grapes of Wrath.*"

Pete fished out one of Aggie's letters to reread. He could almost hear her saying, "I love you with all my heart," and "My life will not be complete until you're back in my arms." That made him long for her all the more. He removed the helmet from his head and gazed at her smiling face.

"Pretty girl," Aldrich said, looking over Pete's shoulder. "I think that picture is even more flattering than the one you had on Tarawa."

Pete nodded slowly.

"And a helluva good letter writer," he said. "She makes me feel things I've never felt before. I can't explain it."

"Women in love are masterful writers," Aldrich said. "Just

ask Jane Austin. 'In vain have I struggled. It will not do. My feelings will not be repressed. You must allow me to tell you how ardently I admire and love you.' *Pride and Prejudice*."

"Well, I don't understand all that poetic mumbo jumbo, but a lot of times Aggie and I even think alike, and that's scary," Pete said.

The Professor stood and clapped Pete on the shoulder.

"I'll check on the new boys in case they're having first-night jitters," Aldrich said and walked off.

CHAPTER 11

The sun was up for about an hour, promising another hot day.

The squad sat on the ground munching on their K-ration breakfasts. The main entrée was a round can of some alien form of meat. Pete's meal allegedly contained veal and pork loaf. Outside, Scrap Iron was making coffee for the squad, boiling water in the steel portion of his helmet, into which he had dumped multiple packets of the Nescafé coffee from several ration boxes. As the men awaited the coffee, many pocketed the chewing gum and cigarettes for later use.

From the north came the sharp snapping sounds of small arms fire and the thump of mortars. The fight that Dog Company heard yesterday was still in progress.

Pete was repacking his LMO in anticipation of the next move. He saw the three new replacements nervously sitting in a corner the hut, talking softly among themselves. Pete wasn't surprised that the trio gravitated toward each other. They'd come from the same replacement battalion on New Caledonia and

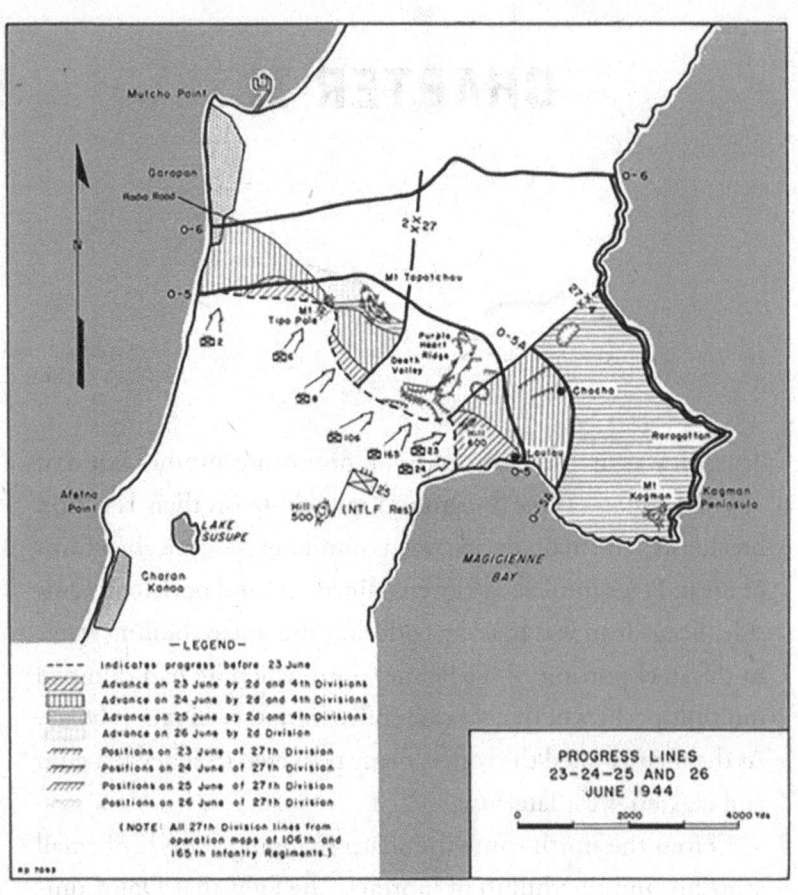

-LEGEND-

- - - -   Indicates progress before 23 June

Advance on 23 June by 2d and 4th Divisions

Advance on 24 June by 2d and 4th Divisions

Advance on 25 June by 2d and 4th Divisions

Advance on 26 June by 2d Division

Positions on 23 June of 27th Division

Positions on 24 June of 27th Division

Positions on 25 June of 27th Division

Positions on 26 June of 27th Division

(NOTE: All 27th Division lines from
operation maps of 106th and
165th Infantry Regiments.)

PROGRESS LINES
23-24-25 AND 26
JUNE 1944

0   2000   4000 Yds

had been trucked to Dog Company together. Pete stood up and crossed the room.

"You fellas have a difficult job, and I'm not just talkin' about fighting the Japs," he said. "You're also gonna be in a fight for acceptance in the squad. With the possible exception of Sergeant Aldrich, these guys aren't gonna cozy up to you, and that's especially true of the Tarawa veterans."

"So what can we do, Sergeant?" Perkins asked.

Pete pegged him as the leader of the group since he seemed to be more on the ball.

"Just do your job," Pete said. "Listen to me. Listen to your NCOs. Don't bitch and get the red-ass when you're given some crappy task to perform, because the squad will be measuring you. More important, I'll be measuring you, and you don't want to get on my bad side." He paused for a moment, eyeing them up. "How much combat training did you have with the replacement battalion?"

"Two days," Perkins said.

Pete nodded grimly. Two days. The kid might as well have said none.

"Was Tarawa as bad as we heard?" Simpson asked.

"Worse," Pete said, recalling the carnage. "Take the most horrible story you heard and multiply it by a hundred. We lost more Marines in seventy-six hours on that damned island than we lost in six months on Guadalcanal. I went in as a part of an oversized squad of sixteen guys. Two hours before the fight ended, I was wounded in the leg and carried off. So our squad had just four guys left standing: Aldrich, Hullihen, Marshall, and Harnish. Harnish was wounded here on Saipan."

The rookies looked suitably frightened.

"Look, the odds are in your favor," Pete counseled. "Just listen to your fire team leaders. When they move up, you move up. When they hit the ground for cover, you do too. Don't try to outguess the Japs, because you can't anticipate what they will do. They are courageous soldiers, so don't sell them short. They are perfectly willing to die, especially if they can take you along. If you come across a dead Jap, shoot him again. And no souvenir hunting." He stood. "Did you guys eat breakfast yet?"

"No, Sergeant," they replied almost in unison.

"Then do," Pete said. "You never know when you'll get another chance."

Pete returned to his place in the shack. As he sat down, he removed Aggie's letter and reread it. God, how he missed her.

His mind took him back to January 28, 1941. That night was their first date that did not involve dragging his kid brother, Charlie, along. Pete was seventeen and Aggie sixteen. Pete, who'd just gotten his driver's license, had cajoled his father into letting him borrow the family's ten-year-old Essex. They took in a movie, then ice cream at Pete's favorite malt shop. When he dropped Aggie off at her house, she gave him his first serious kiss on the lips.

He smiled at the memory, and of coming home and upstairs to his room. Charlie joined him and noticed a smudge of red on his brother's lips.

"Oohh, it's lipstick," Charlie said. Then he broke into a singsong with, "You kissed Aggie. You kissed Aggie."

"Shut up, runt," Pete said jokingly, and the brothers wrestled on the bed.

Pete smiled sadly at the memory.

Pete had reread the letter three more times, when he heard Nicholson's voice outside. He rose and left the hut.

"Get your boys ready," Nicholson told him.

"Where are we goin'?" Pete asked.

Nicholson pointed toward the north and the ridgeline that loomed ahead.

"Up into the hills," he said. "We'll link up with the rest of the battalion. Easy and Fox have been beating their heads against a stony hill that's like a Jap ant nest. The bastards pop out of holes all over the place from caves, gullies, spider holes, you name it." He lowered his voice so only Pete could hear. "The last attack launched by Fox Company cost Capt. Wallace eight killed and eleven wounded. And they didn't even get a quarter of the way up the slope before they fell back."

Nicholson returned to company HQ as Pete readied his squad. He then ordered the men to fill their canteens at some fifty-gallon drums that had been brought up by seagoing trucks called DUKWs, or, more commonly, Ducks. Before they were filled with drinking water, these drums had held gasoline. The men assigned to regimental supply had done a hasty job of cleaning the drums afterward, for the petroleum smell was pungent. Some of the men gagged on the water, but everyone drank. It was the only supply they had.

Ten minutes after refilling canteens came the order to advance. Dog Company began moving into column, men walking single file along both shoulders of the dirt road. It was ten o'clock, according to Aggie's glow-in-the-dark watch.

Pete found himself beside Sgt. Biff Hodges, formally in charge of First Squad. Hodges, who'd been in the Corps since '38, had been booted up to platoon sergeant when Nicholson became the new company Top Knocker. A veteran, Hodges had originally been with the First Division until he got seriously wounded on Guadalcanal. He spent nearly a year in military hospitals and then in rehabilitation. Upon returning to duty, he was reassigned to Second Division just in time for Tarawa.

Pete was feeling queasy as they walked, and Hodges noted it.

"You're looking green at the gills, Hardball," Hodges said. "You're not getting nervous in the service, are you?"

"It's my gut," Pete replied. "I don't know if it's from this damned gasoline cocktail in my canteen or my breakfast. I had a can of that veal shit, but I never saw meat that color. I swear the *K* in *K-ration* stands for *kennel*. I'd rather eat dog crap."

Hodges laughed.

"You haven't lived until you tried balut," he said. "I had it in the Philippines. You take a fertilized duck egg with the baby duck still inside, steam it, then crack open the shell and eat."

"Jesus Christ, you ate that shit?" Pete marveled.

"Being drunk off your ass helps," Hodges replied.

"You were hit on the 'Canal, right?" Pete asked.

"August 21, 1942," Hodges said. "Battle of the Tenaru."

"I remember reading about that in the paper back home," Pete said. "At the time I couldn't imagine anyone, even those crazy Japs, charging into machine gun fire. To be honest, I thought it was government propaganda meant to boost enlistments. You know, Uncle Sam's way of saying, 'Join the Marines and have fun killing Japs by the bushels.' Of course, that was before I saw Tarawa."

"Yeah," Hodges said. "They just came at us over and over, screaming and hollering to beat the band, and we just mowed them down. I always thought the phrase 'the water ran red with blood' was just some old saying. But it's true. I saw it."

"How'd you get hit?" Pete asked.

"I was in a foxhole with two buddies," he said. "A Nip mortar round hit us. The blast lifted me up into the air and tossed me out of the hole. I had twenty-four pieces of shrapnel in my body, but survived. My friends took the brunt of the explosion. They never knew what hit 'em. If I ever buy it, that's how I want to go. No muss, no fuss."

They walked on in silence. Their hike to the front took about thirty minutes.

The terrain ahead was every bit as vile as the enemy soldiers defending it. That's what Pete thought as he scanned the hill he and the rest of Dog Company were expected to attack and seize. The undulating face of the hill's southern slope was a jumble of limestone boulders and jagged outcroppings of black-and-gray coral.

At one time knee-high clumps of grass and some scraggly trees grew in the gaps between rocks, but now well over half the slope was cratered and many of the trees shattered. Topping off this hellish topography were multiple caves ranging in size from those big enough to accommodate two men and a machine gun to those the size of small apartments, with room for a 37mm anti-tank gun, its four-man crew, and supporting infantry. The crest of the hill was clear of rocks and vegetation. The hill was dubbed by HQ as Hill 450 due to its elevation above sea level, but to the men of the battalion who had to storm its summit, it was simply called the Gumdrop.

This heavily defended hill was what Fox Company had been confronting for two days, and what had cost them sixteen dead and thirty wounded in two assaults. In order to even reach the slopes, the men had to attack across a broad expanse of field, every inch of which seemed to be zeroed in by mortars and machine guns with interlocking fields of fire.

The Gumdrop was the largest of three hills, all capable of supporting each other if attacked. The configuration was called the Steel Triangle.

Easy Company tried to support Fox by outflanking the

Gumdrop and attacking its western slope, only to come under heavy fire from the supporting hill. Instead, they were pinned down for the better part of a day until darkness allowed them to pull back. Easy's losses were seven dead and eleven wounded, with nothing to show for the blood spilled.

All the dead from Fox and Easy had been recovered during the night, for leaving them to lie meant almost certain mutilation by the Japanese, who were known to work over Marine dead with knives, butchering them like deer and usually severing arms, legs, and even genitals. For that reason, many Marines refused to take enemy prisoners.

Now it was Dog's turn to test the meat grinder. As a preview of what was in store, while Fox Company left their defensive position and Dog filled in the vacancy, D Company suffered three men wounded and Fox Company one.

The only positive note to this whole fiasco was the fact that Fox had managed to push the Japanese out of an extensive trench system three hundred yards from the base of the hill. Even though the works were still within sniper range, they gave a modicum of protection and were an ideal base of operations for the main assault.

The plan of attack so far was straightforward. Artillery and mortars would blast the hill with as heavy a fire as possible for twenty to thirty minutes. The mortars would continue firing to help cover the attack, laying high explosives on the Japanese and dropping smoke rounds on the field Dog Company had to cross. Instructions to the men of Dog Company were just as simple. Cross the field quickly. Once the Gumdrop's slope was reached, keep going up as fast and far as possible.

This was pretty much the plan Fox Company had followed—twice. Pete wasn't sure this attempt by Dog would have any more success than Fox experienced.

Some three miles directly east of where Pete sat contemplating the ugly hill before him, there was nervous tension of a similar nature radiating through the command cave. The well-worn map of the Philippine Sea and surrounding islands laid spread out on a wooden table. Nagumo stared at the paper map as if he expected it to come alive and tell him what was happening in the naval battle that he knew must be raging four hundred miles beyond the western horizon.

Turning toward the radio operator, Nagumo snapped, "Have you heard any news?" The man shook his head. "Damned radio silence," Nagumo said. "The battle is happening now. I can feel it. We have the Navy's finest ships and enough airplanes between the carriers and those from Tinian and Iwo Jima to eradicate the Americans. We should hear from Admiral Ozawa as soon as victory is achieved."

At another table, Tadashi sat doing some computations of his own. The Americans have been ashore five days, and so far much of the fighting has gone their way. Yes, he knew their casualties have been heavy, but they seemed to have an endless supply of replacements. Nippon did not have that luxury, Tadashi said to himself. Repeated counterattacks on the nights of June 15–16 and 16–17 in the island's northern sector cost the 136th Regiment and the First Yokosuka Special Naval Landing Force dearly. A thousand or more corpses lay bloating on the sunbaked coastal plain south of Garapan. For that loss, the best the Japanese commanders could say is they slowed the Americans' inland drive, but in no way did they stop it.

Worse, just as Tadashi had feared, the enemy had captured both the emergency airfield near Charan Kanoa as well as Aslito airfield and were on the verge of making Aslito operational. To compound the disaster of that loss, the enemy had pushed clear across the island at Magicienne Bay, isolating or destroying thousands of troops of the Third Battalion of the 136th Regiment and Colonel Oka's Forty-Seventh Independent Mixed Brigade. He also estimated that Colonel Goto's Ninth Tank Battalion, which lost nearly forty tanks in two nights of counterattacks south of Garapan, was all but eliminated. Indeed, since that last attack no one had seen nor heard from Goto. The colonel was most likely as dead as his armored unit. Meanwhile, the battle situation worsened as elements of the two American divisions that had turned north, identified as the Fourth and Twenty-Seventh, would soon link up with the Second Division.

To offset the gloom that was overtaking him, Tadashi sought solace with General Saito and Admiral Nagumo's steadfast belief that should the Imperial Fleet defeat the Americans, then infantry reinforcements left stranded onshore could be ferried from Tinian, three miles to the south, and Guam, a hundred miles to the southwest, with no enemy navy to stop them.

He prayed for the island's deliverance. After all, everyone from the General Staff in Tokyo to the lowliest private defending a cave on Saipan knew that the Marianas were designated as part of Tokyo's Absolute Defense Line. Tadashi knew this line must be held at all costs, or Japan was doomed.

———

Pete was still studying the rocky hill before them when he saw Hodges approaching.

"Lt. Stehman is calling a meeting of all squad leaders

at his CP," Hodges said. "Round up Malloy and bring him along."

"What's up?" Pete asked.

"No one tells me shit," he said. "Just get Malloy and do it quick."

Pete found newly promoted Sgt. Terry Malloy with First Squad, and together they made their way through the trenches to a bunker Stehman had procured for his HQ. Stehman got right down to business.

"We have a new plan of attack," he said. "It seems that when they sent Fox Company in against the Japs, the plan was to blanket the hill with heavy fire for twenty minutes, then drop smoke on the open ground out in front and attack through it. Of course, as soon as the barrage lifted, the Japs came out of their holes and plastered Fox Company and drove them back. The next attack was conducted exactly the same way, with the exact same results. This time Captain Stacey, after clearing it with battalion, is making a change. Artillery will pound the hell out of the hill. That'll drive the Japs into hiding. When the barrage lifts, they will most likely come back out and await our charge. We'll give every indication that we're coming. We'll be blowing whistles and shouting orders, and Pogey Bait's mortars will drop smoke rounds." He stopped briefly to gulp down some water to soothe his sun-parched lips. Then he continued. "Here's the change: Instead of us attacking, our artillery and mortars will again blanket the hill. The captain is also hoping to line up some air support. Hopefully, we'll catch the Nips totally off guard and out in the open. When we go, the smoke wagons will focus on the upper slope and crest of the hill, then lift as we start the ascent. Do not stop to fire at the enemy. We need to get across this open ground quickly. We will not have smoke cover this time. Instead, the stovepipe boys will be dropping high-explosive rounds ahead of us."

"What about my machine guns?" asked newly promoted Corporal "Yaz" Yastremski, who took over as chief of the platoon's machine gun section after Moxley Pope's wounding. "Should we still provide covering fire?"

"No," Stehman said. "Stacey wants you to advance with the company and take up positions of opportunity as we attack up the slope."

Stehman scanned the faces around him.

"Do we have flamethrowers and satchel charges?" Pete asked.

"We will by the time we attack," Stehman said. "Each squad will be assigned a flamethrower and a bazooka team from Weapons Platoon, and satchel charges are being brought up, along with more grenades. Cleaning out those caves will likely eat up our supply of pineapples pretty damned quick."

"There might be civilians hiding in some of those larger caves, sir," Hodges said. "How do we handle that?"

Stehman thought long and hard. Then, reluctantly, he said, "We can't let that interfere with our objective. Don't harm civilians if you can help it, but if they get in the way, and it becomes unavoidable, then do your duty." He looked at his watch. "It is now 1130. We're set to start the first bombardment in one hour. That will last about twenty minutes. We'll spend the next ten minutes or so making as if we are starting our attack, and the second bombardment will commence around 1310 hours. We gotta take this hill. Capt. Stacey believes that if we take the Gumdrop, its loss will make the other two supporting hills untenable. Our jump-off will follow at about 1330. Dismissed."

Pete was soon back with the squad.

"So what's up?" the Professor asked. Pete filled him in. Aldrich listened with interest. "That's an intelligent plan Stacey cooked up. It might even work."

"If not, our asses are cooked," Pete said bitterly.

CHAPTER 12

Softening up the Gumdrop's defenses began precisely at noon. Behind the Marine line, 105s and 155s roared as they sent high-explosive shells screaming overhead. Three hundred yards from the base of the ugly hill the men of Dog Company crouched low in their earthworks.

Pete kept a wary eye on his squad, especially the new men—Perkins, Simpson, and McCready—who were experiencing the violence of war for the first time. Two of the men—Simpson and McCready—were curled up like armadillos, eyes pinched shut and clutching their rifles to their bodies. Perkins looked scared, as could be expected, but he also looked resolute.

As the pounding continued, Pete poked his head up a few times to determine, if he could, what effect the smoke wagons were having. Close by he saw Yastremski and Wealand getting their .30-cal ready for the advance. Yaz held the thirty-six-pound gun firmly, ammo already fed into the belt feed slide and locked in place so it was ready for use instantly. Wheels readied the twelve-pound tripod while also lugging two additional ammo cans, each holding 250 rounds. Machine guns could not only lay down a heavy amount of covering fire, but they also drew enemy marksmen. MG teams—there were four teams attached to the platoon—were a prime target, so it was not just a joke when the men referred to them as "suicide squads." On Tarawa, the life expectancy of a machine gunner was measured in minutes.

In the midst of the shelling, two half-tracks carrying 75mm howitzers arrived to bolster the Dog Company attack. Accompanying them was a third vehicle, a modified flatbed International four-by-four truck sporting three box-shaped rocket launchers. Inside each launcher were a dozen 4.5-inch missiles. Nicknamed "Old Faithful," each of these twenty-nine-pound rockets carried a six-and-a-half-pound warhead of high explosives. All thirty-six rounds could be fired in seconds by a well-trained crew of "Buck Rogers Men," as their fellow Marines called them. That barrage of rockets created a hellish world for those unfortunate enough to be on the receiving end. The three vehicles took up a position behind the company and waited. They would support the infantry assault.

Half an hour after it began, the artillery fire ceased, and a curtain of silence drew over the field. Whistles now began to blow, and officers shouted orders as they moved back and forth along the trench. The company began to take on the look of men ready to charge into action. Moments later came the dull thump of 60mm and 81mm mortars. Out on the deadly expanse of open ground the company would have to cross, the shells struck the earth and began spewing heavy gray-and-black smoke. More shells landed, and more smoke rapidly obscured the field.

On the Gumdrop's forward slope and crest, the Japanese defenders hurriedly crawled out from their shelters to take up their assigned positions. Weapons were cocked and ready. A few eager beavers commenced firing blindly into the smoke, certain of striking some of the American devils they believed were making their attack.

Suddenly, shells of all calibers blanketed the hill. Behind Dog Company, the two howitzers opened fire as well. With the harsh ripping sound of tearing fabric, the Buck Rogers Men loosed a thirty-six-round "ripple" from their launchers. Pete watched as a swarm of 30-inch rockets winged their way toward the Gumdrop. Then the rocket trucks' biggest weakness was demonstrated. The thick, smoky discharge created by three banks of tubes became a potential aiming stake for the enemy's 37mm guns. Nicholson knew it too, as he quickly moved along the trench, saying, "Keep your heads down. Stay low."

But the Japanese were not firing on anyone. Caught flat-footed out of their shelters, the 37mm gun crews were too occupied by the unexpected bombardment to fire at the launch truck even though it was well within their range.

Taking no chances, the Buck Rogers Men, their rockets exhausted, quickly departed for the rear to get out of range and rearm.

The men of Dog Company remained huddled in the trench, awaiting the signal to advance. After half an hour, as the barrage slackened, the men heard aircraft engines. Risking a look, they could see six cumbersome fighter planes. Although Pete and the men of the company were unaware, the Japanese airfield at the southern end of the island had been taken and was quickly made operational by Navy Seabees. The six planes were land-based P-47 Thunderbolts, the first to be assigned to Saipan.

One by one, the "Jugs" swooped in fast and as low as they dared, considering the deadly load they carried. Pete watched as each plane loosed a silver cylinder.

"Napalm," he said to himself.

Napalm it was, and the D Company men watched with grim satisfaction as the fireballs from six cylinders of the jellied gasoline saturated much of the hill.

"Let's go!" came the shout. "Move out. Double time."

Instantly, Dog Company ran forward, weapons at the ready. Behind them, the two howitzers continued to strike the Gum-drop. Out in front, Pogey Bait's mortars began dropping rounds on the defenders ahead of Dog Company's advance.

Initially, no opposing fire came at the Marines. Hopefully, Pete thought, the Japs were too stunned by the unexpected barrage and napalm attack. Even if they were, he told himself, they'll recover soon.

The race across the open expanse was easier than any man hoped but was not totally unopposed. Explosions from one of the 37mm guns blossomed among the charging men, sending two Marines soaring several feet into the air. Enemy machine guns began to speak. Along the company front, five men fell, three with wounds and two killed. The latter included Third Pla-toon's CO, First Lt. Raymond Pickering. Wounded on D-Day, he now took a bullet through the heart and was dead before he dropped to the ground.

Hitting the base of the hill, the Marines began the grueling climb. Bullets fired by Japanese soldiers now slowly regaining their senses pinged off rocks or dug themselves into the earth. Though they were warned against it, some Marines began to fire back, shooting at puffs of smoke or suspected enemy rifle pits.

Before the attack, Pete had spread out Second Squad, with Steve Aldrich's Fire Team One on the right, Honeybun's Fire

Team Two on the left, and Reb's Fire Team Three in the center. Pete attached himself to this team to put himself in a position to best control the squad.

Pete pointed up the hill, most of it still smoldering from being doused with napalm. "Go! Go!" he yelled. "Keep moving."

Pete's urgings were not his alone, but rather a mantra for every NCO and officer in the company as they encouraged, cajoled, and in some cases, shoved their men up the hillside.

The ruse of luring the enemy from his bunkers only to pound him with a second barrage seemed to have worked as the company, despite rocks, felled trees, patches of burning vegetation, and charred corpses, took the first third of the hill in one forward rush. The covering fire from the mortars and artillery, wary of dropping rounds on friends, suddenly ceased. From here on Dog Company was on its own.

As he scrambled up the hillside, Pete had yet to fire a shot. The only Japanese he had seen was the mangled remains of three men and their badly bent Type 92 machine gun sprawled in a smoldering crater, victims of a direct hit by a large-caliber shell. Advancing past the shattered enemy position, he scampered for cover by the stump of a felled tree as a Jap machine gunner sent a burst in his direction. Woodchips flew as the rounds stippled the trunk. Unable to strike his intended victim, the gunner soon swerved his weapon as he sought for easier targets. Pete glanced around for Reb and McCready, only to discover that, in the frantic climb, he had drifted away from Fire Team Three. He picked himself up and continued climbing.

All along the line, Marines clambered up the hill through greasy clouds of smoke, coming under fire from Japanese caves and rifle pits. Flamethrowers flared as enemy strongpoints missed by the napalm were incinerated, and satchel charges with eight pounds of plastic explosives roared after being tossed into caves, killing or entombing their defenders.

Pete hunkered down as heavy fire poured from Japanese troops manning a trench cut into the slope of the hill only ten feet away. Pete removed two grenades from his belt and yanked the pins. He tossed one toward the trench. When he heard the resulting explosion, he quickly tossed the second. As it burst, he scrambled uphill across that slim ten-foot stretch, Thompson cocked and at the ready. The trench was empty. A quick search revealed a tunnel made by burying empty fifty-gallon fuel drums end to end. He didn't know how far the tunnel extended. Sometimes they honeycombed all through the mountain. Pete fired a burst from the Thompson into the tunnel, hoping to hit anyone hiding inside, and moved on.

Ahead he saw a small cave. As Pete crouched low to avoid being spotted, two rifle shots rang out, clipping a boulder by Pete's left shoulder. Slipping a grenade from his belt, he yanked the pin and tossed it into the cave. As soon as the grenade burst, Pete was up and approaching the cave with caution. A Japanese soldier, bloodied and wounded, staggered out. Pete quickly shot the man, then continued climbing.

To Pete's right, the fire team of Aldrich, Perkins, and Rosie had just stormed through the charred remains of a machine gun crew. Huddled now in the protective shadow of a rocky protrusion, they found themselves pinned down by four enemy riflemen located behind a rock formation ten yards above them. Every time the Professor attempted to rise up a bit in order to confirm their position so he could toss a grenade, their bullets sent him ducking.

After half a dozen attempts to spot their exact location, he told Rosie, "Get ready to spray them when they come back up."

With that, he heaved a grenade in the approximate direction of the enemy. As Aldrich had hoped, the Japanese ducked when they saw the grenade coming at them, then rose after the explosion in order to fend off a possible lunge forward by the Americans. Instead, they saw Rosie, BAR poised. For two of them, that image was the last thing they saw as a burst from the BAR cut them down. The other two turned and seemed to disappear among the rocks. Aldrich shot at them but missed. Then he, Perkins, and Rosie climbed as fast as they could. Reaching the enemy position, they stepped over the two dead men. Aldrich was prepared to shoot, when he realized this was not just a rifle pit. There was also a cave.

"Cover me," Aldrich said to his team.

Approaching the cave, he carefully entered. Casting his mind back to their brief schooling on handy Japanese phrases, Aldrich urged anyone inside to come out, guaranteeing their safety.

"Dareka imasu ka?" he called into the cave, careful to enunciate each word clearly and hoping he'd gotten the correct phrase. *"Te wo agete detekite."*

At first there was no response, so he repeated the words. From the depths of the cave, Aldrich thought he heard faint voices, male and female. He slipped his Marine Corps issued flashlight off his belt.

"Are you going in there?" Rosie asked, horrified.

Aldrich nodded.

With his men holding their weapons ready, the Professor aimed the flashlight beam straight ahead. Moving with caution, he'd gone just a short distance when he heard sobbing. From the gloom emerged seven civilians of varying ages, including two young children. In the harsh glow of the flashlight beam, they all looked terrified, so Aldrich softened his voice and told them again that they wouldn't be hurt.

They reluctantly continued forward until a guttural voice from the rear of the dark cave barked, *"Tomare. Modotte!"*

The civilians hesitated nervously, obviously in reaction to the commanding voice behind them. One man began to turn back, but an older man seemed to urge them all forward. An automatic weapon suddenly blazed, its bullets raking the civilians. Instinctively, Aldrich hit the ground as bullets zinged overhead. Rounds continued to strike the civilian bodies even after they'd fallen. The Professor slipped a grenade from his belt and yanked the pin. He allowed the spoon to fly off, counted to three, and heaved the pineapple into the depths of the cave. The detonation was thunderous in the enclosed confines of the cavern. Even before the sound died away, the Professor was on his feet and racing forward. Several yards beyond where the civilians lay in a bloody tangle, his flashlight beam fell on four bodies, all Japanese soldiers. Three, including the riflemen he'd seen outside, lay sprawled on the cave's floor. A fourth man, a sergeant, was also lying prostrate. He began to stir, slowly raising himself up so he could lean against the back of the cave. In the beam of the flashlight, the two sergeants locked gazes. The Japanese sergeant was badly hurt. His right arm and shoulder, as well as the shirt covering his chest, were torn and bloody. His right hand rested on a Type 100 Nambu submachine gun, but the damage to his arm probably made it impossible to lift the nearly ten-pound weapon.

Staring at each other, the Professor had never seen such an intense expression of hatred as he saw reflected in those eyes. In his mind, Aldrich saw the civilians lying dead behind him, shot down because they sought safety for themselves and the children. A cold rage overtook Aldrich, and he fired three rounds into the man's chest. Then he put a round into the head of each corpse, just to make sure. Walking slowly back toward the cave's mouth, he stopped by the civilian bodies. Staring down at them, the man who never cursed absentmindedly muttered, "What the fuck is this all about?"

In the center of the squad's line, Fire Team Three, consisting of Reb, Miller, McCready, and Simpson, was crouched behind a coral ridge that protruded from the hillside like a crooked finger. Further up the hill, a sniper, occasionally concealed by clouds of drifting napalm smoke, occupied a prime location among some boulders, forcing the Marines to keep their heads down.

"Wheah the hell is that bastard?" Reb complained.

"I don't see him either, Corporal," McCready said as he carefully scanned the hillside using the scope from his rifle. "Damned smoke. But if I get a clear shot, I can take him out."

Reb tried to get another fix by quickly making himself visible and then ducking low. For his efforts, he got creased across the cheek when a bullet sent rock fragments flying. For Reb, it was reminiscent of Tarawa, where a bullet nicked his cheek and ear, both of which still sported scars.

"Goddamn," Reb snarled. "I wanna kill that sumbitch."

"I think I know where he is," McCready said. "There's a notch between the first two rocks. If I were him, that's where I'd be. Now if he'll just show himself."

A rustling noise from behind made Reb turn his head. It was Lt. Stehman and his runner, Pfc. Eduardo Sanchez, dubbed Bongo for his love of Latin music. Keeping at a crouch, the two caught up with Reb's small group.

"We gotta keep moving, Corporal," Stehman ordered. "We can't hesitate."

"We will as soon as we get tha' theah sniper up ahead, sur," Reb said. "He's a crackerjack shot, he is."

"Where?" Stehman asked, craning his neck for a glance up ahead.

The two simultaneous rifle shots sounded like a single hand-clap. The sniper's bullet struck Stehman square in the forehead. The lieutenant never knew he'd been killed. He just toppled to the ground in front of the horrified Sanchez. McCready's slug hit the sniper in the left eye. He, too, was dead before he knew it, his rifle slipping away and dropping to the ground in front of the boulders.

"I got him, Corporal," McCready said, but the grin of delight froze when he saw Lt. Stehman lying dead.

Miller, Simpson, McCready, and Sanchez were stunned to immobility at the officer's death.

"Bongo," Reb ordered, snapping them all back to the present. "Get yore ass back to company and tell the skipper wha' happened to Stehman. My team, follow me."

Fire Team Three rose from behind the coral outcropping and again started up the hill.

Honeybun's Fire Team Two on the left of the squad line seemed to be ahead of any other unit in the entire Second Battalion as they advanced on one of the Gumdrop's small terraces about a third of the way from the top. At the opening of the attack, the enemy had two machine guns set up among coral outcroppings. One had been silenced by the hot breath of the napalm, but the other poured a steady stream of lead down on the heads of the advancing Marines.

Honeybun noted the location of the firing and led his team to a position west of the partially blackened terrace. This put him in position to approach the enemy unseen, using the cover provided by a shallow crevice that snaked up the slope. The ground around the team was still hot from the napalm.

As Honeybun's men reached a still-smoldering shell crater ten feet from the terrace, Honeybun risked another look. The terrace was in fact an uneven patch of ground a few feet in width. At the rear of the terrace, against the hillside, was a stand of scraggly bushes the napalm had somehow missed. In front of him lay the mangled gun crew, hit by mortar fire. Across the terrace, about twenty feet, was the second gun, its operator concentrating on the Marines coming up the fire-blackened slope. Honeybun ducked back down and turned to Dembrowski.

"There are four of them on that gun, Scrap Iron," he said. "Take them. We'll cover you."

Dembrowski nodded, then cautiously climbed to the edge of the crater and eased himself over the lip of the terrace. The rest of the team followed. Taking about half a dozen steps forward, Scrap Iron raised his Thompson and cut loose with a sustained burst that mowed down the four men at the machine gun. He barely had time to turn back to his friends with a satisfied grin when a throaty cry of "Banzai!" erupted to his right.

A dozen Japanese soldiers, some armed with just clubs, led by a pistol-wielding officer, seemed to emerge from the mountain itself and charge the Marines on the terrace. The next few seconds felt eternal, as both sides exchanged fire at close range. Scrap Iron, his finger automatically tightening on the trigger of the Thompson, seemed imperturbable as he shot down three of the enemy at the outset. Goodman and Dubbs each accounted for two more. As for Goodman, one Japanese bullet tore through his shirt but missed his skin, while a second punctured his canteen. Honeybun shot two of the enemy before his rifle jammed. The officer, seeing Honeybun's dilemma, aimed his pistol and fired. Honeybun jerked at the last second, so the bullet aimed at his chest instead grazed the inside of his left upper arm. In response, he threw his Garand horizontally at the officer. The rifle struck the man in the face and sent him sprawling. Honeybun unsheathed his Ka-Bar, pounced on the man, and slit his throat. The two surviving Japanese ran for their lives up the slope.

The fight quickly over, Dubbs discovered a cave cleverly concealed behind the tangled bushes at the rear of the terrace. From inside, he heard moaning. Continuing forward, he came across four wounded Japanese, three badly injured and lying side by side, while one man was seated upright, back against the cave wall, a bloody bandage across his gut. Upon seeing an American entering the cave, the seated man pulled out a grenade. Dubbs raced out of the cave as the man yanked the arming fork and activated it by slamming it against the cave wall. Then the wounded soldier threw his own body atop the other three as the grenade went off. The four men died together.

Outside, Dubbs leaned wearily against a large rock.

Honeybun stood close by, cradling his injured arm.

"I'll get ya a corpsman," Goodman said.

"No time now," Hullihen said. He tossed his first aid pouch to Dembrowski. "Scrap Iron, bind my arm up as tight as you can. We still got this hill to take."

Pete came across Stehman's body. A short distance ahead, he could see Reb's fire team as they approached the cave containing one of the Gumdrop's two 37mm anti-tank guns. Reb's team was huddled by a ripple in the ground that protected them from the artillery piece; however, the angle of the slope in front of the gun made Reb's approach extremely difficult. Worse, an enemy machine gun above and to the right of the 37mm piece could obliterate anyone charging the cave.

As Pete studied the situation, Nicholson came up, accompanied by three men. Richard Crosley toted the sixty-eight-pound flamethrower, its three malevolent tanks, two containing napalm and the third a nitrogen propellant, strapped to his back. The other two men were Carl McComsey, lugging a bazooka, and Fred Mosely, McComsey's loader, with a pouch of 3.5-inch rockets hanging at his side.

Nicholson barely cast a glance at Stehman's corpse.

"Bongo Sanchez came back to company HQ with the news," he said. He pointed up the hill. "I saw your men up there and figured you could use some help."

Pete nodded.

"Reb's pretty close to that 37mm gun," Pete said. "Too close." Pete turned to Crosley. "Dick. Do you think you could reach Reb?"

Crosley glanced out ahead, nodded, and asked, "Then what?"

Nicholson said, "Why not flank the Nips?" He pointed to the left. "There's a gully there, probably rain washout. It goes almost clear to the top. If McComsey can get his bazooka up that gully . . . but it's a tough angle."

Pete turned to McComsey.

"How good are you with that overgrown drainpipe, Fred?" he asked.

"He could shoot a cigarette out of your mouth," Mosley boasted.

"Okay, let's do it," Pete said. "Dick, when you get to Reb, tell him to wait until McComsey fires this sewer pipe, then move in and burn that cave."

Preparing the bazooka for action, McComsey unfolded the two-piece barrel assembly and used the barrel coupling lock lever to align the tube sections before latching them in place.

Mosley fished a 3.5-inch rocket from the pouch, partially inserted the rocket, and stripped off the safety band. Fully inserting the rocket, he removed the insulated tube from the end and attached the wire to the bazooka's contact springs.

"You're hot," he told McComsey.

Leaving the bazooka's safety engaged, McComsey nodded to Pete and Nicholson.

Pete turned to Mosley.

"Fred, give me that bag," he said.

Mosley shed the rocket pouch, and Pete put it over his shoulder. It'd been about a year since he'd loaded a bazooka during a training exercise.

"On me," he said to McComsey, and they were off.

Staying low, the two picked their way across the slope and reached the gully without drawing fire. The ditch, one of many carved into this hill after centuries of heavy rainfall, was not as deep as Pete would have liked, but it would serve. It took just a few minutes for them to reach a height that allowed them to see their target. Pete was dismayed that the angle was so severe. He could not see more than six or eight feet of the cave's far wall and just a foot or two of the 37mm gun's snout protruding over a sandbag parapet that blocked the cave's mouth.

Pete turned to McComsey.

"What do you think?"

"I can hit that cave wall and ring their chimes real good," he said. "The explosion might even damage the gun. But we'd better take out the MG first."

"That'll give away our position, but you're right," Pete said.

To make sure his hit was on target, McComsey risked lowering the bipod legs near the front of the tube. Unsetting the safety, he placed the weapon firmly on the ground and put his eye to the sights. Pete made sure he was away from the rear of the tube and the inevitable blowback. Then the rocket was off, closing the space in an instant as the machine gun and its crew disappeared in a blast of smoke and fire. The explosion was still echoing as Pete pulled a new round from the bag and began the reloading process.

Attaching the final wire to the contact spring, he gave the ready sign by tapping McComsey on the helmet.

An alert soldier positioned at the sandbag parapet that protected the cave's mouth spotted them and gave a warning shout. An instant later, bullets began singing through the air and stitching the ground around them. With nerves of steel, McComsey ignored the bullets and kept his eye glued to the sight. Then a squeeze of the trigger and the bazooka spat fire from both ends. The rocket closed the distance in a heartbeat. It struck the cave wall solidly, and the resultant explosion ended the Japanese rifle fire, but not before two slugs struck the bazooka tube, rendering the weapon useless.

Before the echo of the rocket's detonation died away, Reb and his team, along with Dick Crosley, were on their feet and racing forward. The infantrymen fired into the cave, then stopped as Crosley sent a stream of fire into the cavern's depths. Agonized screams split the air, and three men with blue-and-orange flames enveloping their bodies ran out. Reb's team did not feel merciful and allowed the enemy to burn to death. The cave threat now eliminated, the team quickly took cover as angered Japanese soldiers elsewhere along the face of the Gumdrop expressed their wrath in a hail of bullets.

"I think theah mad at us," Reb observed.

Five hours of slow, hard fighting found Dog Company scattered about the southern slope of the Gumdrop. Men, individually or in small groups, struggled uphill between patches of rocks, felled or shattered trees, and around shell craters, all while under fire. In some places, the climb was relatively easy; in others it required using rocks and bushes for handholds. Along the way, there had been caves to clear and machine gun nests to eliminate. Those five hours cost D Company eleven dead and twenty-eight wounded, and the hill was still unconquered.

As the hour for a final push drew near, Capt. Stacey called a meeting of his officers and NCOs. Stacey had set up a temporary command post at the protective base of a trio of rocks that had come to be called the Three Sisters. After taking stock of his casualties, Stacey concluded that Second Platoon had suffered the smallest losses. That distinction meant Second Platoon would lead the final assault to the top of the Gumdrop.

"I understand why you want us in the front, sir," Biff Hodges was saying. "But we're without an officer in command."

Stacey nodded. He was running out of officers.

"I'm putting Lt. Shimada in command of Second Platoon," he said.

"About the hill, sir," Lt. Michael Jones of First Platoon said. "It's a safe bet that their defenses on that hill are all facing south. Can we swing a platoon around to outflank them?"

"Not easily," Stacey said. "Remember: the Gumdrop is a part of a three-hill line, so the rear and flanks are covered by interlocking fire from hills to the east and west."

Stacey next asked Jones, "How close are your guys to the crest?"

"Thirty yards," Jones replied. "Maybe a little more."

"Hodges," Stacey said. "Where is the head of your platoon?"

Hodges looked to Pete, who said, "I've got a fire team dug

in less than twenty yards from the top, but they can't get any closer without support."

Stacey nodded.

Pete had a thought.

"Maybe we could get some air support, sir," he said.

"We can't risk strafing runs," Nicholson injected. "Your lead team is too close."

"Not strafing, Gunny," Pete said. "Just have them come in low and buzz the bastards. Keep their attention and have them looking at the sky instead of the ground. That would give my guys the chance to storm the top."

Stacey smiled.

"You'd better be careful, Talbot," he said. "They might make an officer out of you yet."

He turned to Shimada. "Jim, get your boys up there as fast as you can, and when you hit the top, fan out, kill all the enemy, and dig in. The rest of the company will follow."

Shimada nodded.

"As soon as we take the crest, I'll also get the men to dig in on the reverse slope," he said. "Our friends might want their hill back."

Stacey nodded. He looked at his watch.

"We go at 1800," he said. "Watch for the purple smoke. We want to secure the hill as fast as possible. Some engineers arrived down below and will be bringing up barbed wire. So by dark we'll be able to wire up tight in case of a counterat-tack. Meanwhile, I'll contact HQ about getting some planes in the air."

The aircraft arrived just before jump-off time, four Thunderbolts coming in low and fast. After making its pass, each plane looped around and came screaming down once again. The planes drew some angry return fire from Japanese infantrymen who, as was hoped, seemed to be looking skyward.

At precisely 1800, Stacey ignited a purple smoke grenade, and with Second Platoon in the lead, the company rushed forward, many yelling and whooping like attacking Indians in a western movie. Led by Reb and Fire Team Three, the Marines swept over the napalm-blackened crest of the hill, being met with unexpectedly light resistance. Most of the enemy garrison, knowing the hill could not be held, had already made for more defensible positions rearward, and only about twenty die-hard soldiers remained. Few in number, they were still determined to make the Americans pay for this real estate. One of the first Marines to fall was "Wheels" Wealand, Yastremski's machine gun assistant. The tow truck driver from Allentown, Pennsylvania, took a burst of fire from a Nambu just as he topped the ridge.

Vivian Miller got hit next. The former pharmacy delivery boy had just shot down a knife-wielding attacker when a bullet struck his left buttocks and passed clean through the right one.

The fresh-faced shavetail lieutenant in command of Third Platoon, Simon Eppley, along with one of his men, were attacked by a Japanese soldier clutching a live grenade. The three of them entered eternity together.

The fight for the crest was bitter but mercifully short. Just minutes after the Marines topped the ridge, the defenders all lay sprawled on the bloody ground. As the Americans surveyed the carnage, Simpson spotted the body of a Japanese officer. Lying partly under the man, Simpson saw the gleaming blade of a samurai sword.

"Hey, looky!" he shouted with joy. "I got me a Jap sword."

Alarmed, Reb cried out, "No, Simpson! Leave it."

Overcome with the idea of such a sought-after souvenir, Simpson knelt by the officer and began to free the sword from beneath the body. The officer suddenly rolled over, a snarl on his face. He grabbed Simpson by his shirt with one hand while using the other to smack a grenade against his helmet to activate it. Before anyone could react, he pulled the terrified Simpson close just as the grenade went off between them. The blast sent Simpson flying backward, his chest torn open, and his dead eyes casting a horrified look at the sky. Reb walked over to the Japanese officer, whose torso was also ripped apart.

"You fuckin' sumbitch," he snarled and loosed a burst from his BAR into the corpse.

The entire squad seemed stunned. Perkins and McCready, seeing their friend die, had two different reactions. McCready screamed and covered his eyes, while Perkins knelt by the body and wept. Pete watched Perkins vent his grief, recalling the day he knelt in the surf at Tarawa, holding Ted Giovanni's body in his arms and bawling his eyes out. He let the two men grieve for a few moments. Then he stooped over the former Chalfont Hotel bellboy from Cape May, New Jersey, removed the camouflage poncho from his backpack, and covered the body after first removing one of the dead man's identity tags.

"This is why we don't souvenir hunt," Pete snarled at his squad. "Remember it."

With the hill now secured, the company set up a defensive perimeter, mostly by using the vacated Japanese works. Wary of the threat of snipers on the two hills to the north, engineers brought up spools of barbed concertina wire, and the Dog Company men began to string it out thirty yards below the crest. For added security, some trip wires attached to flares were planted along the line, and empty K-ration tins filled with small stones were tied to the barbed wire.

The wounded were attended to by medical corpsmen, including Honeybun, who had a fresh bandage applied to his wound. He refused to go to the rear.

"How do I tell my dad I got shot in the butt?" Miller moaned as Doc Magruder applied sulfa powder and bandages to the ass in question.

Magruder laughed.

"Just show him the four bullet holes you got—two entrance wounds and two exit wounds," he said. "But before that happens, you'll be back here. An ass wound is not a ticket home."

Elsewhere on the hilltop, the dead Marines were carried rearward by stretcher-bearers. At the base of the hill, they were loaded onto amtracs and carted off to the cemetery near Charan Kanoa.

Retaliatory enemy barrages were largely ineffective as the Marines sought the safety of the expertly built bomb shelters the previous owners had constructed.

By 2000 hours, the sun was settling over the western horizon, painting the sky with magnificent hues of purple, orange, and blue. The Professor found Pete sitting apart from the company, perched on a rock, staring off at nature's easel.

"Penny for your thoughts?"

"I'd be overcharging you," Pete snorted. He got quiet, then said, "I was thinking about what I'm going to say to Simpson's folks. I barely knew the kid." He was silent again. Then snapped, "Goddamn it. I told him not to souvenir hunt. All for a damned sword."

"You helped me get a sword on Tarawa for my kid brother," Aldrich reminded Pete.

"I was dumber back then," Pete replied. "Plus, the guy'd

been dead for most of the day." Pete fired up a smoke, knowing it'd be his last before darkness fell.

"Look at that," he said, pointing at the sunset. "What balls God must have to create so lovely a scene and then have it hang over a slice of hell like Saipan. All the pain. All the misery. It's so damned senseless, and I can't help but wonder if God gives a shit."

"I don't claim to know God's intentions," Aldrich said. "But I know a little bit about man's behavior, and we're the only ones who can end this madness. God has His limitations."

Pete did not respond at first. Then he said, "You know, growing up in a blue-collar city, I used to hate college boys. I thought they were all a bunch of uppity assholes who thought they knew everything but who couldn't find their nuts with both hands."

Aldrich laughed.

"Hope you don't think that of me," he said.

"Did you know that befriending you was not my idea?" Pete asked. "It was Giovanni's. He saw you sitting alone on the train seat when we were heading out on liberty after boot camp. He chatted you up, not me. But now I am so glad he did."

Aldrich looked at his friend and smiled.

"Me too," he said, then added, "you are perhaps the most complex, yet the most straightforward person I've ever known."

"When this is all over," Pete said, "I want us to stay friends. You know me. I don't say that lightly."

"Of course we'll stay friends," Aldrich said. "Who can go through what we've experienced together and not stay close?"

Pete nodded with satisfaction as the sun dipped below the horizon.

Three miles to the east, Tadashi Tanimura was watching that same sunset. Out there, where the sun was setting, the great naval battle that Nagumo and Saito were pinning their hopes on was raging.

Or was it? Tadashi did not know. But one thing was certain: the outcome of that battle would determine the Saipan garrison's deliverance or its demise. Today he had seen American land-based planes in the sky over Saipan. That could only mean that Aslito was back in operation, but as an enemy field. That was a very bad sign.

Nippon was the land of the rising sun, Tadashi thought. But was he now witnessing the Empire's sun setting?

CHAPTER 13

It was about 0200 when one of the K-ration cans filled with pebbles in front of First Platoon gave the first warning that the expected Japanese attempt to retake the Gumdrop was approaching.

Pete had been hunched down in his foxhole just behind Honeybun's Fire Team Two. Since most of the fortifications erected by the Gumdrop's former owners faced south, Dog Company had scraped shallow foxholes into the rock-hard soil that allowed them to kneel but not stand up. Dog Company's line was stretched thin, so it was one man per foxhole.

The next alarm came from a pebble-filled can to Pete's immediate left in front of Third Squad. Moments later a loud "pop" broke the night as a trip wire ignited two red flares. The flares sizzled as they lit up the surrounding ground. In their harsh glare, Dog Company saw a mass of Japanese coming up the hill. The Americans responded with a blaze of gunfire.

The racket following the silence of the night was earsplitting.

The Japanese, their presence discovered, surged up the hill

with a roar of "Banzai" and "Marines die tonight." Despite their courage and aggressiveness, the charge quickly fell into disarray when they reached the barbed wire. Unprepared for this obstacle, they began stacking up at the wire. Some tried picking their way among the sharp coils while the braver of them began diving onto the wire, using their bodies as human bridges for their comrades to cross. But many simply died by the wire.

Perkins froze as he saw the mass of Japanese soldiers streaming up the hillside seemingly coming directly at him. He was so scared he didn't even see the bullets kicking up dirt around him.

"Shoot, Perkins!" Rosie cried out over the roar of his BAR. "Goddamn it, fire your piece!"

His fear driven away by Rosie's commands, Perkins opened fire.

Dubbs's shoulder wound worsened under the pounding recoil as he fired his rifle. A wetness under his shirt told him it had started to bleed again. As the enemy attack pressed, Dubbs thought briefly of Bethlehem and his family and his desire to see them again. If getting back depended upon him killing these men, he resolved to do just that.

Eventually the weight of bodies dropping on the wire caused gaps in its length. The surviving Japanese, determined now more than ever to kill the Americans, poured across.

The delay at the wire gave Capt. Stacey a few moments more to get on the radio to Pogey Bait, whose mortars began launching a succession of dull gray-and-yellow illumination shells overhead. With the attackers now well-lit in the harsh greenish-white glare, the volleys coming at them from Dog Company were even more deadly. Along with the rifle fire, Yaz's machine guns were adding to the carnage. Placed so that their fire overlapped, these "coffee grinders" cut down scores of the enemy across the entire company line.

Despite the incredible losses they were taking and with the deadly barbed wire obstacle now behind them, the Japanese attack bore down on the Marines.

Pete left his meager foxhole and moved along his squad line giving encouragement to his men, taking up a position behind Steve Aldrich's foxhole and emptying his Thompson at a trio of Japanese just yards from the line. A blood-curdling roar of rage sounded above the din of the battle as an officer, samurai sword in hand, ran forward. Yanking his pistol from his holster, Pete fired two rounds into the man. The impact of the heavy slugs staggered him, but he kept his feet and continued onward. The Professor put a third round into the angry face and the man dropped to his knees before pitching forward, the tip of his sword just inches from the foxhole.

The attackers pressed on. Pogey Bait had assigned a few of his mortar crews to launch star shells while others dropped the olive-drab and yellow high-explosive rounds on the slope in front of Dog Company. The range was risky. A slight miscalculation would see 60mm shells falling on the Marines. But earlier, while the line was being fortified to fend off an expected attack, Pogey Bait had dutifully walked the slope, computing degrees of elevation and deflection, adjusting mils left or right to put his rounds on target when needed. Those calculations were now at work as explosions enveloped the Japanese front and rear.

Under such an onslaught, the attack faltered, then broke as the bloodied remains of the once determined Japanese horde stumbled back down the hill and darkness once again overtook the field.

At a crouch, Pete again made his way along his line of foxholes, checking his men and taking stock of how they were holding up. To his relief, no one was injured.

Kneeling by McCready, Pete said, "Scuttlebutt says your DI was 'Bull Moose' Blakely."

"Yeah," the boy replied. "He was tough. He once boasted how he'd once caught a boot goofing off on latrine duty and made him clean the toilets and drink the water."

"He wasn't just boasting," Pete said. "I was that boot."

McCready looked at him with astonishment as Pete stood up. He'd seen Nicholson approach, so he joined the gunny. The two walked a short piece. As they passed Dubbs's position, Pete saw the young man examining bloodstains on his shirt.

"You hit, Dubbs?" he asked.

"No, Sergeant," he replied. "My wound from the other day reopened."

"Go see the doc," Pete ordered.

Dubbs nodded and was off for the platoon CP, set up a short distance behind the line. As he watched Dubbs go, Pete asked Nicholson, "How badly did we get mauled?"

"The company had three killed and nine wounded in the attack," Nicholson said. "But it's been a tough day. Overall, we lost sixty-six guys, including eighteen dead."

"Ouch," Pete said.

"We stacked the Nips up pretty good though," Nicholson added. "We doubt they'll be back since the whole damned Jap Army in front of us seems to be pulling back to set up a new MLR."

Great, Pete thought, another main line of resistance to storm. This whole damned island is one big MLR.

————

The new line being set up was under the direction of Colonel Yukimatsu Ogawa, w ho outlined it on the table in Saito's HQ cave. The line he showed to his superiors stretched from the western coast a mile south of Garapan, passed eastward between Mount Tipo Pale and Mount Tapochau, crossed the eastern stretch of the coastal road, then dipped south to the village of Laulau on the northern shore of Magicienne Bay.

"The position is a strong one, and the rugged terrain works to our favor," Ogawa was saying.

Saito looked over the map.

"It seems like a secure place to stage a defense until the Decisive Battle is won, and our transports can bring us reinforcements," he said. He looked up at the radio operator. "No word yet from Admiral Ozawa?"

"No, General," the man said. "Nothing. I'm still trying."

Saito looked disappointed but not dispirited. Nagumo seemed more perturbed. Saito looked to Tadashi.

"What do you think of Colonel Ogawa's line, Major Tanimura?" he asked.

Tadashi walked to the table, brushing by Colonel Suzuki, Saito's chief of staff, who was clearly miffed that Tadashi's opinion had been asked and not his own.

Tadashi looked at the map and said, "With all due respect to Colonel Ogawa." He stopped and gave Ogawa a polite bow of recognition. "I think the line should be moved north, with its right anchored on the northern end of Garapan, then across to take in Tapochau and on to the east coast between Chacha and Mount Donnay."

"Why do you say that?" Saito asked.

"Perhaps the major wants his American friends to take a bigger slice of ground and give them the city he calls home for safekeeping," Suzuki said, his contempt for Tadashi laid bare.

Nagumo opened his mouth to speak, but Tadashi replied first.

"If you are angry that I have an understanding of our enemies, I am sorry," he said tersely. "But if you cared to study the American advance, you will know that they have great numbers of vehicles, especially tanks, and motorized artillery. As for us,

Colonel Goto is dead and so are most of his tanks. The line I am recommending is rugged, with jagged coral and limestone spines and ridges. It could severely reduce the American advantage in tanks. Also, there is Garapan itself. Rather than hand over what you rightly call my home, on the contrary, my line makes Garapan a battlefield. Having to fight there will further delay and entangle the American advance and buy us time."

"That will be enough," Saito injected, heading off further antagonism. He turned to Ogawa. "Establish the line you suggested but also draw up a plan to fall back to a position recommended by Major Tanimura."

Tadashi and Ogawa bowed to Saito. Suzuki just glared. Tadashi turned and left the cave. Hanaya trailed along with him.

"Colonel Suzuki's behavior was reprehensible," he said angrily. "It was unbecoming of one of the emperor's officers."

"Whether or not he likes me means as much to me as a speck of dust on a table," he replied. "I am much more concerned over whether or not Admiral Ozawa is successful."

"You think he might not be successful?" Hanaya asked.

Tadashi did not reply.

The glow of the morning sun illuminated a scene of devastation. Japanese bodies lay scattered all across Dog Company's front, thickest along the line of barbed wire.

By the time the sun was up for an hour, swarms of flies had already gathered around the gory feast. Under the building heat, bodies began to bloat, and it wasn't long before Capt. Stacey ordered burial details to get as many corpses as possible underground swiftly. The men groused mightily but all knew it was necessary.

While this grisly work was underway, Steve Aldrich approached Pete's position. Pete noticed he was carrying a samurai sword. He extended the sword toward Pete.

"Is that the one Simpson was trying to retrieve?" Pete asked.

"No," Aldrich replied. "The grenade explosion blew it apart. This is yours. You shot the guy."

Pete took the sword and studied its highly lacquered black scabbard and the neatly black carved handle delicately wrapped by a thin red fabric. He drew the gleaming steel blade partway out, then shoved it back inside.

"What the hell do I want with it?" he fumed. "I'll send it back to the Holy Joes along with my letter and mail it all to Simpson's folks with his personal affects. It's the least the Japs owe them." He laid the sword down none too gently. "I just hope it doesn't get snatched and end up on some rear echelon asshole's trophy wall."

"You seem especially angry," Aldrich said. "What's up?"

Pete considered, then said, "It was exactly a year ago today that the Navy removed the USS *Grampus* from its roles and closed the book on Charlie and all his shipmates." He lit a cigarette. "According to a letter my mom got from the Navy, they think the sub was damaged from a previous action and was on the surface doing repairs when two Nip destroyers found her. No one knows the precise coordinates where she went down, but she was last spotted in Blackett Strait at six degrees fifteen minutes south, one hundred fifty-six degrees thirty-five minutes east."

"You remember the coordinates?" Aldrich asked.

"Why not? It's as close as Charlie will ever come to having a gravesite."

He lapsed into silence.

———

Sitting on the trunk of a fallen tree close to his tent, Tadashi listened to the distant rumble of artillery fire. Being half American and half Japanese, he felt like a man without a country. Saipan was the only place he ever felt he belonged, and now he was sure Saipan would be the place where he would die.

While Chacha was outside the enemy's grasp at present, he felt that situation would change in a matter of days. That sound of the enemy's artillery was a death knell to Tadashi and his comrades.

Somehow Tadashi felt that dying in war on a Pacific island was a strange fate for soldiers living during what the emperor himself had dubbed the *Showa* reign. To Tadashi, calling this rule "Enlightened Peace" seemed a mockery. But then again, hadn't he and other children been schooled in the idea of glorious death in war almost from birth?

He recalled his teacher declaring, "What is your dearest ambition?" To which the student response was: "To die for the emperor."

Did he really believe that?

Sadly, he also felt he did not fit into the American side of his heritage. In American schools, he pledged allegiance to a flag that was not his own and prayed to a "Father who art in heaven." He didn't understand his mother's explanations about God and heaven, yet he wondered if her spirit was there waiting for him.

———

By 1300 hours, Pete was back at the company CP, having been summoned by Capt. Stacey's runner, Pfc. Ernie Flint. All the company officers and every man with three or more stripes were present. A map was laid out across a stack of ammo crates.

"I just want to brief you fellas so you know what to expect,"

Stacey said. "First off, we will be moving off this hill today. Sometime. We'll be going back to the coastal plain and our positions here will be taken over by the Army." This was greeted by moans all around. "I said sometime today because we don't know when that will happen. The plan calls for the Fourth Marines to come up and push north along the eastern coast while we head up the western coast for Garapan. The Army is to occupy the center of this line, but they've been slowed."

"What happened?" Nicholson asked. "Did they run into a sniper?"

"Nothing so dramatic," Stacey replied. "Army training, by its nature, is less . . ." he sought for the right word, "aggressive than ours and that has our General Smith about ready to chew their General Smith a new asshole. Anyway, when they come up—today we're promised—we will shift west."

He pointed a finger to a spot on the map along the west coast.

"That's our objective—Garapan," Stacey announced. "That hasn't changed since we landed, except it was expected that we'd have the city in our possession by this time. Garapan is the largest town on the island, and we do not know what to expect. It could be defended by a platoon, by a company, or a battalion. Hell, there could be an entire regiment up there. The damned place has been leveled so most of it's just broken chunks of debris and hollowed-out buildings. But one thing is for sure. It will be a style of fighting none of you has ever encountered—block to block, house to house, hell, maybe even floor to floor."

"What about air support?" Lt. Shimada asked. "I know there are some Army planes at that airfield to the south, but when is the Navy coming back?"

"That airfield is now called Isely Field after a Marine pilot was killed during the preinvasion softening-up," Stacey said. "As for the Navy, they are on their way back. Some are dropping the hook offshore as we speak. Evidently they fought some big sea battle about five hundred miles to the west and cleaned the Japs' clock. They sank a few enemy carriers and, if you listen to those blowhard carrier pilots who think they get a kill every time they squeeze the trigger, they blasted about a thousand Nip planes." He stopped as a flight of six Grumman Hellcats roared by overhead. Pointing skyward, he said, "Speak of the devil."

———

Tadashi heard the roar of the Grummans as well. Standing up, he moved to where he could see the sky just in time to catch a glimpse of the Hellcats.

"Carrier planes," he said to himself. "Those are carrier planes. Their fleet is returning."

He hurried to the command cave. Bursting inside, he said, "American carrier planes are overhead. I fear for our fleet."

Inside the cavern, the sound of the planes had been heard, and every man realized their importance. At the radio table, the operator was banging on the transmitter key, trying to get some sort of response from someone. Finally, the key began clicking.

Tadashi watched these frantic actions with a quiet sense of finality. He felt disaster had befallen the fleet.

CHAPTER 14

It had been a long night at the headquarters of General Saito and Admiral Nagumo. Their spirits dipped lower and lower as the radio transmitter clicked off message after message, all indicating that the long-awaited Decisive Battle that would determine the outcome of the war had been lost.

"The dispatches say most of our carriers have been damaged," Tadashi grimly read, summing up the reports. "Six other ships have been damaged as well." He balked at the next line. "Nearly our entire naval air arm was destroyed as well as many land-based planes."

After a heavy silence, Nagumo asked, "What was the extent of damage to the carriers?"

"There is no information on that yet," Tadashi said.

"What about the American fleet?" Saito inquired. "Surely Ozawa must have some details on any damage he inflicted upon the enemy."

"The messages claim to have caused heavy damage to the

Americans," Tadashi said. "Pilots coming back from attacks say they sank as many as ten American carriers."

"Then maybe things are not as bad as the messages seem to indicate," Saito said. "Maybe the Americans will pull back to lick their wounds. We may still have an opportunity."

Everyone nodded and agreed they must wait for further reports from Ozawa or Tokyo. Tadashi hoped his superiors were correct, but the tone of the messages he'd read left little room for optimism.

"We must prepare for the worst," Saito said, echoing Tadashi's thoughts. "If we can't get the needed reinforcements from the fleet, we must get them elsewhere." He looked to the radio operator.

"Contact the command center on Truk," he ordered. "Tell them to relay a request for us to obtain soldiers from Tinian and Guam. They can be sent here in a matter of hours."

The radio man nodded. He wrote out the request, coded it, and sent it on its way.

———

Around midafternoon, the sound of antiaircraft guns at sea reached the ears of Pete and his squad. Faintly, they could also hear the drone of Japanese bombers from Rabaul in New Britain. Watching the air raid from atop the Gumdrop meant the planes looked like fly specks. Still, the men of Dog Company cheered when a black dot in the sky burst with orange flames and began to spiral toward the sea, trailing black smoke. Then an explosion at sea rumbled inland as a ship was struck by a bomb or torpedo. The air raid was soon over, but smoke poured from the damaged ship, which turned out to be the USS *Maryland*. Struck by a deadly Long Lance torpedo just aft of the starboard

anchor, the blast tore a hole in the twenty-four-year-old battleship's starboard bow. She limped back to Pearl Harbor, cruising
in reverse all the way to avoid further bow damage. From their
vantage point, the company knew nothing of this.

Dog Company moved off the Gumdrop at 1700 hours. As
they descended the hill they had fought so hard to take, all were
aware of the cost. A final tally was a solid fourth of the company, which included eighteen dead and forty-one wounded.

Their new position found them digging foxholes in a
farm field about half a mile inland from the coastline and a
mile west of Mount Tipo Pale. It was a bleak farmstead with
a tumbled-down wood and thatch house, a surprisingly intact
barn, and battered fields of what had been sugarcane and corn.
As the men undid their entrenching tools from their packs and
began to hack at the soil, they discovered that, for all the action
they'd seen and all the men they'd lost, they were barely a mile
north of where they had come ashore a week ago.

"It looks like we're gonna be fighting a holding action while
we wait until the Fourth Marines and the Doggies align on our
right flank," Pete told the squad. "Once we have that solid line
done, then we all advance together. In our case, that means
Garapan."

"Well, I expect the Fourth will be in position on time, but
I wouldn't place much faith in the goddamn Doggies," Dembrowski hissed.

Scrap Iron had a visceral hatred of the Army, much more
intense than the usual interservice rivalry between different
branches of the military.

"It'll be dark soon," Pete said. "Smoking lamp is out. Watch
for any infiltrators overnight. They've been bad along this part
of the line."

As the squad meeting broke up, Pete corralled Marshall.

"Reb," he said. "Your fire team is down to just you and McCready."

"Ah know," he drawled. "But he's a good man."

"Agreed," Pete said, "but I'm gonna put in a request with Nicholson for dibs on any replacements he gets his hands on. The gunny should be making his evening rounds soon. I'd like you back to at least three."

Pete returned to the foxhole he shared with Aldrich. While he still had light to read, he took out Aggie's last letter and scanned over it again. He chuckled.

"Aggie said she and my mom and her mom have a joint victory garden in the yard behind our house," he told Aldrich. "I can see Aggie and her mom working in a garden, but my poor mom would be a terrible gardener. Every flower she ever brought into our house died a slow and painful death."

"I guess you miss Aggie now more than ever," the Professor said.

Pete nodded.

Nicholson arrived for his final round of the line before darkness. Pete put in his request for any replacements coming in.

"Reb's fire team is down to two men," he said.

"I'll do what I can," Nicholson said. "Everyone is screaming for replacements, so they're as scarce as nuns at a cathouse." He rose to leave. "Put your men on fifty percent alert." He disappeared in the gathering darkness.

Pete put the letter away and wriggled down in the foxhole.

After a brief silence, the Professor said, "Hardball. What do you think you're going to do after the war?"

"To start with, I'll probably spend the first six months in the sack with Aggie while I figure out my next move," Pete said. "But I sure as hell won't go back to crewin' on the Chester ferries. I didn't mind loading cars and trucks and making sure the load's balanced so the damned boat don't tip over, or wrestling with hawser lines, but I also had to scrub the toilets. Between that and cleanin' heads in boot camp, that ain't gonna happen anymore. Now I got three stripes that tell me from now on, someone else will be scrubbin' the fuckin' commodes." Pete paused. "I suppose you're going back to college to become a shrink?"

"A psychologist," Aldrich corrected. "There's a difference." He slightly waved the letter in his right hand. "My mother, however, seems intent on having me make my living off the Chesapeake, like almost everyone else in town. She knows when I get my degree and become a professional psychologist that a small town like Rock Hall won't be enough to hold me down. I'll be off to Baltimore or some other city." He turned to Pete. "You remember that I told you how ever since I was a teenager, I worked summers on a fishing boat for a salty old coot named Captain Jack?"

"Yeah, I remember," Pete said. "Haulin' crab traps up out of the water and dumping them into baskets. Is that how she wants you to spend the rest of your life?"

"I think so," he said. "She's telling me that Captain Jack is hinting that after the war he'd like me to come on full-time to help him out, how he's getting older and that maybe I could even take over and run his operation. I enjoyed helping him, and the *Jacks or Better* is a strong, sound boat, but that's not where my dreams lie."

"No," Pete agreed. "An oaf like me could take to that work and quite possibly even enjoy it. But a guy like you? With your brains? You're destined for better things. That's why I gotta look out for you in combat. To protect you."

"Protect me?" Steve raged in mock indignation. "Why, you . . . you . . . I shot more than one Jap off your keister on Tarawa."

"Whoa, Professor," Pete laughed. "Watch your mouth. You damned near swore there, and we can't have any of that."

"Thass true," Reb Marshall added from the next foxhole. "Ya'll get to cussin', Perfessor, and this whole damned company's goin' to hell."

Pete rolled over and said, "Wake me in two hours."

Throughout the night, Colonel Ogawa busily set about establishing both the line of resistance he had formulated as well as the Line of Security proposed by Major Tanimura, which would run from just below Garapan across the southern slope of Mount Tapochau to Magicienne Bay. His pride had been stung when Saito second-guessed him and made him adopt Major Tanimura's plan as a fallback line. He needed to regain face before his commanders, and the best way to do that, he determined, was to be daring and launch a predawn attack to break through the American line and drive the Marines into the sea. Yes, a success like that was just what the Army needed. He drew up the plans, laying out the two defensive lines as ordered, and tucked them inside his tunic in case he needed them, but for now he was going to take matters into his own hands.

At the command cave above Chacha, Colonel Suzuki, acting on orders from Saito, radioed, "The Army is consolidating its battle lines and has decided to prepare for a showdown."

It was in the wee hours of the morning that orders arrived from Imperial Army Headquarters.

"You will hold beaches still in your possession so reinforcements being dispatched to your command can be landed," the orders read. "Also, you are to block all enemy attempts to use the airfields now under their control. Use your artillery to make the fields unusable."

Saito looked to Tadashi, whose personal forays into areas of the island still occupied by the Japanese forces gave him the best grip on the overall military situation. Tadashi sadly shook his head.

"That is not possible," he said. "They firmly hold Aslito field. With the men we have, we can disrupt operations, but we cannot seize and hold the airstrip for any considerable time. As for using artillery, most of our heavier pieces have either been destroyed by enemy aircraft or overrun by their ground forces."

Saito turned back to the radio operator.

"Tell Tokyo that we have no artillery, but we will use infiltration tactics to penetrate the enemy lines and destroy what we can," he directed. "Tell them we have only the unfinished airfield at Marpi Point and that we are working to get it fit for aircraft. Stress the need for those reinforcements."

The operator went back to sending, and Saito strode across the cave to Tadashi.

"It may soon come to a point where we cannot remain at this location," he said. "Do you know of a good place to establish a new headquarters?"

Tadashi nodded.

"Colonel Suzuki and I discussed possible locations," Tadashi said. "There is a large cave about seven miles north of Garapan and well out of the reach of the Americans, but that is a last resort. There are two other caves nearer by—one in the white cliffs on the east side of Mount Tapochau and another further north that we recommend."

"We will hold here as long as we can, then pull back to Tapochau," Saito said.

It was just after midnight when the Japanese infiltrators made their presence known. Filtering through the Second Battalion line, two of them made their way to one of several Second Division ammo dumps. The dump went up with a roar, sending plumes of fire and smoke roiling two hundred feet into the sky. The concussion from the blast vibrated through ships offshore. The flames lit up the whole battalion line, inviting enemy sniper fire. All along the American line, NCOs began shouting, "Everybody out! Grab your shovels and follow me."

Before long, a hundred men were heaving shovels full of dirt onto the conflagration, but the hungry flames would not be satiated. Finally, the effort was abandoned.

"Back in your foxholes," was the cry now. "Keep alert! Watch for a Nip attack!"

The dump burned all night. The crackle of the flames, accompanied by the snapping and popping of bullets, gave it the air of a Chinese New Year celebration. In the dawning light, bodies of several Marines who'd been manning the dump were dragged out, the corpses charred beyond recognition. Two of the bodies belonged to the enemy infiltrators who sacrificed themselves as human torches to ignite the ammo.

At 0600, the Second Division began to move forward toward the Japanese main line. The hope was to take Mount Tipo Pale on the right and advance into the outskirts of Garapan with the left and center. Pete was more than happy that his battalion occupied the center of the advance, and not the right flank, with its mountainous foothills. The division advanced with little opposition and few casualties for about eight hundred yards before drawing heavy fire.

Japanese infantry located four hundred yards further on had entrenched well, using the downed sugarcane stalks that blanketed the surrounding fields to construct well-camouflaged rifle pits and *Takotsubo*, a one-man octopus trap that allowed a sniper to lift a hidden lid to fire at the enemy. Punctuating the defensive line were several low reinforced concrete pillboxes, each with one or two machine guns. These were set up in a spiderweb defense, with the trenches and rifle pits radiating out.

Second Battalion advanced, each fire team in a wedge formation, with one man at the point, two men five paces behind him on the left and right, and the fire team leader in the rear at center another two paces between the flankers. Since Reb's fire team consisted only of him and McCready, Pete temporarily dissolved it, folding McCready in with Aldrich and Reb with Honeybun. As the battalion approached the largely concealed line, the Japanese defenses opened fire, felling a number of Marines walking at point. The rest either dropped to a knee or fell prone in the face of the fusillade.

Japanese Type 89 grenade launchers that the Marines referred to inaccurately as "knee mortars" began dropping their shells among the advancing Americans. Shards of razor-sharp steel zinged through the air. Some struck flesh, and the cries of "Corpsman" rang out.

In First Platoon, four men were hit, with one dead from a bullet through the head. Platoon Sergeant Tom Woodson took a round near his collarbone by the right shoulder. Two corpsmen responded to the call and stemmed the bleeding, although, for the moment, evacuation to the rear was almost suicidal.

In Second Platoon, Third Squad leader Marty Manson caught a bullet in the fleshy part of his left thigh.

"Patch it up, Doc," Manson angrily told the corpsman. "I ain't leaving the company."

All along the battalion line, Marines returned a desultory fire; desultory because they had no clear targets to shoot at, except for the concrete pillboxes, and even there some were concealed by sugarcane and tree branches.

Yaz's machine guns were brought to the front and began sweeping fire left to right across the Japanese lines. While seemingly on target—so far as could be seen from this distance, at least—the enemy fire did not noticeably slacken. The Marines resumed their forward motion, only now it was in short spurts of a few feet at a time while hunched over or crawling on their bellies.

Marine artillery commenced firing as the Americans sought a breakthrough. Some 105mm as well as large ninety-pound 155mm projectiles whistled and hummed as they passed overhead. Pete watched the barrages burst along the Japanese front and hoped they were hitting their targets.

By early afternoon, the advance had bogged down, well short of its intended goal. Just as disastrous was the fact that Marine units advancing across the more rugged terrain on the right were stopped by steep cliffs. Attempts to flank the enemy failed.

The order went out to dig in and await the Army's advance regiment. The Marines again used their entrenching tools to scratch foxholes out of the stubborn earth.

As evening approached, Pete found Aldrich sitting in his foxhole, pencil in hand, scribbling a letter. Pete nudged him in the ribs.

"Sugar report?" he queried.

"You know I don't have a girlfriend," the Professor replied.

"The hell I do," Pete said back. "I've been away for six months. You coulda shacked up with some khaki whacky hula babe from Hilo and gotten drunk on bootleg okolehao."

"Unlikely," Aldrich said. "So, are we moving anywhere anytime soon?"

"No," Pete said. "I'm told the Army's having a lot of problems moving into position on our right flank. The terrain is pretty rugged, and they're getting bloodied at such delightful places as Hell's Pocket and Death Valley."

"It's just a difference in philosophies when it comes to training," Aldrich reasoned. "The Army prefers to be more cautious and limit casualties, where we Marines tend to push harder and be more aggressive, sometimes at a higher cost. In the end, it's all about fire and maneuver. Personally, I don't look on Army guys disparagingly. Heck, I even think of them as allies."

"So if it's not a girl, who are you writing that letter to? Your mom?" Pete asked.

The Professor nodded.

"Yes," he said. "She gets on me about writing more often."

"She's really hoping that you'll choose to be a boat captain on the Chesapeake, right?"

"Yeah," Aldrich said.

He stopped writing.

"I've been thinking," he mused. "Why not come to Rock Hall and let me introduce you to Captain Jack?"

Pete grimaced.

"You told me an 'oaf' like you might enjoy it."

"Come on, I don't know a damned thing about crabbing and net fishing," Pete said. "Or any boat smaller than a ferry."

"You'd learn from Jack just like I did," Aldrich said. "I'll help you. With my endorsement, I think Jack will go for it. The work's hard, but the money's pretty good."

"Hard work doesn't scare me," Pete said. "But I don't know."

"Think about it," Aldrich urged. "If not for yourself, then for Aggie."

"Okay, I'll think about it."

CHAPTER 15

As the hour of action drew near, Colonel Ogawa's longing for a glorious attack that would drive the enemy into the sea made him decide to accompany his men. He was certain that, with the element of surprise, they'd be successful, especially since he'd rounded up six of the late Colonel Goto's tanks to add their weight. He was determined that General Saito would not need the defensive lines laid out in the plans now inside his tunic.

At the appointed hour the attack got underway. Drawing his sword, he waved it overhead.

"For our emperor and our nation!" he called out. "Banzai!"

With a roar, the men moved forward, each one eager to slay the hated Americans before he himself would fall.

The attack was on top of the Marines before they knew it. At 0500, heavy mortar and artillery fire began to blanket the American line. Men hunkered down into their foxholes as deep as they could go and tried to pull the hole in after them. For twenty minutes, the ground heaved under the impact of

Japanese explosives, and when the fire lifted a new sound was heard; tanks.

Six armored beasts—four Type 97 *Chi-Ha* class medium vehicles and two lighter Type 95 *Ha-Go* models—rumbled forward, supporting infantry spread out in between and behind. The Marine line erupted with small arms fire, joined next by the rattle of .30-caliber machine guns that dropped attackers in bloody rows as they advanced. The tanks' main armament spoke as the 57mm guns on the four *Chi-Ha*s barked. One shell whistled over Pete's head so low he felt the air ripple. It burst somewhere behind him.

"Goddammit," he cursed, then saw Carl McComsey and Fred Mosely making their way forward. "McComsey! Get that bastard!" Pete hollered, pointing as the *Chi-Ha* rolled toward the line, its turret traversing in search of targets.

McComsey knelt while Mosely loaded a rocket into the back of the bazooka tube, connected the wires, and tapped his shooter on the helmet. The bazooka belched fire as the rocket streaked across the field, hitting the *Chi-Ha* where the turret and chassis met. The blast lifted the turret nearly two feet into the air, then dropped it back down, so it sat askew on its mounting, smoke rolling up from the interior. The shattered tank rolled to a stop.

A light *Ha-Go* flanked by half a dozen infantrymen charged toward Aldrich's position. Gunfire from Rosie's BAR chopped down four of them, while Perkins took down two with one round each. The Professor got the last, but the tank continued forward. Aldrich decided to let the tank pass through, then attack it from the rear.

As it clanked by his foxhole, Lt. Shimada suddenly appeared, put a hand on Aldrich's shoulder, and said, "Cover me, Professor."

With that, he clambered onto the rear deck of the tank and knocked on the turret lid with the butt end of his M1 carbine.

"Akete kudasai," he yelled so as to be heard inside the steel beast. *"Watashi wa mikata desu."*

Told to open up for a friend, the tank commander cautiously cracked the hatch and peered out. Shimada pointed his carbine at the face and fired twice. Then he lifted the hatch, dropped a grenade inside, and leapt off, rolling as he hit the ground. Inside the confines of the light tank, the grenade went off with a dull ring, and the smoldering tank came to a halt.

On the squad's right, Reb and McCready were charged by a Type 97 *Chi-Ha* flanked by five soldiers. McCready managed to drop one man while Reb turned his BAR on three others advancing together. A burst from Old Jube sent them sprawling. The last man, roaring with rage, fired at the Americans. However, in his zeal to kill McCready and Reb, he stepped in front of the *Chi-Ha,* which knocked him down. He screamed once as the fifteen-ton tank crushed the life out of him. Obliviously, the tank kept coming, its 7.7mm machine gun just below and to the left of the main gun spitting out round after round.

With the tank coming at them, Reb raised himself and yelled, "McCready! Get out!"

McCready did as ordered, but three bullets from the machine gun struck Reb and sent him crashing back into the foxhole. Wounded in the back and right shoulder, he watched in horror as the tank approached. As it drew close enough for him to count the rivets in its armored skin, a rocket from Mc-Comsey's bazooka struck the *Chi-Ha.* The vehicle exploded, its flaming corpse continuing toward the wounded Marine.

"Goodbye, Momma," Reb muttered.

Suddenly, hands grabbed him under his shoulders and

yanked him from the hole. Moments later the tank's right tread entered the foxhole and the armored beast jarred to a stop.

"Corpsman! Corpsman!" McCready yelled as he pulled Reb away from the burning wreck.

Pete heard the cry and found McCready sobbing as he dragged Reb to safety.

"Jesus Christ!" Pete muttered when he saw his bloodied friend and noticed the tank that now occupied Reb's foxhole.

Pete applied a compression bandage from Reb's first aid kit and muttered, "Don't you die on me, goddamn it."

"You ain't that lucky," Reb said through the pain.

Magruder arrived and dropped to his knees.

"I got him, Hardball," he said. Then to his patient he said, "What's the matter, Reb? You trying for a ticket home?"

Initially, the attack was all Ogawa had hoped it would be. Under cover of the preliminary bombardment, his attackers had covered half the distance that separated the two sides before the Americans were aware of them. Onward they pressed. Ogawa saw some of his men fall as American machine guns blazed. Running around or jumping over bodies of the fallen, Ogawa's attack kept rolling. To his left, Ogawa saw his aide, Major Sakamaki, drop as bullets stitched his torso. Ahead of him, a man's head exploded as he was struck by two enemy slugs. But Ogawa was in his element. His success here, he felt, would atone for the failures of his June 16 and 17 assaults.

That thought was Colonel Ogawa's last as a bullet slammed into his heart.

The glorious assault Ogawa thought would turn the fortunes of the battle around in favor of Nippon, for which he sacrificed his own life and the lives of about two hundred of his men, was over in about an hour. Wearied, the Marines watched the enemy depart.

Pete hadn't left Magruder's side as he watched the corpsman tend to Reb.

"Fish a morphine syrette from my bag," Magruder said as he tried to stem the bleeding. Pete did. "Open it and jab him in the left thigh."

Pete removed the plastic cover and used the wire ring inside to pierce open the needle. Pete jammed it hard into Reb's leg in order to penetrate the trousers. Meanwhile, Magruder ripped open a pouch of sulfa powder and sprinkled it on the wounds to help the blood clot.

"Am ah goin' home to Momma or home to Jesus?" Reb asked through the morphine fog.

"You'll see your momma long before you see Jesus," Magruder said as he continued working.

Hearing Reb was hit, Aldrich rounded up a team of mortarmen and transformed them into stretcher-bearers. Once Magruder gave the nod, Pete and Aldrich gently lifted their friend and laid him on the stretcher. Magruder attached the empty morphine syrette to Reb's uniform to alert the medics at the field hospital that the drug had been given.

"I'm mad as hell at you," Pete said to Reb. "You get hit when I need every man I can get?"

Reb gave a groggy smile.

"You had your vacation, now it's mah turn," he slurred.

Then he grasped Pete's arm.

"Ya know, you ain't too bad . . . fer a Yank." He smiled.

"He should make it," Doc said. "Hell, he might even be back if the war lasts long enough."

For the Japanese commanders inside the cave at Chacha, the day began badly and then got worse. First came more news about the naval battle. The receiver clacked nonstop for several minutes. When it stopped, the operator decoded the message and handed it to Tadashi, whose face sagged as he read.

"It is from Truk," he said. "Admiral Ozawa's fleet has been turned back. Three of our carriers—*Zuikaku*, *Junyo*, and *Chiyoda*—were damaged, along with battleship *Haruna*. Three others—*Shokaku*, *Hiyo*, and . . ." he paused. ". . . *Taiho*—have been sunk."

"*Taiho* is gone?" Nagumo said in a disbelieving whisper. "That was her first battle. With her armored flight deck, we thought her to be invincible."

"There's more," Tadashi said. "Our loss in aircraft is more than four hundred. Maybe as high as five hundred in carrier-borne and land-based aircraft. Casualties exceed three thousand seamen."

"The enemy's loss?" Saito asked.

Tadashi shook his head as he replied, "Unknown."

The radioman handed Tadashi one more sheet of decoded paper. After reading it, he said, "Tokyo says it will try to get us reinforcements by submarine or fast destroyers, like was done on Guadalcanal, but they can't promise."

"What about help from Guam and Tinian?" Saito asked. "They promised us that."

"There is no mention," Tadashi replied.

Saito strode to a table. Taking paper from his portable writing desk, he scribbled a note and handed it to Tadashi.

"Send this to Imperial Headquarters in Tokyo," he ordered. "I want them to know our situation."

Tadashi looked to the paper and read, "Though our forces have called on all kinds of methods to hinder the enemy advance, we are regrettably reduced to the condition that we cannot carry on successfully with our present fighting strength."

Our fate is now in Tokyo's hands, Tadashi thought.

———————

Pete and the squad barely had time to absorb the loss of one of their old-timers when orders came to saddle up; the division was advancing all along its front. With armor up ahead, the men spaced ten paces apart as they walked across the blasted farm fields littered with smashed crops, bullet-riddled trees, and dead Japanese from the earlier attack.

Behind the advancing American line, artillery pounded the enemy entrenchments ahead, creating a steady drumbeat. Support for the advancing Marines was also bolstered by a number of rocket trucks. These emptied their pods within seconds, filling the sky with a wave of deadly missiles.

The American attack drove forward some fifteen hundred yards before encountering stiffening resistance. On the right side of the line, Marines assaulting Mount Tapochau halted as well, as they were confronted by steep ridges peppered with caves that had to be burned out. Their attack, which had more ground to cover, had advanced twenty-six hundred yards.

East of Second Division, a coordinated thrust by the Fourth Marine Division pushed forty-four hundred yards along to the tip of Kagman Peninsula. Unknown to these men, they were closing in on Saito's CP above Chacha.

The American Twenty-Seventh Division, which was supposed to move up between the two Marine divisions, began their attack late and lagged behind. This delay meant commanders of both the Second and Fourth Marines fretted about their flanks being exposed to counterattacks.

By 1900 hours, the assault was over, and the order was passed to dig in.

———————

All afternoon and into the evening runners from various units around Saipan had reached the command cave, but none bore good news. Early reports stated that, except for contingents of Colonel Yoshira Oka's Forty-Seventh Independent Mixed Brigade trapped on Nafutan Point at the southern tip of the island, the Americans controlled the entire lower half of Saipan. That included Aslito airfield.

Then close to dark came the shocking account of Colonel Ogawa's charge. Saito took the news of the attack, its repulse, and the death of his trusted subordinate with solemnity.

"I understand his enthusiasm to defeat the enemy," Saito said, restraining his anger at his subordinate's rash attack. "But his brashness has cost us dearly, and his loss will be missed."

"Sir, there is worse news," Tadashi said. "We have a report that the Americans have launched an offensive and are pushing north all along their front. Chacha is threatened. Men of the Homare Division are holding their own for now, but they have less than two battalions against an enemy division, and the Americans are on the verge of breaking through. Please, we must pull back to the cave and bunker northeast of Mount Tapochau."

"You think we are in imminent danger here?" Saito inquired.

"Yes sir," Tadashi replied.

Turning to Colonel Suzuki, Saito told his chief of staff, "Tomorrow morning we will break down the headquarters and relocate to Tapochau."

Dog Company's situation meeting that night was inside a rag-
gedy shack that occupied what had been a farmer's field. Capt.
Stacey stood at one end of a table constructed by laying an old
door across four empty ammo crates. As the discussion started,
Stacey looked at Pete.

"Sorry to hear about your rebel friend," he said in a sincere
voice. "How is he?"

"Doc says he'll make it, but as for coming back here, that's
anybody's guess," Pete replied.

"Tough," Stacey said. "He was a damned fine BAR man."
He now spoke to everyone. "The Japs were pushed back, pretty
far in some spots. But they still have a very strong line stretched
out ahead of us running coast to coast. We know that because one of our guys came across a dead Jap officer a couple
of hours ago, and he kindly had a copy of the Nip defenses
tucked inside his tunic, showing the line we just crossed and
the one ahead of us."

"If we know their defenses, what are we waiting for, sir?"
asked Second Lt. Charles Manly, who'd taken over command
of Third Platoon after Lt. Pickering's death on the Gumdrop.

"The Army got a slow start and hit a brick wall in their
attack," Stacey said. Around him, men moaned. "I know. I know.
Our General Smith is spitting nails over it. Anyway, for now,
their absence on our right means that flank is open, and we've
had to bend our line back to cover as much as we can in case
the Nips come out of their holes again. Meanwhile, we have to
wait here for God knows how long."

"Exactly where are we, sir?" Nicholson inquired.

"About three-quarters of a mile from the outskirts of Garapan," Stacey said. "Anyway, a supply depot is being set up

to our rear, so dispatch some men to grab a spool or two of barbed wire and wire up tight. They've attacked our lines the last two nights, and there's no reason not to assume they might try again."

After the meeting, Pete returned to the squad. He stopped at Aldrich's foxhole, where the Professor was back to letter writing, and Pete filled him in on the discussion.

"Doc told me Reb will be okay but doesn't know if he'll be coming back to us," Pete said. "I'm gonna miss that hillbilly."

Aldrich nodded.

"They keep whittling us down," Aldrich said. "Of the sixteen men in our squad when we hit Tarawa, you, me, Rosie, and Honeybun are all that's left."

"Scary thought," Pete said. Then he turned to look at Aldrich. "Are you still writing that letter to your mom? Jesus Christ. The Founding Fathers spent less time on the Declaration of Independence."

"She's an inquisitive lady," Aldrich said. "Why don't you write to Aggie?"

"And tell her what?" Pete replied. "I can't tell her where I am. I can't tell her what I'm doing. I can't say, 'Hello, darling, I'm here on Saipan, where I just killed half a dozen Japs.'"

"Would it tax your brain to tell her you love her and wish you were with her?" Aldrich said.

"That goes without saying." Pete shrugged.

"You're a real romantic, aren't you?" the Professor said with exasperation. "'That goes without saying' is not something women want to hear when it comes to romance."

Pete laughed, then strode to the foxhole he occupied alone and took a seat. He thought about what his friend had said. He had promised Aggie he'd write often—a pledge he had so far failed to keep.

Pete reached into his haversack. From it he withdrew a sheet of paper and his pencil. Using his inverted mess plate as a makeshift writing table, he scribbled, "My Darling Aggie." He continued writing until it was too dark to see the paper.

———

Donnay was two miles as the crow flies north of Chacha, although the twisty snakelike coastal road added perhaps another half-mile. Reaching the village of Donnay, the headquarters convoy halted among a thick stand of trees. Whatever was needed, including Saito's field desk, would be transported by hand. The rest would be abandoned.

Led by a ten-man point guard, Saito, Nagumo, and their entourage headed off into the hills.

The cave intended as the new CP for the island's defense had been preplanned and included two concrete bunkers and several machine gun revetments on each side of the cave's mouth. A contingent of twenty-five soldiers assigned to guard the cave by the late Colonel Ogawa stood ready.

The cave itself, located among the white cliffs of Tapochau's eastern foothills, had been prepared with care and was surprisingly comfortable.

Having just been displaced for the third time in nine days, Saito felt he needed to know the strength of the island's remaining defenses and the combat effectiveness of the men manning those positions. He did not wish this information to be relayed via radio. Instead, he gave orders to Tadashi to conduct the mission.

"This may take you two or three days, but try to report back as soon as you are able," Saito told him. "Go carefully. It is our duty to give our lives for the emperor, but for right now I cannot afford for your spirit to make that trip to Ya-sukuni Shrine."

Tadashi bowed deeply. With Hanaya in tow, the two men struck off. Tadashi heard there was a command post between Hashiguro on the coast and the mountain called Charan Danshi, north of the unnamed Hill 700. They would seek out this post for needed information.

CHAPTER 16

It took Tadashi and Hanaya about two and a half hours to travel north toward the headquarters of the First Yokosuka Special Naval Landing Force. Unlike the SNLF units that had sustained heavy loses to the west, these men were well entrenched and in high spirits.

"How many men do you have who are fit for duty?" Tadashi asked. "We must hold the enemy until reinforcements arrive."

"I have about twelve hundred men under my direct command, but another eight hundred who can be called upon," Captain Benjiro Takashina replied.

Tadashi nodded his approval, then he and Hanaya struck off toward the Tapochau foothills to find Major Rikuto Sadamachi, the late Col. Ogawa's successor, whose battered forces were holding back the enemy south of Garapan.

As the two men walked along, they heard the faint buzz of voices, which grew louder with each step. Rounding a bend in the trail, Tadashi saw a pathetic column of soldiers painfully shuffling along. Led by an officer sporting a bloodied bandage wrapped around his upper torso, the column was comprised of about thirty men, all wounded to some degree.

Those who could walk did so, often assisted by crutches, walking sticks, or inverted rifles. Those worse off were being lugged on stretchers carried by wearied comrades or draped over someone's shoulders. A few even rode piggyback on the backs of the strongest men.

"I am Major Tanimura of General Saito's staff," Tadashi said in his most commanding tone of voice. "This is Captain Hanaya. Who are you, and where are you taking these men?"

"I am Lieutenant Murayama, sir," he said. "We are going to Mount Donnay. We're told there is a field hospital near there. Would you know where it is?"

"I do not," Tadashi said, touched by the sight of the suffering men. "But come. We will find it together."

The bloodied column staggered on.

Dog Company happened to be occupying a section of the line close to their CP. It was just after 1000 hours when Pete heard a jeep approaching. The car stopped by Captain Stacey's command center. Pete recognized Major Simon Parke, who had been made battalion commander after Major Clarkson stopped a bullet on D-Day. Pete did a double take when he saw the other two passengers. One man's identity he wasn't totally certain of, but he definitely knew the other. He had met *Time* magazine writer Robert Sherrod on the troop ship heading for Tarawa, and they shared the same landing boat during that bloody invasion. The last time Pete saw the dark-haired, chain-smoking journalist was shortly before the island was declared secure. Pete was on the beach waiting to be evacuated after his leg was peppered by grenade shrapnel.

Pete sauntered over to the jeep, holding a pack of cigarettes.

"Do you want a Camel, or are you still only smoking those trashy Chesterfields?" he asked.

Sherrod turned around, and a smile cracked his weathered face.

"I'll be goddamned," he said. "Talbot from Chester." He pointed at Pete's right leg. "You're looking a damned sight better than the last time I saw you."

"I'm feeling a damned sight better, too," he said. "I heard you came ashore on D-Day again. You just can't stay out of harm's way, can you?"

"I'm like you," Sherrod replied. "I don't get paid to play it safe." He noticed Pete's stripes and said, "You're coming up in the world, Sergeant. You were a private when we came ashore on Betio."

"It's the price I paid for being one of those few who came back alive," he said. He pointed at the man he could not identify but who wore the stars of a brigadier general. "Is that who I think it is?"

"Yeah," Sherrod answered. "That's your division commander, Merritt Edson."

"Goddamn," Pete said. "I remember reading about him in the paper, about the stand he and his First Raider Battalion made on Bloody Ridge on the 'Canal. If those plucky bastards had lost that hill, God knows what might've happened."

"The whole Guadalcanal Campaign might have collapsed," Sherrod said. "If that had happened, the whole course of the war might've changed."

"Like you told me at Tarawa, I'm here because I have to be," Pete said. "But why do you want to be?"

"I've always had a passion for news," he said. "Ever since I was a kid in Clark County, Georgia. I joined *Time* in 1935 and have been doing this ever since."

"Yeah, but you could've picked a safer place than Tarawa and Saipan," Pete said.

"I guess so," he replied. Then he laughed and added, "Maybe I'll be inspired to write a book about my exploits on Saipan and about guys like you," he said. "Hell, my friend Dick Tregaskis did it. He hung around with Vandegrift and Red Mike Edson on the 'Canal and Tulagi. He called the book *Guadalcanal Diary*. Shit, they even made a movie out of it with William Bendix and Preston Foster. Have you seen it?"

"Nope," Pete said. "And I probably won't. War movies have lost their appeal. By the way, newsman, is there truth to the scuttlebutt that our Navy kicked the Nips' ass the other day?"

"It's not scuttlebutt," Sherrod answered. "We sank three carriers and destroyed close to five hundred planes. The flyboys said it was a turkey shoot, and that's what all the newspapers are calling it. We lost about a hundred planes." He leaned forward toward Pete and lowered his voice.

"Here's a real news scoop for you," he said. "General 'Howlin' Mad' Smith just fired the Army's General Smith. He was pissed and blamed the Army for being too slow and lacking aggressive spirit, so he shitcanned the guy."

"Jesus," Pete said. "Once that becomes common knowledge, the Army is more likely to attack us instead of the Nips."

"Keep it under your helmet for now," Sherrod said.

Edson and Parke emerged from Stacey's CP.

"Ready, Bob?" Edson called.

Sherrod waved his affirmative.

"General," Sherrod said. "I'd like you to meet Sgt. Pete Talbot, a tough, raggedy-assed Marine I met on Tarawa. He was just a buck private in those days."

Suddenly in the hot seat, Pete snapped to attention but did not salute in case of snipers.

"General," he said crisply.

"Good job, Sergeant Talbot," Edson said. "I have a deep respect for the men who fought there."

Edson climbed into the jeep while Sherrod piled into the back. With a wave, the jeep was off.

———————

Tadashi smelled the hospital well before he found it.

The makeshift hospital sat in a bowl-shaped area carved into the mountainside by forces of nature. There were no tents to erect, leaving most of the nearly eight hundred casualties exposed to the sunlight as they lay on the open ground, in scattered grassy patches, and among rocks, exposed to the heat and clouds of flies.

Lt. Murayama's pitiful command now dissolved as his weary men broke ranks in search of open places on the ground to rest their weary bodies and get whatever treatment they could.

Tadashi and Hanaya slowly walked along amid the bodies that lay so closely packed that in some spots they had to step over and between moaning, writhing soldiers. About two dozen overworked medics, *eissei-hei*, moved amid the crowds of sufferers.

"Mizu," was the cry of the sun-parched wounded as they pleaded in a hoarse whisper for a sip of water from men who had none to offer. *"Mizu wo kudasai."*

Wading among this sea of human suffering, Tadashi was sickened. Everywhere was heard the chorus of groans and cries of agony.

Tadashi watched two orderlies pick up a man who had obviously died some time earlier.

"Where are you taking him?" Tadashi asked an orderly.

"Dead pit," the man said curtly.

Curious, he followed the orderlies and their mournful burden about fifty yards from the edge of the hospital. There, in a gully worn out by erosion, his spirit was sickened by the sight of a pile of bodies carelessly heaped one on top of another. Tadashi could not even guess the number of rotted, bloated corpses that lay intermingled in this human refuse.

An officer in bloodstained clothes approached. Tadashi recognized him as Colonel Hiroshi Ikeda, a doctor with the Forty-Third Division.

"Not an encouraging sight, is it?" Ikeda asked. "We lose about twenty patients a day, and every day those twenty, plus some additional troops, arrive to take the places of the dead. You are Major Tanimura. Perhaps you have come from General Saito? Is he sending us supplies and assistance?"

"Yes, I have been sent on a mission for General Saito, but sadly I have nothing for your needs," Tadashi said. "I wish it were otherwise, but I've been sent because General Saito wants an assessment of our defenses and manpower for our future operations."

"Future operations," Dr. Ikeda said in a voice oozing with bitter irony. He pointed all around. "There's your manpower count. I am short of bandages. I have just a few boxes of painkiller injections left. I have little food and water, and I am forced to do amputations with little or no anesthesia.

"On top of that, these people are hungry. They are living on a few ration kits. Sometimes we get sweet potatoes and whatever other crops we can collect from abandoned farm fields. I have twenty-six *eissie-hei*, another thirty orderlies, but only two other doctors, one an islander named Suarez. General Saito must make some provisions to help us."

"I know Dr. Suarez," Tadashi said. "He's a good physician. But as I told you, I am on a mission from General Saito. When I report to him, I will make a plea to get you what you need, but please do not put too many hopes on that. Most of our supply dumps have been destroyed or overrun. But I will do what I can. Meanwhile, you may want to make preparations to move your hospital farther north to the vicinity of Charan Danshi."

"I know," Ikeda said. "I am planning to order a move to-morrow, but I am hesitant because I can only take the walking wounded. We don't have enough able-bodied men to help those who must be carried."

That jolted Tadashi.

"What of the others?" he asked.

"Those who cannot walk may die an honorable death. My orderlies will issue grenades, one for every eight men," he said matter-of-factly. "Grenades are one supply I have plenty of."

Glancing around, Tadashi noted that not all the bodies lying in that field of agony were military. Close to two hundred of the injured were civilians—men, women, old people, and children. Nearly all were emaciated from lack of food and drinkable water.

For Tadashi, the suffering of the civilians was a personal agony, and tears welled up in his eyes.

"What about the civilians?" Tadashi inquired. "What's to become of them?"

"I have no grenades for those who cannot follow under their own power," Ikeda replied. "The rest will be expected to commit seppuku. I can leave them some knives but that is all."

Tadashi felt anger toward this pompous man who decided life and death with such ease. He turned and walked off, searching the sea of suffering humanity. Tadashi felt as though he were in a daze. These people were simple islanders. They did not ask for this.

Among the civilians he spotted Dr. Suarez. Antonio Suarez

was Tadashi's family doctor and had mended Tadashi's broken leg when he was ten years old.

"Hello, Doctor," Tadashi said.

Suarez stared, then grinned with satisfaction.

"Tashy," he said, using Tadashi's boyhood nickname. "It is so good to see you." He looked around. "I just wish it was a happier reunion."

They spoke briefly, with Suarez asking about Tadashi's parents. He was sad to know that Tashy's mother had died.

Tadashi wanted to spend more time with his old acquaintance, but the doctor said, "You must excuse me. So many need my help. Maybe we can talk later."

Tadashi nodded sadly as the doctor continued his grim rounds.

Tadashi then spotted another familiar face. Nanami Ikegama had been a neighbor and almost like a second mother. Her son, Yasuyuki, was a close boyhood friend. Yet this was not a happy reunion, for Tadashi knew Yasuyuki was a seaman aboard the carrier *Shokaku*, which had just been reported sunk. Then there was Mamma Ikegama herself. Tadashi knew she was only in her early sixties, but the shriveled woman before him looked twenty years older. She recognized him right away.

"Tashy," she said, her voice weak and shaky. "You are all grown up. How handsome you look in your uniform. Tell me, how are your honorable parents?"

He told her of his mother's death.

"So sad. She was a wonderful woman. She had a good heart, but I guess not a strong one." Then she brightened up. "You know my son and the fleet are coming to rescue us?"

"I know, Mamma Ikegama," Tadashi lied. "We're all eager."

"You were such a good boy," she said. "This terrible war. I hear the Americans are savages and will butcher us all."

"No, Mamma Ikegama," Tadashi soothed. "The Americans will not harm you and may even get you medical help."

Exhausted and still fearful, she lay down on a blanket to rest, and Tadashi moved on.

———

The day passed quietly along the Second Battalion front. Off in the hills, where Mount Tapochau loomed ominously, the rumble of 105mm and 155mm field pieces blending with the karump of heavy mortars could be distinctly heard as men of the Twenty-Seventh Division fought to get into position for the concerted push to the north.

"Sounds like the Army is having a bad time of it," young Pfc. Perkins said, staring off to the east.

"Yeah," said his foxhole partner, Rosie Roseblum, as he took advantage of the lull to clean his BAR. "My hemorrhoids bleed for the Doggies."

Steve Aldrich, crawling on all fours to avoid making a sniper target of himself, approached. He checked in with his team.

"We're fine," Rosie said.

"Okay," Aldrich said. "It'll be dark in a few hours. Fifty percent alert."

"Sergeant," Perkins said. "I heard that you attended college."

"Two years," Aldrich said. "Maryland State Teachers College in Towson, Maryland. Then the war came along."

"You wanted to be a teacher?" the boy asked.

"Actually, I was taking psychology courses to become a licensed psychologist," Aldrich said. "I went to Towson because it's in Baltimore County, just across the Chesapeake from Rock Hall, my hometown."

"After the war I want to go to college and become a teacher,"

Perkins said. "My mom's a high school teacher back home in Florida, in Eagle Lake—that's in Polk County. I was thinking about starting at the Jacksonville Junior College for two years, then going on to the university."

Perkins was quiet for a while, then rather tentatively asked, "Have you known our sergeant very long? You guys fought together on Tarawa, didn't you?"

"Yep," Aldrich said. "Me, Rosie, Honeybun, and Pete. The four of us are all that's left of the original squad."

"Gosh," Perkins said, clearly impressed. "He seems like a tough cookie. He's awfully hard to get to know."

"Yes, and he likes it that way," Rosie chimed in. "But you have the toned-down version. Hardball was a real loner when he joined the squad. The Professor here . . ."

Aldrich cut Rosie off.

"It's not important whether you get to know him or not," Aldrich said. "What's important is that you listen to him and do what he says. You do that and you'll better your chances of making it through this war."

He returned to the foxhole. As he did, Pete walked up to Aldrich.

"Have everyone get comfy," Pete said. "Looks like we're not going anywhere for a day or two."

"I told my team to go to fifty percent alert," Aldrich said.

Pete nodded and said, "I want the squad settled in, but I don't want them to get sloppy."

"I saw you chatting with that reporter earlier," Aldrich said. "You guys got pretty chummy on Tarawa."

"He's interesting," Pete said. "And he's a good source for confirming scuttlebutt."

He told Aldrich about the sea battle and how Sherrod introduced him to Edson.

"It was embarrassing as hell," he said.

Aldrich chuckled.

"He did give me one bit of news but told me to keep it hush-hush. This is between us for now, but Howlin' Mad fired the top Army general because the Doggies were dragging their feet."

"Oh man," Aldrich replied. "That won't go far in improving interservice relations. Should be interesting to see how Dembrowski takes that news."

———

Darkness closed in quickly after the sun went down. Tadashi and Hanaya settled in for the night at the edge of the hospital. Rolling out their blankets on the hard ground about twenty yards from the "Dead Pit," Tadashi was struck by how the decaying corpses emitted a faint phosphorescent glow. Even though it was nighttime, there was no rest in this charnel house disguised as a field hospital. The moans and cries of the suffering never ceased and those aiding the injured got no relief.

Tadashi found his friend sitting on the ground looking up at the moon.

"You seem to be miles away," Tadashi said as he sat down beside Hanaya. "Japan perhaps?"

"No," he replied. "I was just caught up in the moonlight and thinking about my brothers. About Daisuki who's in the Philippines, and praying for the soul of Miyoko who made the journey to Yasukuni Shrine after Tarawa. And what about you? I guess being under a lonely night sky like this, you must miss Kokoro."

Tadashi nodded.

"It's funny," he said. "We really have not had the opportunity to spend much time together, but yet it was like how the hummingbird is attracted to the sweetest flower. We both felt it. I really hope to be able to see her again, but looking around and seeing how our forces appear to be dissolving before the enemy, I have no high prospects of that happening. At least not in this life. But karma is karma, and I cannot control what I do not hold in my hand."

He turned to his friend.

"What about you, Kisaburo-san," he said. "I have known you since the academy, but you talk little about your home. Is there a girl in your life who you'd like to get back to?"

"There was one girl in the village," he said. "Tamiko Fujiwara. If by some miracle I get back home, I may cultivate that field."

Tadashi laughed.

"Let us pray, then, tonight that this fight turns in our favor, and we see Kokoro and Tamiko again," Tadashi said.

Doubting that his prayer would be answered, he lay down to sleep.

CHAPTER 17

It had been a hard night at the hospital as exhausted doctors and orderlies tried to minister to the injured. Tadashi went looking for Mamma Ikegama only to be told her spirit had departed in the night.

"She lost the desire to live," Dr. Suarez said. "This is what she wanted."

As the morning sun began its climb into the sky, preparations to relocate the hospital farther north began. Medics were given the grim task of selecting who would go and who would remain. All stretcher cases were told they would stay behind. To continue, a man had to be able to walk with minimal assistance. If he fell out of the formation en route, he would be left behind. In the end, less than half of the nine hundred patients would be moving on.

A small ration of rice and vegetables was given to those able to walk to provide them with some nourishment. Those who remained got nothing.

Preparations were well underway when the unthinkable happened. Four American F6F Hellcat fighters came screaming down from out of the sun, making them all but invisible to the terrified people on the ground. The first knowledge Tadashi and the others had was when the lead plane's six wing-mounted machine guns began to shower .50-caliber bullets indiscriminately across the hospital grounds.

The hospital had no Red Cross flags or banners to display, so the question of whether the difference could be discerned between a large body of sick and wounded men and a large body of armed infantry to a pilot diving at 380 miles per hour was academic. What wasn't academic was the horror that resulted.

Screams of terror filled the air as the American bullets kicked up pillars of earth and stone when they struck. Everywhere the heavy .50-caliber rounds tore into people, literally ripping some apart.

The attack by the four planes was short but deadly. At least thirty men had been killed and more than a hundred wounded, some for the second or third time. Nearly fifty civilians were also killed in the attack and a hundred more wounded. Tadashi saw one family of four who lay dead on their bullet-ridden blanket. As he stared, he felt rather than saw Dr. Suarez come up beside him.

"I must get the people ready to move," he said darkly. "At least those still able."

Half an hour after the American attack, Dr. Ikeda climbed up on a large rock so he could address the wounded masses.

"We are told that the enemy could reach this location in a matter of days," he cried out loudly. "For that reason, we are moving the hospital farther to the north, where we hope that friendly troops from Guam will come ashore to help fight the Americans and take our wounded off to hospitals for proper care. Sadly, we can only take those who can walk. The rest of you will be expected to die honorably."

Now preparations began in earnest. The somber task of distributing grenades and knives began. Rifle shots cracked as the most helpless were shot through the head by able-bodied wounded who still possessed weapons. Tadashi stopped counting the rifle shots when it reached fifty.

Those doomed to die scrawled notes on scraps of paper or composed final letters home. They begged hospital staff to take their messages and try to see that their families back in Japan knew what had happened to them and that they died with honor.

Tadashi watched as one man whose lower jaw had been shot off scribbled his name and home prefecture into the dirt because he had no paper. Tadashi nodded and wrote the information in his notebook. The wounded man, tears flowing from his eyes, dipped his head in gratitude.

As the sad procession got underway, the doomed began to shout "Goodbye" and "Thank you."

One man began to sing a song that told of a mother who brought her son's medals to Yasukuni Shrine.

From Ueno Station to Kudanzaka
I get impatient, not knowing my way around.
It has taken me all day, leaning on my cane,
To come and see you, my son, at Kudanzaka.
The great torii *looming up in the sky*
Leads to a magnificent shrine
That enrolls my son among the gods.
Your unworthy mother weeps for joy.

Tadashi was struck by the beautiful simplicity of the song.

He knew the song but had never heard it. It was not one his American mother would've known.

Tadashi had hoped that Japan could inflict enough casualties on America that they would seek peace. No more. The speed with which the enemy had landed, and the number of men they had put ashore on just the first day of the invasion, made him realize Japan's folly in taking on the United States.

He had seen General Saito's force decimated by futile charges, and driven back as the island was cut in two. But it was here in the hospital amid the dead and dying, and seeing the hopelessness in the faces of many of the wounded as they realized no help would be coming to their aid, that he understood Japan's plight. This was a broken army. The increasing rumble of American artillery moving ever closer confirmed the hopelessness. This despair was confirmed when the first of the grenades went off. Then the next grenade went off. Then the next, and the next, and the next.

As Tadashi turned and walked away, the sounds of futile death pursued him.

———

The news roared along the Second Battalion line like a prairie wildfire. Men jerked their heads up and thought maybe they'd misheard, but no. It was true. Howlin' Mad Smith had fired the Army's top general, Ralph Smith. Already pissed off at the Twenty-Seventh Infantry Division for what he perceived as a lack of aggressiveness, Howlin' Mad criticized the Army's fighting spirit and contended that they had "failed to attack on time," unnecessarily costing Marine lives.

Major General Sanderford Jarman was put in temporary command.

Second Squad was trying to absorb the news over noonday chow. Earlier in the morning, Gunny Nicholson sought out Pete.

"Division is setting up a field kitchen in the farmyard about a hundred yards east of the CP," he said. "At 1230 hours, take your boys back for a hot meal."

"Hot chow?" Pete asked in amazement. "After ten days of boxed rations, our stomachs won't know what to make of it."

"I know," Nicholson replied. "Maybe someone in the rear got confused and thought we were the Army." He fidgeted a bit, then repeated the news about General Holland Smith firing Ralph Smith. Pete did not let on that he already knew this.

"Wow," Pete said. "Howlin' Mad really put his ass in a sling, didn't he?"

"That's putting it lightly," Gunny said. "Get your guys fed and back on the line by 1300."

The field kitchen's menu included fresh bread with butter and a hearty beef stew washed down with steaming hot black coffee or cold powdered lemonade. Man after man passed along the cook line, aluminum plates in hand, as a mess orderly ladled a pile of stew onto the plate. There seemed to be more potatoes and carrots working to conceal the sparseness of any actual beef, but to men who'd been living on K-rations for the past ten days the stew, for all its shortcomings, was like dining at the Waldorf Astoria.

The main topic of discussion was the firing by Howlin' Mad.

"That's gonna piss off a bunch of Army guys," Rosie said as the men sat cross-legged on the ground, tin mess plates in hand, and trying to ingest as few of the ever-present flies as possible with each spoonful of stew. Veterans were adept at swatting flies away with one hand while shoveling food into their mouths with the other.

"Do you think maybe Howlin' Mad jumped the gun?"

Honeybun inquired. "I'm not defending the Army, understand, but from all I've heard they had really rough terrain with a lot of valleys to cross while Japs held the high ground."

"Fuck the Army," Dembrowski growled. "Fuck 'em all. Only thing any of them are good for is Jap bayonet practice."

There was a brief silence that Pete soon broke.

"OK, Dembrowski," Pete said. "You've been bitching about the Army since we landed. Let's have it. What did they do to you?"

Dembrowski looked at the faces seated around him and shrugged.

"It's a long story," he said. "But here goes. You fellas remember the Bonus Army's so-called 'riot' back in '32? Well, I was there. I was five at the time. Pop was in the Army in the first war, and after that he came home and opened a small corner grocery store in Chicago, where we lived. All was hunky-dory until the Depression hit. Small businesses like my dad's suffered as unemployment soared and cash got scarce. By '31, Dad's store and his dreams went belly-up. In '32 we lost the house." Finishing his stew, he lit a cigarette. "That's why the Bonus Army thing became so important."

After the First World War, Dembrowski recounted, Congress wanted to establish a bonus for men who fought overseas as a thank-you for their service. Under the act, Dembrowski's dad was due to receive $625.

He related how his father joined thousands of other veterans in marching on Washington to demand the money. They built a "Hooverville" across the Anacostia River at Anacostia Flats using old lumber, packing boxes, and scrap tin covered with roofs of straw or corrugated iron.

"So how did you, a five-year-old, end up there?" Aldrich asked.

"We had no place else to go," Dembrowski said. "And we

weren't the only ones. Ten thousand men, women, and children lived in that Hooverville."

Dembrowski's face darkened.

"Then came June 15," he said. "Congress voted to approve the bonus bill, but the goddamned Republican-controlled Senate voted it down. It was a real kick in the ass to men who put themselves on the line to defend this nation."

"Then Hoover—who also never served a fuckin' day in uniform—wanted us gone, so he called on Dugout Doug MacArthur, who hated the Bonus guys and accused them of being disloyal and infiltrated by commies. He even doubted that they were veterans. On July 28, MacArthur sent in his goons, infantry, cavalry, and even six tanks led by the biggest asshole in the Army, Patton. Yeah, and MacArthur's lackey, Eisenhower, was there as well. The Army attacked, drove us out of Washington by force and back across the river. They followed the Bonus guys across and torched the Hooverville, burning and smashing everything. I remember gripping my mother's hand tight as we ran out of the path of a cavalryman with a saber he was swinging around."

"Hooverville was leveled," Dembrowski said heavily. "Most of what little we still owned got burned up. But there was worse. One hundred thirty-five veterans were arrested and another fifty-five wounded. This included my father, whose leg got run through by a bayonet thrust by an eighteen-year-old private."

Dembrowski was silent, his story finished.

"Well," Pete said. "If anyone has the right to hate the Army, it's you." Rising, he added, "Let's get back to the line."

The men stood and followed Pete to a row of three sawed-off fifty-five-gallon drums sitting on iron grates over a fire, boiling water in each one. This was the "dunk-and-swoosh" method of dishwashing, with one barrel containing soapy water for washing and the other two straight water for a first and second rinse. That done, the squad returned to their foxholes.

The parade of wounded and sick men slogged along at a slow but remarkably steady pace. Dr. Ikeda had told Tadashi that his goal was the village of San Roque. While it was just two miles as a crow would fly, the twisty road combined with rugged terrain made it a daunting task. Tadashi doubted if more than half the men would finish the march. But Ikeda was adamant.

"It's almost on the beach and just a short distance from Tanapag Harbor," he told Tadashi. "If the Imperial Navy can bring in troops and land them there, they will also bring supplies."

All Ikeda was buying by this move, Tadashi was certain, was time. San Roque was a good three miles north of the fighting line. Tadashi and Hanaya were headed for the command center of the western forces, which occupied a former civilian radio station on the southern outskirts of Garapan.

While crossing the southern foothills west of Charan Danshi, Tadashi and Hanaya parted company with Dr. Ikeda's group. Tadashi and Hanaya struck out on their own,

With no road to follow, their path was cross-country, which meant maneuvering around rocky outcroppings of coral or limestone, through or around ravines and up and down hills.

"Tadashi," Hanaya said. "I heard you tell that old lady last night that the Americans would not kill and rape like we've been told. Was that just to make her feel less afraid?"

"No," Tadashi said. "That was *honto*. True. Of course, there are likely some bad ones who might do that. You were in Nanking when I was. You know we have the same type of men in our Army—men without pity or remorse. But I am convinced that most Americans would not kill out of hand. Especially civilians. Their male children are taught to respect women. I learned that from my boyhood friends."

"What was it like?" Hanaya asked after a brief silence. "Living in America."

Tadashi paused in thought.

"Remarkable," he finally said. "When we'd fly by airplane from Washington, DC, where my father was posted, to visit my mother's parents in Nebraska, which is in the Midwest, we would fly over fields that stretched as far as the eye could see across nearly perfectly flat land. But it was the cities that truly amazed me. Washington was a beautiful city, but New York impressed me most. They have a building a thousand feet tall. The Empire State Building. My mother took me to an observation deck on the 102nd floor, and I felt like my head was in the clouds while a cool breeze passed under my wings."

"I thought that was propaganda," Hanaya said.

"No," Tadashi said. "And millions of Americans own cars, and in cities everyone has electricity in their homes."

Hanaya felt nervous because of Tadashi's enthusiasm over an enemy land.

"You may talk to me like this, and you will be safe, Tadashi-san," Hanaya said. "But be careful because it sounds as though you love America more than Japan. If anyone from the *Kempeitai* hears you, it could be disastrous. They might arrest you."

Tadashi laughed. He knew the secret military police, including a small detachment on Saipan, were always on the lookout for suspected traitors or defeatists, but with friends in high places, including General Saito, Admiral Nagumo, and Prince Kaya Tsunenori, Tadashi held them more in contempt than fear.

"I loved being in America," Tadashi admitted. "But I would not live there permanently. I love Japan. But my heart is here on Saipan, where I came of age. This is my home, so I am not afraid to die here."

It was an hour before dusk when Tadashi and Hanaya reached the radio station south of Garapan; a grouping of five structures including one low concrete building with a tall metal antenna standing close by and a recently built wooden barracks for staff and accompanying security forces.

This is all well and good, Tadashi thought. *But this headquarters is less than half a mile from the American positions.*

Inside, the two men reported to Fifth Special Base Force Rear Admiral Tsujimura Takahisa, who had taken over command from Major Rikuto Sadamachi after that officer had assumed command of the 136th Regiment, following the fall of Colonel Ogawa.

As soon as they entered the building, both men sensed an atmosphere of despair. Takahisa greeted the two men. He had been apprised by Nagumo of their arrival and their mission.

"I sense something terrible has happened, sir," Tadashi said after the admiral returned his salute.

Takahisa nodded and handed Tadashi a slip of paper.

"That message was sent out from General Saito to Imperial Headquarters in Tokyo early today," he said.

Tadashi read. "We are menaced by brazenly low flying planes and the enemy blasts us from all sides with fierce naval and artillery cross fire. As a result, even if we remove units from the front line and send them to the rear, their fighting strength is cut down every day. The men's spirits remain high. Can we expect assistance any time soon?"

Tadashi finished, then looked at Takahisa, who handed him a second note.

"This reply came in a short time ago," he said.

Tadashi read, "No further attempts to reinforce the Saipan garrison are possible. You must defeat the enemy with the forces you have at hand, or die gloriously if need be."

Tokyo had abandoned them.

CHAPTER 18

Tadashi spent most of Monday morning leaning over a rickety table in the old radio station, poring over a map provided by Rear Admiral Takahisa. The map outlined the defensive line that stretched from the coast just south of Garapan westward across the foothills of Mount Tapochau and extending to Hashigoru on the island's east coast.

"I have about seven thousand men manning the line," Takahisa said. "There are another two thousand men entrenched in Garapan."

Tadashi nodded. Not content to take Takahisa's word for it, and knowing he'd be questioned by Saito, after he finished studying the map Tadashi personally walked much of the line.

All along his trek, Tadashi saw stout pillboxes of reinforced concrete and cleverly hidden machine gun positions. Most heartening, the men were in high spirits and ready to slaughter the American enemy. All seemed ready.

Satisfied that all that could be readied was readied, including a supply of food, water, and ammunition, Tadashi and Hanaya departed.

———————

The jeep barreled into camp at almost straight-up noon and came to a halt so suddenly that the man seated in the rear was almost thrown out. Recovering, he stood up and yelled, "Mail call! Dog Company, mail call."

If he had said the war is over, he could not have gotten a more joyous response. Men came running, mobbing the jeep in anticipation of their first mail call since leaving Hawaii on May 30. The mail clerk began to shout out names.

"Parker! Aikens! Masters! Bonfield!" he called and on and on across the company's three platoons.

Some names received no answer. They were either on a hospital ship or lying in the ever-expanding cemetery. Others took their mail.

"Lt. Stehman!" the clerk called. Gunny Nicholson took two letters addressed to the dead officer.

Pete intercepted some too.

"Simpson!" the clerk hollered.

"I'll take it," Pete said, reaching for three envelopes neatly addressed to the dead boy from Cape May, New Jersey. He did the same when the names of Morales and Potter were called. These he would turn over unopened to Stacey who would forward them to the chaplain. Not all the nonresponders were dead. Pete also took mail addressed to Baumgartner, Miller, Bucket, and Reb Marshall. These would also end up with the Holy Joe to forward on.

"Aldrich!" the clerk bellowed, and the Professor was handed four envelopes.

246   LARRY ALEXANDER

"You're a fuckin' show-off," Pete said as Aldrich waved the envelopes in his face and grinned.

Pete's name was called out three times. Two of the letters were from Aggie and the third from his mother.

The men were now engaged in sitting on the ground, letters in hand, absorbing the news from home. Pete sought out Aldrich, who was perched on the edge of his foxhole, and sat down beside him. The Professor had already opened one of his letters.

"My mother is a rather prolific letter writer," he explained. "Although one is from my uncle. He was a Marine in the First World War."

Pete took his Ka-Bar and slit open his envelopes. He scanned over his mother's letter first and grunted.

"What's up?" Aldrich asked.

"It's from my mother," he said. "Evidently my father has not been doing so well. He was in the hospital recently, and they say his liver function is down and they're concerned. The way he drinks, that doesn't surprise me."

"I'm sorry to hear that," Aldrich said. "Maybe sorrier than you are."

"He wasn't too bad at the start, but as he grew older and the drinking got worse, he terrorized Charlie and me," Pete said, then added, "and Mom too, I guess."

"How about you?" Pete asked, veering the conversation elsewhere. "Is your mom still badgering you to give up on being a shrink and become a fisherman?"

"You just do that to get my goat, don't you?" Aldrich said. "And yes, she is."

Pete laughed and slit open the first of Aggie's two letters.

"My darling Pete," she opened. "As always, I am praying this letter finds you safe." After updating him on family news, she poured out her heart.

"I'm missing you so much and dream of the day you come home to me. I often feel so lonely, but then I think about how it will feel when I'm back in your arms again. I know you might think I am getting sort of mushy, and maybe I am. But now that we're married, and we've joined our lives together, being with you is all I can think about. I pray this war ends soon so we can spend the rest of our lives together."

Finishing, he folded up the letter, slipped it back into the envelope, and tucked it into a pocket. Then he turned to the second letter. After her "My darling Pete" opening, Aggie spent two paragraphs scolding him for not writing often.

"It is so lonely here without you, and your letters are comforting," she wrote. "I'm pretty sure, from the newspapers, that your division is on Saipan and that you are probably in the thick of the horrible fighting, which is all the more reason that I need to hear from you. I'm terrified for you.

"But I don't want to dwell on that too long. Your mom, my mom, and me have planted another victory garden, this one is in the park. The city council has made the land available for those wanting to plant crops. It's coming along very nicely. We already have harvested peas, carrots, and lettuce, and our sweet corn is close to being ready as well. I feel like the Farmer in the Dell. Also, I used some of my ration points to buy some fabric that I will use to make a dress I plan to wear when you come home. It's blue, your favorite color. My mom will help me because, let's face it, she's a much better seamstress than me.

"Your mother and mine have been most helpful and kind and they try very hard to keep me occupied so I don't just sit around and dwell about how much I miss you. Sometimes they take me to a movie.

"But I miss you, especially at night when you are not lying

beside me, your hand gently on me to comfort and reassure me. Please take care and write me as soon as you can. Forever, Aggie."

Pete reread the letter and could hear Aggie's voice doing the narration.

"How is she doing?" Aldrich asked. "Is she still working at the Navy Yard?"

"For now," Pete replied. "But she's living back with her folks, so she has no rent to pay. Plus, since I'm overseas, she gets a twenty-dollars-a-week allotment as my wife."

"So she's an Allotment Annie, huh?" Aldrich teased. "Fleecing servicemen."

"Hardly," Pete said. "But even with the allotment, she's making almost as much a month as I am." Pete pointed to the letters Aldrich was holding. "So what's the news on the Aldrich family front?"

"My brother Todd had a close shave, Mom says," Aldrich replied, holding up one particular note. "Todd's two years older than me, and he's doing convoy duty in the North Atlantic on a destroyer escort named the USS *Donnell*. Last month his ship took a torpedo from a Nazi U-boat, and a few guys were killed and wounded. Todd's okay, and they managed to save the ship, so as of this letter he's marooned in England until his ship is repaired or he's reassigned."

"I'm glad to hear he's okay," Pete replied. "And being marooned in England can't be all that bad, unless all the women there look like Churchill. You have a brother at Pearl Harbor too, right?"

"Simon," Aldrich said. "He's the oldest. He works in the Navy's ordnance section. Mike and Sadie are both younger and still in high school, although Mike says he wants to join the Corps after graduation. I have mixed feelings about that. So does Mom, according to her letters."

"Maybe you'll luck out, and the war will be over by then," Pete said.

"My father is busier than ever," Aldrich continued. "I told you he's a master boatbuilder, and right now he's doing a lot of work across the bay near Annapolis building whaleboats for the Coast Guard. He's a supervisor. And, of course, he's still doing work for the boatmen in town."

Pete briefly went back to scanning Aggie's letter.

"Have you given any more thought to coming to Rock Hall after the war and taking up the life of a waterman?" Aldrich mused.

"Thanks, Professor, but I really don't know enough about that way of life, and I'm not sure I could do it," he replied.

"What if we both dive into it?" Aldrich asked. "A partnership. You and me. We start with *Jacks or Better* and build up our business, then maybe get another boat. Maybe two more, and hire a couple of crewmen and start a seafood company. I told you there's good money in seafood for two young guys like us who aren't afraid of hard work."

"Whoa," Pete said. "What about your dream of being a psychologist and opening your own office?"

"Well, you could be my full-time client," Aldrich replied, and they both laughed. "Seriously, there's nothing that says that after a few years, when we've built up the business and you've become an experienced waterman, that I can't go back and take the courses I need on a part-time basis. You'd make my mom awfully happy if I stayed in Rock Hall, and you'd make a good living for yourself and Aggie and any little Talbots who come along."

Pete thought long and hard.

"You make it sound pretty good," he said to his friend. "I'll think on it and ask Aggie for her thoughts." Pete pointed a finger at Aldrich. "If I say yes, you have to promise not to get yourself killed."

"I'll do my best," Aldrich replied.

Aldrich slit open the last of the four envelopes he'd received, and as he withdrew two folded sheets of paper, an object slipped out and fell to the ground. Aldrich did not see it fall, so Pete retrieved it. The object was a photograph of a young woman dressed in her Sunday best posed by a large boat, a very warm smile on her face.

"You lyin' sonofabitch," Pete scolded. "You told me you don't have a girlfriend back home."

"I don't," Aldrich replied without looking up from the letter.

Pete held out the photo and said, "Then this is a helluva strange-looking boy."

"Gimme that," Aldrich said and snatched the photo away. "She's just the daughter of a family friend," Aldrich said peevishly. "Her dad is a shell fisherman in Rock Hall. Bill Bachman's also a customer of my dad's."

"That's very nice," Pete said sarcastically. "But that doesn't explain the babe and the cheesecake picture."

Aldrich heaved an exasperated sigh.

"Her name is Veronica Bachman," he said. "We went through high school together, and in our senior year I took her to the prom. Then I went off to Towson, and she went to work for her dad as his bookkeeper. Her mom asked my mom if Veronica could write to me, so don't read between the lines."

"Looking at that shape and that smile on her face, I don't have to read between the lines," Pete said. "Strange. It's almost as if you're keeping Veronica at bay the way I did with Aggie."

"Idiot," Aldrich groused, and Pete chuckled.

Then Pete saw Gunny Nicholson and Lt. Shimada approach,

so he folded up his letter and tucked it away for later. The two squatted down beside Pete and Aldrich.

"I just got the word," Shimada said. "The Fourth Marines and the Army are in position, and tomorrow we start the push on the enemy line." Pete noticed that Shimada never used the words Jap or Nip. "Artillery will commence at 0500. The Navy will join in. The goal is to blast a hole through the enemy line and get into Garapan as quickly as possible. It's not going to be a cakewalk. They seem to have a strong defensive line stretched out in front of us and they will not give up Garapan without a fight. Jump-off will be at 0800, and we will have armor support."

Shimada gave the men an encouraging wink. Then he and Nicholson struck out to brief the rest of the platoon. Pete thought about the upcoming action.

"I gotta write a letter," he said, walking back to his foxhole and fishing out a letter he'd begun but hadn't finished.

That's where Pete was twenty minutes later when Nicholson stopped by.

"How'd you like to get off the line for about two hours?" he asked.

"Next to being at home with Aggie, I can't think of anything I'd like better," Pete replied. "Are we goin' AWOL?"

"Nothing so dramatic," Nicholson replied. "Captain Stacey asked me to go to the rear and see if we can shake loose some replacements. I thought maybe you'd like to go along and visit your rebel buddy. He's still in the main hospital at Charan Kanoa, but they're taking him out tomorrow."

Pete jumped to his feet, stashed the half-written letter into his haversack, and told Aldrich he's in charge of the squad until his return.

"Give Reb my best," Aldrich called as Pete and Nicholson headed for the company CP.

A jeep was assigned to take Nicholson to the rear, so he and Pete piled in.

"Why did Stacey give you this job?" Pete asked as the jeep rolled south on the coastal road.

"It goes back to when I was a floating bellhop on the battleship *California*," he said. "General Smith was on the same ship, although he wasn't a general then. We Marines were just a small detachment amid two thousand swabbies, so we got to know each other very well."

During the trip, the jeep rolled past the Red Beaches where Pete's battalion had landed on D-Day. Tanks and trucks were parked everywhere, and Pete saw amtracs sitting on the sand while gyrenes, including Black Marines, the first he'd ever seen, stacked up crates labeled "K-rations" or ".30-caliber rounds" or "hand grenades" for shipment to the front.

Charan Kanoa had been taken early in the battle. Like its larger sibling, Garapan, it had suffered greatly. Many structures, wood and concrete alike, were reduced to rubble. Streets had been cleared of debris to allow military traffic to roll through. On the outskirts of the town, Pete saw the twisted skeletal remains of the large sugarcane refinery that once processed and prepared for shipment the island's cash crop.

Passing Lake Susupe, which lay just inland from the landing beach labeled "Blue 2," was a large compound covering over fifty acres. Hundreds of people milled about inside the compound.

"That's Stockade Number One," the jeep driver said. "It's also called Camp Susupe. It's for civilians. They've been coming in by the dozens and even by the hundreds."

The jeep drew to a halt in front of several large wall tents. A Red Cross flag hung out in front, and medical personnel, nurses, and orderlies scampered about.

"Be back here in thirty minutes," Nicholson said. "We'll pick you up on the return."

After about ten minutes of asking around, Pete found the tent where Reb Marshall and about fifty other wounded men lay on a row of canvas cots. As he approached his friend, Pete saw an orderly marking a bedside chart.

"So I'm on the line defending the Republic, and you're here being waited on by a pretty nurse," Pete joked.

The bedpan commando gave a bemused smile and left.

"That's Ricky," Reb said. "He's okay." He stuck out a hand. "It's good to see ya, Hardball."

Pete clutched the hand and shook it.

"How come you're not aboard a hospital ship?" Pete asked.

"Navy done ran outta them," he replied. "Hell, they even outfitted a coupla transports as temporary hospitals and then filled them as well. Anyway, a hospital ship is due back tomorrow and Ah'm slated to go on board, then it'll be mah turn to see Hawaii. You had yours." He paused, then said, "So how's the squad?"

Pete filled him in on the squad, assuring him everyone was all right although they knew a massive push north was about to begin. Reb nodded in response.

"Yawl take care of 'em," he said. "Especially that McCready kid. He may be a Yankee but he saved this rebel boy's ass. Bastard Jap woulda run raht over me."

They spoke for a few more minutes, then Pete said goodbye.

"I gotta get back on time or Nicholson will make me walk back to the line," he said.

They shook hands.

"Sorry to be runnin' out on ya, but I'll be back as soon as I can," Reb said.

"I know you will," Pete replied.

"I never thought I'd say this to a Yankee, but I feel privileged to serve with you." Reb smiled.

Choked with emotion, Pete's only reply was a nod of agreement.

The jeep picked Pete up on schedule, and as they journeyed back, Pete said, "So where are our replacements?"

Nicholson snorted.

"General Smith said he was glad to see me, but he has no replacements to send us at present," Nicholson said. "But part of a replacement battalion is scheduled to land in two days, and he'll see what he can do."

———

Tadashi and Hanaya arrived back at Saito's headquarters under Tapochau's white cliffs late in the afternoon. Instantly they realized choosing this location to establish a headquarters had not been wise. American naval vessels cruising along Saipan's eastern coast frequently shelled the area, including the cave complex. The area around the cave had been churned up by exploding shells and twenty-one bodies, including three of General Saito's personal aides, lay piled in a shell crater where they'd been dragged.

As Tadashi relayed the findings of his mission, Saito marked those troop dispositions and defenses on his map.

"That is all good," Saito said. "We have a strong line holding across the island. But I fear we must leave this location."

"I have been to the cave at Makunsha," Tadashi said. "All is ready there and it is a good place. When do you propose to move your base there?"

"We will leave here after midnight," Saito said.

Saito handed a note to Tadashi.

"This directive came a few hours ago from His Imperial Majesty," Saito said.

With due reverence, Tadashi read the emperor's words.

"Although the frontline officers are fighting splendidly, if Saipan is lost, air raids on Tokyo will take place often. Therefore, you absolutely must hold Saipan."

As Tadashi finished reading it, Saito handed him a second note.

"This addition is from the prime minister," he said.

"Destroy the enemy gallantly and persistently and thus alleviate the anxiety of our emperor," Tojo had directed.

"Your response, sir?" Tadashi asked.

Colonel Suzuki said, "We told the prime minister to be assured that Saipan's defenders are prepared to sacrifice all on behalf of the Empire. With ten thousand deaths, we hope to requite the Imperial favor."

Saito looked morose.

"I hesitate moving so far to the north," he said. "It will be my last headquarters because there is nowhere else for us to go."

————

Back on the line, Pete sat alone in his foxhole, knees raised up to form a steady place to lay his mess plate, which now served as a writing desk. He apologized to Aggie for not being a better letter writer, saying, "You know what a pain in the butt I can be about that. But I will try to do better." Then he laid out Aldrich's proposal to her.

"It sounds goofy, I know, but I gotta do something, not just for me, but for you and our future," he wrote. "I sure as hell am not going back to the ferry job, and this sounds interesting and maybe profitable. You know me. I am not afraid to work.

But even more than the work and the money, this sounds especially great to me because it would keep me and the Professor together. I can't explain it, darling, but Steve has become like a brother to me. Not a replacement for Charlie. That could never happen. But more like another brother. Does that make sense?"

He folded the letter, placed it in an envelope he'd addressed earlier, and slipped it into his haversack, where it would remain until he could mail it.

Whenever that may be.

CHAPTER 19

The push on Garapan got off to a promising start as artillery and naval gunfire "walked" back and forth across the Japanese defensive positions. Three battalions of Marines began their sweep north astride the coastal highway while three more battalions took on the difficult task of slogging up and down the steep ridges and ravines of Tapochau's jagged slope.

But the openness and less hostile terrain of the coastal region didn't mean that the going was any easier. The absence of steep ridges was offset by stiffer artillery, mortar, and machine gun fire. As the advance got underway, Second Battalion, including Pete and the men of Dog Company, positioned on the right flank, were blasted not only from Japanese guns in front of them, but by enemy positions on Tapochau's wooded foothills to the east.

Straddling what had been the coastal highway but was now marked Middle Road on most maps, the battalion had pushed forward about a quarter mile and into the southernmost edge of Garapan itself. There the heavy volume of enemy fire slamming

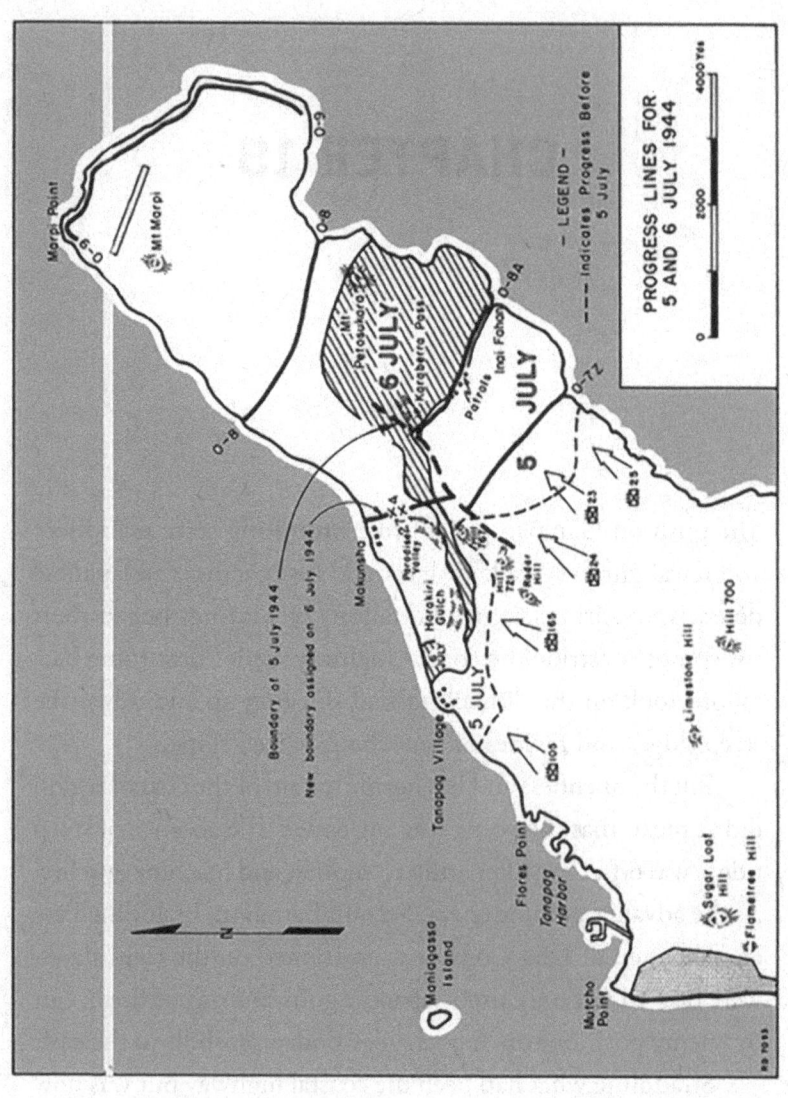

into its front and right flank jarred it to a halt. With forward movement stalled, Dog Company found itself in a bare, rutted field about two hundred yards from several low structures, one of them concrete. Alongside this latter building was what looked like wreckage of a tall radio antenna.

"Looks uninhabited," Captain Stacey mumbled as he scanned his glasses along the opposing line. "That worries me."

He was talking to Lt. Shimada. Accompanying Shimada was Second Platoon's squad leaders, Pete of Second Squad, Terry Malloy of First Squad, and Third Squad's Marty Manson, still limping from a grazing wound to his right thigh five days ago.

"Battalion HQ wants that radio station secured," Stacey said. "The thought is that it might've served as a Jap command center. Then again, it might have been just an old radio station that played Bing Crosby records. We don't know."

"The platoon's gonna be damned near naked out there in that field if there are Japs in there," said Nicholson who was beside Stacey. "How about if I get Pogey Bait's stovepipes to drop their 60s on those buildings and maybe some smokies in the field to cover the advance?"

"Do it," Stacey nodded.

With his glasses, Stacey panned right where a thickly weeded meadow ended at a forest-covered slope.

Shimada read his mind.

"If the enemy is in there, we could be outflanked real fast," he said.

"The 1/6 is supposed to be on our flank," Stacey said.

"Are they?" Shimada asked.

"Damned if I know," Stacey replied. "Just keep one eye peeled on that flank." He looked at Shimada. "It's almost 1100 hours. Go at noon. Take along a bazooka team and that flame-thrower, Crosley. I'll have Yaz set up his MG section to give you a base of fire to advance or, if need be, pull back under." Stacey turned to face Shimada. "I don't like this, Shim, I don't like it at all. But I have my orders. If you so much as smell a trap, beat it back here fast. We'll provide covering fire."

Returning to the squad, Pete assembled Honeybun and Aldrich and explained what was up. Both men looked highly skeptical.

"We're going out there?" Aldrich asked. "Maybe you and I won't have to worry about that fishing business after all."

———

From the cave, amid the cliffs of Mount Tapochau now being lit by the dawn sun, Tadashi heard the rumble of American artillery. The barrage, which he could tell included heavy naval guns, was more intense than anything he had heard since the invasion began thirteen days ago. To him, that meant only one thing: the Americans were starting their offensive aimed at sweeping away all Japanese defenses and at last seizing Saipan.

"It begins," he told Hanaya, as the two men stood at the cave mouth.

Saito hesitated falling back as far as Makunsha.

"To go there is to admit defeat," he said. "I still have faith in Imperial Headquarters. They know how important Saipan is to the defense of *Yamato* itself."

Before dismantling the radio for transit, a report came in about a surprise attack on the American-held Aslito airfield south of Charan Kanoa, launched by Captain Mosahito Sasaki, the highest-ranking officer still surviving in the southern sector of Saipan.

"The battalion will carry out an attack tonight, causing confusion at the airfield," read the radio orders to his troops. "Casualties will remain in their present positions and defend

Mount Nafutan. Those who cannot participate in combat will commit suicide. We will carry the maximum number of weapons and supplies left."

At fifteen minutes before noon, "Pogey Bait" Baker's crews began dropping 60mm rounds on the collection of buildings. Pillars of smoke began rising into the sky as debris from shattered wood and masonry was hurled in all directions. Flames began licking the already ruined wooden buildings.

"Second Platoon, follow me," Lt. Shimada yelled, and thirty-three men left their foxholes to press forward.

A little more than halfway across the field, rifles and machine guns hidden among the buildings erupted. Two men fell, one of them Fred Mosely, the loader for the bazooka team. The other was "Farmer" Goodman, who took two bullets in his upper left thigh. Howling in pain, he fell to the ground. The rest of the platoon dropped as well, hugging the earth for cover and returning fire in the general direction of their invisible enemies.

Shimada started slinking forward on his belly and the platoon began to follow, only to be stopped by a machine gun so close that one round swept away the lieutenant's Bulova watch without breaking the skin.

Pete, who was next to Shimada, saw a frightening sight; men coming from the woods and into the field of tall weeds to the platoon's right.

"Sir," Pete yelled above the fire and pointed. "They're on our flank."

Shimada took one look.

"Goddammit," he cursed. "Fall back!" he bellowed. "Fall back!"

Firing at both the Japanese in the buildings as well as those coming through the weeds, the platoon began its retreat.

Terrified of being abandoned, Goodman cried, "Don't leave me!"

Honeybun dropped to a knee beside him.

"Not a chance," he said, and hoisted Goodman over his shoulder. Grunting over his load, Honeybun rose and began running back. A trio of Japanese soldiers in the field opened fire on them. Scrap Iron Dembrowski placed himself between the Japanese and his fellow fire team members and cut loose with a sustained burst of his Tommy gun. Two of the enemy dropped like flour sacks, causing the remaining man to reassess his commitment to die for the emperor and flee.

For the platoon, the dash back to the trees became a footrace with the Marines, pitted against the enemy troops coming at them from the right. Members of the platoon fired in the general direction of the enemy and kept running. As the Japanese attempted to isolate the Marines, they also opened themselves up to the men of Dog Company as well as Yastremski's machine guns. With a clear field of fire to avoid his comrades, Yaz's two-gun section began to chatter.

Except for Mosley and one man from Third Squad, who took a bullet through the head, the rest made it back safely under covering fire. About a dozen Japanese fell as they tried to swamp the Americans. Three Marines were wounded, including Goodman and two men, one each from First and Third Squads. Several Japanese converged around the body of Mosely and began plunging bayonets into him. Mosely began to scream as the enemy jabbed and jabbed.

"Jesus Christ," his bazookaman, Carl McComsey, shouted. "Fred's still alive."

Frantically, Marines began firing at the men torturing their comrade, and while two fell, the rest finished their grisly work. They then pulled back with their retreating comrades, who'd given up the chase.

Pete sagged back into his foxhole, gasping for breath after the headlong withdrawal. Then he went in search of Honeybun, who had lugged Goodman back. A corpsman, not Ryan Magruder, was working on Farmer by attaching a plasma bottle to Goodman's upturned rifle.

"Where's Magruder, Frank?" Pete asked Pharmacist Mate First Class Frank Lamont, who had joined the company just before D-Day.

"Battalion aid getting an ankle bandage," he said. "He sprained an ankle this morning."

"How's Farmer?" Pete asked.

"Lost a lot of blood, but I've got him stabilized," Lamont said.

"I'm real sorry, Sarge," Goodman croaked weakly.

"You didn't ask to get hit, so don't worry and just focus on gettin' well," Pete said.

Looking around at the men of Second Platoon, who were trying to regain their composure, Pete got boiling mad and went in search of Lt. Shimada. He found the Japanese American officer in conference with Captain Stacey. Nicholson was there as well.

"I hope the stupid bastard back at HQ is happy," Pete said, practically frothing at the mouth. "Goddamn brass hats."

"At ease, Sergeant," Stacey barked. "I let it go because you needed to blow off steam, but that's enough. You're a good Marine, Hardball, but goddamn it, sometimes you need to remember your station and rank."

Pete calmed down, at least physically. Inside, he still seethed.

"I'm sorry, Skipper," he said.

"Okay," Stacey said. "The operation was a fuckup, but at

least we know where the Japs are, and we know the 1/6 is not
yet on our flank, so we'll have to guard that as well. Dig in. I
think we're stuck here until our supporting forces on the right
show up." He turned to Shimada.

"Shim," he said. "Do you think they'll try to infiltrate us
tonight."

The Nisei shrugged, "Not necessarily. They don't have to.
They're strongly entrenched. We have to go to them."

"We're knocking them back on their heels," Stacey said.
"But they're still dangerous. Last night about five hundred of
them attacked the airfield south of Charan Kanoa. They blew
up a couple of planes. The Marines finally wiped them out and
killed their commander."

The gathering dismissed and Pete returned to the squad,
plopping down beside Aldrich, who was leaning against a felled
tree trunk.

Pete made his way toward Fire Team Two. Honeybun and
the wounded Goodman were both gone. Only Scrap Iron Dembrowski was present. He explained that Lamont regretfully told
them there was no stretcher available at present to carry Goodman back to battalion aid. So Honeybun and the corpsman
picked up Goodman in a two-man carry and lugged him back.

Pete sat down beside Dembrowski.

"I saw what you did out there today, putting yourself between your buddies and giving them cover," he said. "It took
guts. Thank you."

"That's why they pay me fifty-four scooties a month," Dembrowski replied sourly.

Pete thought for a moment.

"When you first joined the squad, I took a look at your
service record, and I thought you'd be a dope-off at best, and
at worst a loose cannon looking out just for yourself," Pete

said. "In short, your two-oh-one looked pretty much like mine when I first arrived in the squad, and I decided I'd have to ride your ass."

Dembrowski looked at Pete and cracked a smile.

"I'm sorry about that incident at the farm the other day, when I wanted to shoot that prisoner," Scrap Iron said. "I was out of line."

Pete nodded.

"I'm gonna request you get corporal stripes," Pete said.

Pete headed back for his foxhole.

Since the move to Makunsha would take at least forty-eight hours, a small cave along the route was selected as a short-term HQ.

Without needing instructions, the staff busily went about converting the cave into a headquarters for military operations, setting up the radio and making the place as comfortable as possible given the primitive surroundings. With the furnishings left behind, the situation map was spread out on a canvas sheet laid upon the ground, with the senior officers seated or kneeling around it. While they studied the map by lantern light, a series of reports from the frontline units began clicking off on the radio. The operator scribbled frantically to keep up, handing messages to Tadashi as soon as each was finished. Tadashi read them through as he approached the map. Kneeling next to Saito, Tadashi pointed at the map.

"Thankfully the American assault has been brought to a stop," he announced, allowing some optimism into his voice. "Our best success has been in the center where the Army division, because of the terrain and our hardened defenses, has been delayed. This has caused dissention in the enemy forces and the Marine general in overall command has relieved the Army general for not being aggressive enough. This could work to our advantage."

"How so?" Saito asked.

"The longer we cause the center units to delay, the more anger we create," Tadashi said. "And the more anger we create, the more it sows interservice distrust, which will likely slow the enemy drive. There is already animosity in the way Marine, Navy, and Army commanders view each other." He almost said, "Just like our Army and Navy leaders," but he caught himself in time. "So any way we can disrupt their cooperation and protect our thinly held lines benefits us and buys us time."

"I see what you are saying," Saito said. "If they break our line, they can get behind us and cut us off from the northern part of the island, where most of our remaining food and am-munition is stored." He paused in thought. Then he glanced at Nagumo and at his chief of staff, Colonel Suzuki. "Do we need to create another, stronger line farther north where the island is narrower so we can defend in depth?"

"Yes," Nagumo said glumly. "But understand, if that line gets broken, there can be no other. There would not be time or room. This would be a last stand line."

That knowledge weighed on everyone.

"If Tokyo cannot provide us with support, perhaps we can get reinforcements from elsewhere," Tadashi said.

Saito looked at his young aide-de-camp.

"Two days ago, Colonel Kiyochi Ogata, who is in command on Tinian, tried to send help," he said. "He dispatched eleven barges filled with troops, but the Americans intercepted them. One was sunk, but thank the gods, the rest got back with min-imal damage and loss."

"What about some of the other commands?" Tadashi

asked. "Can we not get assistance from Guam, or Rota, or Yap? Surely someone besides us must see the importance of holding Saipan."

"I have tried them all, but no one has been able to help," Saito replied.

"The only positive response we've gotten is from the Navy," Nagumo said with a hint of pride. "They have offered to bring in supplies by submarine and land at Marpi Point."

"Can they also land troops?" Tadashi asked.

"Some perhaps," he replied. "Imperial class submarines have adequate space."

"It's not just that," Suzuki said. "It is the heavy bombardments from their large fleet that are so deadly and slowly chip away our strength. It's as if they have an unlimited supply of ammunition. Meanwhile, our artillery and mortar attacks on them grow weaker and less effective every day."

"Let us not forget their air superiority, my dear Colonel Suzuki," Saito said. "Since the defeat of the Imperial Fleet last week, we've been constantly attacked by enemy fighters." He turned to Tadashi.

"Is there any place where we can establish another line of defense?"

Looking at the map, Tadashi said, "Your headquarters will be here." He stabbed the map just above Makunsha. "It's about three-quarters of a mile northeast of the village and west of Karaberra Pass. I have confirmed that the new headquarters is ready and waiting."

On a notepad, Tadashi drew a rough line with a pencil and marked coordinates, then handed it to Saito who turned the sketch over to Suzuki.

"Under your orders, we have directed the Fifth Construction Unit and the Seventh Independent Engineers to prepare gun emplacements and pillboxes as quickly as possible. Unfortunately, their numbers are greatly depleted."

Saito digested what he had been told. Then he leaned toward Nagumo for a one-on-one chat. As they conferred, Tadashi prayed to the *kamisama* of war, "Allow us time to prepare to receive our enemies and proudly stand against them in our defense of the Land of the Gods."

As darkness began to settle, Pete checked in with the squad. Dembrowski was still hot under the collar and sat cleaning his Thompson while muttering about asshole officers. Pete found Honeybun perusing one of the three letters he'd received at mail call.

"Anything new on the home front?" Pete asked as he sat down beside Honeybun.

"Mom says all is fine there, but they're a little concerned because my older brother Rick hasn't written recently," he said. "I'm not too worried. Rick's like you; he hates writing. He was with the Seventh Army in Italy. He came in as a replacement after North Africa. But he did serve under Patton until Old Blood and Guts got his ass in a sling for slapping soldiers in a hospital for havin' combat fatigue. Rick's still in the Seventh Army, and so far as I know they haven't landed in France. At least not yet." He put the letter back in the envelope. "I'm the third of four Hullihens. I also have two sisters, Theresa and Emily."

Pete watched as Honeybun opened another envelope and slipped a photo out of it. The picture was of a fair-haired girl sporting a broad smile and a ponytail.

"I didn't know you have a girl back home," Pete observed.

"You didn't ask," Honeybun replied. "Her name's Margaret,"

he said. "We met in high school. These days she's volunteering at a Red Cross blood bank."

"Do you think your folks know where you're at?" Pete asked.

"I'm certain they do," he replied. "Dad's a geography teacher and he follows news on the radio and in the papers and plots out on maps wherever his kids are in the world, be it Tarawa, Saipan, or Italy."

Pete nodded and moved on. At the end of the squad line, he came across Yaz Yastremski with Pfc. Mark Reilly, his loader since the death of "Wheels" Wealand on the Gumdrop. Pete knelt beside him.

"I want to thank you, Yaz, for supporting us out there," he said. "We were fucked until you put this coffee grinder to work."

"It was payback for what happened to Wheels," Yaz replied. "He and I been together since boot camp. He was married. Her name's Faye. They got hitched right after boot camp. I was best man at his wedding. Now I gotta write her a letter. The captain offered, but I said no. It has to come from me."

Pete understood and thought for a moment about Ted Giovanni.

———

Less than two miles from Dog Company's position, Captain Kisaburo Hanaya was seated on the ground at the cave's mouth, staring up at the darkening sky. Around him, those soldiers of the guard detachment not doing sentry duty around the camp's perimeter were settling in under their shelter halves. Hanaya, Tadashi, and other staff officers spread blanket rolls on the ground inside the cramped cave. Tadashi sat beside his friend.

"I sense that your mind and heart are back in Ishikari Prefecture," he said.

"Yes," Hanaya nodded. "I was thinking about the karma that led me from my home to this faraway island where I am most likely going to die."

"The fight is not over yet," Tadashi said, not sure if he believed it. "Besides, death is little more than a rebirth. You know that, don't you?"

"Yes," Hanaya answered. "That would be most satisfactory. I'd be joining my older brother, Miyoko. I don't talk about it much, but Miyoko died heroically with the rest of his comrades on Tarawa while fighting the American Marine Second Division." He paused, then pointed. "The Second Division is out there now. Maybe one of them killed Miyoko." He looked at his friend. "What about you? This is your home. Wouldn't your spirit be more at ease staying here?"

"I don't know that we have a choice," Tadashi said. "My father always believed, and still does, that the spirit resides where it is most at ease. My mother's Christian religion says my spirit, and my father's when he dies, will go to this grand place called heaven, where her spirit is waiting for us, and we will all be reunited."

"Those are two very different beliefs," Hanaya said. "Which do you hope is true? Yasukuni? Or this Christian heaven?"

Tadashi had thought about this many times, especially of late. He'd love to see his mother again. He recalled as a sixteen-year-old youth, sitting on the stones surrounding the koi pond in front of their house in Garapan, watching large gold and white fish glide gracefully through the water. Peggy Driscoll, her heart problem becoming more and more concerning, sat down beside her son.

———

"Tashy, you know how your father always says that life is as fragile as a cherry blossom?" she said. "That's so true. We will not always be together in this world. But I want you to know that even after I am gone, I will be with you. Maybe I will appear to you as a spirit or maybe a gentle breeze that strokes your cheek, but it will be me. And also know that someday, you, me, and your father will again reunite in a new world and a life beyond death."

He did not understand, but vowed to honor it and therefore also honor his mother.

Peggy removed a gold chain from around her neck, a golden cross dangling from it. He knew of this necklace, having seen it many times. She handed it to him.

"Wear this, my darling Tashy," she said. "And always think of me."

That was in 1930, two years before he left for Japan for the Army preparatory school. Fourteen years later, he still didn't understand his mother's belief in the afterlife. To him, heaven was a dwelling place of the gods, not a place of reunion with one's ancestors.

"I don't know which I want to be true, Kisaburo-san," Tadashi answered, feeling the gold cross on the chain beneath his shirt. "I don't know."

CHAPTER 20

The radio station was taken the next morning. Overnight the 1/6 had moved up on Dog Company's right flank, so this time Stacey's men went forward in force. Preceded by a barrage of artillery and Pogey Bait's mortars, the company surged across the two hundred yards of open field. They were met by only sporadic return fire that wounded one man in Third Platoon. The company swarmed among the buildings, firing at the remaining snipers, and tossing grenades into windows. Eight Japanese holdouts were killed. The rest had evidently pulled back earlier.

Pete burst into the partially collapsed concrete building along with his squad. He found himself in what had plainly been a headquarters of some sort, evidenced by smashed radio equipment on a table and littering the floor, upturned chairs and tables, and strewn papers scattered randomly about like snow.

"Check this paper shit," Pete ordered the squad. "See if anything looks important."

Pete saw Lt. Shimada enter the room.

"This was a CP," he told the officer. "A couple of these dead guys look like high-ranking mucky-mucks."

Both of the "mucky-muck" bodies lay close to a broken table. Shimada knelt by the two and examined their uniforms.

"This guy's a major," Shimada said. "That other one is wearing a Navy uniform. I don't know naval insignia, but he has considerable rank."

"Nagumo?" Aldrich asked.

"Too short," Shimada said as he accepted some papers from Aldrich that the Professor had found by an upturned table.

He rifled through some of the papers in his hand, then stopped and tapped one with a forefinger. "I think he's this guy. Rear Admiral Takahisa. Based on these messages, that other fellow is probably Major Sadamachi."

Honeybun walked over from the radio carrying a large piece of paper.

"I found this map, Skipper," he said.

Shimada took it and scanned it quickly.

"This is some sort of defensive line," he said. "But it's not the line we're up against. This one is a good four miles north of here. Good find, Honeybun. I need to get these to Captain Stacey." He turned to Perkins and said, "Get these to the skipper."

The squad spent a few more minutes sifting through the wreckage.

"Here are some orders from Saito to Sadamachi requesting troop strength," Shimada said. "It was issued under Saito's name by a Major Tadashi Tanimura."

"Who do you think he is?" Pete inquired.

Shimada shrugged.

"Since he's signing orders, I assume he must be a top aide to Saito, maybe his aide-de-camp," Shimada said.

Gunny Nicholson popped his head into the room.

"Heads-up," he barked. "Battalion's moving out. Hubba-hubba."

After leaving the radio station, Dog Company took up a position on the right of the battalion. Second Squad was shaken out to form a skirmish line. The eight men left advanced forward cautiously about ten paces apart. As he walked, Pete could see a large farmhouse that stood along Middle Road, which pointed like a dagger into the heart of Garapan itself. The farmhouse, along with a smaller outbuilding, was surrounded by a low stone wall. Beyond the wall and to the rear was a sugarcane field, now heavily pockmarked, that extended about a hundred yards to a large barn. Beyond the barn, the field ended and became a meadow of tangled weeds and vines.

Just ahead, a dried streambed cut across the field over which the battalion was advancing. Pete had no sooner noticed this when the gully erupted in machine gun fire. The squad hit the ground as a series of 7.7mm rounds from at least two machine guns dug in along the stream bank chewed up the earth. Pete and Second Squad returned fire as the rest of Dog Company crawled forward on their bellies. The next thing Pete knew, Captain Stacey was by his side along with Miguel Ramos, Stacey's radioman.

"What do we have?" he asked as the firing let up.

"Machine gun in the streambed ahead, and another one about forty paces to the right," Pete said. "Probably a third one further on."

"Heavy or light?" Stacey asked.

"Heavy," Pete replied. "My guess is Type 92s."

Stacey nodded.

"They're not belt fed," he said, thinking out loud. "They're fed by a thirty-round metal strip, so there's a brief gap as strips are changed. Kill the loader and you slow down the gunner."

"If you can get close enough," Pete said. "Which we're not. Besides, they may not be alone in that streambed. A whole battalion could be lying low there."

"Only one way to find out," Stacey said. He removed a small notepad from a pocket and scribbled some numbers, then turned to Ramos who carried the handheld SCR-536 walkie-talkie.

"Get Pogey Bait on the horn and give him these coordinates." He handed over the sheet of paper. "Have him drop a couple of rounds for range."

Moments later, two 60mm rounds burst in front of the streambed.

"Add twenty and fire for effect," Stacey barked to Ramos who relayed the change.

The six shells that followed straddled both banks of the streambed with two dropping in among the defenders. Doggedly, the Japanese heavy machine guns resumed their fire, which was lethal despite the mortar rounds bursting around them. The fire from one gun killed a man in First Squad, a replacement who came up the other day with McCready, Simpson, and Perkins.

One of Pogey Bait's 60s landed a shell directly on the machine guns nearest the road, touching off ammunition and creating a small fireworks show.

About ten minutes of hammering was all the enemy could take. They abandoned the streambed and fled north toward the farmhouse and sugarcane field, most making for a long, low earthen ridge that cut across the cane field about 250 yards away. Instantly, Stacey had Dog Company rush the vacated streambed, even as more enemy machine gun and rifle fire came at them from the house and the stone wall. The company dropped into the streambed and put their heads down as bullets puckered the ground in front of them.

The banks of the stream were shallow, ranging twenty-four

to thirty-six inches in depth. It wasn't much, but at least it was something. A few feet to Pete's right, a heavily damaged Japanese machine gun was perched across the corpse of its former gunner. Beheaded by shrapnel, he lay sprawled on his back. His dead loader was two feet away, his body also torn by flying steel.

The sight of such grisly death sickened young McCready, who unfortunately dove into the streambed at the former gun position and was confronted with the severed head. To be rid of the grisly object, Honeybun grabbed the head where the helmet strap was attached to the steel pot and hurled it out in the direction of the farmhouse.

"Take care of your buddy!" he shouted. "He's wounded."

Watching this play out, Pete knew that Honeybun was probably just as repelled as McCready, yet to ease the boy's fears, he did something that a year ago he would never have dreamed of doing. The same was true for a lot of Marines who were doing bizarre acts of violence, some bordering on depravity, which they would never have done had it not been for their exposure to the brutality of war. Pete had seen men searching the mouths of enemy dead, knives in hand, to dig out gold teeth. Some also cut off fingers to retrieve gold rings. One Marine in Third Platoon was making a necklace of gold teeth for his girlfriend back home.

We've become immune to violence, Pete thought. *We're like animals.*

The roar of engines coming up from behind drew Pete's attention, and he saw a squad of Sherman tanks rolling along Middle Road. The road was on Dog Company's immediate left with Easy Company deployed just beyond. Pete watched the Shermans clanking along the dirt highway, their turrets sweeping left to right and back again, their 75mm guns probing for trouble. They soon found it. The lead tank had just crossed a small stone bridge that spanned the streambed and had advanced about ten yards when it exploded. Smoke billowed from the armored beast as it continued forward a few more feet before rolling down a slight embankment and coming to a stop in the meadow some twenty paces in front of First Squad. None of the crew climbed out.

The shell came from a gun cleverly hidden at the farmhouse where the stone wall met the road. The enemy gun crew had a clear line of sight along the road to the bridge, making it a perfect bottleneck for approaching vehicles. The next round hit a half-track. Carrying a 75mm howitzer on its bed, it had been following the Sherman across the bridge when the shell smashed into its cabin, killing the driver and a loader. Four survivors leaped from the back of the twenty-thousand-pound vehicle as it came to rest, blocking the bridge.

The gun that claimed this second victim proved to be a 75mm piece dug in a bit further up the road and on the opposite side.

Unable to cross the bridge, the rest of the armored platoon fanned out into the fields on both sides of the bridge. The firing was now joined by other enemy guns, possibly 75mm field pieces concealed on both sides of the road. At least three of these guns were placed on a long, low mound just beyond the farm and cane field. This seemingly harmless ridge of dirt was now recognized as a defensive trench with artillery revetments.

Three Shermans and four self-propelled guns took up position behind Dog Company and the streambed. The tanks seemed to have targeted the farm while the self-propelled guns poured their fire on the man-made ridge. The 37mm enemy gun at the farmhouse that had knocked out the first American tank took a direct hit. Yet it was the larger caliber guns, firing from earth and wood revetments that inflicted the most damage.

A second Sherman took a direct hit, killing three of its crew. A second self-propelled gun was also struck. The driver and two of the five-man gun crew took refuge in the streambed as flames devoured the vehicle.

The artillery duel lasted close to thirty minutes, with the Americans seemingly taking the brunt of the punishment. Through it all, Dog Company stayed low in the gully and returned what was probably ineffective small arms fire.

The Japanese suddenly ceased firing. The Americans did likewise, and an eerie calm settled over the tortured fields.

Then came a dreadful sound—the crunching of many feet clomping unseen through the sugarcane. Now a mass of figures emerged from the cane onto the meadow leading to the streambed; charging forward with shouts of "Banzai" and "Death to Marines."

With the enemy 250 yards and closing steadily, the horrified Americans saw that it wasn't just Japanese soldiers making this attack.

"Oh my God," Pete heard Lt. Shimada say as he peered through his binoculars. "They're driving civilians ahead of them."

Pete risked a look. His face paled as he saw men and women of various ages, as well as children, being prodded forward by the tips of gleaming bayonets held by men behind them. Many were screaming in terror. Children were crying.

Beyond Shimada, Pete could see Captain Stacey's face register the sick decision he was about to make. Hardening his resolve, Stacey shouted, "Fire on my command!" He swallowed hard. "Fire!"

The first volley tore through the civilians, who dropped in windrows.

"Keep firing," Shimada yelled. "Keep firing! Pour it on!" He had tears in his eyes.

Pete crawled along the squad line encouraging his men. Each reacted differently to the slaughter of innocents. With every burst he fired, Dembrowski muttered, "Goddamn it. Goddamn it." Veterans of Tarawa like Rosie and Aldrich did what they needed to do, although the Professor had tears in his eyes as he emptied his Garand, reloaded, and continued firing. When Pete got to Perkins, he found the boy huddled below the stream bank, clutching his unfired rifle, and crying like a baby. He shook Perkins roughly.

"Stop it, damn it, stop," he barked. "Snap to, Private. Fire your goddamn rifle. If the Japs overrun us, we're done for. Get to it."

He grabbed Perkins by the collar, raising him up, then shoved him into firing position.

"Squeeze that trigger, man," Pete said. "Do it."

With tears flowing freely, Perkins fired off a round. Then he fired another and kept going.

Pete took up a position next to Perkins and began to fire, hating every round he squeezed off.

By the time the wave had crossed half of the 250-yard distance, civilian bodies littered the meadow. Now it was just the soldiers, some firing rifles from the hip as they advanced, others running with bayonets thrust toward their hated enemy.

Angered at having to slaughter unarmed noncombatants, the Marine fire seemed to have a new intensity. Enemy soldiers fell rapidly with very few reaching the streambed. One Japanese soldier crashed into Rosie, knocking aside his BAR, and trying to maneuver his bayonet around to impale the American. Having felt the agony of a bayonet on Tarawa, Rosie fought like a wildcat. As they scrabbled together, Rosie finally freed his Ka-Bar and plunged it into his attacker's chest.

Another landed in the stream gully next to McCready. He

stabbed at the boy with his bayonet, but McCready managed to knock the rifle away with his own weapon, then fired a round from his Springfield at point-blank range directly into the angry face.

After what seemed like hours, but was less than thirty minutes, the attack was spent and the bloodied remnants of the Japanese assault filtered back to their jump-off position. The field in front of Dog Company was dotted by bodies, probably a two-to-one ratio between civilians and soldiers, Pete guessed.

Among that field of dead, Pete saw an elderly man struggle to his feet. Obviously injured, the man hobbled toward the road, possibly seeking a place of safety. A rifle shot from the Japanese lines rang out and the old man fell. He did not rise again.

Pete rose to his knees and called out, "Have you no compassion?"

Another rifle shot rang.

"Idiot," Pete cursed himself and sat back down.

———

At the mouth of the jungle cave command post, Tadashi listened to the sound of heavy fighting to the west that wafted inland on the warm breeze. He knew the gunfire came from the direction of Garapan.

Sadly, he recalled walking into town with his mother. Peggy Driscoll loved Garapan. Its simplicity and sense of community reminded her of growing up in her small hometown outside of Omaha. Even though she was a Caucasian, the locals would greet her on the street with a smile. Her son was also embraced by the local population, Japanese and Chamorro, and was accepted by his playmates even though he was a head higher than the tallest among them.

He remembered Mr. Izumi's store where he could get

American candy such as Hershey bars, imported regularly from American controlled Guam.

His favorite location was the town's theater. Small and primitive by American standards, he enjoyed going there to see movies. Like chocolate candy, while in America he'd acquired a taste for movies, in particular cowboy films starring Tom Mix. He swooned over films like *The Trouble Shooter*, *Riders of the Purple Sage*, and *The Arizona Wildcat* and had seen each one several times. In fact, one Christmas his parents gave him a set of Hubley cap pistols, complete with double holsters and topped off with a cowboy hat.

Returning to the cave, Tadashi saw the radio operator hand a sheet of paper to Col. Suzuki, whose face darkened as he read.

"This message has just arrived from Imperial Headquarters," he announced. "Thirteen days ago, on June 15, more than sixty heavy American bombers struck Imperial Iron and Steel Works at Yawata. It is said these are gigantic aircraft, larger than anything we've ever seen. Headquarters believes they were based in China."

The homelands were no longer impervious to air raids. If Saipan fell, Tadashi feared that these monster bombers could fly the sixteen hundred miles to Japan and back. The effects and damage caused on Japan by these planes could be devastating. Tokyo alone contained twenty-two square miles of paper houses, many set just inches apart. Should the Americans resort to firebombs, the city would be burned to cinders.

Tadashi remembered the words of the late Admiral Isoroku Yamamoto about America's potential to create a juggernaut against which Japan would be powerless to stop and would be crushed under. Even as a boy, Tadashi knew this as well. In his travels with his father, he saw steel mills and factories and shipyards. He wished the Imperial command had done the same before they leaped so recklessly into war. He recalled how his father felt about men who so cavalierly made war without studying their enemy's strength.

"A frog in a well knows nothing of the sea," he said.

Because of your brashness and foolhardiness, we are all doomed to die, he thought.

————

As the sun swept past noontime and began slipping toward the western horizon, the stench from the corpse-studded battlefield in front of Dog Company was overpowering. Both sides seemed content to sit back and lick their wounds. Stacey had lost five men killed and eleven wounded, nine of whom required evacuation. The armored boys had lost even more, including two Shermans knocked out, two M3 half-tracks KO'd, and a third damaged to the point where it could only serve as a stationary battery. At least a dozen men of the armored regiment had died.

Based on what could be seen, the Japanese had been hurt worse. Pete guessed a hundred Japanese lay dead on that field. At least a hundred civilians, and probably more, lay bloating under the hot sun as well.

What Pete found so irritating was that the battalion's attack, which had started off so well that morning, was bogged down. It wasn't just on the coastal plain. Up in the high ground among the caves and ridges, the attack was also stalled, hampered both by stiff enemy resistance and by their own casualties.

Pete settled back and made himself as comfortable as possible amid the heat and stench. Reaching into his haversack, he pulled out the letter to Aggie he had started yesterday. As he did, Gunny Nicholson came crawling up, careful to stay low.

"How are your boys doing?" he asked.

"Fine," Pete replied. "You know what pisses me off so much

is that Garapan, our objective since we landed on this shithole island, is just a mile ahead and here we sit on our asses, stuck."

Nicholson chuckled and said, "War is hell." Then he moved on.

Pete got back to letter writing but quickly stalled, not knowing what to say that would get past the censors. As he struggled, the Professor crawled by.

"How's Perkins?" he asked.

"Rattled," Pete replied. "But he'll get over it."

He saw the letter and pencil in Pete's hand and said, "I'll let you get back to your letter."

"Why?" Pete said. "I want to tell her I'm okay and where I'm at. But most of what I'd like to say will get penciled out by the goddamn censors so what's the use?" Angrily, he started to put the letter away. "Damn it. We'd be together if not for this damned war."

"Remember it was 'this damned war' that brought you two together," the Professor said. "Otherwise, you'd still be hemming and hawing over your feelings for her. You're a very lucky guy and you know it."

Pete was silent as his mind conjured up an image of Aggie and her infectious smile. He took the letter back up again and said, "This won't write itself."

"Send her my best wishes and tell her she deserves a medal for marrying an oaf like you," Aldrich laughed, then left.

CHAPTER 21

"Aggie, my love," the letter began. Yes, he liked that opening.

Pete had written this letter to Aggie last evening before the sun disappeared, taking its light with it. Now the light was returning, giving him an opportunity to look the letter over to make sure it reflected his feelings and related any news he could.

This missive was the third incarnation of the letter, the first two having been ripped up in disgust because they didn't say what he had wanted to say.

He opened with hope that she was doing well and not worrying too much about him.

"I can't tell you where I am," he said, "but if you read the papers, you can probably guess. But rest assured that I am fine, and I intend to stay that way. You have given me your love, the strongest motive for coming home safe and sound."

Without going into detail, which would probably be blacked out, he mentioned that both Bucket Harnish and Reb Marshall had been wounded. He didn't tell her the extent of the wounds.

He told her that Steve Aldrich was fine and that he had told Pete to send his greetings to her. He also wrote more about Aldrich's suggestion that they go into business together after the war.

"It sounds interesting, and I might do it," he told her. "I just hope you don't mind if we live on the eastern shore of the Chesapeake Bay."

Then he came to the conclusion.

"I love you with all that's in me," he had written. "That kind of stuff is not easy for me to say but I want you to know it. And when I get home, and note I said 'when' and not 'if,' I don't ever plan to be apart from you like this again. Please stay well, and I will do the same. Your loving husband, Pete."

He stared at the letter for a few minutes, digesting the words before placing it in the already addressed envelope, sealing it, and writing "Free" in the upper right corner. He also scribbled "MMRLH" for Marine Mail, Rush Like Hell. Then he placed it back in his haversack until he could pass it along.

On Middle Road just to the west of Dog Company, boys from the armor support unit using the dark of night for cover, affixed chains to the ruined half-track blocking the bridge. A Sherman was brought up and the other ends of the chains attached. With a little coaxing, the thirty-ton Sherman dragged the wrecked vehicle backward off the bridge, clearing the way once the American attack was renewed. Surprisingly, the Japanese did not challenge the bridge clearing task.

It was 0600 and Pete moved along the streambed to check in with the squad. Most were having breakfast, spooning down chopped ham and scrambled eggs from the tins inside their K-ration breakfast boxes. At the far right of the squad line, he found the Professor and Rosie, both finishing off their biscuits and chatting as if it were afternoon teatime.

"So what's the topic for today, ladies?" Pete jabbed as he settled down beside them.

"We were remembering the old squad," Rosie said. "The guys we landed with on Tarawa."

"We were saying how it's just us three and Honeybun who are left," Aldrich added.

Pete nodded soberly.

"Then there was Ray Colby," Aldrich said. "Radio Ray."

"He wasn't in our squad," Pete corrected. "He was with headquarters. Stacey's radioman."

"I know," Aldrich replied. "But he hung out with us so much he might as well have been. I got to know him pretty well. He once told me his pop had a radio sales and repair business back in Indiana, I think it was, so Ray learned from an expert. Given enough time, he probably could've picked up radio reception on your canteen."

"He went Asiatic on us," Rosie remembered.

Aldrich looked at Pete.

"You found him, didn't you?" he asked.

Pete nodded.

"Curled up in a ball at the seawall," Pete said. "Even your battlefield psychoanalysis couldn't have helped him, Professor. I just hope the poor bastard snaps out of it and doesn't spend the rest of his life in a padded room."

"I think about Mickey Mouse," Rosie said in reference to Miklos Kuzaka. "Run through by a samurai sword. God. Makes that bayonet in the shoulder I received seem like I just cut myself shaving. At least it didn't kill him."

"I wonder about us," Aldrich mused. "We four who are left. Were we just lucky? But then again, this war is far from over."

"I don't know about you guys," Pete said, "but the day before I got my leg loaded up with Jap shrapnel, I wouldn't have given you a plug nickel for my chances. I heard that voice in my head loud and clear telling me I wasn't gonna leave that goddamned island. My clothes had been hit by bullets several times. My Garand took a hit intended for me and got busted all to hell. Shrapnel tore my camo cover on my helmet. My entrenching tool and LMO pack each got hit once and a Jap bayonet creased my forearm. Because of all that, I thought my number had to be coming up. Gunny spotted the symptoms and talked me back."

"I talked about this with Honeybun last night, and do you know what he's thinking?" Aldrich said. "He's convinced that the four of us who are left will come through the rest of the war okay because, he said, the odds against all sixteen of us being killed or wounded are implausible. And it makes sense."

"I hope you and Honeybun are right," Pete said.

"We four," Aldrich mused. "We happy four. We band of brothers." He looked at his friends and grinned. "My apologies to Shakespeare."

Pete was about to head back along the streambed to his position on the squad's left when he saw Gunny Nicholson approaching.

"Just got the word from the skipper," he announced. "The battalion is getting ready to assault the Japs. Second Platoon's objective will be that farmhouse across the way. First and Third Platoons will attack across that cane field behind the farm, using that big barn out there as a marker with First to the left and Third to the right of it. They will assault the Nip earthworks beyond. The artillery, including the self-propelled pieces, will pound the Jap positions for half an hour prior to our jump-off, and the mortars will precede our attack. The tanks will advance with us, rolling across the streambed once we've cleared it. Jump-off time depends on the artillery, but you'll get the signal when we're ready to go."

It had been an uneasy night in the command cave. The sound of heavy fighting from the direction of Garapan during the day faded, but the drumming of artillery in the hills to the immediate south meant the Americans were exerting extreme pressure on Japanese forces already stretched thin.

Tadashi had difficulty sleeping, and at around 0300 he gave up. Sitting up on his blanket, he noticed that he was not the only one for whom sleep was elusive. Admiral Nagumo was sitting erect on his blanket and bedding, leaning against the cave wall and apparently lost in thought.

"Are you all right, sir?" he gently inquired.

"I am fine, Tadashi-san," he replied, a faint smile on his lips. "I am just indulging in an old man's fancy of reliving past glories. Especially since the prospect of future glories is, shall we say, uncertain."

Tadashi rose, went to a chest along one cave wall, and opened it. From there he withdrew the admiral's last bottle of Suntory whisky and poured some into a tin cup. The admiral reached for the cup gratefully.

"*Domo*, my young samurai," he said. Then he went on.

"Did you know I have been to America?"

"No, I did not," Tadashi said.

"Briefly," Nagumo said. "In 1925 and 1926, I was part of a mission sent to study naval tactics, strategies, and equipment in Europe and the United States. I must admit that, at the time, I was not impressed by the American Navy as a worthy foe. They allowed postwar isolationism to rot their military. But considering what I have seen in this war, the Americans adapted quickly."

He paused to allow Tadashi to savor the irony.

"When I led *Kido Butai* from Hitokappu Bay to strike at

Pearl Harbor, what a glorious time that was. I had six powerful aircraft carriers, two battleships plus cruisers, destroyers, submarines, and over four hundred aircraft. There wasn't a force in the world that could take us on and survive. Now, except for *Zuikaku*, all those aircraft carriers are gone, as are most of the brave men who flew their planes. Afterward, I considered committing seppuku, but my staff dissuaded me. Now here I am, facing my own karma. Still, I feel I have done my duty to the emperor, and if I am to die here, then it shall be so."

Nagumo turned to face Tadashi.

"Try to get some rest," Nagumo said. "There are hard times coming."

Stalled and rebuffed several times over the last five days, the Marines' latest effort to take Garapan began around midmorning as batteries of 105s began roaring, sending a stream of shells whistling overhead.

The Japanese weren't about to sit still and get hammered. Their artillery farther to the rear and out of sight across the gently rising field began targeting the Marine forces still in the cover of the streambed.

This thirty-minute duel of howitzers felt like an eternity. Then whistles blew and all along the battalion line men rose up as the attack rolled forward. The heavy guns to the rear ceased their deep-throated roar as mortars took up the cause, dropping rounds ahead of the advancing gyrenes.

Despite the pounding coming down on their heads, machine guns inside the Japanese entrenchments and the stone farmhouse came alive. A few advancing Marines were struck and fell while many others dove to the ground for cover and began returning fire. For the men of First and Third Platoons, this had a disturbing effect as they had been advancing among the corpses slain the day before. Moving forward involved crawling on their bellies over torn bodies as enemy rounds kicked up dirt geysers all around them. The dead jerked repeatedly under the impact of bullets.

In spite of the number of hits the stone farmhouse and its surrounding walls had sustained, heavy fire continued to come from that location. Captain Stacey grabbed his radio from Ramos and quickly ordered Pogey Bait to concentrate his fire on the house and farmyard. The mortarmen complied, and a flurry of shells began blasting the house and farmyard. Soon the entire southern portion of the dwelling was reduced to rubble as the wall and part of the roof collapsed. That caused enemy fire to slacken somewhat but it never entirely ceased. Still, Dog Company crept forward, using what cover nature provided.

As the Marines pushed ahead, five Sherman tanks clanked across the streambed and rolled toward the cane field. Two of the behemoths veered off in support of the attack on the farm and the other three toward the distant trench line. Japanese gunners soon began targeting the armor and shells started bursting around them. The racket of the battle ratcheted up as artillery dueled with artillery, tanks blasted away at anti-tank guns, and small arms fire from men of both sides swept the field.

Finally, Second Platoon had closed to within thirty yards of the wall, and Lt. Shimada ordered a straight on assault. This was carried out using a leapfrog technique as First and Third Squads provided covering fire while Pete's Second Squad advanced ten paces. Then they hit the ground and provided cover to allow the other two squads to advance through them to a point ten paces out in front.

Using this technique, the platoon quickly reached the wall,

although calling it a wall any longer was misleading. It was more a collection of bullet-scarred and shattered rocks strewn with dead Japanese, some partially buried by the rubble. Enemy soldiers began to pour out of the still standing northern portion of the house and hurried rearward, firing their weapons as they fled. The Marines brought down several of the fugitives whose bodies began to litter the farmyard.

His adrenaline pumping, Pete crossed over the wall and dashed to a wooden two-wheeled cart that lay abandoned in the farmyard. With one wheel shattered, the cart sat partially on the ground and Pete sought cover there. He realized the folly of this when he came under fire from a sniper still inside the house, his slugs piercing the brittle wood. Pete sent several bursts from his Thompson at the nearest window without success as the sniper's slugs continued to chew through the aging wooden cart. Each round got closer. Pete realized the sniper was changing positions among the rubble of the house in order to get a clearer shot. Realizing the man would soon be on his open flank, Pete rose slightly to fire again. He saw the enemy soldier who had taken up position at the corner of the house nearest to himself. In that split second, Pete knew he had made an error, and expected a bullet as his reward when a burst from a Tommy gun cut loose from behind him, tearing into the sniper. Looking behind him, Pete saw Scrap Iron Dembrowski give him a thumbs-up salute.

By now, the rest of Second Battalion had begun entering the farmyard. Pete got Honeybun's attention and pointing said, "Clear the house!"

Honeybun directed his team through a doorway and into what remained of the dwelling. Inside, men poked through three rooms littered with household furnishings. Lying among the debris was half a dozen dead Japanese soldiers. There was no sign of any civilians. Moments later, Honeybun signaled the "OK" sign to Pete.

The Japanese who had occupied the farm had fled, some heading toward the entrenchment about forty yards to the rear while the others pulled back no further than the stone wall that bordered the northern portion of the farmyard. Pete raced from the meager protection of the cart and into the house. Both of his fire teams were there now as well, and he took stock of the squad's situation. Except for Rosie, all his men were accounted for, but not without injury. The Professor sat on a chair he had righted and was trying to stem blood flowing from his right arm.

"How bad is it?" Pete asked with grave concern.

"I don't think it's too bad," Aldrich replied. "Rosie went for a corpsman."

As if on cue, Rosie and Magruder rushed into the house, enemy bullets following close behind.

"A guy could get hurt this close to the Japs," Magruder said as he knelt on the floor by his patient. "Stopped one, eh?"

"I had to give you something to do," Aldrich retorted. "Didn't want you getting lazy."

Most of Second Squad was at the northern wall of the house. In the farmyard, First and Third Squads were securely dug in. The enemy was about twenty yards ahead taking cover behind the stone wall. The bloated carcasses of three cows lay between the two forces, legs stiffened in death. Behind the house, the outbuilding, possibly containing the landowner's meager farm implements, continued to burn fiercely, sending billows of black smoke eastward across the cane field.

Having finished patching up Aldrich, Magruder began replacing his supplies in his Unit 2 bag.

"How is he?" Pete asked.

"Bullet entered the fleshy part of his upper arm," Magruder said. "Passed clean through."

Doc shouldered his bag and prepared to leave.

"I wouldn't leave until you're called," Pete advised. "The Nips know a corpsman's value and I'm sure they'd love to shoot you in the leg in order to bag a few Marines who'd be running out to save your ass."

"You've got a charmed group here, Hardball," Magruder said as he righted a chair and sat down. "Except for a scratch to the Professor, you guys were lucky. Too bad I can't say the same for First and Third Squads. First Squad lost two men wounded and Third Squad had one killed and one wounded. Third Platoon took the biggest hit out there in that sugarcane. They lost their commander."

"Lt. Manly got hit?" he asked.

Magruder nodded.

"Machine gun ripped him up badly," Doc said. "He was in agony and begging for my help, so I gave him two syrettes of morphine."

Pete understood. One for pain, two for eternity.

"Charlie was a good leader," Pete reflected. "Got a battlefield promotion on Tarawa." He paused again. "At least the squad still has Billy Trent. Trent's also a Tarawa vet, so the squad will be fine. But damn! Charlie Manly."

A burst of increased firing from the Japanese erupted from the stone wall as Lt. Shimada dashed through the doorway, followed by Sergeants Terry Malloy of First Squad and Marty Manson of Third. Close behind came Platoon Sergeant Biff Hodges and Carl McComsey with his bazooka accompanied by his new loader, a young Marine who Pete did not recognize.

"This is straight from the skipper," Shimada said. "There is a strong enemy line about forty yards beyond this house. It's heavily manned and includes at least three bunkers containing machine guns and maybe small field pieces. The good news is that the trench does not apparently stretch the whole way to the road, meaning all we have before us is those guys at the stone wall. Artillery is going to plaster the enemy trench line starting in about fifteen minutes. We'll also have some air cover when we attack. Corsairs, so that means Marines will be flying them." That brought smiles to the faces of everyone. "Our job is to clear that wall of its defenders and attempt to flank the enemy's position. It's hoped that our appearance on their flank, coupled with renewed attacks by First and Third Platoons, will force the enemy to retreat."

"What about our left flank?" Pete asked. "Won't we be open to attack ourselves? There's a house up ahead across the road that could take us under enfilading fire."

"Easy Company across the road from us will be attacking as well," Shimada said. "The enemy at that house will be too busy keeping them away. As for that wall in front of us, Carl will use his stovepipe to punch a hole or two."

"We could also burn our way through, Skipper," Pete said. "We're close enough that Crosley's Zippo would be damned effective."

Shimada nodded.

"I'll send him in," Shimada replied.

He was about to leave when Dubbs called out, "Sir, we got some civilians here!"

Dubbs had stumbled across a trapdoor in the floor at the southwest corner of the house. With Perkins and McCready standing by with rifles aimed, Dubbs opened it cautiously. He found himself staring down into the terrified eyes of a man, a woman, and several children, all of them trembling in fear. The children began to cry.

Standing over the doorway, Shimada urged the family out. "*Ikou*," he said, motioning. "*Shimpai shinaide. Korosanai.*"

Shimada had to coax the civilians several times before the family began to move. Shimada indicated that the man come up first. The woman helped the children go up next, two small boys and a girl, all still crying from fear. The woman emerged last, an infant strapped to her back by blankets. Once out of the cellar, the family still looked terrified. Pete could imagine what they'd been told by the Japanese military authorities about how the Americans would treat them. He'd be afraid, too, in their place.

Clearly, the family was perplexed by Lt. Shimada.

"*Anata wa Amerika-jin desu ka?*" the man asked nervously.

"*Hai,*" Shimada confirmed. "*Amerika-jin desu.*"

Looking at his men, Shimada said, "He asked if I was an American."

Pete picked up a doll that was laying amid the rubble and handed it to the girl. Still frightened, she snatched it away and hugged it tightly.

Shimada took the family aside and told them to stay hidden, that the Americans would soon move on to the north in pursuit of the Japanese soldiers. The man and his wife, obviously relieved, thanked him profusely.

"You handled that well, Lieutenant," Aldrich complimented. "These poor souls surely are getting the crappy end of the stick."

"The man said his family has operated this farm for a hundred years," Shimada told the men. "They have damned little left."

"What was he telling you?" Pete inquired. "Did he think we were going to murder him and his family?"

Shimada nodded and said, "Bastards! Makes me ashamed of my heritage."

"You don't need to feel that way, sir," Aldrich said. "You were raised in a country that allows personal freedom and individuality. They've never known that."

Shimada smiled.

"I've heard about your passion for psychoanalysis, Professor," he said. "But you're right. Their lives are regimented. In their culture, the nail that sticks up gets hammered down." He looked at his watch. "I understand their fear. Back home in Hawaii, we had a large contingent of Japanese, and we were accepted. But when I was in San Diego and San Francisco, it was a different world. I was a 'damned Jap' and spit at. I wasn't even allowed into some restaurants despite being a Marine officer."

Then he said, "Enough gab. Let's get ready. The curtain rises in five minutes."

At the command cave there was turmoil. It began when an American fighter plane spotted their location and made a strafing run on the camp. A junior aide to Nagumo was killed and three men were wounded. Five more men were killed shortly after that when the place was hit by a mortar barrage. Mortars meant the enemy was close, and Tadashi urged Saito to relocate to the cave at Makunsha.

"Getting there could take two days, sir," Tadashi said. "But I feel we need to do it and do it quickly."

Saito knew Tadashi was correct, but he was growing tired at constantly having to fall back.

"The Americans have chased me around this island like a hawk after a field mouse," he said sadly. "I am weary of the chase. Is the new defensive line near Makunsha strong enough to hold the Americans back?"

"I'm told they have worked around the clock."

Saito turned to his radioman.

"Has there been any response yet to my request for help?" he asked.

The message Saito had dispatched made their predicament quite clear.

"Our reserve units, hospital units, equipment maintenance, and supply units are either completely wiped out or reduced to the point where no fighting strength can be expected from them," he had wired. "Food and ammunition are nearly exhausted. Since there is no hope for victory in places where we do not have control of the air, we are also requesting aerial reinforcements. Praying for the good health of the emperor we all cry banzai."

The radioman said there had been no response.

"We need to attack," Colonel Suzuki exclaimed, his voice dripping with anger. "We should die gloriously in battle with a final charge."

"Don't be so eager," Saito said soothingly. "You must not rush death. If we must die, the time will come. But for now, our service to the emperor is not complete."

Suzuki, his blood up, glared at Tadashi.

"I wonder if all of us here share that sentiment," he said through clenched teeth.

Tadashi met Suzuki's glare.

"I am sorry," he said tersely, "but if you are referring to me, I am a Japanese officer first and foremost. Prince Tsunenori did not question my loyalty when he made me his aide-de-camp. Now I serve General Saito and if he mistrusts me, all he needs to do is tell me, and I will immediately commit seppuku."

"Remember your places, both of you," Saito snapped. "This is not the time for a falling out among ourselves. We need to work together to plan our next moves to block the Americans from seizing this island. As for Makunsha, Major Tanimura will alert them we are coming. We will start out after midnight and take advantage of the dark."

Tadashi stepped forward.

"What about Garapan?" Tadashi asked. "Do we defend it?"

"Yes," Saito said. "Tell Admiral Takahisa . . ."

"Excuse me, sir," Tadashi said. "I fear the admiral is dead and his headquarters overrun."

Saito nodded. He had lost so many senior officers he was forgetting who was left.

"Garapan can be held with a small force," Saito said. "Tell Colonel Sumimoto to leave two companies to defend the town and pull the rest back. That will buy us the time we need to solidify our line. Tell all commanders they must chew up the Americans and make them pay in blood for every inch of ground. They are to begin their withdrawals tonight."

———

Right on schedule, American mortars began dropping 60mm and 81mm rounds on the Japanese lines. The ground around the enemy trench was torn by explosions that sent up pillars of dirt and debris. Colored identification panels were stretched out in front of First and Third Platoons just in time to alert a trio of Marine Corsairs. The blue gull-winged fighters nosed over and made diving runs at the trench ahead, their machine guns raking the Japanese line. The mortar barrage went on for about a quarter hour. As it ended, Pete saw First and Third Platoons start their advance.

In the farmyard, Lt. Shimada ordered Second Platoon forward. Inside the house, McComsey's bazooka roared as a rocket zipped across the open space between the house and the wall. It burst against the stones, sending rocks and men flying. The smoke hadn't yet cleared when Dick Crosley put his flamethrower to work. Pete opened up the valve on the tanks to get the lethal diesel fuel mixture flowing and patted Crosley on the helmet. Crosley hosed down the wall left to right as if he was watering a garden. Horrific screams came from behind the flaming wall. The survivors, some with their clothes afire, ran rearward. The men of Second Squad leaped from the farmhouse windows to join the rest of the platoon as they charged ahead.

Not every Japanese soldier at the wall fell back. Some stood their ground and fought. Dubbs shot down two stalwarts and Perkins accounted for one more. To his right, Pete saw a Japanese soldier leap to his feet directly in front of Lt. Shimada. The soldier paused, obviously confused by a man who looked like him dressed in American combat gear. But before he could recover from this shock, Shimada raised his automatic pistol and shot the man in the heart. Shimada kept going.

"Come on, Second Squad!" he cried. "Follow me!"

Shimada led the way forward as the platoon charged across the field and over a score of dead Japanese, some still wrapped in flickering blue-and-orange tongues of fire. Shimada led his men on a flank attack that soon had them taking the Japanese trench under heavy fire. Their efforts were supplemented by McComsey's bazooka, which knocked out a machine gun crew trying to shift their weapon to take on this unexpected threat.

Out in the sprawling cane field beyond the house, the attack by First and Third Platoons was bolstered when the tanks moved up from the streambed. The Shermans rolled forward, crushing down stands of sugarcane as they blasted away at three enemy bunkers. An anti-tank gun in one of the bunkers struck a Sherman, which threw a tread. Unable to move, the crew opted to continue firing its main gun and its machine guns until a second shell hit, persuading the crew to get out. One tanker never emerged.

The fight among the sugarcane lasted close to an hour. Another Sherman rolled up from the rear. Stopping a hundred yards from the trench, it suddenly loosed a stream of fire that engulfed the enemy pillbox. Unearthly screams pierced the air as the three men manning the piece were cremated alive. That taken care of, the tank, dubbed a "Ronson," turned and ground its way toward the second pillbox. A round from the position's 37mm gun glanced off the Ronson's sloped three-and-a-half-inch forward armor. That was the Japanese gun crew's last chance as the flames from the tank engulfed them.

This last horror gave the Japanese sufficient reason to leave. The remaining enemy soldiers leaped from the trench and began falling back as quickly as their legs could carry them. They were chased the whole way by fire from the Marines.

Word came down to dig in, so Dog Company settled into the former enemy trench after clearing it of the dead. With a strong enemy defensive line some 250 yards away, the Japanese slain in the recently captured trench were heaped up in front of the line to serve as human sandbags.

When the battalion jumped off this morning, Pete thought as he settled back, they were just over a mile from the outskirts of Garapan. A day's fighting had advanced them only a third of the distance.

As the afternoon began fading into evening, Platoon Sgt. Biff Hodges made the rounds.

"Keep your guys at fifty percent alert tonight, Hardball," he said. "We're not expecting an attack, but you know the Nips. Tomorrow is shaping up to be a tough day. That Jap line crossing this open field up ahead is longer and stronger than the one we just took."

Pete nodded.

"Thanks for the good news, Biff," he said. "I'll sleep better tonight."

CHAPTER 22

The last day of June was barely an hour old when Tadashi, General Saito, and Colonel Suzuki led the headquarters column away from the small cave. Tadashi knew that further north the jungle would thin out as the elevation increased. The northern part of Saipan consisted of sharp ridges and deep ravines, mostly emanating from Mount Tapochau like octopus tentacles. Yes, Tadashi thought, the uphill climb will be difficult, especially for Nagumo. It was hoped that the procession would cover half of the four-mile trek the first night, but staff members voiced concern about the grueling pace over rugged terrain, especially for Saito and Nagumo. For that reason, ten-minute breaks were made every hour.

As predicted, the dense foliage began to thin noticeably as the column began moving up the slopes of Tapochau's ridges. There the jungle growth was replaced by scrub trees and tangles of vines and grasses. This terrain shift was evidence they were approaching the island's northern plateau, which ended in sheer cliffs, especially to the west and in the north at Marpi Point. The point, Tadashi knew, was also the site of Japan's final airfield on Saipan. Incomplete at the time of the invasion, orders had been given to do whatever work was needed to make it possible to land planes to bring in reinforcements, ammunition, and food. Without these much-needed items, Tadashi knew, the forces on the island could not fight for much longer. After that, there could be no effective resistance. That would leave the garrison with two choices. One was surrender, which Tadashi knew was unthinkable. As for the other, it could well mean a maneuver unseen in this or any other war. *Gyokusai.*

Gyokusai. Shatter the jade. An all-in, do-or-die attack designed to kill as many of the enemy as one can while seeking a glorious death.

Yes, Tadashi thought. *It had come to that.*

Pete Talbot greeted the new day bleary-eyed. Despite being fatigued from yesterday's fight, he found it difficult to sleep. How would that affect his actions today, he wondered. The battalion was going up against that heavy line of Japs and he needed to be sharp. Pete left his foxhole and crawled along the squad line, wary of enemy soldiers in the works ahead.

Arriving at the Professor's foxhole, Pete found Aldrich studying the field ahead.

"How's the arm?" Pete asked.

"I hardly notice it," the Professor replied.

"At least it should get you into the Purple Heart club," Pete joked.

"Possibly," Aldrich snorted. "Compared to Rosie getting bayoneted and Mickey Mouse getting run through by a sword and Bucket getting a leg almost blown off, I feel like I'm cheating. I've had worse wounds from paper cuts."

"It's a club I didn't want to get into myself," Pete said. "I thought I was gonna lose my leg for a while. Scared the shit outta me."

"Seeing a Jap bayonet coming at me was scary as hell, too," Rosie said. "And seeing it stuck in my shoulder was even more horrible."

Turning their attention back to the job ahead, the Professor nodded toward the distant line they'd be attacking later that day.

"What do you think is waiting for us there?" he asked.

"I have no clue," Pete answered. "I heard noises during the night. Sounded like troops moving around. Maybe they were reinforcing the line, gearing up to blow our asses away when we come at them."

"I heard those noises, too," Aldrich said. Then after a moment's thought added, "Do you think maybe they were pulling out?"

"I wouldn't know why," Pete answered. "They can kill a lot of us today when we attack that position. Why give it up?"

"I'm thinking about that map we found the other day," Aldrich said. "I heard Lt. Shimada call it a fallback line. Maybe those guys are on their way to that line."

"I don't know," Pete said. "The Japs on Tarawa didn't pull back and give us anything. We had to pay in blood for every inch we took. Besides, there's Garapan. They're not about to just hand over the largest town on the island without a fight. They can tie us up for weeks with house-to-house fighting."

"You're probably right," Aldrich said. "Call it wishful thinking, but I've been watching that line and have seen no signs of movement."

———

The sun was up when the headquarters column reached the road that linked Saipan's east and west coasts. At Tadashi's direction, the lead scouts located a rocky defile that would provide adequate protection against being spotted by enemy pilots.

"Their planes are like birds of prey looking for mice on the ground," Tadashi remarked as he and Hanaya laid out their blankets on the ground.

"I wish we still had a way to bite them back," his friend replied. "I don't like playing the role of a mouse."

Even though Nagumo had his own Navy aide-de-camp, Tadashi made a point of checking in on the man. He found the admiral not just settled in, but also sound asleep, so Tadashi returned to Saito's side. When told Nagumo was asleep, Saito chuckled.

"For a sailor, he holds up well on a forced march," Saito observed. "Maybe better than me. Perhaps I spent too many years on horseback exercising my backside instead of my feet and legs."

"Sir?" Tadashi inquired.

"Forgive me, Major," Saito said. "Most of my Army career was with the cavalry. I was assigned there right after my graduation from the academy in 1912. Even as recently as five years ago, when I was assigned to the Kwantung Army under General Umezu, I served as his chief of cavalry operations. I rode a fiery horse as black as coal. I called him Yokaze."

"Night Wind," Tadashi said. "A strong name for a strong warrior."

"Unfortunately, he and I never fought together," Saito said sadly. "This fight is my first combat command. Now if you'll pardon an old soldier, I need to get some rest."

———

The word came down. The attack on the Japanese works would commence with a softening-up barrage to start at 0830. The attack would follow at 0900. As the Marines waited, Pete passed along his squad line, making sure everyone had taken advantage of the morning lull to resupply. Ration crates and boxes of ammunition arrived, and the men loaded up on grenades and bandoliers of ammo.

As he checked his line, Pete joined Aldrich.

"Still watching the Japs and hoping they all went away, huh?" Pete said.

"I haven't seen anyone or anything up there," Aldrich said. He chuckled. "Did you ever hear of the Kellogg Briand Pact of 1928? It was a document that banned war as a way of settling problems between nations. Over sixty nations signed it including Germany, Italy, and Japan."

"Where do you pick this shit up?" Pete asked.

"It's called school," Aldrich said. "All you have to do is listen and study."

"My teachers were boring as hell," Pete said. "They had us memorize idiotic poems about crap like seeing anything as lovely as a tree."

"Joyce Kilmer," Aldrich said.

"I hate you," Pete replied and headed for his foxhole, with Aldrich's laughter in his ears.

At 0830 hours, right on schedule, the artillery of the Tenth Marines began pounding the ground ahead. The earth heaved, and billows of smoke drifted across the field. The roar was comforting to those about to cross 250 yards of meadow and flattened sugarcane.

Thirty minutes after they began, the heavy guns went silent. Now the mortars started up, blanketing the field with high explosives and smoke. Whistles blew. Four .30-caliber machine guns placed along the line began laying down a base of fire as Dog Company lifted themselves up and began a cautious advance.

With every step he took, Pete expected to be swept by rifle fire and the chattering of Nambus, but none came. To his left, Pete suspiciously eyed an abandoned car sitting partway on the road, its bullet-riddled carcass giving mute testimony that it had been strafed by a fighter plane. It was just the sort of thing the enemy liked to convert into a machine gun nest. He held his Thompson ready to spray the car at the first sign of life. But it was empty, and Pete moved on past the wreck.

Clearing the ruined cane field, the Marines broke into a run to cover the last hundred yards and get in among the enemy as quickly as possible. However, as they neared the trench, it became apparent that there was no enemy to get among. As Aldrich had suspected, the Japanese had withdrawn in the night. When the Americans occupied the trench, they found only discarded ration packages, empty ammo clips, spent casings, and damaged weapons, including a Nambu machine gun and several Arisaka rifles. Near the position of Pete's squad, there were also half a dozen unburied corpses.

"No souvenir hunting," Pete told his squad. "Five will get you ten; they left some goodies behind."

Taking this position without a fight was not what the top brass had expected, so the men were told to consolidate their gains and await further orders. Part of this delay was because across Middle Road, Easy Company was having a tougher time of it. A machine gun inside the skeletal remains of a bus blocking the highway plus Japanese thoroughly dug in along a side road that branched to the left bogged down the attack.

Watching out ahead, Pete's experience told him the rest of the day would not go as smoothly. In front of Second Platoon were a number of structures on both sides of the dirt highway, the closest being a large badly shot-up L-shaped wooden building. To the platoon's right, an ominous-looking clump of woods confronted First and Third Platoons. Pete moved along the trench to find Aldrich.

"Too bad you're not a gambling man, Professor," Pete told him. "You know how to spot a bluff when you see one. Have you any more feelings about what's in front of us?"

"No," Aldrich said. "But my best guess is that they at least left a skeleton defense behind."

"This time we're on the same page," Pete replied.

He eyed the large building about forty yards ahead, half of which had collapsed into a jumble of wood and corrugated iron roofing.

"When we advance, we'll be hitting that first building end on, which would be good if the goddamned flyboys and cannon cockers hadn't blasted everything and created piles of rubble for the Japs to hide in," Pete observed.

Aldrich nodded his agreement as Lt. Shimada came up.

"The enemy threw us a curveball but don't get too comfy," he said. "We're continuing the push, so get your squad ready."

"Sergeant Aldrich and I were just discussing that building ahead," Pete said.

Shimada nodded and said, "When we go, you and Malloy will take Second and First Squads straight in. Third Squad will attack on an angle to hit the flank and rear."

"What about Third Squad's rear?" Pete said. "They'll practically have their backs facing those woods."

"The rest of the company will keep them occupied," Shimada said. "Get your guys ready. We go on my command."

It took a few minutes for the machine guns to displace from their previous positions and get resituated to cover the next phase of the advance. As soon as Yaz's coffee grinders were set up and loaded, the signal was given, and the men once again left the protection of a trench and advanced on the enemy. This time it would be no cakewalk. In front of Second Platoon, Japanese fire erupted from the ruined building. The Marines hugged the ground for whatever cover could be found and returned fire, their bullets smacking into the piled debris and sending wood chips flying. Not everyone got to cover in time. First Squad's leader Terry Malloy took a round to the gut. Command fell to the next ranking man, Corporal Frank Zulicky.

"Corpsman!" the call rang out.

Bullets dug into the ground all around the Americans from an unknown number of Japanese soldiers cleverly concealed among the detritus. Amid the confusion of the firefight, Pete noticed a gap opening up between First and Second Squads. Pete worked his way to the right until he spotted Zulicky.

"Zoo-Zoo," he shouted amid the din of battle. "Zoo-Zoo! You're drifting right! Close on me!"

Zulicky waved his acknowledgment and veered his squad to their left. The gap began to close.

Progress by the Marines was slow, but was considerably aided when Carl McComsey brought his bazooka to bear. The explosion tore into the rubble, and at least two enemy bodies were flung from the ruins and out onto the ground. Pete slipped a grenade off his belt and called to Dembrowski, who was the man closest to him. Pantomiming the throwing of a grenade, Dembrowski nodded and slipped one off his web belt. On Pete's signal, both men yanked the pins, released the spoons, and hurled the weapons into the rubble, where both burst simultaneously.

Pete shouted, "Let's go!" and led Second Squad in a rush toward the house. Clambering amid the rubble, Pete and his men, now joined by First Squad, flushed out the enemy. Fleeing the structure, many were shot before they could escape. Third Squad joined the fracas pushing in through the rear of the house and bursting into the L-shaped annex. The surviving Japanese fled, leaving about a dozen of their slain comrades behind. Three Marines, including Malloy, had been wounded. Pete's squad suffered no casualties. Pete wondered how long their luck would hold.

While First and Third Platoons continued their fight with the Japanese amid the small, wooded area to the east, Pete used the lull to investigate the building. Amid the scattered furnishings were tables, a few broken chairs, and what appeared to be counters and shelving. Combined with copious amounts of broken glass, emptied tins, and slashed burlap sacks and other wrappings. Aldrich joined Pete.

"Village grocery store," Aldrich observed.

"Yeah," Pete replied. "This poor bastard is out of business. Countryman or not, judging by the debris, it looks like the Japs ate everything that wasn't nailed down."

"Maybe it's because he wasn't Japanese," Aldrich said and pointed to a crucifix hanging on a wall. "This guy was Catholic."

Biff Hodges arrived, and Shimada asked both to follow him. They picked their way through the jumbled room to two windows facing north. Staying to each side of the window so as not to attract any sniper fire, they peeked out.

Immediately outside was a rusty but still serviceable flatbed Ford truck that Pete assumed was the store owner's vehicle. A two-seater with an enclosed cab, Pete guessed its age at around 1920. Beyond the old Ford, Pete and Shimada could see five wooden structures, three on the east side of the road and two on the west. All bore bullet and shrapnel scars on their walls and torn roofs. Two had partially collapsed.

"That row of houses is our next objective," Shimada said.

"It'll be tough with Easy still stalled," Hodges said. "Their Third Platoon needs to be on our flank."

"I'm aware of that, Sergeant," Shimada replied. "Just as I'm aware that our First and Third Platoons need to secure those woods to our right. We'll catch our breath here and move as soon as we can. Biff, brief Zoo-Zoo and Manson. Tell them to give their squads a break but stand by to move on a moment's notice."

The respite was brief. Within ten minutes, First and Third Platoons secured the woods while on Second Platoon's left across the highway, Easy Company broke across the open side road that had stalled their assault. Renewing their attack, the Easy men drove the Japanese defenders back.

With the line now restored and both their flanks secured, Lt. Shimada led his men out of their temporary refuge in the ruined store and against the next house some twenty yards across open ground. The Japanese defenders gave it up quickly and raced for the next building in line. As a precaution in case all the defenders hadn't fled, grenades were lobbed into the windows and men burst through doorways, weapons at the ready. Simple furnishings, like chairs and tables, were strewn about and pottery smashed. Pete found a few framed photos depicting an Oriental couple and three children. He briefly wondered if they were among the dead civilians killed in yesterday's attack.

The next building in the row was more stoutly defended. The platoon peppered the south-facing wall of the structure with fire from the BARs wielded by Rosie and Dubbs, who had inherited the weapon on a permanent basis after Reb was hit. Their heavy bursts tore into the flimsy wood and thatched walls. The building, larger than the one Pete's men had just taken, had a front and rear door and as the Japanese inside fled from the front, the Marines charged through the back. Several of the enemy had not gotten out and now exchanged fire with the Americans. Pete was the first one in, kicking open the door and charging through, followed by Biff Hodges.

As he raced inside, Pete saw two Japanese soldiers rise up from beyond a store counter. Pete loosed a six-round burst from his Thompson that struck both men. Before they died, one got off a round. The slug barely missed Pete's body, striking Hodges in the left shoulder and tearing through flesh and bone on its way through.

More men from the platoon entered the store. Dubbs cut down two enemy soldiers making a break for the doorway and Honeybun shot another.

Pete knelt beside Hodges while Aldrich yelled for a corpsman. Frank Lamont answered the call, bursting into the house as enemy fire from the next building whizzed past.

"Wow!" he exclaimed in a voice laced with excitement and relief. "That was close."

He got to work immediately, quipping, "I thought you were bulletproof, Biff."

The joke went unanswered. Everyone knew that while Magruder generally got right to business, Lamont liked to banter with his patients when possible. He felt it relieved their anxieties as well as his own. Shimada entered, and upon seeing Hodges down, he hurried over. Lamont saw the concern on Shimada's face.

"Sorry, Lieutenant," the corpsman said. "I've gotta send him back. His collarbone is shattered."

Shimada nodded somberly, then looked at Pete who was kneeling by Hodges.

"Looks like you're my new platoon sergeant, Hardball," he announced. "Turn your squad over to Aldrich. Then have everyone get ready. We're slowly making progress, and Captain Stacey wants us to keep moving."

Keeping low, Pete moved back to his squad to give Aldrich the news.

"Biff's hit," he said. "Shimada made me platoon sergeant, so the squad's yours."

Aldrich nodded, then went to inform the squad while Pete returned to Lt. Shimada.

The fourth and last building in the row, a former dry goods store from the look of the debris strewn about, fell almost without a shot being fired as the enemy pulled back to a dirt lane that branched off Middle Road. The lane had a three-foot deep shoulder that formed a ready-made trench, which the Japanese put to good use. Crouched behind this protective wall of earth while also fortifying several houses beyond, the enemy laid down a heavy volume of fire as Dog Company attacked all along its front. The attack was quickly stopped by heavy enemy fire.

Across Middle Road, Easy Company attacked in unison with Dog pushing across almost three hundred yards of terrain that included a small clump of scrub trees and a battered sugarcane field. They made headway until running up against a heavily defended three-story stone building that appeared to be an inn. Japanese riflemen seemed to fire from every window. Cleverly concealed machine guns also helped bring Easy Company's drive to a shuddering halt.

Lt. Shimada was crawling on his belly along his platoon line. Reaching Pete's position he said, "Keep the pressure on them. Captain Stacey is trying to get some tanks up here."

Dog Company kept steady pressure on the Japanese in a firefight that was rapidly reaching two hours in duration. That's when, above the rattle of the small arms, was heard the growl of engines coming up from behind. Pete turned and saw six Shermans clanking along the main road. Three tanks peeled off to assist Easy Company, their 75mm guns slamming into the

stone walls of the inn. Of the other three Shermans, one drew
to a halt on the road by the dry goods store while the other two
drove between the store and the house. Reaching the rear of the
millinery shop, both vehicles opened up with their main guns
and raked the ground ahead with their machine guns.

"Dog Company, let's go!" Captain Stacey called, and the
attack resumed.

The fury of this assault overwhelmed the defenders, many
of whom died at their posts. The rest fled as the tanks reached
the road, their machine guns chopping down the refugees whose
bodies flopped to the ground in a bloody tangle.

Dog Company reached the dirt lane. The road and shoulder were thick with bodies of the slain.

A sniper opened up from one of the houses along the road.
One of the Shermans traversed his turret and elevated his 75mm
piece. The gun roared as its round tore into the flimsy wooden
house. The walls burst open as smoke and flames poured out.

The American attack had built up an unstoppable momentum. After two days of being held at a standstill just one mile
from Garapan, the Marines were determined they would not
be halted. Fifty yards ahead of Dog Company was another side
road. Perched at the intersection of this road and Middle Road
was the largest structure the Americans had seen so far. Made
of wood and concrete blocks, the building had an attached stee-
ple. Even as the Americans closed in on the intersection, two
dozen civilians, mostly Chamorro, poured out of the doors,
many wailing and waving crucifixes and rosary beads at the Marines and yelling, "Chamorro!" "Christian!" and "No shoot!"
to identify themselves.

As he approached the church, Pete worried that the Japanese
would begin shooting the civilians as they tried to surrender.

"Second Platoon, follow me," Pete yelled.

Reaching the church, Pete led the platoon through the throng of civilians. Some clutched at their liberators' arms to thank them, but the Marines hurried around the corner into the cemetery. Japanese soldiers ran helter-skelter amid the tombstones, some stopping to fire while others seemed more eager to get away.

Two Japanese tried to make a stand by a large stone grave marker, but a burst from Dembrowski's Tommy gun dropped them both. McCready was rattled when a bullet caromed off his steel helmet.

The battle for the cemetery was short as the enemy fled north toward Garapan, leaving Dog Company in command of the field.

It was nearly 1800 hours now. The battalion had been fighting eyeball-to-eyeball combat for nearly nine hours. Captain Stacey called a halt and ordered his platoon and squad leaders to the church where he had set up his CP. As Pete entered the church alongside Aldrich, the two men were stopped by Gunny Nicholson.

"I was watching you both during the last part of the fight," Nicholson said. "Professor, you did a good job leading the squad on that last charge to the church. Talbot, you showed command ability when you ordered Second Platoon through that wall of civvies and into the cemetery to drive the Japs out. It looks like those new jobs you guys have will be permanent. Hodges is being sent back. Also, Talbot, I gotta tell you that Malloy didn't make it. Corpsmen couldn't stop the bleeding, so Zoo-Zoo will stay in command of Third Squad unless you want to make a change."

"Me?" Pete said.

"You're platoon sergeant," Nicholson said. "You can recommend anyone you want."

"Zulicky is a 'Canal vet," Pete observed. "He's the most

experienced guy in the squad next to Malloy, so I'm not going to rock any boats."

"Malloy was a good man," Nicholson mused. "I always called him '158.' During the first peacetime draft back in 1940, the first number drawn was 158."

A gathering of the company's officers and NCOs was convening in the church. Stacey thanked all for their determined action that day.

"We took some knocks, and we lost a couple of good men," he said. "But we pushed the enemy back to the gates of Garapan." Several of the men looked quizzical. "Tomorrow we'll move into the town and kick their asses out. It won't be easy. Before the invasion about fifteen thousand people lived in Garapan. That's one hell of a lot of houses and other buildings. Since the preinvasion softening-up began, Garapan has been smashed flat as a bug so there are a thousand places to hide a sniper or a machine gun or an entire battalion of infantrymen, so it will be slow going. Be careful. These bastards are tricky, and I want to see all of you fellows alive and well when the job is done. One reason for that is once we've taken Garapan, the Second Division is going into reserve." The men gaped in disbelief. "This isn't totally official yet, but the plan is that we take Garapan, consolidate our position, and then stand fast while the Fourth Marines and the Army push on to the north shore of Saipan."

"We're done, then?" Aldrich asked.

"I don't know, Professor," Stacey said. "Let's hope so."

CHAPTER 23

General Saito arrived at what would be his final headquarters at about 0300, walking past a double row of soldiers all standing ramrod straight at attention. The contingent consisted of fifty men under Lt. Tatsuo Kadashi, handpicked by Colonel Suzuki, to serve as bodyguards.

Aware of the enormous honor, he bowed deeply to Saito and said, "My men and I will protect you to the death."

The last leg of the journey was eased since vehicles were provided when Saito reached Tanapag Harbor. Still, by the time the column reached the new command cave, all were exhausted from both physical and emotional strain. Many men just collapsed and slept where they fell. Saito, fatigued, looked the place over and nodded approvingly.

Compared to the last few places he'd been forced to occupy, this cave, selected by Tadashi and outfitted by Suzuki, was luxurious. Tadashi liked that it included two smaller caverns for senior staff. Suzuki made sure there was a gas generator and

two electric lights, as well as cots for the senior officers and a
table for maps and dining. It was Tadashi's foresight that led to
the construction of a concrete bunker adjoining the cave with
a 75mm gun placed inside to assist in the defense if attacked.
Since the cave overlooked a valley, the gun could shell any approaching American forces.

To enter his new headquarters, Saito pushed aside a large
dark tarp that had been strung across the cave mouth to keep
stray beams of light inside from escaping into the night. Saito
smiled with satisfaction. Even though the electric light bulbs
were each just twenty-five watts, their low warm glow made the
cave's interior feel cheery.

"This is most satisfactory," Saito remarked, then walked
to one of the cots and sat down. "From here we will fight the
battle to its end. Send a message to all commands. Tell them
that the line now being established is the final one. Each man
will defend his position to the death."

"Why don't you lie down and rest, sir," Tadashi said. "It
was a long journey."

Saito smiled and lay on the cot. If he slept, Tadashi did not
notice it.

The long-awaited move into Garapan began at first light. A
shift in Second Battalion's front found First and Second Platoons astride Middle Road, now referred to by the Marines as
Broadway since it cut through the center of town. With First
Platoon on the west side of the road and Second on the east
and Third Platoon to the rear of both, the Marines cautiously
advanced through the town's outskirts toward a crossroad that
contained a cluster of wood and thatch houses. If any resistance

was to be met during this initial penetration, everyone knew it would come from here.

It did.

Just as McCready and Wally Bright of First Squad, walking at point, drew near the intersection of what the maps labeled as Gualo Rai Road, gunfire erupted from huts directly in front of them. At the same time, First Platoon on the west side of Broadway also came under fire. Marines on both sides of the highway hit the ground.

Since many of the houses in Garapan, as elsewhere on Saipan, stood on short stilts, Marines used that to their advantage and crawled under the huts to return fire. Behind the two stalled platoons, Third Platoon was ordered to hold in reserve although two of its .30-cals came forward to lend support. It quickly became obvious that all the shacks lining both the north and south sides of Gualo Rai Road were occupied, and a hot firefight soon developed.

The rumbling of engines and clanking of caterpillar treads announced that two of the Sherman tanks that had been following the lead platoons were joining the fight. Pete saw Lt. Shimada hurry up to one of the tanks and give the commander instructions. With a nod, the turrets on both tanks swiveled right. Moments later their 75mm guns barked. Their targets were the two huts sitting atop stilts on the northern side of Gualo Rai Road directly in front of Second Platoon. One shell dropped short but the second scored a direct hit. The hut's flimsy walls blew apart in a cloud of shattered wood as sections of the corrugated iron roof fell inward. The tank that missed its mark reloaded for a second try. The Japanese inside weren't about to see if the gunner's aim had improved and began to flee. This time the gunner scored a bull's-eye and the explosion ripped through the house.

Approaching the row of blasted and burning huts lining the south side of Gualo Rai Road, the lead tank smashed through what remained of one of them, crushing under its treads scattered household furnishings and personal belongings. What was left of the wooden roof frame and corrugated iron sheets tumbled down onto the armored intruder but did not slow its progress. Instead, the beast burst through the northern wall and fired its 75mm gun directly into the house across the road. Bodies were flung into the air as the shell exploded.

The second Sherman had remained on Broadway and now turned right onto Gualo Rai Road to join its companion.

As the tanks blasted their way forward, Pete saw Shimada shouting something in his direction and pointing ahead. He knew what was being said without hearing the words.

"Second Platoon, let's go," Pete shouted. "On me!"

The men rose and attacked the ruined row of houses. Finding no enemy left alive, they charged through the shacks and raced across Gualo Rai Road to storm the huts on the other side of the street. There were four of these although the tanks had already dealt with half of them.

"Keep going!" Pete yelled as he plucked a grenade off his web belt. Arming it while still running, he kicked open a flimsy wooden door on one hut and lobbed the pineapple inside. Ducking out of the doorway to shield himself from the blast, as soon as the grenade detonated, he rushed in with Rosie right behind him. Many of the defenders were already headed rearward, jarred by the fury of the Marine assault. Inside, two enemy soldiers crouched in a corner, lifting their weapons to fire, but Rosie leveled the BAR and riddled both defenders.

It took Second Platoon just a few minutes to clear all the huts lining Gualo Rai Road. But the fight was not over. Directly behind these shacks were three more, one a large house along

Broadway and two small ones behind it facing south. The small-
ness of these latter two shacks belied their danger as the sharp
boom of a 37mm anti-tank gun hidden inside struck the lead
Sherman. Smoke billowed from the vehicle as the crew slid out
of the emergency hatch in the tank's belly.

"Suppressing fire!" Pete yelled. The platoon opened up on
the huts, making the enemy duck while the tankers scurried for
cover. Four made it. The fifth fell, badly wounded. He writhed
in pain, panic, or both as Marines hollered, "Don't move! Don't
move." But he did move, and the Japanese did not neglect the
target. Rifle fire riddled the man until he lay silent.

Not able to spot where the round had come from, the second
Sherman prudently reversed to a less exposed position between
two of the ruined shacks. Pete, however, had seen the slight puff
of white smoke when the anti-tank gun discharged, and he raced
over to the tank. Opening a small call box on the tank's rear
panel, he picked up the receiver. A voice from inside said, "Yeah?"

"First hut on the left," Pete said sharply. "Southwest corner.
The AT gun is there. Give me two minutes to get my platoon
ready to attack."

"You got it, Mac."

Pete hurried off to alert his squad leaders that they would
attack the Jap position the minute the Sherman blew the
anti-tank gun out of existence. As he finished that task, Lt. Shimada came up with Dick Crosley and his precious flamethrower.

"Dick, you're a sight for sore eyes," Pete said. The two men
had been part of the same training platoon at Parris Island. To
Shimada Pete added, "The Sherman is gonna blast that gun,
then we're going. I've alerted the platoon."

"Yeah," Shimada said. "Keep the pressure on them. Don't
give them time to think. When their plans are thrown off, they
don't adapt well."

The engine of the Sherman roared as the vehicle rolled out from its cover. The turret swung right a few degrees and the gun fired. The shell closed the distance in a flash, ripping into the hut, which caught fire. The dried wood and thatch rapidly spread the flames, and moments later 37mm rounds stored inside began to detonate.

As instructed, the platoon emerged from its cover and charged across the field. Pete had told First and Third Squads to take the two huts directly in front of them, including the one that had held the anti-tank weapon. Second Squad would attack the larger house facing Broadway. Pete had Crosley accompany Second Squad. A fireman from Wheeling, West Virginia, before the war, Crosley knew exactly where to torch the house. With two squirts from the nozzle of his Zippo, he left two walls burning. The squad closed the distance rapidly. Tossing grenades into windows, they followed up after the explosions by crashing into the house and finishing off any of the remaining Japanese. In the confines of the burning house, the fight was brief but deadly. When the shooting stopped, eleven of the enemy lay dead along with one American. Caught up in the rush, Crosley had foolishly followed the squad into the house.

"Get down!" Pete had yelled, fearing that a bullet would ignite the tanks on Crosley's back and immolate half the squad. Before Crosley could react, a bullet pierced his helmet and entered his brain. Pete saw the brief but final expression on Crosley's face. It was one of surprise.

With the fall of these shacks, the enemy fell back to another cluster of houses about a hundred yards away. Dragging Crosley's body with him before the flames reached the fuel tanks still strapped to the dead man's back, Pete exited the burning house and was about to order the platoon to move forward against that next Japanese line of defense.

"Hold up!" Lt. Shimada called, sticking up a hand as a visual signal. Turning to Pete he said, "We've outrun the rest of the company, so we'll hold here."

"Aye aye, sir," Pete said.

"By the way, Hardball," said Shimada who rarely called Pete by his nickname, "the platoon performed well so far today. Keep it up."

Pete nodded and felt a little puff of pride.

Shimada looked down at Crosley. Ryan Magruder had hurried up, seeing a man down. Heaving a deep sigh when he discovered Crosley was dead, he removed the man's identity tag and handed it to Shimada.

"He was a good man," Shimada said. "He'll be tough to replace."

"I knew him since boot camp," Pete said. "He and I and a guy we called Feather Merchant were assigned to clean the heads. I was a hotshot back then and felt it was beneath me, so I goofed off until our DI came to inspect. He caught me and had me clean the toilets alone, then dipped a tin cup into one commode and had me drink the water. I'm the only one of the three left."

Shimada said, "Better see to the men."

Aldrich had gotten the Second Squad well situated, placing his two BAR men, Rosie and Dubbs, at either end of the squad line and the others spread out in between.

Moving in a crouch, Pete made his way toward First Squad. With nine men, including Zoo-Zoo, this was now the largest squad in the platoon. Yesterday evening, after he'd been made platoon sergeant and while he had some quiet moments, Pete visited his new command. Some of the men he knew quite well, others not so much. Pete made it his job to rectify that situation starting with First Squad.

Pete recalled that Frank Zulicky had been a salesman in Rehoboth Beach, Delaware, selling new and used Ford automobiles until he got bored and enlisted in the Marines in early 1941.

Corporal Bill Francis, operating a BAR, had been a Pittsburgh steel worker. It was a job that could have exempted him from military duty, but Francis enlisted anyway. Miguel "Siesta" Minozo of New Mexico earned the nickname because he could fall asleep almost anywhere.

Fritz "Kraut" Schuler was practically a next-door neighbor to Pete, hailing from Philadelphia where he worked as a cop. He boasted that his ancestry went back to German immigrants who came to America before the Revolutionary War.

Wallace "Wally" Bright was an eager-beaver kid from Schenectady, New York, where he had worked at a bowling alley as a pinspotter. Myron White worked in a butcher shop in Lebanon, Pennsylvania, making the region's famous Lebanon Bologna.

Pete knew little about the rest of the squad. Stuart Pierson was from Indiana, Claude "Wings" Wingenroth was a BAR man and hailed from New Hampshire, and Morris "Moose" Shay, also toting a BAR, came from Tennessee. He vowed to learn about them provided there was time.

"Dig in but stay alert for another move," Pete told Zoo-Zoo.

On the platoon's right was Third Squad, led by Marty Manson. Manson had taken a flesh wound to the thigh nine days ago but refused evacuation. Pete knew that Marty, who was from Los Angeles, had worked in Hollywood as an assistant gaffer, or electrician, on a number of Warner Brothers films. He never tired of saying how he'd befriended Humphrey Bogart when they worked together on several films, including *The Maltese Falcon*.

"Bogey liked subdued lighting, and I was good at that," he'd say.

Besides Manson, the squad had seven men. Pete barely knew the members of this squad. Corporal Clarence "Cal" Coleman of Wyoming had been wounded on Guadalcanal during the closing days of the six-month campaign in January 1943. He and Nicholson had served together in the same company and Coleman was hit as the Marines took the ridge called the Galloping Horse.

BAR man Thomas Standish was from Massachusetts and, despite his not being in any way descended from the Pilgrims, was still tagged with the nickname of "Miles."

Michael "Chief" Grayhawk was a Lakota Sioux from the Standing Rock Reservation in South Dakota. A jack-of-all-trades, he worked whatever jobs that would hire an Indian—usually construction work.

Bruce Toler had worked as the head cook in a restaurant called The Top Hat until the draft came along. Evidently being a chef at a fancy Manhattan eatery did not exempt one from military service. "Chef" Toler, as he was dubbed, was bitter about it and let everyone know.

Mark "Boomer" Borden, a BAR man, was from Missouri, Warren Mayer hailed from Illinois, and Andy "Buff" Buffenmyer was from Easton, Pennsylvania, not too far from Sammy Dubbs's home. During the division's stay in Hawaii, the two had become friends.

After making his rounds, Pete returned to Second Squad and shared a foxhole with Aldrich.

———

The message that crackled over the radio in the headquarters cave was grim.

"The enemy has entered Garapan," the message read. "Our

men are fighting courageously but are slowly being pushed back. We pray for the emperor."

"Why are the cowards falling back?" Suzuki fumed. "Why don't they stand and die?"

"Don't be so impulsive, Colonel," Saito admonished. "When it is time for us to die, we shall all die together. Until then, we fight on, luring the American devils closer and closer to our massing troops. Then we will smash them in a most dramatic and glorious fashion. The spirit of Japan, the *Yamato Damashi*, is instilled in our men. It will give them spiritual strength to win over superior manpower and resources."

Yes, Tadashi thought, every man believed in the strict code of never be captured, never break down, and never surrender. Each soldier was trained to fight to the death and was expected to die before suffering dishonor.

How about you, Tadashi? he asked himself. *You pledged to that same code when you became an officer. Are you still willing to die for the emperor? For Japan?*

Yes, he answered himself. *I'm Japanese, and I will do my duty.*

Still, he inwardly cursed generals and politicians who so cavalierly made war on a great and powerful nation without knowing its capabilities, who depend on past glories to carry them through to victory. To him, they were like the mythical bird that flies backward because it likes where it has been and does not want to see where it is going.

Still mulling over the battle that all knew was raging to a climax, Saito said, "I will not be pushed back any further. We will win or lose from here."

"Sir," Suzuki urged, "if the situation continues to deteriorate, let us radio Imperial Headquarters for a submarine to rendezvous with us at Marpi Point and take you to safety. You have gained valuable tactical knowledge of the enemy that can be shared with our generals. If you perish, that knowledge and experience will be lost to Japan."

Saito looked to Suzuki.

"No. I will retreat no further."

"Then we of your staff will also fight to the death," Suzuki said firmly.

"I would expect nothing less," Saito said.

By noon the Marines had pushed seven hundred yards into Garapan. Now the Americans were getting into the more populated areas of the town. In addition to the typical wood and thatch houses with tin roofs, more and more structures were constructed of concrete blocks and limestone rocks mined from the island's hills and ridges. But the war had handled Garapan roughly. "Little Tokyo," as residents used to refer to Garapan, was flattened like a fly on a window.

Pressed against the remaining wall of a building that had once, according to the charred remains of a sign, been the medical office of a Chamorro doctor named Antonio Suarez, Pete peeked around the corner.

Looking along Broadway toward the busiest section of town, Pete saw avenues clogged by piles of debris. There were a few wrecked or burned-out cars, a bus turned on its side, broken animal-drawn carts and wagons. Some of it was still burning, emitting dark smoke.

"Not much left, is there?" Pete mused aloud.

"No," said Lt. Shimada, who was kneeling beside Pete and also peeking ahead. "I can't help but feel sorry for the civilians living here. Before the war, this must've seemed like an island paradise. Now their homes, their lives, and their dreams lie scattered on the ground for us to step on and roll our tanks over."

"I understand what you mean, sir," Pete replied. "And I feel badly for the natives here, the Chamorro like this Dr. Suarez here, and the Carolinians and Chinese. But most of the rest are Japs and I can't feel bad for them. No offense, sir."

"None taken, Sergeant," Shimada replied.

"Begging your pardon, sir, but how does it feel for you to fight against and kill men who . . . uhmmm . . . look like you?"

"A legitimate question," Shimada replied. "How would it feel for you to be fighting in Europe against the Germans?"

Pete thought for a moment, then said, "I never thought of it that way."

"I don't know those men out there, Hardball," Shimada said. "I was born in Hawaii so those men are as foreign to me as they are to you. Oh, and by the way, I have a brother, Nick, who is in Europe. He's with the 'One Puka Puka,' the 100th Infantry Battalion."

"No shit?" Pete said. "I've heard of them. Gutsy bastards."

Shimada just smiled.

"Begging your pardon again, sir, but I heard you describe how you were treated in California. Was that true?"

"Yes," Shimada replied. "Being a Japanese American in Hawaii is a whole different thing than in California. Even in the Marines, there are men who take a look at my Oriental face and sneer. I am called 'Nip' and 'Dirty Jap,' and some say they want to 'slap a Jap.'"

"No Marine better say that within my earshot," Pete said.

Shimada just smiled.

Pete again peeked around the corner of the building.

Roughly a hundred yards ahead of Second Platoon was the crossroad of Broadway and Kopa Di Oru Street. While many small houses and sheds had once stood on the ground, all had been flattened by artillery and bombs to the point where it was impossible to say how many there had been. Their shattered remains were scattered far and wide between Kopa Di Oru Street and the Marines. However, a pair of large two-story concrete buildings dominated the southeast and northwest corners, placing them in a good position to cover the debris-covered field with sniper and machine gun fire. The northeast corner of this intersection featured wide open green spaces. Pete asked about it.

"That's Sugar King Park," Shimada replied after a quick glance at his map. "It's named for the guy who began the sugarcane industry here. By the way, I just tapped Marty Manson to be your guide sergeant just in case you up and get hit."

"I have no intention of getting shot," Pete replied.

He pointed at the large buildings that dominated the intersection. "I'm more worried about them. From where they sit, they have a clear field of fire if we move on the park."

"In a few minutes that shouldn't be a problem," Shimada said. "The captain is on the horn to get us some air support."

They didn't have long to wait. Within ten minutes of laying out their identification panels, the Marines heard a flight of three Grumman Hellcats screaming down from the sky. Their wing-mounted machine guns chewed up the already destroyed structures plus the two large buildings. With a whooshing sound, each plane fired a spread of four High Velocity Aircraft Rockets. Each "Holy Moses" streaked toward its target at over thirteen hundred feet per second. Three of the twelve hit home, two into the structure on the southeast corner and one in the other building. Carrying seven-and-a-half pounds of Composition B explosive in each, the resultant blasts tore into the structures, sending chunks of concrete and wooden beams hurling into the air. Part of the first building began to fold up and then collapse. The eight remaining rockets erupted around the Japanese line along Kopa Di Oru Street and amid the debris-riddled field.

The order to move up came from Captain Stacey and Dog Company, its platoons straddling Broadway, First on the left, Second in the center, and Third to the right. Fox Company took its place on Dog's left flank while Easy Company brought up the rear as battalion reserve.

Supporting the advance, two platoons of tanks, mostly Shermans with a few Stuarts thrown in, rolled along Broadway, ready to be called up at a moment's notice.

The Japanese response was quick. Rifle and machine gun fire came at Second Platoon, forcing Pete and the rest to seek cover amid the field of charred and shattered debris. Across Broadway, the advancing Marines faced similar resistance. Movement was a matter of crawling from one pile of rubble to the next as bullets pinged off broken masonry or clanged into charred sheets of metal roofing. One sniper seemed to have homed in on Pete. Stuck behind a pile of burnt timbers, he tried first to move to his right for better cover, and then tried going left. Both times bullets thunked into the wood just inches from his face.

"Goddamn it," he swore. "Does anyone see where this bastard is?"

"I do, Sergeant," McCready said.

The youngster was behind some chunks of limestone rock blasted from a house. Pete noted with satisfaction that the boy had his eight-power scope attached to his Springfield.

"He's about forty yards in front of you, under a pile of wood and covered by a sheet of metal," he said as he peered through the scope. Then he pulled the rifle back and fine-tuned his aim. "Two clicks right windage," he muttered to himself. "And one click up."

Then he sighted in again and said, "Okay, Mr. Jap. Put your

head up one more time."

"Let me help," Pete said. "This guy has a real hard-on for me."

Pete made a quick movement as if he was going to try to shift positions. As he pulled his head back, McCready's rifle barked. The boy smiled.

"You can move now, Sergeant," he said proudly.

"Call me Hardball," Pete replied.

Moving forward through the debris and toward the Japanese line along the road was slow and painful. In First Squad, Stuart Pierson was grazed by a bullet that sliced through his shirt and along his rib cage. After being patched up by Corpsman Frank Lamont, the Ohioan refused to go back to the field hospital.

In Third Squad, Warren Mayer had no choice after a bullet tore through his chest. Corpsman Ryan Magruder, still limping with a bad ankle, performed a quick patch-up job and commandeered a stretcher to take the wounded Illinoisan to the rear. Standing there with Mayer's blood smearing his arms almost to the elbows, he watched as the boy was carried away. Then, wiping his hands on his already bloodstained uniform, he went back to work.

The Japanese manning the Kopa Di Oru Street defense were persistent. Even the large structures in the intersection, both now heavily battle damaged, remained a beehive of enemy fire. Behind Second Platoon, Pete saw four of the supporting tanks, all Shermans, roll into the field. While two of them concentrated on the Japanese along the road, the other two swiveled their turrets toward the large building on the southeast corner. Beyond Broadway, other tanks were doing the same thing to the remaining concrete structures.

From the rear, Dog Company's mortar section began dropping rounds on the Japanese line while the Americans inched forward. When the fire lifted, Captain Stacey ordered an attack. Rising up, the company came on in a rush. Japanese soldiers began abandoning their positions and raced rearward across Kopa Di Oru Street and into Sugar King Park.

As the Marines neared the road, Aldrich hollered, "Second Squad follow me!"

The squad made for the large building directly ahead of them. Reaching the door facing Broadway, Aldrich, Perkins, and Dubbs lobbed grenades through the doorway and front windows. After the grenades exploded, the men ran inside.

"Honeybun! Second floor!" the Professor yelled.

Hullihen led his fire team up a flight of stairs to the left of the front door. At the top they found themselves in the center of a long hallway that ran the length of the structure north to south. Sections of the roof and debris from broken masonry littered the floor. The tanks had done a thorough job.

"Dembrowski," Aldrich said. "You go right. Check those rooms." He pointed south. "McCready, go with him. Dubbs and I will go this way."

There were four rooms in both the north and south wings of the building, and each was cleared the same way—a grenade followed by a rush through the doorway, weapons blazing. Not every Japanese soldier positioned inside these rooms calmly waited as the grenade explosions came closer and closer. From a room at the far end of the southern corridor, three Japanese burst out yelling some unintelligible oath and firing their rifles. One bullet thudded into the wall just two inches from McCready's face while a second smashed the scope still attached to his Springfield. Dembrowski opened up with his Thompson and chopped them down.

By the time the second story was cleared, fourteen enemy bodies lay sprawled on the floor. Two of the rooms also contained Nambu machine guns knocked out by tank fire.

The downstairs was easier to clear. Most of the enemy here

had escaped before this latest attack. Only four holdouts were killed by the squad, and one young man, to the shock of everyone, put up his hands in surrender. He was clearly terrified.

"What do we do, Sarge?" Perkins asked nervously.

Drawing on the few phrases the men had been taught en route to Saipan, Aldrich said, *"Kega wo suru koto wa arimasen."*

After assuring the man he would not be hurt, Aldrich sent Perkins out to find Lt. Shimada while Rosie thoroughly searched the man for hidden weapons. He found none. All he came up with was his paybook and two letters from home.

Perkins soon returned, followed by Lt. Shimada and Pete.

Shimada walked up to the young soldier, who was clearly surprised to see a Japanese man in a Marine uniform.

"Think he knows anything about the Jap defenses?" Pete asked.

Studying the captured paybook, Shimada said, "This man is a private. He knows less than nothing. He just does what he's told." Still consulting the paybook, he said, "Junyu Immato. Fifth Special Base Force."

After a few moments, he offered the man a cigarette and said, *"Tabako hashi desu ka?"*

"Domo, domo," the man said, bowing deeply several times.

Having gained the man's confidence, Shimada said, "Let's see what he does know."

"Think he'll tell us?" Pete asked.

"His commanders expected him to die in combat, according to their interpretation of Bushido," Shimada replied. "He was never instructed not to tell us what he knows. The company is holding here, so I will take this man back to company HQ for interrogation." He turned to Pete. "Get the platoon dug in along the southern edge of the park. If the enemy launches a counterattack, we want them to have to cross that open ground."

Shimada looked to McCready, who was in the process of removing the remains of his shattered scope from his rifle and said, "I'll see if I can scare you up a replacement, Private."

Telling the prisoner to stand up and clasp his hands atop his head, Shimada prodded him toward the doorway and to the rear.

Second Platoon cautiously moved across Kopa Di Oru Street, stepping over and around corpses of dead defenders and abandoned or battered weapons and discarded equipment. Entering Sugar King Park, shovels came off LMO packs and the men dug in. Aldrich had begun deploying Second Squad on line when the first Japanese mortar rounds began falling. Now it was the Marines' turn to hunker down in whatever cover they could find as explosions blossomed all around them. The bombardment was short but vicious, and while Second and Third Platoons escaped with only jangled nerves, First Platoon had one man killed by a direct hit on his foxhole and two wounded including a man who had a foot blown off. As everyone tried to compose themselves following the mortar attack, a new sound came from dead ahead. Seven Japanese tanks, including four medium fourteen-ton Type 97 *Chi-Ha* vehicles and three small Type 95 *Ha-Go* vehicles, were rolling down Broadway, maneuvering around piles of debris, toward the Marines' line. Where Rosa Street intersected Broadway, three of the tanks peeled off, turning right onto Rosa Street. Then the trio, including one *Ha-Go*, wheeled left and drove over and between residential homes, many of wood, as they attacked First Platoon on Kopa Di Oru. The other four tanks, three *Chi-Ha* models and one *Ha-Go*, spun left and entered Sugar King Park.

Shaken by the unexpected appearance of Japanese armor, Pete glanced around for Carl McComsey and his bazooka. When Pete spotted him dug in with Third Squad, he yelled and pointed. The heads-up was not needed. McComsey had seen the tanks and knew what needed to be done. With a whoosh, the bazooka discharged its rocket. The light *Ha-Go* took a direct hit and exploded. Smoke billowed from every gunport and from the Dutch door–style top hatch, which was partly open.

But the bazooka had been spotted by the sharp-eyed commander of one of the *Chi-Ha* tanks, who traversed his turret around and lowered his main 57mm gun.

"McComsey!" Pete yelled. "Displace! Get out of there!"

Pete would never know if McComsey heard or not, for a moment later, the main gun roared, and the shell scored almost a direct hit on the bazooka's position.

"Son of a bitch!" Pete yelled and emptied a thirty-round clip from his Thompson at the tank, probably doing the tank no harm other than scratching the paint. The three surviving medium tanks kept coming, their 7.7mm machine guns, two per tank, firing incessantly, and their main guns firing as fast as they could be loaded.

The *Chi-Ha*s had traveled about halfway across the park when a blast from behind the Marines resulted in one of the tanks almost disappearing in a spectacular explosion. Reduced to junk, it rolled to a stop, burning furiously.

The blast that killed the tank came from a Sherman, one of six that had been advancing behind the Marines. Responding to frantic radio pleas, the Shermans hurried forward. Now three of them moved to the left to take on the Japanese vehicles approaching from Rosa Street while the other three rolled into Sugar King Park.

One *Chi-Ha* spun its turret and fired at a Sherman, but the blow ricocheted off the Sherman's forward-sloping armor. The *Chi-Ha* did not get a second shot as a 75mm shell from one of the American vehicles punched through the enemy tank's armored skin and exploded inside the turret.

The last Japanese tank in the park was a newer and more lethal *Shinhoto* variation, with a long, high-velocity 47mm gun, which its commander put to good use. As the Sherman that had knocked out the *Ha-Go* tried to maneuver to line up a shot, the *Shinhoto* got off the first round that penetrated the Sherman's engine compartment. Powerless, the Sherman came to a stop. Before the other two Shermans could get into position to help, the *Shinhoto* got off another round that penetrated the American armor, killing the tank driver and wounding two other crewmen. The remaining Shermans took revenge, each one putting a 75mm round through the enemy's armor plating. The battered vehicle rolled to a stop. No crewmen emerged.

Across Broadway, two of the three attacking Japanese tanks sat silent and smoldering. The third, a *Chi-Ha*, had escaped.

An eerie silence fell over Garapan. The only battle sounds were from Flame Tree Hill halfway up the sloping ridge east of Pete's position. Pete remembered coming ashore on D-Day and seeing the large patch of lush red foliage that made it seem as if the hillside was on fire.

Leaving his position, Pete walked to where McComsey and Woolson had been posted. Shrapnel had torn both bodies open and one of Woolson's legs had been severed in the blast. The twisted remains of the bazooka lay nearby. Pete stared at the two bodies as Corpsman Ryan Magruder removed one identity tag from each corpse, then using camouflaged ponchos he'd gotten from God-knows-where, he gently covered both men until Graves Registration could come and claim them as they went about their grisly task. Their loss made Pete think of Dick Crosley, killed earlier that day.

"I don't know about you, Doc," Pete said wearily. "But I am getting so damned sick and tired of watching friends get killed.

I am getting damned sick and tired of watching Marines I don't know getting killed. Hell, I'm even sick and tired of watching Japs get killed. It just fuckin' never ends. It was so much easier on Tarawa. I was a private, just taking orders, until they made me squad leader. Now here I am heading the platoon. Good Christ. Men like McComsey and Woolson are under my command, so how do I not feel responsible when they get killed?"

Magruder stood up and pocketed the tags in order to give them to Captain Stacey.

"I understand, Hardball, but you can't shoulder the blame and still do your job effectively," he said sympathetically. "We're all doing a job we despise. I never in a million years imagined a time where my job would involve sticking my hands deep into some guy's guts trying to pinch off a severed artery. This is not why I joined the Navy."

"Well, you're good, damned good," Pete said. "You've saved God knows how many guys' lives, not to mention my leg. I admire you, and coming from me, that's something."

"I'll send you the bill," Magruder said and headed rearward.

After Magruder left, Pete spotted a bronze statue towering over the park a short distance from where McComsey and Woolson had died. Curious about who it was on this damned island who inspired the statue, he carefully walked closer. The statue was of a man in a business suit, his jacket open and his left hand in his trouser pocket. The statue, maybe eight feet in height, was mounted atop a granite pedestal ten or twelve feet high, which itself stood upon a square granite slab. Five steps led up to the obelisk. A plaque on the pedestal, naturally enough, was in Japanese. Pete could only read one thing, the name Haruji Matsue. He recalled Lt. Shimada mentioning the man's name as the driving force behind the sugar industry on the island.

"So you're the bastard," Pete scowled.

Pete returned to the platoon. He knew tomorrow they were going to continue the drive through Garapan, the most heavily populated portion of the town. That meant buildings and houses crammed together, all now reduced to rubble and all probably hiding enemy snipers just itching to put a bullet through a US Marine or two.

Oh yeah, Pete thought. *The fun never ends.*

CHAPTER 24

Tadashi Tanimura stood outside the cave in the midnight darkness, listening to the steady rumble of American artillery in the hills to the south. The sound was gradually getting closer as the Marines inched nearer to the newly established Japanese line.

About three hours earlier, news had come that the Americans attacking Garapan had reached Sugar King Park. Perhaps more ominously, the news arrived by runner and not over the radio. In fact, there had been no radio messages from the Garapan area for at least ten hours. Tadashi frowned. He heard General Saito come up from behind and stand beside him.

"The news about the fighting in Garapan saddens you," Saito said.

"Yes sir," he said. "As a boy I used to join my friends in playing baseball in Sugar King Park. Quite often the other boys chose me as a team captain because I was the only one who had been to America and actually saw a real baseball game."

The two stepped back inside the cave.

"That must have been most enjoyable," Saito said.

"Yes," Tadashi agreed. "So the concept of Sugar King Park as a battlefield staggers my mind. Memories can be a two-edged sword."

"When I was a child, we lived near the town of Misato, but my mother would take me to Sendai for the festival," Saito said, a note of sadness in his voice. "She firmly clung to the old ways, traditional dance and music. She played the shamisen with a delicacy that would make the gods smile. She also knew almost every old folktale there is and would recite them to me at night. I especially enjoyed the *Issun Boshi*, the One Sun Boy who was just three centimeters tall yet managed to defeat a demon and save the girl he loved."

"I don't know that story," Tadashi said.

"Maybe your favorite was Momotarō," Saito said. "A lot of people like the story of the Peach Boy."

"I don't know any of the traditional Japanese folktales," Tadashi admitted. "My mother was American, remember? The traditional folktales she read to me at night were from a mythical author named Mother Goose and two German brothers named Grimm."

Suzuki, clearly irked about the rapport between his boss and a man he inwardly considered a half-breed with questionable allegiance growled, "It's best that your mother did not know our cherished folktales. An enemy alien should not be permitted to corrupt our heritage."

Tadashi glowered at Suzuki.

"My mother was not an enemy alien," he said tersely. "She was a loving woman from a different culture, who was devoted to her family, her heritage, and to Japan, her adopted country. By calling her an enemy alien, you bring disrespect upon her, but you also bring disrespect down upon yourself."

The two men glowered at each other, anger in their eyes.

"That's enough," Saito said. "You are like the cobra and the mongoose. I need your help to fight this battle, and there is no time for you to fight each other."

Tadashi turned and bowed deeply to Saito, saying, "My apologies, General."

Suzuki grudgingly followed suit.

Tadashi stormed out of the cave, followed by Hanaya.

"The man's a mud turtle," Hanaya growled.

"An idiot can only be cured when he dies," Tadashi said.

————

Lt. Shimada called his squad leaders together in a tumbled-down hut he had claimed as his CP. In his hand he held a sheet of paper with lines pointing left to right and up and down. Some had scribbling beside them.

"Battalion wants to wrap this up today so we're throwing our entire force against Garapan," he said. "I know there's been some scuttlebutt that the Japanese are setting a trap for us in Garapan, that they have a great number of heavy and light machine guns strategically placed. Captain Stacey doubts that and so do I. We both feel that since the enemy is known to be strengthening a line up ahead, they have probably left just a skeleton force to hold the town in an attempt to slow us down and buy them time to strengthen their works. So the problem is not the number of Japanese left behind, but how to root them out."

He pointed to some of the lines running left to right on the paper.

"Right now, we're here." Shimada pointed to his map where two lines intersected. "We're calling it Twenty-Seventh and Broadway. The heaviest concentration of buildings is between

Broadway and westward to Beach Road, which skirts the coast. From where we are now, that's about a thousand feet, but as we go north it widens to half a mile or more. Dog Company and Easy Company on our left will lead the way with Fox in reserve. In our sector here on the right of the battalion line, First and Second Platoons will advance together while Third Platoon will be reserve. But once we cross this street"—he pointed to one of the horizontal lines marked Kadena Di Amor Street— "Third Platoon will move up and take position between First and Second because Broadway starts to curve northeast, widening the gap between it and the coast. Our area of responsibility will be the space between Broadway and this north–south road, Asusena Avenue. Elements of the 1/6 will advance on the east side of Broadway across from us."

He now pointed to a spot where heavier pencil lines intersected.

"This is the brass ring," Shimada said, circling the spot with a stubby pencil. "The town's major roadways, Middle Road—or Broadway—running north to south, Garapan Road intersecting from the west, and Sugar King Road approaching from the east merge here. This is Times Square. After that, the buildings become sparser as do places for snipers to hide. We take Times Square, and Garapan is pretty much ours. Questions?"

"Yes sir," Pete chimed in. "Armor support? All those hollowed-out buildings with second-floor windows, it'd be useful if we could throw a couple of 75s into them. I'm also concerned that we lost both our flamethrower and our bazooka team."

"I haven't forgotten that, Sergeant," Shimada said. "Captain Stacey is trying to get us a new bazooka team. Flamethrowers are a little harder to come by, they're more in demand, but we're trying. As for armor, we'll be supported by at least two platoons of Shermans and one of Stuarts."

"Sir," Marty Manson piped up. "With the buildings we've been clearing so far, we've been burning through grenades like wildfire. I'll bet there aren't five left in my entire squad."

Zoo-Zoo gave a "Hear! Hear!"

"Everyone has been running low," Shimada said. "Captain Stacey has Flint trying to track some down. You know Ernie. He'll get them if he has to do it at gunpoint."

The supplies arrived at 0740 and Flint outdid himself. Besides crates of .30-cal and .45-cal ammunition, there were enough grenades to give each platoon three crates. For Second Platoon, these seventy-five grenades were enough to give at least three per man.

"I love that little bastard Flint," Zoo-Zoo told Pete as they sorted crates for the platoon. "He should get the Medal of Honor."

At 0800, with artillery and naval fire blanketing the town ahead, the Marines began their push.

As expected, resistance was light initially as the battalion crossed Rosa Street and reached Dama Di Noche Street. After crossing this road, Pete got Second Platoon deployed between Broadway and Asusena Avenue. He sent Manson's squad up Asusena, Second Squad along Broadway, and gave Zoo-Zoo's squad, the largest of the three, the admittedly shitty job of picking their way forward between the two streets, traversing rubble-filled backyards and alleyways. Cautiously, the platoon began inching their way forward, doorway to doorway, ducking into hollowed-out buildings and dashing across ground strewn with the ruins of what had once been peoples' lives.

Pete moved with Aldrich and Second Squad. On Broadway, in front of what he suspected had been a clothing shop, Pete spotted a female mannequin lying in the street, nude except for brown shoes and a wig. He chuckled out loud when he saw the tanks politely swerve around the unclad lady. Further along, bloated corpses of two cows were lying in the street, legs stiffened in death.

The deeper into town they probed, the more it seemed that for all intents and purposes, Garapan had been all but flattened. Shattered concrete and wood spilled out onto the streets from collapsed buildings. Sheets of twisted corrugated iron roofs, burnt-out homes and businesses, charred timbers, broken glass, furniture, clothing, shoes, and children's toys all spoke of the devastation and heartache suffered by the inhabitants of what was once their homes and businesses. As he followed Pete, Rosie stooped to pick up several pieces of flat cardboard.

"I'll be damned," he said. "Look at this, Hardball."

Rosie held half a dozen baseball cards featuring Japanese players. Amused, Rosie pocketed the sum of his looting.

Resistance began in earnest as the Marines approached Kadena Di Amor Street. It started when an explosion erupted from one of the tanks as the vehicle struck an aerial bomb that had been adapted for use as a land mine. As if that were the signal, rifle fire suddenly poured out of the battered buildings lining Kadena Di Amor. Now the rubble piles that had been obstacles became a haven for the Marines avoiding enemy fire. As two other tanks maneuvered around their wounded colleagues to provide the crew a safe escape, the infantry took cover among the ruins and returned fire. Japanese bullets pinged off broken concrete and splintered wood.

Gutsy tank commanders led their vehicles forward, turning off Broadway and onto Kadena Di Amor. With enemy bullets clanging off their armor, the tankers began firing their main guns point-blank into the houses that concealed the enemy. Still, the stubborn Japanese held their ground.

Tiring of the back-and-forth, whistles began blowing. Dog

and Easy Companies surged forward across the street. Pete rallied Second Platoon and together they burst into doorways, shooting and yelling at the top of their lungs. The fight was now room to room, floor to floor. A grenade would be followed by men crashing through doorways, weapons blazing.

Entering a two-story structure, Aldrich's Second Squad went through it textbook style, clearing it from the top floor down. Handicapped by having only two fire teams instead of three, the Professor sent Honeybun's team to secure the exterior perimeter of the structure. The remaining team gained access to the building through a partially collapsed wall. Aldrich and Dubbs stayed by the entrance to secure an exit in case things went wrong and sent Rosie and Perkins up the stairs. The two men stormed up the stairway. At the top, a Japanese soldier appeared, looked down, then ducked back. Rosie knew that a grenade was coming, so he readied himself. He was right. Hearing the "thunk" as the soldier activated his grenade by striking its arming rod against his helmet, Rosie saw the grenade coming their way. Making a one-handed grab that would've made Joe DiMaggio proud, in one motion he hurled the lethal missile back upstairs. As the grenade exploded, he bounded up the remaining steps. One Japanese soldier lay dead in the hallway while another one, dazed by the blast, tried to regain his feet. Rosie shot him dead. With Perkins behind him, they swept through four rooms, killing two more of the enemy.

An overeager Dubbs ran up to a closed door, intent on bursting through. Surprised by Dubbs's disregard of tactics, Pete hurried after him just as Dubbs crashed into the room. Inside were two Japanese soldiers. The first one immediately raised his hands in surrender. Dubbs let up his vigilance for just a second.

It was a decoy. As the first man feigned surrender, the second man yanked a hidden pistol from the waistband of his comrade's trousers and fired twice. Both bullets hit Dubbs, who was slammed against the wall. With a surprised look on his face, he slid to the floor. Pete raised his Tommy gun and riddled both men with bullets, their corpses falling one atop the other.

"Get a corpsman!" Pete yelled as he knelt beside Dubbs. He removed Dubbs's first aid pouch, ripped open some bandages, and tried his best to stem the bleeding.

Dembrowski, hearing the call for help, raced into the room.

"Fuck," he cursed as he saw his friend lying on the floor bleeding. He knelt beside Dubbs.

Dubbs, his eyes partially opened, seemed to be watching the process, but Pete wasn't sure if he comprehended what was going on.

"Take it easy, Dubbsy," Dembrowski kept muttering. "Take it easy."

Aldrich arrived, followed by Magruder.

"Get outta my way, guys," he said hurriedly. "Let me get in here."

As Magruder worked frantically over Dubbs, Pete turned to Aldrich.

"We gotta keep going," he said to the Professor. "Get the squad moving."

Aldrich nodded and rallied his men.

"You too, Dembrowski," Aldrich said, and the man reluctantly rose and followed. Aldrich gathered his squad outside, and they returned to the fight.

"You might as well go too, Hardball," Magruder said.

Pete looked at Magruder, his eyes asking a silent question. Magruder understood and just slowly shook his head.

The fighting intensified as the Marines drew closer to the next cross street, Flores Rosa Avenue. They were now entering "Center City Garapan," the town's two most populated blocks, which meant even more debris for the enemy to hide among.

One tank, a light Stuart, had been destroyed on Kadena Di Amor Street when a Japanese soldier, clutching a mine, hurled himself under the tank's right tread. He and the tank's forward gunner were killed in the blast that left the Stuart a smoking wreck. The other three crewmen were wounded. Undaunted, the remainder of the tanks emerged from Kadena Di Amor and headed for Flores Rosa where they sent more 75mm shells into more buildings, adding to the debris.

Second Squad took refuge in the corner house at Flores Rosa and Broadway, exchanging fire with several of the enemy. Pete rejoined the squad. Dembrowski looked at Pete.

"Dubbsy?" he asked.

Pete just shook his head.

"What happened?" Scrap Iron asked. Pete told him. "I told him not to trust the bastards. Every goddamn Jap should be killed."

"Lt. Shimada is Japanese," Pete reminded Scrap Iron.

"You know what I mean," he replied and resumed firing.

Pete left the house from the back and carefully went on to the next one, which was occupied by First Squad. This was a red frame structure with moderate battle damage. Inside, he found Zoo-Zoo directing his squad's fire on a stone house across the way that contained a Nambu machine gun. Firing through a hole in the front wall from his position on an upper floor gave the gunner a wide field of fire. Zoo-Zoo directed his BAR men, Wings and Bill Francis, to concentrate their fire on the upper floor, but the enemy gunner's cleverly constructed position using concrete and heavy wooden beams seemed impregnable.

"Lieutenant Shimada went back to try to scare up a bazooka or a tank," Zoo-Zoo said to Pete. "We can't seem to hit the bastard. He has a little bunker up there. How're the other guys?"

"Dubbs was hit," Pete said. "I don't think he's gonna make it."

Zoo-Zoo shook his head sadly.

For the next several minutes, the men of First Squad played hide and seek with the machine gunner until Shimada finally returned with a bazooka team in tow. Zoo-Zoo led the man carrying the tube to a front window and carefully directed his aim.

"Give me some covering fire," the bazookaman told Zoo-Zoo, whose men obligingly unleashed a heavy fire into the building to make the gunner duck his head. Then the bazookaman raised the weapon, sighted in, and pressed the trigger. The rocket zoomed through the hole in the opposing wall and slammed into the gunner's homemade blockhouse. With a roar, concrete, wood, and pieces of the gunner's body flew into the air, some of it, including a leg, dropping to the street.

"Pays to have the right equipment," Zoo-Zoo said. Then he turned to Pete.

"While you're here, take a look at this place," he said.

Careful to avoid showing themselves to any other Japanese who might want to use them for target practice, Zoo-Zoo and Pete crossed the room. From the amount of broken china and glassware scattered about, Pete thought it might have been some type of café.

Zoo-Zoo stooped over and picked up several once elegant kimonos in shades of red, blue, green, and purple, all adorned with delicately painted images of birds, flowers, and willow trees. Sadly, most were badly ripped and dirty.

"And what do you think of this?" Zoo-Zoo asked. He directed Pete's attention to a pile containing thousands of condoms, most still in wrappers, piled on the floor. There were also sake bottles, all of which were empty, to the chagrin of the Americans.

"What was this?" Pete asked. "A cathouse?"

"No," Zoo-Zoo said. Then, indicating Lt. Shimada, he

added, "The Lieutenant says it's a geisha house, although I'm not sure what the difference is. From what this looks like, all the Japs did here was drink and screw."

"It says geisha house on the building," Shimada injected. "Although this might have been a place of prostitution. Traditionally geishas are hostesses and entertainers, not hookers. Real prostitutes sometimes ply their trade by calling themselves geishas."

Shimada signaled Pete to join him.

"Magruder wanted me to tell you Dubbs didn't make it," Shimada said.

Pete could only nod.

"The next cross street is Garapan Street, the main east–west artery," Shimada said. "Easy is being sent back to reserve and Fox is moving up. When they are in position, about half an hour from now, we'll push onto Garapan Street and take Times Square. Besides Broadway, five streets cross Garapan and connect with Flores Rosa. The first two, Kala Chucha and Bukiki Avenues, are ours to take, while Filooris, Puti Tainobui, and Alaihai Avenues are Fox's responsibility. When we get to Times Square, on the northwest corner is a large two-story concrete building. That's the town post office. Do you think Second Squad can handle it?"

"With the loss of Dubbs, they only have six men," Pete said. "Seven if I go along."

Shimada thought for a moment.

"Once we get there, I'll send you a fire team from Zulicky's squad," he said. "They'll be your covering party. You lead the search party inside, establish a base of fire, and send searchers up the stairs."

Pete nodded.

By now, the enemy's Flores Rosa defensive line was giving

way and enemy soldiers began filtering rearward toward Garapan Street. On every street as the Americans advanced, they
trod upon the detritus of people's lives. In a house along Broadway, Aldrich came across phonograph records produced by the
Nipponphone Company and a record player from the Teitoku
Gramophone Company. Flipping through a stack of records that
had survived intact, Aldrich was amused to see that the musical
tastes of the people were eclectic, ranging from traditional Japanese to Bach and Wagner to Bing Crosby and Rudy Vallee to
the big band sounds of Glenn Miller and the Dorsey Brothers.

The homes, or what was left of them, told a little about the
family. Most Japanese homes had some sort of Shinto shrine or
Kamidana. These were usually made of intricately hand carved
wood, some with delicate artwork and colorful banners. Chamorro
homes were identifiable since they usually displayed Christ on the
cross. But war does not discriminate and most of the religious
articles in private homes were smashed or missing altogether, possibly stolen by looters or Marines out souvenir hunting.

Tanks and infantrymen moved slowly but steadily along the
streets leading to Garapan Street. Since jump-off that morning
from the area of Sugar King Park to Garapan Street, a distance
of about four hundred yards, the battalion had lost fourteen
men killed and 109 wounded. They counted at least sixty enemy
bodies. Now they had to cross Garapan Street, the widest road
in the town.

Pete sat in a concealed position inside a stoutly built concrete structure on the southwest corner of Times Square looking
out of a window. He was struck by how forbidding the intersection looked, especially when one considered that men with
rifles and machine guns probably had the junction covered by
overlapping fields of fire.

The building Pete was in had served Garapan as a bank.

There were several tables, chairs, and a row of teller windows. A large safe stood against the back wall and the heavy door was wide open. There was no money in the safe but there was some paper currency scattered about. Pete assumed Japanese soldiers stumbled across the bank and grabbed what they could carry. But to him and his men, it was worthless. In fact, the squad laughingly tossed it around like confetti and referred to it as "monkey money." Dembrowski took some to use as toilet paper.

Aldrich and Pete weren't thinking about the money. They were both studying the two-story structure directly across Garapan Street. The post office building showed battle holes from bullets fired by American fighters and shrapnel scars from naval shells and artillery.

Besides the six men left in Second Squad, Lt. Shimada had borrowed three from First Squad, including Stuart Pierson, Wings Wingenroth, and Moose Shay. These last two were armed with BARs.

"How do we want to play this?" Aldrich asked.

"How 'bout we attach Zoo-Zoo's boys to Honeybun's fire team," Pete said.

"Yeah," the Professor agreed. "With two BARs and Scrap Iron's Tommy gun, they'll make a strong covering party. We'll take the search party into the building. You set up the foothold position right inside the door with Perkins while Rosie and I go upstairs and clear that floor."

Pete looked at his friend.

"You take the foothold position," Pete said. "I'll take Rosie to the second floor."

Aldrich shook his head.

"According to the book, the foothold position is established by the fire team leader," he said. "You're the ranking NCO so it's your job to hold the potential escape route open."

Pete knew his friend was correct, so he just nodded.

"Just don't get killed," Pete said. "I don't want to write any Dear Veronica letter."

"I told you . . ." Aldrich said.

"I know. I know," Pete said, grinning. "She's just a friend."

Like the preceding assaults, this one was accompanied by armor that ranged along Broadway, swerving around piles of debris and firing point-blank into suspected Japanese hiding places. Even as 75mm shells burst through walls, Japanese infantry in the buildings sent a steady fire at the Marines of Dog and Fox Companies, who were now racing across Garapan Street. Pete led Second Squad across the broad avenue as bullets kicked up dust from the roadway. Under such heavy fire, the road felt as if it were a mile wide. Finally reaching the other side, Pete used hand signals to tell Honeybun to position his team around the west side of the building and Corporal Wings's team around the eastern side. Their job was to secure the perimeter in the event the Japanese tried to rush reinforcements to the post office.

Once the covering teams were in position, Pete and Aldrich each armed a grenade and tossed them through the vacant window frames. Then, along with Rosie and Perkins, they hurried up the concrete steps after the grenades exploded. On the stoop, they were confronted by a set of double wooden doors. Without pause, Pete kicked the doors open. A Japanese soldier standing about twenty feet inside the doors raised his rifle to fire, but Rosie loosed a three-round burst that bowled the man over.

Pete saw a stairway to the right of the doors and pointed to Aldrich.

"Rosie, on me," Aldrich barked.

As Aldrich and Rosie took the stairs two at a time, Pete and

Perkins took up a position behind a heavy wooden table just left inside the door.

The lobby was wide and ran almost the length of the building before ending at a long counter. The right side of the lobby had two offices, with windows overlooking Broadway. The doors of both were closed. When the searching party was through upstairs, these rooms would be cleared.

"Think there are Nips in those rooms?" Perkins whispered.

Pete was about to answer the question when one of the doors burst open and four enemy soldiers came out in a rush, yelling and firing randomly. When they saw the two Americans, they yelled again and adjusted their aim.

Too late.

Perkins fired twice, both rounds striking the Japanese soldier on the right. Pete's Tommy gun cut down the others.

Upstairs, Aldrich and Rosie found a board meeting room, its door yawning open. Aldrich reached the boardroom doors and peeked inside. He saw a long mahogany meeting table, its polished surface now dirty and scarred. A dozen mahogany chairs, some upended, others broken, were scattered about.

A dead man lay on the once posh table. Four or five others lay dead on the floor, showing the clear signs of suicide by grenade. Aldrich had seen it on Tarawa. Rather than be captured, men activated grenades and held them to their chest or head. It was a gruesome but efficient way to die.

In addition to the boardroom, there were three closed office doors. Carefully approaching the first, Aldrich threw it open, following up with a grenade. He burst in right behind the explosion but found the room empty. The next room was the same. In the third office, one wounded man remained. As Aldrich stormed in, the man squeezed off a shot that missed the Professor by inches, striking the wall behind him. Rosie entered and fired four quick rounds from his BAR that slammed the soldier back and he bounced off the wall before hitting the floor.

With the upstairs secured, the two went back down the steps. Pete pointed to the remaining unopened office. Aldrich and Rosie crossed the lobby and reached the far wall. Sideling up to the door, Rosie took a grenade from his belt. Aldrich reached out and turned the doorknob and threw open the door. Rosie tossed the grenade, and both braced for the blast. After the explosion, they rushed the room where they were greeted by two dead Japanese manning a Nambu machine gun pointed at the door. Had they just burst in without the grenade, the gunner would've easily shot them down.

Outside, Pete reassembled the entire team. By this point Fox and Dog Companies had crossed Garapan Street in force, although at the cost of another tank that stood disabled in the middle of the road. The men of Easy Company were moving up Broadway and filing into position to assist Fox Company in securing the final block of the town of Garapan.

Lt. Shimada spotted Pete and hurried over.

"Captain Stacey's orders," he said. "We're to hold in place. We're officially in reserve. We'll spend the night here, and by dawn the field kitchen will be up, and the men will get a hot breakfast. Then we sit tight for orders."

Pete decided to billet the platoon in the bank. It was a sturdy structure plus it had carpet, albeit well-worn carpet, that would be more comfortable to sleep on than the ground.

With the death of Dubbs, a pall had fallen over Second Squad. Dembrowski took it especially hard. Pete knelt beside him.

"I didn't want to get close to anyone," Dembrowski said. "But I did. I liked the guy. I really did."

"For what it's worth, I know what you're feeling," he said, and told Scrap Iron about Ted Giovanni.

"We can mourn for our friends," Pete told him. "But we're here to do a dirty, stinking job, and that's our first priority. If we forget that, someone will end up mourning us."

"I'm okay, Sergeant," he said.

"We got some time off, so that'll help," Pete told him. "But if you need to talk, I suggest you chat up the Professor. He talked me through some difficult times."

Dembrowski nodded.

Pete walked back across the room and sat down beside Aldrich.

"How's Dembrowski?" he asked.

"I think he's okay, but keep an eye on him," Pete said.

"I think we're all stressed," Aldrich said. "Thank God for reserve."

Pete smiled and curled up in a corner. Relaxed for the first time in what seemed like a week, he thought of Aggie. Then he drifted off to sleep.

CHAPTER 25

Tadashi was deeply concerned. It was now ten o'clock at night and it had been twenty-four hours since he heard any radio reports from the Garapan area. The last he had heard was that the Americans had reached Sugar King Park. Repeated attempts to contact the 136th Regiment had failed. The regiment was positioned just north of Garapan to bolster the forces engaged in the town and hold the door open for their withdrawal as well as the withdrawal of the Fifth Special Base Force and the 135th Regiment still fighting on Tapochau.

Shortly after midnight, a runner arrived from the Garapan command post with a note. Tadashi took the message and read it, consternation on his face.

Just as anxious for information, Colonel Suzuki hurried over to Tadashi.

"Garapan has fallen," Tadashi said.

The news jolted Suzuki.

"We thought they'd hold out at least another day or two to

give us every opportunity to prepare our new works," he snarled. "What happened?"

"With no radio communication, the 136th Regiment is withdrawing," Tadashi said.

A horrified look came over Suzuki who, though he was Saito's chief of staff, was also technically in command of the 136th.

"What fool ordered that?" He stormed, then turned to the runner and ordered him to hurry back and stop the movement.

Terrified, the runner, a private, said he wasn't sure where the 136th was since it had taken him an hour to find Saito's HQ.

Irritated, he snapped, "Wait here for orders."

Suzuki turned to Tadashi. Both men knew what this message meant. The overall strategic plan that Saito and Nagumo had been working on called for the 135th, 136th, and assorted naval forces fighting around Garapan and Tapochau to link up with the line Saito had established. To assist them, supplies had been hoarded in caves near Makunsha to be funneled to these forces to bolster their resistance. With the 136th pulling back prematurely, the forces fighting stubbornly in Garapan, and the men of the 135th on Tapochau would be cut off and isolated. Resupply and armed assistance would no longer be possible. His men were being left to wither on Tapochau.

Tadashi felt embarrassed by the news. In 1940, before the war with the Allies, he had served with the 136th as an interpreter to read intercepted American and British messages.

"I must see General Saito," Suzuki said through clenched teeth. "I need to rally the 136th. I want to return to my old command or what's left of it. If I am to die on this island, then it will be at the head of my men."

He began throwing his personal items together.

"You can't just leave him, Colonel," Tadashi said urgently. "I will wake the general."

Tadashi gently nudged Saito awake, then showed him the message and told him of Colonel Suzuki's desire to return to his former command.

"I cannot spare you," Saito told Suzuki. "I understand your duty to your regiment. But you also have your duty to me. Since the line north of Garapan is collapsing, dispatch runners to tell all commanders to fall back to the Tanapag–Tarahoho Line. With the loss of Garapan and the collapse of the 136th, our situation grows worse by the minute."

Suzuki bowed deeply.

As promised, the field kitchen had set up on Broadway at Flora Rosa Street, making it an easy walk for the men being served while keeping the kitchen away from the front and the threat of being shelled by Japanese mortars. The morning fare was shit on a shingle. Yes, there was more cream than dry beef in the glop, but it was hot and relatively tasty. After getting his plate filled, Pete stopped by a table where a mess man was pouring fresh hot joe.

"Blonde and sweet?" the bean jockey asked.

"Black as the devil's soul," Pete replied.

Pete spotted Aldrich, Honeybun, and Rosie sitting together on the curb of the sidewalk along Broadway directly in front of a building that had served as the local movie theater. Abandoned lobby cards still on display in showcases facing the sidewalk showed sword-wielding men in kimonos. Unfortunately, no one could read the title until Lt. Shimada walked by.

"Lieutenant," Pete called out. "This movie sure looks exciting. What the hell is it?"

Shimada walked up to the theater doors and studied the lobby cards.

"*The 47 Ronin*," he announced. "It stars Chōjuro Kawara-saki."

"He's one of my favorites," Pete said sarcastically.

"If it isn't Roy Rogers, I'm not interested," Honeybun said.

Shimada laughed, then said, "Hardball, after morning chow, have the men get ready to move out. We're being relocated to Tanapag Harbor and the Flores Point seaplane base. We'll still be reserve, but it puts us closer to the front in case we're needed."

The hike to Flores Point should have been an easy one for the veterans of Dog Company. The road they were walking along was like an old friend. It was the same one they'd been following since their initial landings. At that time it was just the coastal road, then it became Middle Road, followed by Broadway, and now back again to the coastal road. However, what should have been a walk in the park became a muck-filled challenge when the heavens opened up to release a downpour. Men who had them donned ponchos to keep as much of their gear and themselves as dry as possible. The friendly coastal road turned into a quagmire, where mud tried to suck the boondockers off men's feet.

Slogging past Tanapag Harbor, the men saw the smashed remains of landing barges and ruined seaplanes. Overlooking the harbor was Observatory Hill, with its fifty-foot lighthouse topped by a copper roof that stood unscathed.

Two hours after leaving Tanapag Harbor behind them, the column arrived at Flores Point. Like the harbor, American shells and bombs had done their job. So had the men of the Army's 105th Regiment, who had fought over this ground previously. Japanese corpses, so fresh that they had not yet begun to blacken under the harsh sun, lay scattered where they fell. Any American casualties had been carried off.

The column halted and fell out with orders to make themselves as comfortable as practicable but still be ready to move on a moment's notice. A few of the base's structures remained relatively intact and the thoroughly soaked Marines took advantage of this. The Second Platoon utilized a damaged building whose three remaining walls managed to hold up most of the roof. Toppled tables, benches, and ruined cooking equipment in a kitchen told that this had been a mess hall. The men staked out dry spots and settled in.

Typical of the tropics, the heavy rain that had sprung up so quickly disappeared the same way. The sun came back in all its blazing glory and the soaked earth began to emit steam under the warm sunshine.

Pete used this time to look around. Standing on the beach just above the tide line, Pete studied the charred carcass of a ninety-two-foot-long *Kawanishi* flying boat that had drifted ashore, probably after an American air raid, and burned on the beach. Out in the harbor, Pete saw three more of the aircraft, dubbed "Emily" by the Americans, partially submerged at their moorings. Close by were the remains of two *Nakajima*, "Float Zeros" or "Rufes."

As the afternoon wore on, the sound of battle to the north and east grew dimmer as the front line pushed northward through Tanapag. Pete sat by himself, composing a letter to the family of Private Sammy Dubbs of Bethlehem, Pennsylvania. He told them how Sammy was so well liked in the squad, that his humor always left the men laughing, and of his heroic sacrifice during the taking of a major enemy position. He hoped they'd believe it and that they'd find comfort. He sure as hell didn't.

Finishing, Pete watched Gunny Nicholson approach. The gunny also noticed the gunfire moving away from the company's position.

"After coming so far in this fight, part of me would like

to be in for the kill," Nicholson said. "But another part of me hopes they can wrap this thing up without us."

Changing the topic, Nicholson said, "At 1600, bring your platoon back to the CP to stock up on ammo and supplies." He saw concern in Pete's face. "No, we're not moving up. Not yet anyway. It's just a precaution. Also, tomorrow we're going to be receiving replacements. The company should be getting at least forty guys. That'll put us up to about one hundred twenty. I think your platoon is in for eight or ten guys straight off the boat, so disperse them wisely."

"More cannon fodder," Pete said. "Do you realize that of six replacements I had when the squad left Hawaii in May, only Dembrowski is left. And of the four I got a few days ago, I have only Perkins and McCready."

Nicholson nodded.

"It could get worse before it gets better," he said. "Have your platoon on fifty percent alert tonight. The front line may be ahead of us, but there are still Jap stragglers behind us, and they're trying to move north to rejoin their friends. This coastal area is a prime route for them to take. Password is Luscious Lips."

He paused to light up a Lucky Strike. Pete took his cue. He removed a pack of Camels from an empty ammo pouch and fired one up.

"Keep this under your hat," Nicholson said softly. "After Saipan is secured, there's an island five miles to the south called Tinian. It's a lot smaller than Saipan and not as heavily defended, but someone's gotta take it, and you can bet old Howlin' Mad isn't going to give that job to the Army."

After Nicholson departed, Pete went looking for Lt. Shimada. Finding him at the platoon CP, he mentioned Nicholson's talk about replacements.

"Yes," Shimada said. "In fact, I was just thinking about how to disperse them. You've obviously given it some thought."

"Yes sir," Pete said. "If I get enough, I'd like to revive Fire Team Three in Second Squad." Shimada nodded agreement. "Put two new guys in that team and bring McCready back in as well."

"Who would you suggest to lead it?" Shimada asked.

"Rosie," Pete stated. "He's the most logical choice. Dembrowski's been a Marine longer and he's real good in a fight, but he's a loose cannon. I also suggest boosting Rosie to corporal, but I don't have that kind of power. He's earned it. You can bet he won't like leading a team, and he'll bitch about it, but I'll deal with that. Dembrowski also deserves consideration for corporal stripes. As for the other four replacements, two men per team will bring us back to full strength."

"Those are good suggestions, and along the line of what I was considering," Shimada said. "Let's see what the division sends us, and we'll go from there."

————

Tadashi sat cross-legged on his blanket, eyes closed as he tried to reconcile in his mind today's sudden downturns. Yes, Garapan would fall. There was no preventing it. But not at least for another day or maybe two. The sudden collapse would pressure efforts to make the Tanapag–Tarahoho Line as impregnable as possible.

The loss of Garapan involved more than just real estate. Besides the losses in men and materials, gone now were three 140mm guns mounted on railroad cars. These had proved very effective against American ships and landing beaches. Also lost were three 5-inch coastal guns, thirty-two 120mm dual purpose guns, six 200mm mortars, hundreds of spools of barbed wire that could've been used to bolster the Tanapag Line, twenty large searchlights, and boxes of canned crab that had been imported from Hamburg, Germany.

Perhaps even worse than the capture of Garapan and the materials was a loss of men's spirits. More and more he was seeing soldiers, individually or in groups, straggling back from the front, dispirited, and often weaponless. Some chose not to wait for the final battle to die.

The headquarters complex was also showing signs of deterioration. One of the three caves had become a hospital. More and more it was being filled up by wounded men. Inside the cavern, medical corpsmen worked feverishly to patch up the wounded, especially those who might be able to continue the battle. But with every wounded man patched up, there was that much less medicine and equipment to help the next man.

Some of the men wandering in were near death from thirst. They told stories of how the Americans had used captured maps showing Japanese watering areas as a trap. As men came to fill canteens, presighted artillery or mortar rounds would fall on their heads.

The wandering men also learned to take canteens from the dead while others trapped rainwater.

As a diversion, Tadashi thought of Kokoro, delicate as a spring blossom. Before he left for Saipan, Kokoro had held a small but traditional *chanoyu*. Tea ceremonies had been a part of Japanese history dating back hundreds of years, so it was no surprise that her parents, traditionalists, had a small tea house behind their home.

He wore his best uniform and she her finest *iromuji*, a solid beige kimono adorned with delicately painted branches and cherry blossoms. It had been a wonderful evening, even though some parts of the traditional meal she prepared for him had to be eliminated due to unavailability of supplies.

Bowing deeply, she said, "Please forgive my poor attempt to give you a *chanoyu* worthy of a warrior."

Tadashi looked at her endearingly.

"I'm hardly a warrior, Kokoro-san," he said. "As for your 'poor' attempt, your meal was worthy enough for the emperor himself."

Afterward they had gone for an evening stroll, arriving in a park that had once held the ancient Yonezawa Castle. There, standing on the bank of a moat that had surrounded the castle, he took her into his arms, and they kissed.

That night, she gave herself to him.

Tadashi Tanimura was in love. Of that there could be no doubt. The thought made him happy yet sad because he might not live to enjoy that love. He knew Kokoro felt it too. But as a true Japanese woman, she accepted whatever fate decreed for them both.

Two bodies, same heart.

He hoped the gods would smile on them.

———

Pete had a restless night and sleep was difficult. That was just as well. It was shortly after 0200 hours when he heard a shuffling sound like feet walking through tall grass. It was coming from behind his position.

"Password!" he called. There was no response, so cocking the Thompson he again called, "Password or I fire!"

The enemy, stragglers trying to reach their comrades, fired first. A blaze of muzzle flashes twinkled in the dark, and Pete heard invisible bullets streak by. He cut loose with a long burst from the Thompson, sweeping the weapon left to right. With an unintelligible yell, dark figures charged from the night. Gunfire erupted from rifles mounted with bayonets. All around Pete, men of Second Platoon jolted awake and joined the fray.

The enemy came screaming out of the night like phantoms, bayonets at the ready. Bullets from the Marines found most before they reached the American line, but a few broke in, slashing and stabbing as they went. Aldrich felt a bayonet tear through his shirt as he fired his Garand into the man's face. An enemy soldier came lunging at McCready. The boy managed to knock the Arisaka away, and they both fell into the foxhole, a tangle of arms and legs. Dembrowski, who shared the foxhole, yanked his Ka-Bar from its sheath. Wrapping an arm around the Japanese soldier, he pulled the man off McCready and plunged the seven-inch carbon steel blade into the Jap's chest.

Pete cut down two enemy soldiers before his magazine ran empty. He pulled the .45 from his shoulder holster just in time to fire at a third man who was charging in his direction.

The melee only lasted five minutes. American casualties were light. One man, "Boomer" Bordon of Third Squad, suffered a minor arm wound. He remained on the line. As for the enemy, twenty-three bodies lay sprawled on the ground. None had escaped.

Half an hour later, another soft sound wafted through the night air, this time from out in front. Pete's finger clenched on the trigger of the Thompson as Rosie called out, "Halt! Password!"

A call came back, "Pas Chamorro."

"Don't fire, but be ready," Pete warned. "Peace Chamorro" was how local natives surrendered to the Americans.

From out of the darkness, a knot of men, women, and children came forth. Some were dressed in well-worn clothes while a few wore more formal attire. All had their hands up, clearly terrified. Pete waved an arm for them to come forward. The grown-ups gave a collective sigh of relief as they were waved into American lines. The children broke into smiles when McCready and Aldrich handed out chocolate bars from their K-ration kits. The children divvied them up eagerly.

"Siesta" Minozo of First Squad spoke Spanish and was dispatched to escort the civilians to a rear area.

Settling back into their positions, the Marines came under attack again. This time it was 105mm stuff from enemy guns on the sloping ridge of Mount Tapochau. The men of Dog Company utilized whatever cover they could find—foxholes, old shell craters, and the ditch that ran beside the coastal road.

Pete had piled into a shell hole with Aldrich.

"Do you think they know today is the Fourth of July?" Aldrich asked between shell bursts.

"Is it?" Pete asked. "I'll be damned."

The barrage was short. The silence of night overtook the men again.

The sun was above the horizon by 0600, and the grisly task of disposing of the dead Japanese began. Marines dragged corpses to nearby shell craters, rolled the bodies into the pits, and shoveled dirt over them. That job finished, the men opened their K-ration breakfast boxes. Pete had an unpleasant task to perform. Finding Rosie sitting with Aldrich on the trunk of a fallen tree, Pete tapped Rosie on the shoulder. Rosie, who had just opened a tin of chopped ham and eggs, looked up.

"I need to talk to you," Pete said, sitting on the log next to the boy from Poughkeepsie. "And you, Professor." Pete saw Hullihen enjoying his breakfast a short distance away.

"Honeybun! Get your ass over here," he called.

Hullihen joined them, also taking a seat on the log. Pete stood and faced the three.

"We're getting replacements today," he said. "I don't know how many. Gunny said our platoon could get eight or ten. The Lieutenant and I have talked about it and he's given me the okay to disperse the replacements among our platoon. Professor, since Second Squad has had the most casualties, I'm gonna try to hopefully get you three or four guys. Revive Fire Team Three. Put McCready back there plus two new guys. The rest of the replacements you'll put into the other teams as needed."

"How about a leader for Team Three?" Aldrich asked.

Pete turned to Rosie.

"That's where you come in . . . Corporal Roseblum," Pete said.

Rosie looked like someone had just crapped on his shoes.

"No, no," he said. "Not me. I don't want the stripes or the job. Keep it."

"I don't think you're going to have a choice," Aldrich said to him in a low tone.

"When the replacements get here, Professor, you disperse them among your fire teams as you think best," Pete said.

Aldrich nodded while Rosie cursed to himself none too quietly.

It was shortly before 1300 hours when Pete saw Lt. Shimada approaching at the head of a single file of Marines, whose uniforms and weapons screamed "fresh fish." Pete counted ten men and gave a silent "Hallelujah." That was two more than he had hoped for. He rounded up all three of the platoon's squad leaders and met with Shimada behind Second Squad's position.

At Shimada's command, the replacements formed a line. Shimada consulted a paper he held in his hand, then gave it to Pete.

"Take roll, Sergeant," he said.

Pete consulted the list.

"Sandina, Pedro," he barked.

"Here, Sergeant," replied a tall, lean, dark-complected man with cheeks scarred by childhood chicken pox.

"Says here you're from Detroit," Pete said.

"Yes, Sergeant," he answered. "I worked in that new Ford plant at Willow Run."

Consulting the list, he said, "Zeamer, George."

"Here!" said the lanky six-footer.

"Gettysburg, Pennsylvania?" Pete asked.

"Yes, Sergeant," he said proudly. "My granddad was in the Union Army and fought in the Wheatfield just two miles from his home."

Pete turned and smiled to Aldrich, who nodded as both men in unison said, "Honeybun."

Moving on, Pete said, "Palmer, Edward. Minnetonka, Minnesota."

"It's a Sioux name, means 'Great Waters,'" replied a slightly pudgy man with a smooth baby face.

"Are you Sioux?" Pete asked.

"My great grandfather was, so I'm one-quarter Sioux," he answered.

Continuing, Pete said, "Summers, Robert. Fullerton, California."

"Here, Sergeant," came the reply.

"We have another Californian. Jones, Galen. Arroyo Grande," Pete said.

"Just call me Jonesy," came the jocular response.

Pete glared at the man for his unsolicited and unwelcomed familiarity.

"I will after you get that spanking new uniform and rifle good and dirty," Pete said.

Next, he read, "Cezon, Manuel. Guadalupe, Arizona."

"Here, Sergeant," said a muscular six-footer with jet black hair peeking out from under his helmet.

Pete nodded. "Carvell, Richard. Grand Island, Nebraska."

"Here, Sergeant," a quiet voice responded. The man, standing about five foot ten, looked as unassuming as his voice.

Going on, Pete said, "Kostecky, Paul. Canterbury, Connecticut."

"Here, Sergeant." The voice came from a barrel-chested man about six feet tall, with a BAR slung over one shoulder.

"You any good with that weapon?" Pete asked.

"I certainly am," the man replied.

"I hope so because I'm damned short of AW men."

Consulting the list, he next read, "Keener, Martin." Pete paused. "Where the hell is Crab Orchard, Tennessee?"

A boyish lad of about eighteen smiled.

"East Tennessee, Sergeant," he said. "Cumberland County. Population is only about five hundred people. It was named after the crab apples that grow every which way."

Pete fought back a chuckle and moved on.

"Balmer, Warren. Teaneck, New Jersey."

"Here, Sergeant."

Completing the roll, Pete scribbled something on the list, then showed it to Lieutenant Shimada. He read the scribblings and nodded.

Turning back to the line of replacements, Pete said, "You new men, listen up. In case you've forgotten, you are now in Second Platoon of Dog Company. You've met Captain Stacey, our CO, and Gunny Nicholson. You've also met our platoon leader, Lieutenant Shimada, who in case you missed it, is an American Marine officer of Japanese descent. Just to avoid confusion." He signaled for Zoo-Zoo to step forward.

"This is Corporal Zulicky of First Squad," Pete said. "Palmer, Jones, you two will go with him."

After Zoo-Zoo led his two off, Pete had Manson step out. "This is Corporal Manson of Third Squad. Summers, Cezon, and Carvell, you three will go with him."

Once they were gone, Pete addressed the remaining five men.

"You men will be assigned to Second Squad. This is Sergeant Aldrich; he is the squad leader. He's competent, he's got guts, and he's smart as hell. Listen to him."

With a nod, Aldrich told his new replacements to follow him, and they headed back to the squad area. Pete was elated. With the replacements, all three squads were each just one man short of full strength.

Tadashi was aware that the slow but steady advance of the battle lines northward made the cave at Makunsha untenable.

Tadashi was outside the cave, standing with Hanaya as the two listened to the artillery banging away beyond the ridge.

"They seem to have an endless supply of explosives," Hanaya said.

"It does seem louder today than usual," Tadashi mused. "Maybe because today is the Fourth of July." Hanaya looked quizzical. "American Independence Day," Tadashi elaborated. "When their leaders signed the Declaration of Independence from the British. In the United States, they celebrate this day with flags and banners and fireworks."

About that time, General Saito emerged from the cave. He wasn't outside more than ten minutes when several American shells came streaking in. The first landed between two of the cave's guards who were sitting together on the ground brewing tea. The blast sent one shredded body tumbling into the air while the second man disappeared completely. Another shell struck near the hospital cave, killing three previously wounded men lying near the entrance. The last shell killed no one, but shrapnel from the explosion sliced across Saito's upper right arm. The officer grunted and staggered but did not fall. Tadashi and Hanaya were at his side instantly.

"It's a grazing wound, sir," Tadashi said. "Let's get you inside. Somebody fetch a doctor from the hospital cave."

Colonel Suzuki joined them, visibly relieved to find Saito had suffered only a minor injury. They managed to get Saito to sit on his cot. The doctor hurried in and began treating the general's arm.

Knowing Saito was being tended to, Tadashi walked back to the cave entrance and stared across the valley. Earlier that day, he had seen men digging in on the slope and along the crest of the distant ridge, but assumed they were friendly. Now he knew that enemy spotters were there. Thankfully they had no idea of Saito's presence.

Knowing Americans were on that ridge just across the valley made Tadashi feel like they were entirely surrounded. Here was more evidence that defeat and death were looming.

Hanaya hurried up to Tadashi.

"General Saito wants you and me to make a physical check of our defensive line, to see how strong it is, and if it can hold the Americans back," he said.

Tadashi nodded. The general was correct. While orders had been issued to form a new line, no one from staff had ever followed it up personally. Tadashi quickly went into the cave to retrieve his pistol, strapped the leather belt around his waist, and then he and Hanaya were off.

What they found was horrifying. The defensive line that was

to stymie the American advance barely existed. Trenches were either lightly held or entirely vacant. Pillboxes were practically empty and camps vacated. In one camp, the men had fled so hastily they left a fresh half-butchered water buffalo lying on the ground. The fact that hungry men could flee before such a feast was a chilling omen.

Reaching the shore, Tadashi and Hanaya ran north along the beach and found the same situation everywhere. They spoke to local commanders and the story from each was the same; they simply did not have enough troops. Some said they might be able to hold the American attack off for a day or maybe two, but no longer. Others feared their lines would dissolve at the initial enemy contact.

Returning to the command cave after dark, Tadashi reported the sad news that the Tanapag Line had dissolved if, indeed, it had ever been formed. Saito looked pensive. Then he looked resolute.

"How many troops do we have to man the defenses?" he asked.

"Five thousand," Tadashi answered. "No more."

"Then we have only two choices," Saito said. "To stand here and fight and be captured or to attack and die a glorious death. Tomorrow morning we will begin to assemble all remaining troops in our area for the final attack."

Tadashi knew what that meant. The end of them all. The end of everything.

It meant *gyokusai*.

CHAPTER 26

In his heart, Tadashi always knew this fight would end in *gyoku-sai*. The term meant "shatter the jade" and stemmed from the belief that all Japanese, being a pious and gentle people akin to precious gems, would be destroyed in a final, desperate assault.

The phrase had been floated loosely for the last few days, at least on a philosophical level. Now it was on the verge of becoming a reality. What made it so sad, Tadashi thought, was that the end result of such an action would not defeat the Americans. That opportunity had melted away like the morning mist before a rising sun. Rather, the intent was for each man to kill as many of the enemy as possible before finding his own glorious death.

Tadashi had joined the Imperial Army with the lofty goal of preserving the Empire. That it could mean losing his life was understood. Now that moment appeared to be at hand, and he wondered if he was ready to die. He would if he had to, of course, but is any man truly ready to die? He was sworn to make the ultimate sacrifice for the Empire, but was it unpatriotic to

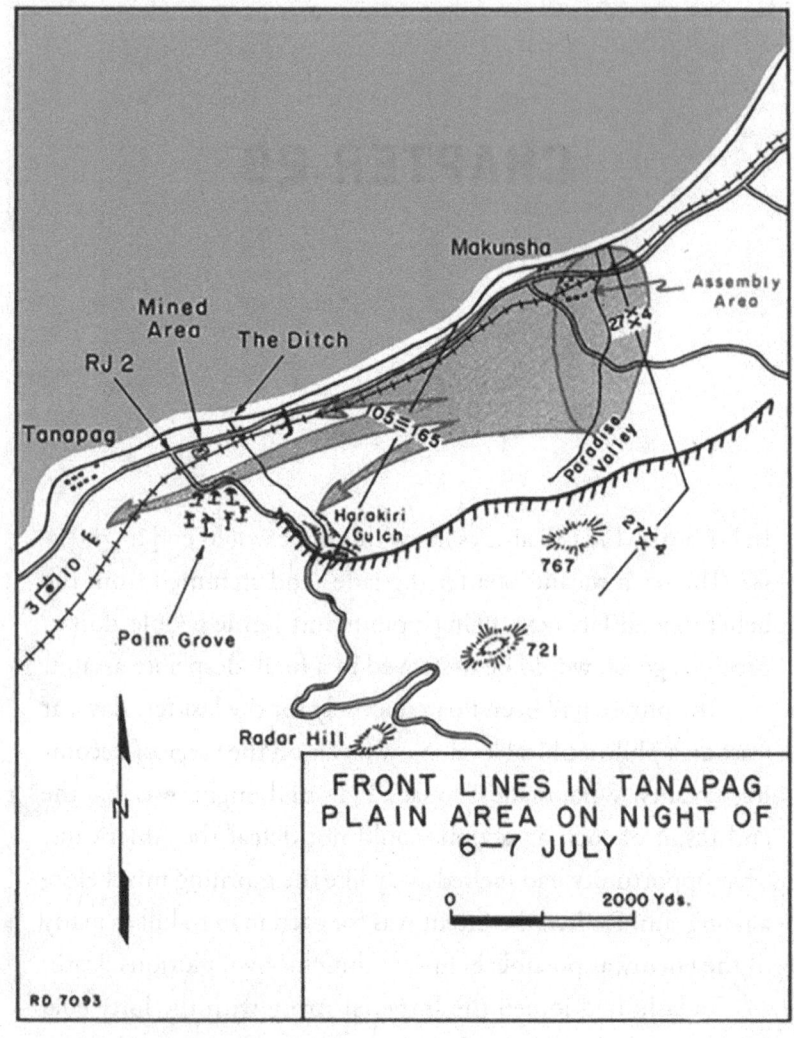

FRONT LINES IN TANAPAG
PLAIN AREA ON NIGHT OF
6-7 JULY

0   2000 Yds.

RD 7093

want to live? Or was that just his mother's Christian faith playing with his mind?

He thought about his parents. He knew his father would be saddened by the death of his only child, but would Hideo Tanimura also be proud of Tadashi's heroic sacrifice? And if Tadashi should be captured, would his father feel relief that his son had survived, or would he experience humiliation at his son's disgrace?

What about Kokoro? Beautiful Kokoro. He once told her she was as delicate as a rose petal. She replied that if that were so, his presence provides the needed sunshine to nourish the flower. Thoughts of her saddened him and brought him the deepest pain.

And what of Saipan? His beautiful island home, where he had spent the happiest years of his youth—a land he had come to love more than Japan itself. Looking around, he felt despair. Everywhere he looked, he saw not just the destruction of the land, but the total annihilation of a way of life. The economy, the infrastructure, the very fabric of society had been decimated. Its gentle people had become animals, living in caves and scavenging the war-ravaged countryside for food. At the northern side of the island, he had heard that entire families were throwing themselves off cliffs. So real was their fear of the Americans—a fear, he knew from his own past, was unjustified.

Tadashi knew it would take Saipan decades to recover from the war, if recovery was even possible. He felt deep remorse at being a part of that destruction.

The previous afternoon, US planes had scattered leaflets addressed to General Saito, offering an opportunity to save the lives of noncombatants on Saipan.

"If the Japanese troops want to sacrifice themselves uselessly, that is their affair, but the American forces do not want to kill noncombatants," the leaflet read. It explained that civilians and other noncombatants should gather on Bandero Road, near Tanapag, at nine o'clock waving white flags.

Saito would not consider the plea.

Having made the ultimate decision, Saito and Admiral Nagumo were now hunched over maps and unit reports as they formulated a plan. Saito summoned Tadashi.

"I want you to take a message and send it to Imperial Headquarters," he said. Tadashi took up a notepad and pencil. Then Saito dictated, "On July 7, the day after tomorrow, we will advance to attack the American forces and will all die an honorable death. Each man will kill ten Americans."

"What if Tokyo overrules you?" Suzuki asked.

"Unless they can promise to send me ample reinforcements, my orders stand," Saito replied grimly.

"What about the civilians, sir?" Tadashi asked. "There are thousands of them hiding in this part of the island. Shall we warn them to move further north?"

Saito thought for a moment, then said, "There is no longer a distinction between civilians and troops. It will be better for them to join the attack with bamboo spears than to be captured. Write out instructions to that effect."

Tadashi bowed, but he felt ill at the order.

"We should contact unit commanders by runner so that our orders are followed," Suzuki said.

Saito nodded, then turned to an aide.

"Dispatch runners to contact Colonel Oka, Lieutenant Colonel Naki, and Captain Kazu," Saito commanded. "Have them report to me as soon as possible."

"July 7 is nearly upon us," Suzuki said. "Do you feel we can be ready in time, or should we move the attack back a day or two?"

"No," Saito said. "I have given this much thought. I chose

July 7 because it marks *Tanabata*. What better day to join our ancestors? To my staff, I regret that I have no colored *tanzaku* on which you may write down your final wishes, but I do have white paper you may cut into strips if you so desire."

Hanaya passed, but Tadashi took a sheet of paper, tore off a narrow strip, and composed a note wishing Kokoro a long and happy life. Then he went outside. Not having bamboo branches available, as tradition required, Tadashi attached the note to a sturdy tree. Lost in a deep sense of personal grief, he watched the paper flap in the breeze and hoped the gods would read it after he was dead.

———

Pete, the Professor, Rosie, and Honeybun were sitting together in the shelter of a small clump of trees. It had been a quiet day so far, meaning they'd only been shelled three times. Luckily, the Japanese aim was bad, so all the bombardments did was scare the shit out of the new guys, at least two of whom were curled up in foxholes crying. They'd soon learn.

Then, out of the blue, Aldrich asked Pete, "You have a birthday coming up, right?"

"Yeah," Pete replied. "Day after tomorrow. The seventh. Why?"

"No reason," the Professor answered.

"How old will you be?" Rosie asked.

"Twenty-one," Pete replied.

"Hey, when you get back to the States, you can legally drink," Rosie said.

"Speaking of back home," Aldrich said. "Have you given any more thought to my offer about us partnering up with Captain Jack?"

"I wrote Aggie about it to see what she thinks," Pete replied.

"But what do you think?" Aldrich pressed.

Pete paused, then said, "If Aggie is okay with moving to Maryland, I'll take a look at it. But are you sure you wanna do commercial fishing rather than that psychology stuff? You're pretty damned good at it."

"Who said I have to give up on psychology?" Aldrich replied.

"Who's this Captain Jack guy?" Honeybun asked.

"He's a grizzled old sailor," Aldrich said. "Spanish-American War vet. Served on the USS *Oregon* at the Battle of Santiago de Cuba. Now he's a commercial fisherman I worked with over the summer to raise tuition money."

Aldrich was going to go on when they heard a rumble of engines. The sound was coming up behind them, growing ever closer. Soon a convoy of trucks and jeeps was visible moving north along the coastal road. Some of the trucks carried Marines, and all towed 105mm and 155mm artillery pieces and ammunition.

"That's the Tenth Marines," Pete observed.

"Yeah," Aldrich said. "The Army's up ahead, but I don't get it. The Army has their own artillery."

Aldrich looked at Pete.

"Something's up," he said. Pete just nodded as they all watched the convoy roll past.

The trucks weren't yet out of sight when Nicholson jogged up. He signaled Pete to follow. After collecting Second Lt. Michael Jones of First Platoon and Second Lt. Carl Swanson, Third Platoon's recent replacement leader, Nicholson led them all to the company CP. Captain Stacey was there, along with Lt. Shimada, Yaz Yastremski, and mortar team leader "Pogey Bait" Baker.

Standing beside Captain Stacey was a major Pete did not recognize.

Pete and the other new arrivals snapped to attention.

"At ease," Stacey said. "This is Major Waller, Battalion S2. He's got something to say, so listen up."

Major Waller cleared his throat.

"General Smith and the other top commanders want you to know that while we're aware that this has been a tough fight, tougher than we first anticipated, the end is in sight," Waller said. "To acknowledge that, HQ has issued the following memo." Consulting a sheet of paper in his hand, he read, "The enemy's ability to offer effective resistance has been eliminated. His freedom of movement has been restricted. His centers of resistance have been constrained. The end of the Saipan operation is in view."

"Sir," Nicholson injected. "If I may, why were the Tenth Marines moving several batteries of artillery forward?"

"Just a precaution, Gunny," Waller replied. "Don't read into it. The 105th has just asked for additional support as they push on to the northern tip of the island. Maybe they figure our guys are better shots," he added with a grin. "Any other questions? If not, then carry on."

Everyone began drifting away as Waller climbed back into his jeep. His driver gunned the car and off they went.

"The end is in sight," Pogey Bait scowled. "Don't piss on my shoes and tell me it's raining."

Captain Stacey probably agreed with Pogey Bait, but as an officer he chose his words carefully.

"Don't think for a minute that this fight is over," he said. "Go back to your commands and stay alert."

As Pete walked along the platoon line, Pfc. Eduardo Sanchez flagged him down.

"Sergeant, do you have a minute?" he asked.

Pete asked the boy what was on his mind.

"When I shipped out, I was eager to get into this thing," Sanchez said. "But now that I'm here, and I see dead Japs laying around and can hear the shooting up ahead, I'm scared. Real scared. It's all I can think about."

"I understand the fear," Pete said. "For what it's worth, we all feel it, and I mean every goddamned day that we're on the line. Think about that job at Willow Run. Is the plant as big as they say?"

"Hell yeah," Sanchez said. "It sits on sixty-seven acres of land. The building is a quarter mile wide and half a mile long. To send messages from one end to the other, they have guys driving jeeps. We make B-24 bombers. Do you know there's a hundred thousand parts in a B-24?"

Pete whistled, then said, "You're sharing a foxhole with Scrap Iron. He's a good man in a fight. Listen to him and to Corporal Hullihen, and you'll do fine."

Sanchez nodded his thanks as Pete left.

————————

The response from Tokyo to Saito's message regarding *gyokusai* was not what he had hoped for but was what he expected. It came in just before dark.

"Continue the battle in order to gain time," it read. "Hang on and try to check the enemy. We are trying to send you reinforcements."

Saito crumpled up the paper, not in bitterness, but in despair. Those fools did not appreciate what he was up against.

"You've seen the orders, General," Suzuki said. "What is your plan?"

"Nothing has changed," Saito said. "We will proceed with our preparations for *gyokusai*. Major Tanimura, I will dictate my instructions to you, then I want you to mimeograph three hundred copies for disbursal among all the units."

"Yes, General," Tadashi replied.

Several of Nagumo's staff officers were present and argued against *gyokusai.*

"We have gotten our orders from Imperial Headquarters, and they must be obeyed," said Rear Admiral Hidemasa Igeta, Nagumo's intelligence officer. "We must buy time for our submarines to bring in supplies and troops."

"And how long will that take?" Suzuki shot back. "A day? A week? A month? We can't hold out that long. We must attack in full force and end this battle one way or another."

Nagumo and Saito said nothing during the exchange. In the end, Saito's order stood.

The night of July 5–6 was a beehive of activity in the command cave. Admiral Nagumo, who had relocated his headquarters to another location, sent Tadashi a gift and a note via a runner. The gift was his last bottle of Suntory whisky, two-thirds drunk, with a note to "Tashy" saying, "We will not meet again in this life, but at Yasukuni Shrine or perhaps in our beautiful Yamagata Prefecture. Until then, please enjoy the last of my excellent whisky. You are a fine officer. Too bad you're not in the Navy."

As dawn broke over Saipan, Tadashi split the bottle with Hanaya and the two stood just inside the cave entrance watching the figures of American infantrymen atop the ridge across the valley.

"This could well be the last dawn we see," Hanaya mused, sipping the whisky. "It has been my honor to have been your friend."

Tadashi nodded his appreciation.

"Not many men would say that to me," he replied. "So many like Colonel Suzuki look at me in disdain."

"Do you have any regrets?" Hanaya asked.

"Only in regards to Kokoro," Tadashi mused. "She came into my life too late."

"Maybe in the next life," Hanaya said.

"Perhaps," Tadashi replied, thinking of his mother's Christian faith of reunions in heaven.

He fished out his pack of Hikari cigarettes he'd been given as a parting gift from Prince Tsunenori. There were just three left inside. He offered the pack to Hanaya who declined as expected. Tadashi lit one up.

Saito and his staff had spent the night planning the attack, which was to be launched at 0400, in about twenty-two hours. The sleepless night and the stress of command was showing on Saito. He appeared bedraggled and dispirited.

Earlier he had met with Lt. Colonel Naki, Captain Kazu, and Colonel Oka, all of whom led large numbers of surviving troops. Colonel Suzuki was also present. Saito had the men gather around a map of the Tanapag region. Using his index finger as a pointer, he said, "I have decided to launch *gyokusai*. Your officers will gather every man you can rally and lead them in the attack. Rather than attack on a broad front, we will focus on specific areas in order to smash our enemy and their supply bases. Colonel Naki, your men will attack south along the railroad tracks. Captain Kazu, you will attack along Lt. Col. Naki's left flank, and Colonel Oka, you will attack along the coast. You will press the assault until the last man is dead. Every soldier will do his utmost to kill ten Americans before dying an honorable death. No one is to come back. Any man who finds himself alive by 1300 hours on July 7 is to kill himself. As I plan to depart before the attack, Colonel Suzuki will be in overall command and will issue all orders."

"Excuse me, sir," Suzuki said. "I ask the privilege of accompanying you to Yasukuni."

Saito considered briefly, then nodded.

"Very well, Colonel," he said. "Colonel Oka, you will be in overall command. Turn your troops over to a subordinate. As for me, I am old and cannot make any meaningful contribution to this patriotic effort, so I intend to commit seppuku very soon. It makes little difference whether I die today or tomorrow, so I will die first. Please forgive me for going on ahead. I will be at Yasukuni Shrine to await you all there. But before I make that journey, I will issue a proclamation to be read to all soldiers before the attack."

After the others left, Suzuki said, "I wonder if our sacrifice will help to defeat the Americans in the long run."

Saito thought, then replied, "With many strokes, a large tree can be felled."

———

The morning of July 6 was quiet for Pete and the men of Second Battalion. The rumble of artillery from the hills told that the Japanese were still out there and full of fight. Around 1100 hours, Pete noticed Lt. Shimada making his way along the line.

"I got a bad feeling about this," Pete observed.

Aldrich just nodded.

Shimada knelt beside Pete and the Professor.

"Alert your men—we're moving up in about an hour," he said. "I'm sure you saw the Tenth Marines moving their guns to the north yesterday. They took position about twelve hundred yards southeast of Tanapag. Their CO has requested additional Marines to help protect their flanks. A detachment from the Twenty-Third Marines will set up on the Tenth's right flank, and we'll dig in on the left."

"What's up, Skipper?" Pete asked.

"For the past several days, the Army and Fourth Marines have been picking up more and more POWs as they advance," he said. "Ordinarily they're privates with no information G2 finds useful. However, a few of these men speak of massed troops and something called *gyokusai*."

"And that means what?" Pete asked.

"Shatter the gem, shatter the jade. Something like that," Shimada said. "But it's the date I find more ominous. They say it will take place tomorrow. It's the seventh day of the seventh month. In Japan it's called *Tanabata*. Supposedly the spirits of their dead ancestors return to Earth. They consider it a good day to die."

———

As this longest of days wore on, Saito's decision received approval from the highest level possible. A message arrived from Emperor Hirohito himself saying, "The Saipan defense force should carry out *gyokusai*. It is not possible to conduct the hoped-for direction of the battle. The only thing left is to wait for the enemy to abandon their will to fight in the face of *gyokusai* of the one hundred million."

Tadashi thought, "Was the emperor hinting at *gyokusai* for every man, woman, and child in Japan in case of an American invasion?"

However, the emperor's wishes for Saipan would not have mattered either way. The orders were given.

Saito's proclamation to his men, dated July 6, was actually ready by 2000 hours the night before.

"I am addressing the officers and men of the Imperial Army on Saipan," Saito had written. "For more than twenty days since the American devils attacked, the officers and men and civilian

employees of the Imperial Army and Navy on this island have
fought well and bravely. Everywhere they have demonstrated
the honor and glory of the Imperial forces. I expected that every
man would do his duty. Heaven has not given us an opportunity. We have not been able to fully utilize the terrain. We have
fought in unison up to the present time, but now we have no
materials with which to fight and our artillery for attack has
been completely destroyed. Our comrades have fallen one after
another. Despite the bitterness of defeat, we pledge 'Ten lives
to repay our country.'

"The barbarous attack by the enemy is being continued even
though the enemy has occupied only a corner of Saipan. We are
dying without avail under the violent shelling and bombing.
Whether we attack or stay where we are, there is only death.
However, in death there is life. We must utilize this opportunity
to exalt true Japanese manhood. I will advance with those who
remain to deliver yet another blow to the American devils and
leave my bones on Saipan as a bulwark of the Pacific.

"As it says in the *Senjinshen*, 'I will never suffer the disgrace
of being taken alive, and I will offer up the courage of my soul
and calmly rejoice in living by the eternal principles.'

"Here I pray with you for the eternal life of the emperor
and the welfare of the country. I advance to seek out the enemy.

"Follow me!"

While the proclamation was being disbursed, a messenger
from the Navy communications cave arrived with orders from
Tokyo to "gain time." Reinforcements were promised.

The Navy staff, the messenger said, wanted to obey the
order.

"It is too late now," Suzuki said upon hearing the message.
"The arrow has been shot."

Standing by the cave entrance, in the distance Tadashi could hear men yelling "Banzai" and *"Meiyo no tame no shi,"* meaning "Death for Honor." By this time tomorrow, he thought, those voices will be stilled forever.

Since General Saito had issued his final order, his staff ceased to have any function, so men attached to the general began collecting their personal gear. Tadashi considered rolling up his spare clothes in his blanket, then decided nothing had value anymore. The only property he made sure he took with him, besides his pistol and sword, was an American made Ronson cigarette lighter his father had given him, and the gold cross and chain from his mother that he always wore around his neck.

Tadashi noticed Hanaya fondling a white sash he'd removed from his pack. It was his thousand-stitch belt, meant to protect the warrior in battle. Silently, Hanaya wrapped the *senninbari* around his waist and fastened it. Tadashi admired the belt and its neat rows of stitches, each one indicating a prayer for the wearer. Hanaya's mother walked the streets asking friends, relatives, and passersby to add a stitch.

"That is an elegant *senninbari*," he told his friend. "All the years I've known you, I've never seen you wear it."

"I did in the Philippines," Hanaya said. "Since being on staff, I've never been in any up-close combat, so I did not feel threatened. Now the need for prayer is present." He paused briefly. "Do you have a *senninbari*?"

"No," Tadashi replied. "My mother would never have known how to make one."

"Then how will you pray?" Hanaya asked with deep concern.

Tadashi fished inside his shirt and brought out the gold cross and chain.

"This meant a lot to my mother," he said. "I pray to this."

It was close to 2200 hours. Saito turned to face Tadashi.

"I hope you will excuse me for going first," Saito said.

"I fully understand, General," Tadashi replied. "It is a matter of honor."

"You have been a loyal and faithful aide-de-camp, Major Tanimura," Saito said, then handed Tadashi a folded paper. "This is a battlefield promotion for you to the rank of colonel. Keep it on you so that when the Yankee devils find your body, they will maybe treat you with more respect."

Tadashi bowed deeply.

"Domo arigato gozaimasu, Saito-sama," he said, giving the general high praise by elevating him to the title of lord.

"It is little enough for all your hard work," Saito replied, acknowledging the praise. "Now you can do one more thing for me. I want you to serve as my second. You may use your revolver. Since I do not wish for the Americans to make a spectacle of my body, I want you to take sufficient gasoline stored by the generator and cremate my remains."

Tadashi, choked with emotion, could not speak so he bowed his agreement.

Suzuki stepped forward. He was holding two folded flags in his hands.

"Would you also please burn the regimental colors of the 135th and 136th Regiments?" he implored.

Tadashi nodded and took the flags from Suzuki's hands.

Addressing Tadashi and Suzuki, Saito said, "My faithful assistants. Let us have one last meal together."

Aides had spread a blanket on the ground. On it was one of the final bottles of sake still left unopened and a few tins of sweetened crab meat. One of the headquarters staff opened the sake and the tins and handed them to each officer. A delicate porcelain cup was produced and sake poured into it. This was handed to Saito while Tadashi and Suzuki used tin cups.

Saito lifted his cup in salute.

"Blessings to our emperor," Saito said with a toast. "May Japan live for ten thousand years."

The men drank their sake and consumed the crab meat in absolute silence, each lost in his own thoughts.

The meal finished, Saito rose and walked out of the cave. He entered a smaller adjoining cavern, which until now had served as a barracks for some of the guard garrison. Suzuki went with him, followed by Tadashi and Lt. Sasaki, commander of the headquarters security garrison, who was asked to serve as Suzuki's second. After walking a few paces into the cave, they stopped. Here both Saito and Suzuki sat cross-legged on the rocky floor. Earlier Saito had ordered this area cleaned to make it a fit place for the final act of his life. Sasaki oversaw the work. On the ground before Saito lay three swords, the forty-one-inch-long *katana*, the twenty-seven-inch *wakizashi*, and the sixteen-inch *tanto*. The blade of each was secured in its polished scabbard. Suzuki knelt behind and slightly to Saito's right with his swords laid out before him.

For several long minutes, Saito sat motionless, a resolute expression on his face as he steeled himself. Suzuki did the same. Then Saito took up his *katana* and unsheathed the sword, its forty-one-inch blade gleaming. He gently laid the scabbard aside and then bared his abdomen. Tadashi quickly looked around for water to pour on the blade to purify it and at the same time moisten the blade for a clean cut. But there was no water handy and besides, there wasn't time. Placing the tip of the sword against his bared abdomen, Saito took a deep breath, then rammed the razor-sharp carbon steel into his body. His face remained impassive as he dragged it across his stomach, blood oozing over his hands and into his lap. Tadashi was sickened and wanted to turn away but dared not. He had to watch for the signal from Saito that the pain was unbearable so he could deliver the coup de grace. He removed the 9mm pistol from its holster and aimed the weapon at the back of Saito's head. Then it came. Saito lowered his head, and Tadashi squeezed the trigger. The shot resounded throughout the cave. Tadashi watched the body collapse as if in slow motion. The gunshot was followed by a second report as Suzuki, who'd opted to use his *wakizashi* sword, with its twenty-seven-inch blade, dropped his head, and Sasaki fired. Grieved beyond endurance, Sasaki put the muzzle of his revolver into his mouth and fired again. He dropped dead across the body of Colonel Suzuki.

Tadashi stared down at the three dead men.

Behind him several staff members gathered. Tadashi whirled and barked to one man, "Go to the generator and get me ten liters of gas. Quickly!"

When the gasoline was delivered in two five-liter canisters, Tadashi, with some difficulty, withdrew the *katana* from Saito's body, then laid it and its scabbard by the general's corpse. Then he took one can of gas and poured it liberally over the general's body. Then he did the same with the second can. He ordered more gasoline and doused Colonel Suzuki's body as well, although not that of Lt. Sasaki, who had killed himself without permission. Tadashi had the young man's body dragged aside.

The gasoline was lit by Tadashi using crumpled and now useless reports.

As the flames grew, Tadashi took the flag of the 135th Regiment and dropped it into the growing conflagration. Then he held the 136th's flag. He stared at it briefly, recalling how early in his career he had served under this banner. Then he consigned it to the flames.

Turning on his heels, he told Hanaya, "I need to walk."

"Do you want me to come along?" Hanaya asked.

"No," Tadashi said. "I need to be alone. I will return before the time of the attack."

He left the cave, the crackle of the funeral pyre echoing in his ears.

At this same time, in his command cave, Admiral Nagumo issued his own statement to the naval forces under his command.

"The opportunity to repay the benefits received these many years from our country is now," he said. "Every man will mobilize his full power to annihilate the enemy on the beach, to destroy his plan, and to hold our country's ramparts."

Then he put the barrel of his pistol against his right temple and pulled the trigger. Moments later, Admiral Hideo Yano, Nagumo's chief of staff, put a bullet into his own brain.

Tadashi had no goal in mind when he walked, but somehow he ended up on the shoreline north of Tanapag. Perhaps his coming to the beach was instinctive. As a boy, he had always loved the shoreline, looking out at the horizon, and wondering about the world beyond. He'd comb the beach for seashells and driftwood, and imagine himself as a sailor exploring new undiscovered lands. Now he had seen the world and it was ugly.

He wondered what time it was. It had to be after midnight, making it July 7, the final day for many, including himself. Off to his right he saw shadows in the night. The shadows soon developed into a small knot of five civilians, three men and two women. Tadashi watched as they talked quietly among themselves, ignoring the lone figure standing some thirty yards away. Then as he watched, the five took hands and walked into the sea. One of the women seemed hesitant, but was gently coaxed into going along. Mesmerized, Tadashi watched them go and saw the water around them getting higher and higher as they walked out further and further. One by one the people disappeared until just one head, that of a man, remained. Then it, too, was gone. The mild ocean swells continued unperturbed as if nothing had happened.

Suddenly, Tadashi felt dirty. This is what the war had done to his friends and fellow islanders. Saipan had been good for him and helped him to grow and mature. In return, he and the other soldiers had come back bringing only death and destruction.

Tadashi stripped off his clothes and waded naked into the ocean until he was half immersed, then began scrubbing himself, scrubbing and scrubbing in a frantic urge to get clean. He vigorously bathed himself to the point of physical exhaustion. In some places, his self-purging drew blood. Then he staggered out of the water, exhausted. He dressed and headed back for the command cave. The end was upon him.

Dog Company began moving forward around 1230 hours, slogging along both sides of the roadway. As they neared Tanapag, they came upon the guns of the Tenth Marines as they took up position to support the Army dug in well to their front. Battery H, with its four 155mm Long Toms and two 105s, was set up five hundred yards southeast of Tanapag between the road and the railroad tracks. About 250 yards southeast and beyond the railroad tracks was Battery I, with Battery G four hundred yards to the southeast of that. As Dog Company filed by, they watched the smoke jockeys placing their weapons and preparing for any potential threats from the enemy.

Passing Battery H, Captain Stacey deployed First and Second Platoons about 150 yards beyond the gun line with orders to dig in along a shallow swale on the battery's left flank. Third Platoon would be held in reserve among Battery H's guns.

Stacey called for his platoon leaders to follow him, and they began retracing their steps back to Battery I.

"You may've heard that we've been picking up POWs who keep mumbling about some sort of mass attack to be launched maybe as soon as tomorrow," he said. "We don't know if it's true or if they're just trying to unnerve us, but aerial reconnaissance as well as foot patrols have spotted a lot of Jap troop movement, so we can't take any chances. We expect the Army to hold back the Nips but if they can't and if, God forbid, we're swamped, we have one last ditch defense." He pointed to a stand of trees several hundred yards to the rear. "In that patch of woods, the Japs have a large supply dump, mostly aircraft parts probably intended for the unfinished airfield at Marpi Point. We're calling that Fort Apache. We take up a final position there, and we hold that ground no matter what."

He led them into the woods, where they were confronted by a jumble of wooden crates of various sizes, some stacked on top of others. Even now, Seabees initially assigned to inventory the dump were placing crates to provide an ideal battlement.

After inspecting Fort Apache, the group returned to the company.

It was just after midnight, July 7.

Pete was sitting in a foxhole with Aldrich when the latter began to chuckle.

"What's so funny?" Pete asked.

"I was just recalling our last liberty in Hawaii," he said. "We hopped a ride from the Big Island to Oahu. Master Sergeant O'Leary was with us, and we spotted some female Marines, the first we'd seen. O'Leary said, 'Goddamn it. First the Marines gave us dogs, now it's women.'"

"I miss that crusty old bastard," Pete said.

Aldrich poked his head up and gazed off into the darkness. "I wonder what the Japs are doing out there tonight," he said.

"When they decide, they'll let us know," Pete said, then added sarcastically, "Happy birthday to me."

CHAPTER 27

Returning to the command cave, Tadashi stripped off his clothes and donned his last, and best, uniform. It was time to go to the attack position. Then he took his map case and binoculars and walked outside into the night. Hanaya followed. Stopping at the lip of a steep ravine, he threw the map case over the edge. Then he opened his binocular case, tossed it as well, and studied the binoculars.

"They're beautiful glasses," Hanaya said.

"Zeiss," he said. "My father bought them for me in October of 1940, when he accompanied a contingent of diplomats on a visit to our German ally. My father was there to observe German farm methods, which is silly considering that Germany was at war with England."

"Are you sure you want to destroy them?" Hanaya asked.

"I don't," Tadashi said. "But I'd rather do that than have some American take them off my body and hang them on his wall back in America."

With that, he threw the binoculars out into the darkness. The two returned to the cave.

The rallying spot for the main column attacking along the railroad tracks was by the mouth of the valley below the headquarters cave. Fought over several times in the last few days, the Americans derogatorily called this Paradise Valley. To the Japanese it was known as the Valley of Death, and that name was never more fitting than it was today. Tadashi estimated that at least two thousand men were gathered in this location, called the center column. Guessing that the beach column had another thousand men and the east column perhaps fifteen hundred more, that meant the *gyokusai* was to be launched by approximately forty-five hundred soldiers. A number of civilians, men who until now had been huddled in caves consuming sake, joined in for the charge. Tadashi knew this would be the largest attack ever staged in the Pacific War unless, the gods forbid, the Americans land on the home islands.

Tadashi was impressed by the numbers, but his heart fell when he considered the fighting caliber of these men. True, aside from the civilians they were all Imperial Army and Navy personnel, but hundreds were already wounded and nearly a third had no rifles. Some of these carried sharpened sticks, machetes, and even pitchforks stolen from surrounding farms. The rest would follow a man already armed to pick up his weapon once he fell.

Perhaps worst of all, most were woozy from draining every sake bottle they found, and some were outright drunk. Broken glass from the bottles lay scattered everywhere.

Not all the men agreed to die in one gallant charge. Tadashi overheard one officer, a major, tell his men they were not attacking. Instead, they would head northwest toward the coast and continue the fight there. Others opted to go to Yasukuni ahead of the rest. Tadashi noticed three men, two privates and a corporal. They had been attached to Lt. Sasaki's headquarters garrison.

"Major," the corporal called, "we are going to Yasukuni Shrine together. I have a grenade. Will you accompany us?"

"No, thank you, but you may go ahead," he replied.

The corporal saluted. The men huddled close as he activated the grenade. With a loud bang, the trio of friends died together.

The image that stayed with Tadashi the most was the young lieutenant and his four men pleading with a major to allow them to kill themselves.

"We are the last survivors of our entire battalion," the young officer said, tears of shame streaming down his cheeks. "We pray for the honor of finding death now, together, and rejoining our comrades."

The major was adamant that they take part in the assault. Tadashi intervened.

"Major," Tadashi said. He reached into a pocket and drew out the paper from Saito promoting him to colonel. "I am Colonel Tanimura, aide-de-camp to General Saito. These men will not make a difference in the outcome of our attack one way or the other. Leave us." Looking angered at being overruled, the officer stomped off. Tadashi turned to the lieutenant. "You men may go together into the next world."

"*Domo, domo,*" the officer said.

He turned to his men. Automatically, one knelt before him.

"Cut cleanly, please," he said as the lieutenant raised his sword.

As Tadashi turned to walk away, he heard the blade's swoosh, followed by a dull thump, like someone slapping a melon. He heard two more swooshes, followed by two more thumps. A subsequent pistol shot told Tadashi the young officer had just joined his comrades.

"Such a waste," Tadashi muttered.

"Yes," Hanaya said. "I have been told that one hundred thirteen wounded men of the 135th Regiment have killed themselves by grenade within the last few hours."

By 0330 hours, most of the men making the attack from Paradise Valley and along the beach were gathered. Oka had broken the center force into two waves. He appointed Lt. Colonel Naki to lead the first wave. His job was to smash down the first lines of American defenses.

"I will lead the second wave," Oka announced. "Advancing over your corpses, we will finish the job."

Tadashi decided to attack with the first wave.

By 0400 hours, rain began to fall. Tadashi saw this as a mixed blessing. It would make the attack across muddy ground more cumbersome, but it would serve to muffle the Japanese approach and would decrease the Americans' visibility.

But the GIs were not totally dormant. Reports of Japanese troop movements by men huddled in listening posts brought artillery rounds crashing down on some of the massed units, and men died before ever making the attack.

At 0440 hours, the order was given. "Attack!" Men bid their comrades farewell and promised to meet them at Yasukuni Shrine. Tadashi watched one young private write, "My foxhole is my grave" on a slip of paper and slid it into his pocket to be found on his corpse after the battle.

Eager to strike the hated enemy, the three massive columns of Japanese soldiers headed south like a human tidal wave. Tadashi and Hanaya watched as they moved out with deadly determination, all knowing they would not come back. At this moment, Tadashi was proud to be one of the emperor's soldiers.

"Let us go, my friend," he said to Hanaya. Together they

followed the mass of troops plodding through the rain toward the waiting enemy.

"Goodbye, Father," Tadashi said to himself as he drew his sword from its scabbard.

———

The men of the 105th Regiment of the US Army's Twenty-Seventh Division weren't totally caught off balance. For the past hour, their outposts reported hearing a low murmuring sound, much like the drone of a very large beehive. They called in artillery fire.

Now the faint buzzing grew louder and louder still. Whatever force was building out there was on its way.

For five days there had been speculation that the further the Japanese were pushed into the northern corner of the island, the likelier they were to launch a major assault. So the attack now rolling their way did not surprise the GIs. The size of the assault was the surprise, and it quickly became evident that this was a human steamroller bent on destruction.

As Saito had decreed, machine guns—many firing the last of their ammunition—opened up, their red tracers streaking through the rainy night. American machine guns replied, making themselves targets for the attackers. While dozens of Japanese fell before the blazing muzzles, those who survived swamped the guns, shooting or bayoneting the crews, and trying to turn the captured weapons on the GIs.

The Marines huddled in a rain-soaked swale southeast of Tanapag and listened to the ominous racket from half a mile up ahead. Muzzle flashes from artillery flickered in the darkness like heat lightning, followed moments later by the growl of thunder. Added to all this was the faint crackle of small arms fire. Red and white tracers stitched crisscross patterns through the inky sky.

Moments earlier, the men of Second Platoon had been grous-ing about the rain. Now the rain was the least of their worries.

As Pete moved along the soggy swale, Honeybun said, "The Doggies are really catching hell tonight. Think they can hold the Nips?"

"We'll know the answer to that before the sun comes up," Pete replied.

———

The front ranks of the Japanese assault swept over the Ameri-can 105th Regiment. Foxholes and machine gun nests held for a while, but were soon drowned by the relentless tide. Tadashi noticed the bravery of the Americans as many stayed at their posts and died rather than fall back. He watched in awe as a wounded sergeant ordered his men to pull back while he stayed to cover them. The sergeant killed a dozen attackers before being run through by bayonets.

Time seemed to stand still as the fight swirled, much of it up close and hand to hand. Men were shot. Men were stabbed with bayonets and swords. Tadashi saw one officer attack an American in his foxhole, and with one swoop of his razor-sharp sword, he lopped off the man's head.

While some brave Americans held their positions in the face of certain death, more and more men began to break and flee, having withstood all they could bear.

Twice Tadashi was confronted by the terrified face of a young American soldier. He shot one man with his pistol and ran the second through with his sword.

Hanaya fought by Tadashi's side, his pistol and sword also drawing the blood of the hated enemy.

As he went forward amid the charging soldiers, Tadashi

found that, as an officer, he had attracted a following of about forty enlisted men. American illumination rockets lit the sky, and Tadashi and his self-styled platoon were confronted by a .30-caliber machine gun nest located in an old bomb crater. Tadashi turned to Hanaya.

"Take half the men and get on the flank of that gun," he said. "We'll keep them busy in front."

Hanaya was off, pointing to individual men and ordering them to follow.

"Forward!" Tadashi cried. He and his contingent raced ahead, shouts of "Banzai!" ringing out.

The machine gun reacted instantaneously, its muzzle spitting out a torrent of lead. Several of Tadashi's men were struck and violently hurled to the earth. Tadashi felt one American bullet tear through the sleeve of his tunic, leaving a jagged hole on the fabric but not touching his flesh. At the last minute, one member of the gun crew spotted Hanaya's band of men. He tried to lift a submachine gun to repel the attack, but Hanaya was on the man, his sword flashing. The rest of his soldiers inundated the gun crew. The gunner tried to rise and run but was tackled and bayoneted.

Caught up in a swirl of emotion, Tadashi pointed his sword in the direction of the fleeing enemy and ordered another charge.

"Let us seek out the enemy," he cried. "Follow me. *Totsugeki!*"

By 0600, two battalions of the 105th Regiment had fought to the limits of their endurance. Many men conducted a fighting retreat, while some simply ran for their lives. They had taken severe losses. For a few strange minutes during this wild melee, retreating Americans ran side by side with attacking Japanese.

The battle had raged for over an hour and was drawing perceptively closer. All along the Marine lines, fingers tightened on triggers. The sound of the approaching Japanese steadily increased like an oncoming freight train. Some sang patriotic songs as they charged, the words and melody interspersed with cries of "Banzai" and "Death for Honor."

Nicholson sought Pete out.

"Radio reports say the 105th has been overrun," he said sharply. "Get your boys ready. The Japs punched a hole in the line, and they're coming through. Alert your guys that if the Japs reach us, the smoke jockeys are gonna level their barrels and cut artillery fuses to four-tenths of a second and do ricochet fire. If things get too hot, the cannon boys will pull firing locks from their pieces and pull back on Battery G. We'll cover that displacement."

With dawn starting to streak the eastern sky, the first rattled GIs began streaming past the Marines. Some were weaponless, and all looked shocked and exhausted.

"They're coming," some of the more panicky soldiers called to the Marines. "Millions of 'em. Get out while you can."

None of the Marines moved.

Minutes later the Japanese emerged from the rainy mist, their ranks spread out left and right as far as Pete and his men could see.

"My God," Warren Keener, the Tennessee boy, said in awe. "They look like a swarm of locusts on a Kansas cornfield."

Zeamer of Gettysburg thought about his grandfather and wondered if this was what Pickett's Charge looked like.

Behind the platoon, the guns of Battery H opened fire. With the barrels leveled, Pete could feel the shells zipping by just above his head. Their fuses shortened to the bare minimum, the projectiles sliced through the enemy ranks and exploded amid the horde of attackers. Bodies and pieces of bodies cartwheeled into the air. But the rest pushed on without letting up.

With the distance separating them from the closing Japanese, the cannoneers turned to ricochet fire. Spouts of mud leaped into the air as 155mm shells glanced off the ground and jumped skyward. There they burst, sending a deluge of jagged shrapnel raining down on the heads of the men below. This was the most incredible display of firepower Pete had ever seen. He had witnessed banzai attacks both here and on Tarawa, and felt that under normal circumstances such a tremendous pounding would've turned the attackers away. But this was not a normal banzai attack. The only objective in this assault was death.

The lead elements of the attack had come within a few hundred yards of the American line when the open fire order rang out. The Marines along the swale poured out a steady stream of bullets and attackers fell like rows of wheat before a thresher. Pete moved along his line, loosing bursts from his Thompson as he went.

"Pour it on!" Pete yelled above the din. "Give it to 'em."

Warren Keener had never been so scared in his life. He fired his rifle into the mass, reloading and firing some more. He didn't know if he hit anyone, and he didn't care. They were trying to kill him. This was not the way he'd imagined war. Scenes from his favorite movie, *Guadalcanal Diary*, flashed in his brain. This was not what he'd seen in the movies.

As the Japanese attackers drew near, more and more artillerymen were struck while serving their pieces. Fewer men meant a slower rate of fire and that gave the Japanese the time to draw closer.

In the midst of this desperate fight, First and Second Platoons got the order to "Pull back to the gun line."

Hearing the order, Pete went among his men, echoing the command to displace. Together the two platoons leapfrogged rearward, one platoon passing through the other, firing as they went.

Now it was evident that the enemy was going to steamroll over Battery H. At 0650, the orders came to disable the guns by removing the firing locks and pull back to Battery G, which lay 250 yards southeast. The cannon cockers did as ordered, while Pete and the other Marine infantrymen provided suppressing fire. The attackers, their ranks considerably thinned but no less determined, pushed forward just a hundred yards behind the retreating Marines.

First and Second Platoons paused briefly by the now abandoned guns, fired a few volleys, then fell back some more. The Japanese were hot on their tail, swamping the abandoned artillery like a flooded stream flows over and around rocks.

Zeamer took a round that struck his right buttocks, then curved downward to emerge from the front of his thigh several inches below his groin. Staggered, the Gettysburg boy fell. Pete saw him go down and raced over, but before he got there, Honeybun had scooped Zeamer up and hoisted him over his shoulder. Several Japanese pursued the two men. Pete, now joined by Dembrowski, laid down a covering fire with their Tommy guns, allowing Honeybun to lug his burden rearward.

The fight for Battery H lasted slightly less than an hour.

Having successfully covered the artillerymen's withdrawal, the Marines suddenly found they were in danger of being flanked and overrun as more Japanese appeared on their right.

"We're going to Fort Apache!" Shimada hollered. "Follow me."

Tadashi and his makeshift platoon continued moving south-ward. Of the forty or so men he began with, his numbers were down to twenty-eight. However, their zeal never abated. They'd been in action for over an hour when they encountered a group of over a hundred men who appeared to be dejected and lead-erless. The only officer Tadashi saw was a young lieutenant, his right arm bloody and supported by a crude sling.

"I am Colonel Tanimura, and this is Captain Hanaya," he barked. "You and your men will follow us."

"Lieutenant Ono," he said, bowing. "My men and I are at your service."

The group continued southwest along a stream that quickly earned the nickname Bloody Run. In the gloom ahead, Tadashi saw a large group of Japanese soldiers attacking over a stubbly field littered with corpses. Led by an officer he did not recog-nize, they confronted three light American tanks perched on a small rise. At the officer's command, the men started forward only to be staggered when one of the tanks fired a canister shell, which had the same effect of walking into the path of a giant shotgun. Steel balls from the shell ripped a gaping hole into the Japanese formation. The result was devastating. The young of-ficer, severely wounded, placed his sword tip against his chest, then fell forward, impaling himself.

The tanks' victory was cut short as the steel beasts now came under attack from Japanese soldiers from three direc-tions. Tadashi led his men into the fray, coming up on the right flank of the Americans. Machine guns mounted inside one Stuart opened fire and cut down several of Tadashi's men. The tankers, knowing they were in big trouble, started roll-ing away, seeking safety. Two escaped but a grenade crippled one Stuart by blowing off a tread. Hanaya's echelon climbed all over the stricken vehicle, pounding on the steel in an effort to get inside. Tadashi saw Hanaya and Lieutenant Ono crawl up on the steel hull and try to pry open the main hatch. The steel lid opened slightly, and an American sergeant poked his head up, a pistol in hand. He fired twice, both bullets striking Hanaya in the chest. Tadashi was horrified as he watched his friend topple backward off the tank and plop down into the mud. The American tried to shoot Ono as well, but, despite his injuries, the young officer was quicker. He drove his sword into the American's chest. The top hatch now open, two grenades were dropped inside.

Tadashi hurried over to Hanaya and lifted his friend into his arms. Hanaya's eyes opened slightly, and he smiled.

"I will wait for you at Yasukuni," he said, so softly Tadashi almost could not hear.

Captain Kisaburo Hanaya closed his eyes and died.

Tadashi said a silent prayer for the best friend he ever had.

————

Reaching Fort Apache had been costly. Hastily counting noses among his platoon, Pete discovered First Squad had been hit the hardest. "Kraut" Schuler told Pete that he'd seen Myron White, the Lebanon bologna maker, killed. He also said that a new replacement, "Jonesy" Jones was missing. Wally Bright, the Schenectady pinspotter, had been wounded badly, although Doc Magruder expected him to survive. Veteran Zoo-Zoo Zulicky had been killed by a Jap grenade, leaving Bill Francis in charge of the squad.

In Third Squad, "Chef" Bruce Toler would never get to open his own restaurant, having been bayoneted in his foxhole. Manuel Cezon had suffered what could be a million-dollar wound that would earn him a trip back to

Guadalupe, Arizona. Andy Buffenmyer got lucky. A Jap bullet pierced Buff's helmet through the front, then angled upward to exit through the top of his steel pot without breaking the plastic helmet liner.

Second Squad had been lucky. So far.

———

Tadashi led the remnants of his command forward toward a distant battery of American guns he could faintly see in the morning gloom. The guns had barrels leveled and he watched as two shells literally bounced off the ground and exploded overhead. Shrapnel whizzed by his ears, but he was not touched. Yet three men around him were hit, one of them decapitated. He wondered how long his luck would last.

Another shell ripped into the ground and Tadashi saw Lieutenant Ono hurled through the air to land in a bloody heap a few yards away.

"Forward! Forward!" Tadashi yelled, waving his sword.

Ahead, in the growing daylight, Tadashi could see that the Americans were abandoning their artillery pieces. He saw Marine infantrymen conducting a fighting retreat as Japanese troops swarmed over the weapons even as American mortar rounds began bursting around them.

Reaching a swale about 150 yards from the abandoned artillery, Tadashi once again waved his sword and encouraged his men to charge. He never saw the next mortar shell explode. All he was aware of was the sensation of tumbling through the air, followed by a plunge back to earth. Dazed, he lay in the mud for several minutes as Japanese soldiers charged around him. He struggled to a sitting position and shook his head to clear his vision. He had been struck by shrapnel that had pierced his back, penetrating through to his right shoulder. Blood saturated his shirt and tunic. Blood was also flowing down his face from a gash to the right side of his head.

Looking around, Tadashi saw he was surrounded by bodies. He did not know how many. He attempted to stand but could not. As he tried to regain his senses, Tadashi heard a wild yell and saw men of the second attack wave racing toward the Americans. He saw the familiar figure of Colonel Oka out in front urging them forward. Tadashi smiled in spite of his injuries. Colonel Oka was making what looked to be a most successful attack. Then an American artillery round burst directly in front of him. When the smoke cleared, Oka was gone. Tadashi tried to stand again, but dizziness swept over him, and he fell back into the mud. Giving up, Tadashi crawled back to the swale a few feet behind him. Lying down on the soft bank of the swale, he tried to regain his senses. Tadashi looked up at the sky and saw the first streaks of dawn. He smiled before the darkness took over, and he saw no more.

Inside Fort Apache, the Marines, including about forty men from Battery H who'd inadvertently ran south and not southeast, filtered among the crates looking for discarded weapons and good firing positions. The Seabees had headed rearward by the time the Marines entered the dump. Captain Stacey, shouting commands, pointed and sometimes physically shoved men into the places he wanted them to defend.

The Japanese attackers were giving Stacey little time to organize as they seemed to be coming from three directions. Bullets splintered the wooden crates as the two sides exchanged gunfire. Several Japanese soldiers charged a gap between two very large crates, hoping to penetrate the American defenses. Dembrowski emptied a thirty-round clip, cutting them all down.

Perkins was firing from atop a large crate, using a smaller one for cover. Too busy to be frightened, he had shot and killed two enemy soldiers and winged an officer who scampered rearward. He was feeling secure behind his stout breastwork, which proved not to be as sturdy as he thought. A bullet pierced the front of the small crate, missed whatever might have been inside, and emerged from the back, striking Perkins in the chest. The Florida boy gazed at the bullet hole in the crate in stunned disbelief. Then he rolled onto his side. He would never be a teacher like his mother.

Bullets flew thick as a swarm of hornets between the Marines in their citadel and the Japanese trying to storm the ramparts. Pharmacist Mate First Class Ryan Magruder took a round through his left shoulder near his neck while treating a wounded man. In considerable pain, he refused to stop for treatment while injured men needed his help.

On the line held by First Squad, BAR man "Moose" Shay spotted several Japanese about to pour through an undefended gap. He cut loose with a long burst that emptied his BAR. He dropped all but two of the attackers. One fled while the last Jap came at Shay, bayonet fixed to his rifle. Shay twisted his body to the left just in time. The blade nicked his right ear, then buried itself in a wooden crate. The soldier frantically yanked on the rifle to free it, by which time Shay pulled out his Ka-Bar and rammed it into the man's chest.

Second Squad was also heavily besieged. Warren Balmer was partnered with McCready as the pair held a gap between two stacks of crates. Ten Japanese came at them yelling "Marines die!" The Americans opened fire. Balmer couldn't help but notice that McCready fired off the five rounds in his Springfield, dropping five Japanese. Balmer fired four rounds and dropped two more, by which time McCready had reloaded, shot three times, and hit the remaining three men.

"That's incredible," Balmer said, clearly impressed. "You've hit everything you've shot at."

McCready took a moment to smile and wink. Then the smile froze on his face as he watched a Japanese bullet crash through Balmer's helmet. The Tea Neck, New Jersey, boy was dead before he knew what had hit him.

As the fight raged, several of the wounded gathered at an aid station near the center of the supply dump, crying out for water. Most had no canteens of their own and the men on the line were too occupied to help. Corpsmen picked up used helmets, removed the plastic liners, and gathered water from pools of rainwater that had collected in the tarps that once covered the dump. Two disabled jeeps on a dangerously exposed portion of ground sported five-gallon jerrycans. Two volunteers risked enemy fire to race out to the vehicles. They discovered that some of the cans were full of holes and most of the water had leaked out. At last they located two cans, which, although damaged, still contained sufficient water. They lugged these back to the aid station.

Dog Company headquarters was not immune from attack. With a sudden shout of "Banzai!" a dozen enemy soldiers burst through the defenses and stormed Captain Stacey's position. The very first rounds fired by the enemy killed Stacey's radioman, Miguel Ramos. Without missing a beat, Stacey scooped up Ramos's rifle and killed two attackers. Gunny Nicholson killed three men with his rifle and one with his bayonet. Second Lieutenant Michael Jones of First Platoon used his carbine to deflect a bayonet thrust, then put two bullets into his attacker's face. Two men charged Lt. Shimada. He shot one through the head. The second attacker, stunned at seeing a Japanese face under an

American helmet, stopped suddenly and gaped. His hesitation was long enough for Shimada to fire his carbine.

Knowing they were in the enemy's headquarters, the final three attackers came on hard. Two had received minor wounds but were not to be stopped. Stacey's runner, Ernie Flint, intercepted one man. Ernie, who often boasted about his prowess as a high school football player, neatly blocked the man, then bashed in the angry face with his rifle butt. One of the two survivors fired at Stacey, and his bullet bored through the captain's upper right arm, passing clean through. He tried for a second shot, but Flint fired first. The last man attacked Nicholson with his bayonet. Nicholson neatly spun out of the man's way, then leveled his own rifle and killed the man.

By 0700, the shooting had stopped completely. The sight that met the eyes of Pete and the other Americans as they looked out over the battlefield was jaw-dropping. While they did not know it until later, the approximately two-mile stretch between Paradise Valley, where the charge began, to Tanapag, where it ended, was covered with over four thousand Japanese bodies. Amid this desolation also lay over eight hundred dead Americans, mostly from the Twenty-Seventh Division. The irony was lost on no one as this scene of utter destruction of the Japanese forces on Saipan was being illuminated by the rising sun.

Around Fort Apache, Japanese bodies lay in twisted heaps three and four high. The dead were piled up by the crates like snowdrifts. As Pete surveyed the ground, he spotted a stunned McCready looking at Balmer, who was obviously dead.

"McCready," Pete said.

"I was looking at him and talking to him, then just like that he's dead," the boy said.

"I know, but you gotta put it behind you. You can't let it get to you."

Pete went looking for the Professor, who told him Perkins was also dead.

"The platoon got hit pretty hard," Pete said. "We have five dead, five wounded, and Jones is missing. The skipper lost Ramos as well."

"How is Stonewall?" Aldrich asked. "I heard he took a bullet."

"Arm wound," Pete replied. "I doubt it'll slow him down. Same with Magruder. Neither knows when to quit."

Both men wondered what was next.

They didn't have long to wait. At 0900, Lt. Shimada appeared.

"Pack up," he said. "The artillery guys want their guns back so we're advancing to Battery H. We'll go nice and slow, make sure the enemy soldiers out there are dead. I want no possum players popping up as we go by. Also, keep an eye out for wounded Marines or GIs left behind. Don't take any chances. If you think a guy's playing possum, shoot him."

Dog Company moved out fifteen minutes later. Recrossing the field to the position they'd occupied three hours earlier on this bloody morning, they were forced to step over and around the corpses. The walk was a nightmare, for bullets and shrapnel have no regard for quick, simple death. Instead they tear and shred human flesh indiscriminately. The Marines came across many bodies that had been ripped open, sometimes from chest to groin. Limbs lay several feet from the body they'd once been attached to, and heads rolled away from torsos.

Pete noticed that close to half of the enemy dead sported bandages from earlier wounds.

Reaching Battery H, Dog Company discovered dead men, including about twenty Marines from the artillery unit, intermingled among the four Long Toms.

The dead piled up around the guns was a sad sight, but the men of Second Platoon were especially angered by one. Private "Jonesy" Jones was found tied to one Long Tom. Still alive, the Japanese had worked him over with knives and bayonets, then he was run through by a sword. Jonesy's friend Bob Kostecky hurried away to puke in private.

As the smoke jockeys of Battery H reclaimed their pieces, word arrived for Dog Company to move forward 150 yards to retake the swale they had occupied three hours and thousands of deaths earlier.

Weapons at the ready, the company fanned out to cover a wide area and moved forward.

————

The first sensation Tadashi Tanimura felt was warmth. His face felt very hot. Opening his eyes, he found he was lying in the swale flat on his back, his face getting a full blast of morning sun. As he struggled to get onto his knees, he became aware of the profound silence. Where was the gunfire? Where were the artillery bursts? Where was the throaty yell of determined men sweeping in on the enemy?

Then it occurred to him. It was over. The charge was done. His comrades were all dead or driven into the hills to live in caves like wild animals. That brought on thoughts of his own fate. What was he to do? His duty was to kill himself. That is what General Saito would expect, and that is also what Admiral Nagumo would expect. It's probably what his old boss Prince Kaya Tsunenori would expect. But what good would killing himself do now? He was convinced the battle was over, the island lost. Nothing, least of all his death, added on to the thousands who'd already died, would change that. Was he being a coward? And how should he do it? His pistol was empty, and he had no spare clip. He had only his sword, which lay in the mud where he'd dropped it when he was wounded.

He thought of Colonel Suzuki, who did not consider him a true Japanese soldier prepared to die for the emperor. By not killing himself, was he proving Suzuki to be correct? Slowly, he picked up his sword and gazed at it, its mud-spattered blade glinting in the sunlight. He had no second, so he knew it would be a painful death. Could he do it alone? Even Saito had a second to relieve the agony.

Then the decision was made for him.

Like the rest of Dog Company, Private Robert McCready was advancing over the field of dead. His mind was still on Balmer's death when he spotted movement in the swale up ahead. It was a man on his knees. He swung his rifle up.

"Don't move," he said, trying to sound commanding.

Tadashi heard the order and found himself looking into the face of a nervous looking young Marine in a muddy uniform. The man motioned for him to rise.

"Stand up," the boy said, not realizing that any ordinary Japanese soldier would have no idea what he was saying. "Drop the sword and put your hands up."

As Tadashi complied, McCready yelled, "I got a live Jap!"

In the distance, Tadashi noticed several men running toward him and the young man. The first to get there was an older man with scraggily whiskers, carrying a submachine gun. Tadashi did not like the look on the man's face.

"Son of a bitch," the man said, roughly slipping Tadashi's empty pistol from his holster. "Good catch, McCready. Kill him."

The boy looked horrified.

"What?" he stammered.

"Kill him, goddamn it," Dembrowski growled.

"I can't, Scrap Iron," the boy complained. "It'd be murder."

Dembrowski was about to reply when he saw a gold cross on a chain around Tadashi's neck. Pointing at it, he said, "Where the hell do you think he got that? Off some dead American, you can bet." He reached out to rip it off Tadashi's neck, but the prisoner grasped his wrist. They stared into each other's eyes.

"You fuckin' Nip bastard," Dembrowski snarled and started to unsheathe his Ka-Bar. "I'll cut your balls off."

"That's enough," Aldrich snapped as he and Pete arrived.

Fully expecting to be killed, Tadashi let go of the man's wrist. Dembrowski pointed at the cross.

"I'm saying this bastard took that cross off a dead Marine," he said. "It sure as hell ain't his. There are no fucking Nip Christians."

"I'll have no man in my squad shoot a prisoner," Aldrich said firmly.

"Please tell your angry private that he is incorrect," Tadashi said. "There are Christian . . ." He paused for emphasis. ". . . Nips."

Everyone stared at him.

"You speak English," Pete said.

The prisoner nodded.

"Are you Christian?" Aldrich asked.

"No," was the reply. "My mother was."

Shimada arrived, and now it was Tadashi's turn to be amazed.

"You are Japanese," he said, wonder in his voice.

Shimada pulled up short, obviously taken aback.

"I'm an American," Shimada corrected. "Lieutenant James Shimada."

"You are from California," Tadashi guessed. "No, wait. Hawaii."

Shimada nodded, still taken aback.

"Your English is very good, Major," Shimada said. "Where did you learn it?"

Tadashi considered not answering, but what good would that do?

"Besides being a Christian, my mother was an American," he said. "As a child, I lived in the United States. And just so you know, before he died, General Saito promoted me to colonel. I have his order in my pocket."

Shimada indicated he wanted to see it, and Tadashi handed it over. Shimada opened it to read.

"It's in Japanese, Lieutenant," Tadashi said.

"I'm sure it is," Shimada replied as he read.

Finishing, he said, "Colonel Tadashi Tanimura." He mulled the name over in his mind, then turned to Pete. "Hardball, why does that name ring a bell?" Pete shrugged.

"I got it, Skipper," Aldrich said. "That radio station we took south of Garapan. Those documents scattered all about. That name was on a lot of those papers."

"Major Tanimura," Shimada said. "Of course. You're on General Saito's staff. But you said the general is dead."

Tadashi nodded and said, "He committed seppuku last night. I served as his second."

"Admiral Nagumo too?" Shimada asked.

"So I'm told," he replied.

The realization of being a prisoner, of being disgraced back home, began to sink in and Tadashi said, "I wish to follow them. You understand that by being taken alive I am disgraced. So I beg of you, would you please do me the honor of shooting me? I'm sure your angry private would gladly do the job." He glanced toward Dembrowski who glowered back.

"I understand about your Bushido code," Shimada said. "I understand your sense of honor. But I think you are a very valuable prisoner of war, so I must decline your request. Besides, what would your Christian American mother say?"

"As a prisoner, I will not be welcomed back to Japan with open arms," Tadashi said.

"The world is changing, Colonel," Shimada said.

Resigned to his fate, Tadashi pointed to his sword lying on the ground and asked if he could pick it up.

"Very slowly and very carefully," Shimada said.

Automatically, Pete readied his Tommy gun, just in case.

Tadashi looked at Pete, who appeared mistrustful, then slowly leaned over, wincing at the pain from his wounds. Holding it, he wiped the mud off the blade with the sleeve of his tunic and then sheathed the weapon, removed it from his leather belt, and held it out to Shimada.

"Your angry private wanted my sword," Tadashi said. "He doesn't deserve it. I would like you to take it, Lieutenant Shimada. I know it will be in the hands of someone who understands its significance."

Shimada accepted the sword, saying, "*Domo*, Colonel. Now how about you and I go get your wounds taken care of. You have a date with my captain."

CHAPTER 28

Within thirty minutes of being captured, Tadashi Tanimura was being led into a makeshift command post. The CP was inside a bombed-out farmhouse to the rear of the aircraft supply dump the late Colonel Suzuki had established two months before the American invasion. As he walked across the corpse-riddled battlefield and saw seemingly countless bodies, both American and his own comrades sprawled together and stiffening in death, Tadashi's heart sank in despair.

An officer sporting a bandaged arm looked up as Tadashi and Lt. Shimada entered.

"Captain," Shimada said. "This is Colonel Tanimura, aide-de-camp to the late General Saito."

Stacey studied the prisoner. Noting the bloody tunic and dried blood on the man's face, he turned to an aide and said, "Get a corpsman up here." Looking back at Shimada, Stacey said, "Tell him to sit down and get comfortable."

"You can tell him yourself, Captain," Shimada said. "He speaks perfect English."

Feeling woozy, Tadashi sat down.

"Would you like a cup of coffee, Colonel?" Stacey said.

Tadashi nodded. He had not had coffee in days. Another aide brought him some in a tin cup. He sipped gratefully. Corpsman Frank Lamont arrived and began treating Tadashi's injuries, starting with the gash on his head.

"I couldn't help but notice your eyes, Colonel," Stacey said. "I've never seen a Japanese person with blue eyes. Or one that topped six feet."

"His mother's American," Shimada said.

"Was, Lieutenant," Tadashi corrected. "I lost my honorable mother six years ago. She was from Nebraska."

"Is that where you lived as a child?" Shimada probed.

Tadashi smiled.

"Am I being interrogated?" he said with a grin. "No matter. It is of no military value. My family lived in Virginia. Alexandria. Just across the Potomac River from Washington, DC. My father worked for the Ministry of Agriculture. He is retired now."

"I'm from Fairfax, Virginia," Stacey said. "We were practically neighbors."

Tadashi responded with just a quick nod.

"Skipper," Lamont said after moving from the head wound to the one in Tadashi's back. "I need to take this man to the field hospital. He's got shrapnel in pretty deep. I haven't got the gear to do an adequate job."

Stacey turned to Nicholson.

"Gunny," he said. "Go with Lamont and the prisoner to the hospital. I'll notify the battalion. They will be most anxious to talk to this man."

Lamont helped Tadashi to stand. Once on his feet, he looked to Shimada.

"I have had a most pleasant conversation with you and your captain. I hope we can talk some more," he said. "But understand, the average Japanese soldier if captured will talk freely because he doesn't know any better. I am not your average Japanese soldier, so I will converse with you, but I will not freely reveal any secrets to harm my country."

"I would not expect you to," Stacey said. "But that is between you and the battalion intelligence officer."

Tadashi nodded, then sat down again.

"Please," he said. "May I first have another cup of coffee?"

Reestablishing themselves in the swale, Dog Company and the rest of Second Battalion replenished their ammo and sent men to the rear lugging canteens in search of water drums just brought up on trucks. Every man sensed they were going to be advancing again soon.

Pete stood looking over corpses that were strewn liberally across the field like grass seed. He did not hear Aldrich come up until his friend spoke.

"We're surrounded by an ocean of dead men," Aldrich said.

"It's un-fucking-believable," Pete said. "I thought Tarawa was butchery. All this for islands no one ever heard of."

"Well, you know what Mark Twain said," Aldrich replied. "'God created war so that Americans would learn geography.' I now know where Tarawa and Saipan are. That's for sure."

Then Aldrich said, "I can't get over that Japanese officer Mc-Cready picked up. Top aide to the enemy commander on the island. His English was more refined than half the men in the company. What did you think of him?"

"Not a helluva lot," Pete answered. "Lieutenant Shimada

had two Japanese parents, and he's more of an American than that bastard will ever be."

"Would you have preferred if I'd let Dembrowski shoot him?" Aldrich asked.

"Of course not," Pete replied. "Scrap Iron is a wild card. You gotta keep him reined in. And the prisoner is obviously a prize catch."

"I found the guy intriguing," Aldrich said. "So did the lieutenant."

"That's because all three of you are eggheads," Pete joked. "Let's get the guys ready. I think we're moving out soon."

Pete started to walk away when a voice called out, "Hey, Talbot. Wait up."

Pete stared. It was *Time* magazine reporter Robert Sherrod jogging forward.

"What the hell are you doing here?" Pete asked.

"I came up with General Smith," he said. "Howlin' Mad is back at battalion HQ, so I came on ahead. I wanted to get away from him because he's pissed as hell about the Army's performance so far. First, he fired their commanding general a few days ago; now he's calling them cowards." He opened a notebook. "His exact words were, 'They're yellow. They're not aggressive. They've held up the battle and cost my Marines casualties. I'm sending the Second Division through tomorrow, and I hope the Second doesn't get into a fight passing through. I'm afraid they'll say, 'You yellow bastards.'"

"I hope you're not going to print that, or there will be war between the Army and the Marines," Pete observed.

"Hell no," Sherrod said. "I'll save it for my book."

Sherrod looked at the bloody landscape and scribbled in his notebook. Pete peeked over his shoulder and read, "The whole area seemed to be a mass of stinking bodies, spilled guts, and brains."

"You have a way with words," Pete said.

"I wish I could make it even more graphic," he said. "Then maybe we'd stop making war." He fished a Chesterfield out of his pocket and lit it up. "You're moving up soon. Mind if I tag along?"

"It's your ass," Pete said. "I'd like my boys to see what kind of fool does this type of work when he doesn't have to."

Sherrod laughed.

The battalion soon moved out, picking their way through an obstacle course of bodies. Making the advance even more grisly, Sherman tanks and half-tracks accompanying the Marines mercilessly crushed enemy dead beneath their steel treads.

"What are they going to do with all these dead bandidos?" Private Sandina asked Honeybun.

"Same thing they did with 'em at Tarawa," Hullihen answered. "Dig pits or widen shell craters, shove the bodies in using bulldozers, then cover it over. I just hope to hell they don't ask us to help collect the dead." He looked at the boy walking close beside him. "Now spread out. Ten paces at least. Don't bunch up."

As the battalion advanced, the increased number of corpses wearing US Army olive-drab twill uniforms gave grisly evidence that the fighting here had been extremely heavy and vicious.

By 1300 hours, Dog Company, advancing at point, closed in on a meandering stream that justified its nickname Bloody Run. Here had occurred brutal eyeball-to-eyeball fighting during the height of the enemy charge as the GIs driven from their forward works attempted to make a stand. The dead, both Doughboys and Japanese, lay in heaps; some blocking the stream like a breakwater, and others sprawled across fields and roads. But not all the enemy here were dead. Advancing, the Marines came under a smattering of small arms fire. One of the men on point was struck and fell, and everyone else dropped prone or to a knee.

The firing came from a small band of Japanese soldiers using the run's bank as a breastwork. Either these men were survivors of the charge, or they had not participated. Amid the exchange of gunfire, the Shermans and half-tracks clanked through the Marines, guns blazing. The tank gunners cut down most of those who fled.

Resistance crushed, the armored vehicles rolled across Bloody Run, followed by lines of infantrymen. As impossible as Pete and the others found it to believe, the landscape beyond Bloody Run, closer to where the *gyokusai* collided with the 105th defenders, was even more gruesome than the field they'd just crossed. So many dead covered the ground that one could almost walk the length of the field without touching the earth. Dead Japanese wearing bloody bandages from earlier wounds, some with sharpened spears still clutched in their hands, were even more evident here, where the fighting was thickest.

Close to the 105th's forward line, the advancing Marines could pick out what had been Army strongpoints, such as machine gun emplacements or mortar pits. Each of these told a story of individual heroism as GIs held these positions in the face of overwhelming odds. Enemy dead were piled up knee-deep. Attackers literally climbed over heaps of their own slain to get at the GIs, whose own guns soon became useless as enemy corpses started to block fields of fire.

There were also indications of heartless brutality as the Marines came across a line of dead Americans who had been wounded or captured. Many had been bayoneted and a few were beheaded. Unbridled anger rose among the Marines and some dead enemy soldiers were kicked or shot in the head.

As Second Platoon neared the debris of what had once been a small bungalow, their senses became alert. This was a prime location for an enemy ambush. Sure enough, from out of the rubble popped four Japanese soldiers armed with rifles. They opened fire and at least one bullet struck Third Squad's recent replacement Richard Carvell. He dropped, screaming in pain and fear. As the call went out for a corpsman, the rest of the platoon cut loose. Three of the Japanese died instantly. The fourth removed his bayonet from its scabbard and clutching it with both hands, raised it over his head. He was about to plunge the blade into his own body when Scrap Iron fired a short burst from his Thompson. The man was thrown backward before collapsing to the ground.

"I wasn't about to give that bastard the luxury of dying honorably," Dembrowski announced.

By late afternoon, the Marines reached the line the 105th had occupied prior to the Japanese suicide charge. Told to dig in, just in case any surviving Japanese attempted a second *gyokusai*, they began to remove American dead, carrying them a short distance rearward and lining them up for easier collection. Japanese dead were just shoved aside into shell craters or anyplace else where they'd be out of the way. Some were stacked up to become human breastworks.

As the men worked removing the dead, Nicholson made the rounds.

"Tell your boys they're home for the night," he told Pete. "Tomorrow us and the Fourth Marines will head for Marpi Point and take what remains of this damned island."

Dinner that evening was served via K-ration boxes.

"I don't know where this beef came from," Pete said as he jabbed what the can called a "beef loaf" with his fork. "But I'm sure that the steer is better off dead."

"I agree," Aldrich said. "Beef wasn't meant to have a green tint."

"Quit your bitchin'," Nicholson said. "The shit we had on the 'Canal was far worse."

"Look who's talking," Aldrich said. He turned to Pete. "In Hawaii a bunch of us went on liberty with Gunny here. He led us to the Black Cat Café on Hotel Street. Man oh man, they made the best hamburger I ever had. It was large and juicy and worth every penny of the fifteen cents it cost."

"But do you know what Gunny ate?" Honeybun chimed in. "A fuckin' T-bone steak."

Nicholson smiled and said, "Rank has its privileges. Remember: I make thirty bucks a month more than most of you."

"They had seafood too," Aldrich said. "Thirty-five cents for shrimp or a half dozen oysters, but sadly no steamed crabs."

"Is that your way of asking me if I made a decision on our business venture?" Pete asked Aldrich.

"Did you?"

"I sorta like it," he said. "But I'm waiting to hear from Aggie."

"Just so you know," Aldrich said. "Mom wrote that Captain Jack's on board, no pun intended."

It was 1630 on July 7. Tadashi Tanimura's war had been over for about six hours. Wounds tended, he had been confined to a tent at what he assumed was a battalion headquarters. His furnishings were a single canvas and wood folding cot and a chair. An armed guard stood just outside the tent flaps. Every so often an enlisted man would pop in and ask if he wanted water or something to eat. Stoically, he declined. In his mind his honor was taking a beating. Should he have committed seppuku and died in the Bushido way when he'd had the opportunity? Was it his duty to die for Japan, or was it to live and return to Saipan after the war to help rebuild his beloved island? Here, he thought, he had a better chance of gaining acceptance for being captured. The turmoil caused by his military indoctrination and warrior's code welcoming an honorable death struggled mightily with his Christian mother's upbringing, which appreciated and nurtured life.

He heard a vehicle stop outside the tent and low voices coming nearer. The tent flaps separated, and Captain Stacey entered, accompanied by a tall officer. He introduced himself as Colonel William Bryce.

"I am attached to General Smith's staff," Bryce said. "I'm here to escort you back to HQ. I understand you speak English."

Tadashi nodded.

"And you were General Saito's aide-de-camp?"

Tadashi nodded again.

"And the general is dead?"

"Please don't treat me like a fool, Colonel," he said. "You know all of this already. You are an intelligence officer."

"How do you know that?" Bryce asked, taken aback.

"Because they would not send the quartermaster to pick up a prisoner, especially one from General Saito's inner circle," he said.

Tadashi saw Stacey smile at Bryce's evident discomfort.

"You'll find that Colonel Tanimura is an intelligent man, Colonel Bryce," Stacey said. "Besides, he's half American, remember? I think he knows where we're coming from."

"My apologies, Colonel," Bryce said. "Now, if you will accompany me."

Exiting the tent, Tadashi and an MP guard climbed into the rear of a jeep while Bryce took the front passenger seat. A private was at the wheel. Tadashi turned to Stacey.

"Do you have a cigarette, Captain?" he asked.

Stacey did not smoke, but Nicholson offered him a Lucky Strike. Tadashi beamed.

"I have not had an American cigarette in years," he said. "Thank you, Sergeant. And thank you for your hospitality, Captain."

"It's been a unique experience, Colonel," Stacey said as the jeep roared off.

Turning onto the coastal highway, the jeep headed south. Tadashi asked Colonel Bryce where they were bound. Charan Kanoa was the answer. He settled back.

As the jeep barreled along, everywhere Tadashi looked he felt deeper and deeper sorrow for Japan and her cause. Traffic on the road was heavy with vehicles of all descriptions; tanks, half-tracks, trucks carrying fresh-faced replacements, trucks mounted by rocket launchers or piled high with supplies, ambulances ferrying the wounded, and jeeps carrying injured men on stretchers. Most disheartening was seeing his dead comrades gathered together in piles like rubbish. Nearby bulldozers scooped out trenches in the earth. Tadashi knew those excavations would serve as unmarked graves.

Before long, they entered the skeletal remains of Garapan. For Tadashi, this was the most sorrowful part of his journey. The city was smashed beyond recognition. Only a few buildings; the post office, the bank, the theater, and a few random houses remained at least partially intact. The rest were rubble. Worse was the human cost. Collection parties of American soldiers and ragtag groups of civilians sifted through the rubble for corpses. These bodies were reverently laid along sidewalks. Many were Japanese soldiers, but many others were civilians. Tears flowed from his eyes. Bryce glanced back and saw the tears.

"Are you all right, Colonel?" he asked.

"No, I'm not," Tadashi replied. "After eight years in America, my father was reassigned to Saipan to help build the sugar industry. These people were my friends and neighbors."

"You didn't return to Japan?" Bryce asked.

"I was seventeen years old when I first saw Japan," he replied. "This is my home."

————

The final push for the northern tip of Saipan began early the next day. The Marines advanced steadily but with caution across a tumbled landscape of spindly trees, tall grass, clumps of thick vegetation, and outcroppings of limestone boulders. Among these last were natural caves. Second Platoon came across one of these early on. With First and Third Squads holding, Second Squad spread out while creeping forward, all eyes on the partially concealed cave mouth.

"*Dare ka imasu ka?*" Lt. Shimada called, inquiring if anyone was inside.

Silence.

"*Dare ka imasu ka?*" he repeated. "*Kega wo suru koto wa arimasen.*"

Even his adding that they would not be hurt failed to get a response.

Shimada called one last time, threatening to flush them out with a flamethrower. This was a bluff. The platoon had no flamethrower. Still, the vision of being roasted alive brought a response. A small white cloth waved from the cave mouth.

"*Yukkuri detekite,*" he said, commanding them to come out slowly.

A wide-eyed young soldier slowly materialized, followed by two more. The second man wore a white but bloodstained *hachimaki* headband with a large rising sun painted in the center.

"Honeybun," Aldrich said. "Check them for weapons."

Covered by Dembrowski, Hullihen frisked the first man. Finding nothing, he moved on to the man with the *hachimaki*.

Suddenly, he emitted a guttural "Yaaahhh" and drew out a knife. He raised his arm to plunge the blade into Honeybun, but a bullet from Scrap Iron's Thompson killed him first. As he fell, Scrap Iron shot down the other two prisoners as well.

"They were probably all in on it," he explained.

He removed the *hachimaki* from the dead man and pocketed it.

The platoon happened upon two more caves. From those caves Lt. Shimada coaxed a combined total of one wounded soldier and twenty-one terrified civilians, including eight children. Everyone wore rags indicating that they'd been in hiding for weeks. The children cried from hunger.

"K-rations. Come on," Shimada said to the men.

Pete handed over both a lunch box and a dinner box. Two chocolate bars were produced and split among the children.

As the jeep carrying Tadashi entered Charan Kanoa, he saw that the second-largest settlement on the island had received the same drubbing as had the largest town. Houses and stores were collapsed or burned out. Side streets were clogged by debris, although the main arteries had been opened by men operating cranes and bulldozers. The dockyard where ships once loaded refined sugar bound for Japan had sustained heavy damage, although the vital docks still stood and were being quickly repaired. Tadashi was impressed by the speed of the work crews.

The large sugar refinery stood in ruins, its skeletal steel beams looking naked and forlorn. The iron rails of the sugar train were twisted and blackened.

The jeep finally arrived at a collection of large green tents. A young lieutenant came and led him to a smaller tent.

"This will be your quarters for now, sir," the lieutenant said. "The general is up at the front but is expected back by tomorrow morning. Meanwhile, if you need anything, let the guard outside know. Dinner will be in thirty minutes. I will come and get you."

———

The northern coast of Saipan is a high plateau of low scrub trees; tall, dense grass; and clumps of thick bushes. This plateau ends at steep cliffs that tower from four hundred to more than nine hundred feet above a turbulent sea, where waves relentlessly batter the shore.

That's where Second Platoon, point unit for Dog Company, now found itself. But it wasn't the awe-inspiring sight of magnificently curling waves crashing against a rocky coast that caused them to stare. Nor was it the startling blue of the water. The sight that left many slack-jawed was the hundreds and hundreds of men, women, and children bobbing on the water among the partially submerged rocks like corks on the frothy ocean swells. But more than the dead in the ocean were the corpses of those who miscalculated their jumps and lay smashed among the jagged outcroppings of rock and coral at the base of the cliffs.

"Jesus Christ," Pete said in disbelief.

"How can people do that to themselves?" Aldrich said in wonder.

"I heard this type of thing might be going on up here, but I wouldn't have believed it," Sherrod said.

"Lieutenant, look," Pete said urgently, gently smacking Shimada on the shoulder and pointing.

About fifty yards away, a family of five dashed from the underbrush and hustled to the cliff.

"*Yamete kudasai*," Shimada shouted, urging them to stop. "*Janpu shinaide kudasai.*"

Despite Shimada's plea that they would not be hurt, the father quickly and with no hesitation threw his three screaming children one by one off the edge to their deaths. The mother was babbling in terror until her husband gave her a shove off the precipice. Then he shot a look of absolute hatred at the Marines and followed his family into oblivion.

The platoon stood stunned.

"My God," Shimada muttered aloud. "I am Japanese like them, but I do not understand these people."

Shimada turned to the platoon.

"Fan out," he commanded. "Beat the bushes for more civilians. Round them up. Tackle them. Shoot them in the legs if you have to, but keep any more from jumping."

The task was easier said than done. Pedro Sandina spotted a young mother clutching an infant as she ran for the edge. He hurried forward.

"Stop!" he yelled. "Don't!"

Sandina got within twenty yards of the woman when a shot rang out. The sniper's bullet struck a tree trunk just as Sandina ran by it. A second shot from the concealed enemy and Sandina hit the dirt behind a small line of rocks. Meanwhile, the woman reached the edge. Glaring back at Sandina, she held her baby close and jumped. The sound of gunfire drew Honeybun and Scrap Iron.

"Sniper to my right," Sandina called to his comrades. "I'm pinned down."

The two Marines scrutinized the area. Honeybun saw a slight movement in a tree and called it to Dembrowski's attention. Dembrowski peppered the tree with his Thompson and the sniper fell from the branches.

Rosie spotted a dozen people on a rocky ledge by the water looking indecisive. As they mulled things over, a huge wave rolled in and swept four or five out to sea. Those remaining seemed to lose heart and began walking away from the water.

Suddenly, a Nambu machine gun hidden in a cliffside cave opened fire and shot down the remaining civilians. The angry sea claimed their corpses. Rosie cautiously made his way toward the machine gun. He managed to get into position about ten feet above the gun and dropped a grenade on the crew's heads. The explosion catapulted the gun and two of the three crewmen over the edge and down the cliff.

Pete also heard gunfire. Following the sound, he spotted two of the Second Squad's newest men, Kostecky and Palmer, taking potshots at the bobbing heads on the water below.

"Got one," Kostecky crowed. "That makes four for me and three for you."

Pete stopped them.

"What the fuck is the matter with you two?" he said.

"We're just trying to bag some Nips," Kostecky said. "That's what we're here for, isn't it?"

"We're here to kill Jap soldiers, not helpless civilians," he snarled. "Get the hell back to the squad. Both of you!"

As he watched them retreat, Pete thought about how war can turn kids, even two eighteen-year-olds from Canterbury, Connecticut, and Minnetonka, Minnesota, into heartless killers.

Word came down that the battalion was staying put for the present. Its three companies, Dog, Easy, and Fox, were deployed to guard against Japanese getting through and killing themselves on the cliffs. During the day it was an easy task, but nighttime was a challenge. A few of the more zealous civilians got through. Still, that first day, the company snagged thirty-eight civilians and five soldiers, all trying to reach what was now being called Suicide Cliff.

As the sun went down on July 8, Aldrich related an interesting tidbit of news.

"Do you guys realize this is D+23?" he asked. "Twenty-three days since we landed on Saipan."

"So?" Pete asked.

"Marpi Point, just over yonder," Aldrich said, "was initially our objective for D+9, according to the planners."

"So?" Pete said again.

"Nothing," Aldrich conceded. "I just thought it was interesting about how far planners have their heads shoved up their behinds."

"I thought you'd learned that on Tarawa," Pete joked.

At 1300 hours the next day, July 9, Captain Stacey gathered Dog Company around him. Standing up in the back of his jeep so all could see and hear, he announced, "At 1400, Saipan will be declared secured."

Men cheered and slapped each other's backs.

"We will be marching to the Marpi Point airfield for a flag raising ceremony at 1400 hours."

At precisely 2:00 p.m., men of the Second Division stood in ranks as the American flag was hoisted up a hastily erected flagpole made from a felled tree trunk. *The battle is over*, Pete thought. As the formation broke up, Pete and Second Platoon were called to Stacey's HQ. A special assignment was coming their way.

———

Tadashi Tanimura had been held at Second Division HQ for two days. Granted, his incarceration was not uncomfortable. He had been allowed to write letters to his father and Kokoro, which would be turned over to the Red Cross. There were no promises from his captors that the Japanese government would allow the letters to be delivered. Tadashi said he understood.

He had been treated well. Doctors had tended to his injuries and applied fresh dressings as needed. He was allowed to go outside his tent to get exercise and he ate meals in the division officers' mess tent. He discovered how much he missed American food. General Smith's officers ate well. Tadashi had not had steak since the war began. He had not enjoyed Southern fried chicken since his mother's illness worsened in 1937 and caused her to cease cooking. In the last two days, he had enjoyed both.

He had been subjected to "interrogation time" several hours a day, but even that was not as trying as he had anticipated. He freely gave up information such as the number of troops that had been assigned to Saipan, their deployment, and their current combat effectiveness. Since the battle was clearly over and most of these men were now dead, he felt he was not betraying his country.

"What would you say was General Saito's condition during this time?" he was asked.

"His spirit has gone to Yasukuni, so what difference does it make?" he replied.

"What were your duties?" a major from G2 asked.

"Toward the end, I was to scout the lines," he said. "I was to assess the fighting ability of the men and the strength or weakness of our lines."

He was asked about what type of help Imperial Headquarters promised or how they intended to deliver that assistance.

"Even if I had that information, I would not answer," he said. "Obviously, their efforts failed."

"What about Tinian's defenses?" a captain asked. "How much contact did you have with General . . . ah, what's his name again?"

Tadashi smiled.

"In America, you would call that a cheap trick, Captain," Tadashi said. He knew the forces there were under the command of Colonel Kiyoshi Ogata. "Since you are obviously going to Tinian next, I will let you introduce yourself to the island's commander."

"Come on, Colonel," the captain prodded. "Do you really want to see more of your mother's countrymen die needlessly?"

"Captain," he replied. "I have just watched almost thirty thousand of my father's countrymen die, including my general. This war has been doubly unfortunate for me."

One officer cast suspicion over Tadashi's activities while his father served with the Ministry of Agriculture in the United States. Did his father take a lot of notes? What about photographs of US government facilities?

"My father was a low-level diplomat studying farming techniques," Tadashi said. "He lives and breathes farming techniques. Your insinuation that he was some sort of Japanese superspy is absurd."

On the morning of July 10, the third full day of his captivity, Tadashi was ushered into the headquarters tent of General Holland "Howlin' Mad" Smith. At age sixty-two, the square-jawed Smith's lips seemed to have a permanent downward curve, giving him the grumpy look of a constantly scowling man. He rose from his chair when Tadashi entered.

"Good morning, Colonel Tanimura," Smith said, indicating a chair. "Please be seated."

"Thank you, General," he replied.

"As General Saito's aide, you were at his final headquarters," Smith said. "So you know the circumstances of his death. Correct?"

Tadashi nodded.

"He did not have a proper burial. Am I also correct on that?"

"Yes, General," Tadashi replied. Where was this going?

"If I order out a patrol to recover the body of the general, and Admiral Nagumo as well, in order to give them proper funerals with military honors, would you be willing to show my men the way?"

Tadashi hesitated, in shock. He did not expect such a courtesy.

"If that offer is sincere, then yes sir," Tadashi said. "I would be most honored."

"Very well," Smith said.

"If I may make one request, General," Tadashi added. "May I recommend the men for the patrol?"

Smith's eyebrows rose in surprise, a condition he seldom experienced.

"I would very much appreciate if you would allow Lieutenant Shimada and his men to go with me," Tadashi said. "The lieutenant would retrieve the general's remains with the utmost respect, and he has several men who would also appreciate the solemnity of such a duty."

Smith looked to an aide.

"He's with Dog Company, Second Battalion," the aide said. "He's Nisei."

"Issue the orders," Smith commanded.

The trucks carrying Second Platoon stopped just outside what was left of the village of Makunsha. Fighting here had been heavy both before and during the *gyokusai*. A few battered walls remained. The men jumped down from the trucks and looked to Lt. Shimada who shrugged because he had no idea what was up. The men milled about for thirty minutes before a staff car rolled up. Doors opened and two men stepped out. Eyes widened in amazement when one turned out to be Colonel Tanimura.

The other man, also a colonel, spoke.

"I am Colonel Bryce of G2," he said to Shimada's men. "I think most of you know this man." He indicated Tadashi. "Colonel Tanimura will be acting as your guide. Your orders from General Smith are to go with the colonel to recover the bodies of General Saito and Admiral Nagumo so they can be given military funerals befitting their ranks." He turned to Lt. Shimada. "Lieutenant, you will leave one squad here. The other two will go on the mission."

"Are you going to accompany us as well, Colonel?" Shimada asked.

"Sadly, no," Bryce said. "But you will take a radio to let us know of your arrival and your return. I will have trucks here to take you, your men, and the bodies to Charan Kanoa."

After an exchange of salutes between Shimada and Tadashi, Bryce climbed back into the staff car and was gone. Shimada looked to Tadashi.

"Please forgive me," Tadashi said. "I asked General Smith to assign you and your men. You will appreciate this endeavor."

Shimada smiled and nodded.

"I certainly do," he replied.

Not everyone was pleased.

"Jesus Christ," Dembrowski muttered. "First, we gotta kill 'em, then we gotta drag their dead asses back and bury them with honors." He strolled up to Pete. "How do you feel about this chickenshit assignment, Sergeant?" he said. "These bastards killed your brother, and we're burying them like they're heroes. I'd rather throw their carcasses into the latrine."

"My feelings about this sonofabitch are just that, mine," Pete said. "So leave my brother out of this."

Detaching Third Squad, Shimada, with Tadashi at his side, led the patrol along the Makunsha road, then cross-country toward the mouth of Paradise Valley.

"Tell me, Colonel, what does *gyokusai* mean?" Shimada asked. "What is it to 'shatter the jade?'"

"It is a belief that we Japanese are a special or valuable people," he said. "Jade, you might call us. We remain as such until a great calamity, a disaster from the outside world and not of our making, forces every man, woman, and child to become warriors for a final assault even if it means our total destruction. Shattering the jade. It's a total call to arms."

He paused reflectively as thoughts of General Saito, Admiral Nagumo, Kisaburo Hanaya, and the thousands of others, Japanese and American, who died in the *gyokusai* flowed through his mind.

"In the end," Tadashi said sadly, "perhaps all of us, Japanese and American alike, are little more than shattered jade."

Tadashi dropped back slightly to walk beside Pete and Steve Aldrich.

Tadashi addressed Pete.

"My pardons, Sergeant," he said. "I do not mean to pry, but I overheard the angry private say that you had a brother who died in this war. Was he killed by Japanese?"

"That's not a good subject to get into, Colonel," Aldrich cautioned.

"Pipe down, Professor," Pete said.

"So sorry, Sergeant," Tadashi said. "Please excuse my rudeness."

"My kid brother and his submarine disappeared in the Solomons," Pete said.

"This war is terrible," Tadashi said somberly. "So many have been lost. I do not have a brother to lose, but my home has been lost." Pete and Aldrich looked at Tadashi. "Saipan is my home."

He told of his growing up on the island.

"Now Garapan has been smashed," he said. "Saipan has

been smashed. Many of my friends and neighbors are dead. Almost everything I knew and loved is gone. It is enough to make the gods weep."

Pete looked at Tadashi. From somewhere inside, he suddenly felt compassion for this man.

After assigning two men to carry folded stretchers, Shimada ordered the column forward.

About an hour into the hike, Tadashi pointed and said, "The headquarters cave is just beyond those trees."

The group finally arrived at the headquarters cave. The tarp that had been used to prevent light from escaping from inside the cave had been torn down and men began to enter. Tadashi followed. The headquarters had been ransacked. The table and chairs Saito and Nagumo had used were overturned and broken. The mimeograph machine on which Saito's final proclamation had been copied, and the all-important radio, had both been battered into junk. Four bodies lay sprawled on the dirt floor, killed by self-inflicted gunshot wounds. Tadashi walked over to where he and Hanaya had spent their last night together. Their blankets lay where they had been left. He thought about his friend who was waiting for him at Yasukuni. He picked his up.

"Colonel Tanimura," Shimada said. "Where is General Saito's body?"

"Follow me," he said, and led Shimada, Pete, and Aldrich to the smaller cavern adjacent to the command cave. The charred figure of what had been a man lay on a small rocky ledge. The scorched remains of a samurai sword lay by his side. From appearances, it seemed as if someone had tried to incinerate the corpse even more since there were the still-warm embers of a recent fire on top of the body. Tadashi used his blanket to swipe the embers away.

"Stretcher, up here!" Pete called out.

Keener arrived with the stretcher, and with help from Kostecky, unfolded and secured it. Since no one seemed eager to lift the blackened body with bare hands, scraps of fabric were found to serve as makeshift gloves. Pete and Aldrich exchanged glances, then wrapped their hands. With Pete at the head and Aldrich at the feet, the once proud commander of the Imperial troops on Saipan was gently lifted and placed on the stretcher. Tadashi covered his commander's remains with his own blanket.

That done, a search of the area was made to find Nagumo's CP where his charred remains lay. The cave was found but the body was gone. The corpse had been removed by his staff and secretly buried elsewhere. Giving up the search, Pete pointed at the stretcher holding Saito's body and said, "Keener, Kostecky, Wings, Minozo, grab an end."

The four stretcher-bearers hoisted their load and Shimada led the patrol back the way they'd come, but not before Tadashi took one last look at the cave.

At Makunsha, Second Platoon reboarded the trucks. On the bed of one deuce-and-a-half was the stretcher bearing the general's body. With the starting of engines and shifting of gears, the procession began the drive south to Charan Kanoa.

Two days later, July 13, a procession of Army and Marines assembled in the Twenty-Seventh Division Cemetery at Charan Kanoa, in a section reserved for the bodies of upper-level Japanese officers. A semicircle of men surrounded an open grave that would be General Yoshitsugu Saito's final resting place. At the head of the grave stood the division chaplain as well as General Smith and General George W. Griner, who had taken over command of the Army's Twenty-Seventh Division. At the foot of the grave were seventeen men of the Fourth Marines, constituting a firing squad of sixteen riflemen with one NCO in command. All the other witnesses, including the men of Second Platoon, stood in a semicircle to one side of the grave.

The same four Marines who'd lugged the stretcher down from the cave served as the pallbearers. While every other corpse in the cemetery was buried wrapped in a blanket or poncho, General Saito would repose in a six-foot-long wooden coffin now draped by a large rising sun flag. Following brief words by the chaplain, the flag was removed and folded.

"Ten hut," a loud voice called. "Salute!"

Everyone saluted crisply, including Tadashi, who stood graveside with Lt. Shimada. Taps sounded, and the honor guard fired volleys as the coffin was lowered into the earth. At that moment, as if the gods themselves were saddened, rain began to fall.

At the conclusion of the ceremony, Tadashi stood for a while in the rain and watched as the grave was filled in. Then he walked to where Shimada and his men waited.

"Lieutenant Shimada," he said. "I want to most humbly thank you and your men."

Colonel Bryce tapped Tadashi's arm.

"You need to come with me, Colonel," he said.

Tadashi nodded, then turned to Pete.

"My deepest condolences for the loss of your brother," he said.

Pete nodded.

"And I am sorry for all you have lost," Pete said.

Tadashi allowed himself to be taken away in the custody of Bryce and two MPs. As Pete watched him go, he had the fleeting memory of another Japanese soldier who, amid the flying steel and lead of the Tarawa invasion, took a brief moment to salute Pete for what he saw as an act of courage.

How can a man hate an entire nation and make war against

it and its people, yet have admiration and respect for individual soldiers of that nation?

"What a fucked-up war," Pete muttered as the platoon got ready to return to Dog Company.

CHAPTER 29

The men of Second Squad and Pete's "guest," Robert Sherrod, sat in a circle in the Second Battalion bivouac area just south of Garapan. In a spirit of camaraderie, they hoisted warm olive-drab cans of GI beer in tribute to their squad mates, dead and wounded, who had been lost since landing on Saipan on June 15. This included Paul Kostecky, whose left arm had been sheared off at the elbow by Japanese shrapnel on July 25 during the Tinian operation.

It had been on July 23 when the Second and Fourth Marines left Saipan for the three-and-a-half-mile journey over water to Tinian. The Fourth Marines went via landing boats and the Second by transport. The next day, dubbed "Jig Day," the invasion began. Under cover of naval fire from the battleships *Tennessee* and *Colorado*, the Second faked a landing at Tinian Town, well south of the intended invasion zone. The Second went so far as to scale down cargo nets and drop into landing boats. Then the "attack" was called off and they reboarded. So convinced were the Japanese by this "victory" that Radio Tokyo announced that the Americans had been "repelled."

The Fourth Marines landed on July 24 while the Second came in the next day. The island's two landing beaches, White 1 and White 2, were the only usable ones on Tinian, and then just barely. The amtracs were so constricted by rocks and coral that they could only come in four abreast. The beaches themselves were so narrow that supply dumps, usually established by the shore, had to be set up well inland. Luckily the assault was lightly contested.

It was that same day, July 25, that the Second Battalion saw its biggest action of the entire nine-day struggle for Tinian. Fighting had centered around the four-hundred-foot-tall Mount Maga as Marines closed on one of Tinian's four valuable airfields. Dog Company stormed across the airfield where the blasted carcasses of several Japanese planes sat, along with single engine fighters and twin-engine Betty bombers. Pilots and air crewmen came rushing forth to defend their field, only to be mowed down by the Marines. Enemy troops began pulling back to the heights of Mount Maga itself, covered by mortar and machine gun fire. Second Battalion pressed up the hills, blasting caves with grenades, satchel charges, or flamethrowers.

It was during this assault when Pete heard a scream of terror and pain. Hurrying toward the sound, he came across young Kostecky standing stunned and gazing down at his bloody forearm that lay in the dirt.

"Sit down," Pete said, helping the boy. "Sit down. Corpsman!"

Ryan Magruder, just back from the hospital himself, raced over and took charge.

"I got him, Hardball," Magruder said. "Get back to the platoon."

The battalion eventually took the hill. Barbed wire was

strung in preparation for a banzai attack. It came after midnight in a blaze of screaming oaths and the tearing sound of small arms fire. When the fight was over, five Marines were dead. Over fifteen hundred Japanese were slain.

After that and until the end of the campaign on August 1, the Sixth and Eighth Battalions carried the bulk of the action. That was fine as far as Pete was concerned. He'd seen enough fighting over the past six weeks.

By August 5, he was back on Saipan. The whole operation had cost the Marines 326 killed while the Japanese lost over five thousand men killed with another 250 captured and over two thousand reported missing. Many were probably entombed in collapsed caves.

With the fighting over on Saipan, some semblance of civilization was returning. As soon as Second Division's slop chute opened, Pete raced in and plunked down a buck for two cartons of his beloved Camel cigarettes. He also bought new stationery to answer letters he'd just received from Aggie and his mother.

Meals were served in a mess tent. So what if the typical meal was corned beef, spam, beans, powdered eggs, and dehydrated potatoes. It was still hot food, and they were under a roof in case of rain. Best of all, for the first time since mid-June, Pete and friends weren't in fear for their lives. There were still some Japanese holdouts huddled in the caves and jungle areas of Saipan that had to be flushed out, but for now it was the Twenty-Seventh Division GIs beating the bushes and doing the flushing.

That allowed free time for the men of the squad to relax, drink some beer, and remember.

"Tokyo Rose is on the radio," Rosie chimed in.

"Fuck her," Dembrowski replied.

"We've just been through two island invasions," Rosie reminded him. "That idea may have some appeal."

"You Marines of the Second and Fourth Divisions may think you have won a great victory on Saipan, but the fight is not over," the sultry voice cooed. "A huge naval task force with thousands of Japanese troops is steaming toward the island at this very moment and will sweep you into the sea. Sorry to say, but none of you Marines will get home for another Christmas."

"Go ahead and send 'em, baby," Pete heard Scrap Iron bellow. "We'll send 'em to hell like we did with these other guys."

"Yeah," Aldrich said. "Maybe she forgot that because Saipan fell, Tojo got fired from his prime minister job."

Pete lifted his beer high.

"A toast to Tojo," he said.

The men toasted Tojo.

"I don't know if you guys know this," Sherrod said. "But I'm hearing that back in the States, you Marines are considered to be kill crazy."

That drew howls of laughter.

"No shit, fellas," Sherrod said. "There was a story published on how to deal with Marines after the war. It suggested confining them in what the writer called 'reorientation camps' and maybe locating these camps in the Panama Canal Zone. Returning Marines would be forced to wear an ID patch to alert everyone of their 'lethal instincts.'"

"I heard a rumor that the Navy doesn't post nurses close to the front because we might rape them," Honeybun said.

"Where did you hear that?" Rosie asked.

"Oh, it's going around."

Pete pulled out a letter he'd gotten from Aggie and handed it to Aldrich.

"Read the last paragraph," he said. "And just the last paragraph."

Aldrich took it and read: *I found the idea Steve brought up about the two of you going into the fishing business together very interesting. Your letter sounded as if you felt the same way. If you think it is something you would like to do, darling, you have my full support. Speaking for myself, I think it might be fun to live in a small fishing town by the Chesapeake. Frankly, I'm tired of living in a city. A small town would also be a great place to raise a family. I am so glad you have found such a good friend in Steve. You need that.*

Aldrich handed the letter back.

"Smart girl," he said. "Then we're on?"

"Yeah," Pete replied. "We're on. But I'll tell you something. Now that I've committed myself to this, don't you dare get yourself killed. Because if you do, dead or not, I'll murder you."

Everyone laughed and toasted the partnership with a fresh round of beer.

As he watched the grinning men drink, Pete thought about how far he'd come since he was that angry loner at Parris Island.

Damn, he thought. *I love these men.*

———

Two days after the funeral of General Saito, Tadashi suffered the indignation of having all his military rank and unit affiliation insignia removed from his tunic. Blindfolded, he was taken aboard a ship. Once at sea, the blindfold was removed.

Tadashi was confined in a small room with a metal bunk and chair. Twice a day, MPs escorted him topside for fresh air and exercise. He had no idea where he was going, and no one volunteered information.

"Can you tell me where we're headed?" he asked a young lieutenant who was a part of his escort.

"I'm sorry, Colonel," he replied. "I am not at liberty to do so."

"Well, considering we're sailing an easterly course, I'd say Hawaii or the United States, probably the latter," Tadashi said. "Would that be right?"

The lieutenant just smiled, but Tadashi knew he was correct.

Three weeks later, he got his answer.

Escorted topside, he saw long fingers of land dotted with houses passing by both sides of the ship. Ahead, hovering over the waterway, the Golden Gate Bridge gleamed in the morning sun.

How beautiful, he thought.

Allowed to stand by the ship's rail, he watched Alcatraz slip by. For a while he feared that this hellish place might be his final destination.

When the ship finally docked, Tadashi was led ashore by the MPs. At the base of the gangplank, a tall, well-dressed man in a dark suit stood waiting.

"Colonel Tanimura," the man said. "I am Robert Meacham. I am with the United States Office of Strategic Services."

Tadashi smiled and bowed.

"And what does America's intelligence office want with a humble Army officer?"

"Oh, not too much," Meacham replied. "Mainly, we want to talk with you about your father's activities during the eight years he was stationed here. His movements—any notes or pictures he might have taken."

Tadashi threw back and emitted a raucous laugh.

"I am so sorry," Tadashi said, trying to compose himself. "I do not mean to be disrespectful. I just find it outrageously funny that you think my father might have been a spy. Even if that were true, I was an eight-year-old boy at the time."

Tadashi scanned his eyes around the harbor.

"When my family left for Saipan in 1923, we departed from San Francisco," he said. "Of course, the bridge wasn't here then. I do recall seeing Alcatraz. Now here I am, twenty-one years later."

Tadashi was led away by Meacham and an hour later found himself in the company of two additional men in suits on a train speeding east. As the train crossed the Great Plains on the second day of the three-day trip, Tadashi realized that America was vaster than he remembered.

"My father admired all these fields of wheat and corn stretching out as far as one can see." He turned to face Meacham. "Does that make him a spy?"

Tadashi watched the scenery slip by for a short time, then said, "May I again inquire where I am being taken?"

Meacham thought, then said, "Let's just say PO Box 1142."

"That is very cloak-and-dagger," Tadashi said and then fell silent.

The next day, the scenery was very different. Gone were the sweeping plains ripe with crops and farms. Replacing them was an urban setting of houses, towns, and eventually a city. Tadashi wondered where they were until the train pulled into a station with a sign announcing Fairfax.

"We are in Virginia," he stated matter-of-factly. "May I ask how far we are from Alexandria?"

Meacham gave Tadashi a rare smile.

"Yes, your family lived there for a while," he said. "About twenty miles."

"There is a sad irony that I am returning to the home of my youth as a prisoner of war," he said. "I should like to see Alexandria again, but I do not think that will happen."

From the station, Tadashi was shuffled off into a waiting car with Meacham and a driver. Then they were off.

"So where is this PO Box 1142?" Tadashi asked.

Alone with just the two of them, Meacham's attitude softened. He knew his prisoner would be confined for the duration of the war with strict, limited outside contact.

"You are going to our facility at Fort Hunt," he said. "I think you'll appreciate that the land was once part of George Washington's Mount Vernon property, what he called the River Farm. It's a facility for prisoners we think might possess vital technical or strategic information. You will stand out in the camp. Most of the men held here are German. You will be housed comfortably and fed quality meals. The United States adheres to the Geneva Convention with regard to POWs, so you will not be tortured in any way. You will, however, be interrogated."

Tadashi smiled.

"About my father's 'espionage,' no doubt," Tadashi said. "Suspicion is a cruel mistress. It can cause nations, even civilized ones like America, to mistake a humble public servant, or even thousands of its own loyal citizens, for being spies just because they look different and lock them behind barbed wire."

"It's not just your father's activities," Meacham said, ignoring Tadashi's obvious reference to the treatment and imprisonment of Japanese Americans by their own government. "Colonel, you have a very unique perspective on this war. Your position close to the commander of a strategic island puts you close to the decision-makers in Tokyo."

"I will gladly tell you about my father's so-called espionage activities with regard to crop yield, fertilizer, and growing conditions," Tadashi replied. "But I will not betray anything that could harm my country. I believe your people think I am more important than I truly am."

"That's between you and your interrogators, Colonel," Meacham said.

Half an hour later, the car passed through the gates of Fort Hunt.

———

Two days after Tadashi left Saipan as a prisoner, word came down that the division was shipping out for New Zealand. The men eagerly anticipated liberties in Wellington and the gushing welcome that awaited them from the country's grateful population.

But while the future seemed to be turning away from death and destruction to music, dancing, and swilling beer, there were darker rumblings.

The war was entering its final phase, and that end would most likely involve invading the Japanese home islands. After Saipan, in which many of its Japanese civilians joined the fight with the Army, no one had any illusions that the end would result in an immense bloodbath of both Japanese defenders, military and civilian, and invading American troops. Guys had heard the rumors that civilians, regardless of age or gender, were being trained to repel the invaders using bamboo spears. Guys had heard Japanese leaders pledging "one hundred million die together."

Anticipating huge losses, the Marine Corps was recruiting more men and building a fighting force the size of which had never been seen. It was known that two new divisions would soon be deployed. The Fifth Division, stationed in Hawaii at Camp Tarawa, was activated in January 1944, and the new Sixth was being formed on Guadalcanal. Both divisions were still understrength. To fill those gaps, not only was recruitment being bolstered, but veterans were being pulled from units that had seen action as a way of introducing experience to the new men who had none, and to let them know what they would face in combat.

That was why Pete and the men of Dog Company did not depart for New Zealand with the rest of the division. Dog Company was one of several veteran units plucked from Second and Fourth Divisions and shipped to Hawaii.

The men bitterly groused at being taken away from comrades they had fought beside in two bloody campaigns, but Captain Stacey set them straight as he called them together and broke the news.

"I don't like it any more than you do," he told his men. "But we go where the Corps needs us."

"And where is that?" Pete asked.

"Second Battalion, Twenty-Eighth Marines," he replied.

As Pete absorbed the news of the reassignment, he wondered what Japanese hellhole awaited them.

ACKNOWLEDGMENTS

My heartfelt thanks to my family for their forbearance as I researched and wrote this book. Thanks also to my wife, Barbara, who is my friend and my soulmate as well as my valued proofreader.